D0195759

LOVEFIRE
JULIA GRICE

A PASSION SO GREAT
IT NEEDED A NEW WORD
TO DESCRIBE IT

LOVEFIRE
JULIA GRICE

▲ AVON
PUBLISHERS OF BARD, CAMELOT AND DISCUS BOOKS

LOVEFIRE is an original publication of Avon Books.
This work has never before appeared in book form.

AVON BOOKS
A division of
The Hearst Corporation
959 Eighth Avenue
New York, New York 10019

First Avon Printing, October, 1977

AVON TRADEMARK REG. U.S. PAT. OFF. AND IN
OTHER COUNTRIES, MARCA REGISTRADA,
HECHO EN U.S.A.

Printed in the U.S.A.

For Mike, with love

LOVEFIRE

❧ *Prologue* ❧

BRENNA LAUGHLAN spurred her mare, Portia, to a gallop. The girl's red-gold hair, slipping loose from its ribbon, streamed freely behind her, her full breasts bobbing slightly with the motion of the horse. She rode with a reckless abandon, as if stealing time that was not her own.

For today was her wedding day. In only a few hours, she would be a married woman, with whatever burdens and responsibilities that meant.

To her left lay Dublin, cradled in a cleft of the hills, a few church spires rising above the gray fog that hugged the low ground. In a few minutes, the sun would burn away the mist, revealing the brilliant yellow-green of the hills, dotted with grazing sheep. She loved these hills; had walked and ridden them ever since she could remember.

All summer long she had been stealing out at dawn, dressed in an old pair of her brother's riding breeches, to release her caged-up energy in wild gallops. But today, she sensed, was her last morning for such wild, secret freedom. By one o'clock she would be Lady Brenna Urquhart. And Neall might frown on such dawn wanderings, she thought uneasily. Especially might he object to her riding astride. The Urquharts were a powerful family, with definite ideas on how things should be done.

Not that she herself hadn't her own definite ideas,

Brenna told herself. Hadn't she persuaded her father to give her Portia for her eighteenth birthday in May? Even her groom, Paddy, had said the high-spirited bay mare was too headstrong for her to ride. But she had worked with Portia many long hours, and now the mare was truly hers; the sleek body obedient under Brenna's touch.

Near the top of one of the slanting hills was the ruin of an old monastery, dating from the tenth century. Today the ruins were mostly stones except for a soaring round tower where, it was said, the monks had scrambled to escape the attacking Danes, pulling a rope ladder up behind them. Brenna spurred Portia toward the tower, wondering if any of the monks had ever felt as she did, pent-up and bursting with some feeling she couldn't even name.

As they approached the scattered stones, she thought of her future life as the lady of the manor: sitting with her sewing, chatting with her friends, riding her horse decorously side-saddle. A lady's life was rigidly prescribed in these days of 1819.

A frown crossed Brenna's face. *I won't do it,* she thought rebelliously. *I won't be a lady. I can't.*

But even as she thought it, she knew she would have to. She was eighteen, and it was time she married. She needed someone to take care of her and manage her financial affairs, her father said. And to keep her warm in the chill mornings, too, Brendan Laughlan had added with a smile which told her he was thinking again of her American-born mother, Gwenyth, dead now nine years.

Anyway, wasn't marriage what all women came to? And if she must marry, why not someone like Neall Urquhart, with his tall, spare body and his black eyes which seemed to look right through her, and set her shivering inside.

"If anyone can tame you, Brenna, my girl, it's Neall," her father had commented, with an odd look, as if he were trying to persuade himself this was true. She wasn't quite sure why he had said this. Neall, she knew, was thirty-three years of age, and had been a young man while she herself had been still a child playing with the wooden horses Paddy whittled for her. Neall had attended Merton College, Oxford, then traveled extensively in America and

France, seeing to the financial interests of his family which, it was said, were considerable.

It was whispered that the Urquharts held interests in the American slave market, that Neall had sown youthful wild oats with the beautiful, mixed-blood women of New Orleans and Havana, and that the silver-white scar on his left cheekbone was the result of dueling.

Dueling. Octoroons. Slavery. These were things of which a girl like herself was supposed to be ignorant. But Brenna had a lively curiosity and had sometimes overheard snatches of her brother, Quentin's, conversation with his friends. Thinking of Neall with some brown-skinned girl had made Brenna feel shivery inside, although she could not have explained why. She did know that people said she was one filly who would be led gently to paddock once Neall had put a couple of children in her.

But what they said wasn't true, she told herself now, biting her lower lip until it stung. She might marry Neall, but she wouldn't be led to paddock, and she wouldn't sit in the main hall and do needlepoint. And she might not let him put any children in her, either. Her own mother had died in childbirth.

She was now close to the ruins, the mare's hooves clattering over the rough shards of stone. But Brenna, lost in her thoughts, was barely aware of this.

Suddenly a rabbit dashed out from behind the row of tumbled stones, its small body a blur of fur. One moment Brenna sat erect on Portia's back. Then Portia fell convulsively to one side, her forequarters lashing the air.

Brenna never remembered flying through the air, only the jarring fall on the grass. Pain flashed through her, stabbing her right ankle.

She choked back the sourness that rose in her throat and crawled to her feet, wincing as she put her weight on her ankle.

The mare was standing close by, her sides heaving violently, her eyes rolling in a way that was almost human. Portia held her right foreleg gingerly off the ground.

Why had she ridden so recklessly? Brenna asked herself, forcing back a sob. If she could only go back ten minutes in time, if only the incident hadn't happened at all!

They were more than three miles away from Laughlan, the large home built twenty years ago by Brenna's father. Three miles of walking on a twisted ankle, leading a lamed horse. It would take hours, she thought desperately.

Brenna never knew how much later it was that she and the horse finally staggered back to Laughlan, both limping badly, Brenna's face smudged with dirt and tears. There was a rip in Quentin's riding breeches, where the sharp edge of a rock had jabbed her in the hip. She knew that her thick, red-gold hair was straggling down about her shoulders, that she looked disheveled and even comical, dressed as she was in Quentin's too-big breeches. But none of this mattered. Only Portia.

"Miss Brenna! Miss Brenna! What happened to you?" The first person to notice her return was the old groom, Paddy, running breathlessly across the lawn from the stable. He took her arm, still panting out questions. "What's wrong with Portia?"

"Oh, Paddy!" Brenna felt like a little girl again, ready to sob in Paddy's arms because she had fallen off her pony. "Paddy, Portia is . . . she was frightened by a rabbit, and she threw me, and her leg is hurt."

"Poor beast, I always knew she'd throw you someday. Her and her skittish high-strung ways. Too much like her mistress, sometimes, I'm afeard," Paddy scolded. "But don't worry. Portia will probably be good as new, once I've seen to her."

Brenna turned, seeing her father coming at a half-run across the broad sweep of lawn and garden, followed by Quentin. Quentin, nattily attired in a fawn coat, had ink smears on his fingers. He had been at his poetry again, the solitary pleasure that occupied him when he wasn't out making merry with his friends. He was a year older than Brenna, and she had spent most of her childhood tagging after him, swimming with him, or racing him on her pony.

"Brenna, Brenna, what is this? What's going on?" Her father's voice was sharp with anxiety.

Brenna looked at him. His long face seemed more pale than usual today, the circles under his eyes heavier. He was dressed in a dark blue, broad-collared coat, long trousers and a white linen shirt with pleated front. But the starched whiteness of the shirt only accented the sallow tinge of his face. He hurried toward her now, his eyes taking in the men's breeches, the smudges on her face. Behind him, Quentin's eyes were widening with suppressed mirth.

Quickly, before he could grow angry with her, Brenna told her father what had happened. To her surprise, Brendan Laughlan began to laugh. "Do you mean to tell me that you, my little wild rose, walked three miles on a twisted ankle?"

Brenna nodded.

The smile left Brendan Laughlan's face, leaving it tired and somehow very old.

"Very well, Brenna. It's your own fault for galloping around the hills on your very wedding morning, of all times. I've told you, the ground near the monastery is full of rocks and holes, not a good place for a horse. You will marry Neall today, and I imagine he will not entrust you with another mare as beautiful and as wild as Portia."

Brenna felt a pain twist in her chest. What her father was saying was true. She did not deserve a fine horse. And yet . . . The ache increased. A horse meant freedom to roam the fens and hills as she pleased, freedom to lose herself in wild and breathless gallops. But she said nothing, avoiding Quentin's sympathetic glance.

"As for your attire, young lady, it is disgraceful, as you well know," Brendan Laughlan added, his voice softening only slightly. "It is a good thing that Neall isn't here to see you dressed like a tinker's boy."

"I'll wager Neall wouldn't mind all that much," she said recklessly, in the softly accented voice that combined an Irish lilt and her mother's more forceful American accent.

"Neall Urquhart? Don't be too sure about that. It's a proud family, Brenna. Sometimes I am not certain—" He stopped.

"Not certain about what?"

"Nothing. Marriage is something that must come to all young girls, and the sooner the better, I might add, for one so impetuous as you. So, today it will happen. The arrangements have been made, and that's that." He spoke heavily, his face looking disturbed, as if he saw visions that Brenna could not see.

She stared at him, puzzled for a moment. Then Paddy started to lead the mare gently toward the stables, and Brenna turned to follow him.

"And where do you think you're going?" her father asked.

"I'm going to help take care of Portia," she said.

"You'll do nothing of the kind," her father said. "You are not going to spend any more time with that horse on your wedding day."

"She isn't just a horse, she's Portia. And if it wasn't for me . . . well, I want to be with her, and I'm going to go." When Brenna was stubborn, her lower jaw firmed and her gray-green eyes took on the cold look of the sea on a December morning.

"Very well. But for God's sake come inside soon and dress for your wedding. And have Mary see to that ankle. She should strap it up tightly." Her father turned abruptly and walked across the wide lawn to the big ivy-covered house.

"I'll help you walk, sister," Quentin said, coming up to take her hand. Slightly taller than she, he was auburn-haired, his face long and narrow, with a prominent, straight nose like their father's. Today he smelled of ink and, ever so faintly, of whiskey. It was an odor which Brenna noticed about him more often these days.

"A crazy thing to do on your wedding morning," he could not resist saying, with a wink. "I hope it doesn't bring you bad luck."

Late in the morning it rained briefly, then cleared away in long, glittering beams of sunlight slanting through masses of broken gray and black clouds. After the rain, the air was moist, full of the scent of grasses. It was the kind of day she and Portia loved. She had often rambled in the hills and through the meadows as far as Howth, where the blue sea shimmered in the sun, and where she could tether Portia and balance on the edge of the rough cliffs.

For the rest of this morning, however, she was a numb object, over whom Mary fussed and fluttered, draping her red-gold hair this way and that, finally combing her back curls high and letting the soft ringlets fall around her face. Mary's hairdressing skills were known throughout Dublin, and some of the ladies, Brenna was aware, whispered that such talent was wasted on a boyish girl like Brenna Laughlan.

"Miss Brenna, you're a beautiful bride, a fair sight for any man to see," Mary told her through a mouthful of hairpins. "Now that we've got you cleaned up and that ankle bound, anyway."

Mary, in her forties now, had been with the family since Quentin was born. It was Mary who had raised Brenna after her mother died. Gaunt, square-faced, formidable-looking, Mary had been widowed ten years previously when smallpox had visited Dublin. Her face still bore the pits of the disease. Once, Mary had been a beautiful, fair-skinned girl, Paddy had told Brenna. But smallpox and ten years of widowhood had pared her down to bone.

On Mary's instruction, Brenna turned before the mirror, only half seeing the white taffeta and lace of her wedding gown. Slightly taller than was considered fashionable, Brenna had a slim waist which barely needed to be held in by stays and corsets. Her hips were full, her breasts surprisingly firm and voluptuous for a girl only just eighteen.

Above the taffeta, Brenna's gray-green eyes, framed by thick lashes, seemed smudged and remote, full of dreams. Her complexion, always clear and rosy, was even more flushed today, so that the few freckles across her nose (which Mary had tried valiantly to bleach with a mixture of lemon juice and beeswax) were barely visible. Today her mouth, fully curved and red, was somber.

"Yes, Miss Brenna, you're something a man would want to have and hold today," Mary repeated, her expression turning wistful. "I swear, that serious look becomes you, it does. Not, of course, that I'd want you to fall off your poor horse every day."

Brenna sighed, leaning closer to the mirror as if seeing the stranger in it, that flushed girl, for the first time. She was glad she looked attractive, of course. It would be terrible to be ugly. She thought of Neall's eyes, during the courtship, watching her body with intensity. Would he like her? Would he—

She stopped, unable to say the words even in her own mind. In one more hour, she would be married. She would belong, not to herself, but to a man, to do . . . whatever he wanted. To do the things that Mary had taken pains to explain to her only a few months ago, when she had seen that Neall's attentions to Brenna were serious.

For a second Brenna wanted to clutch Mary's angular arm, to bury her face in the front of her gray dress, to cry out, *I can't! I won't! I don't want to!* But Mary's face was so happily expectant that she couldn't. She couldn't say anything. She could only sit in her room and greet the female wedding guests, some of whom had been staying in the house for two days, as they admired her hair, and fingered the small pearl-and-hair brooch that had been her mother's.

Then it was time. They drove into Dublin and through the cobbled streets to Christ Church Cathedral, with its crypt dating back to Sigtryg, King of Dublin. And she stood beside her father, her perspiring hand resting on his coat sleeve, hearing the sound of the organ, and the rumble and expectant whisper of voices.

"Are you all right, Brenna?" Brendan Laughlan whispered. "You look so white. I don't want you to swoon with that ankle of yours."

"I won't swoon, and my ankle is all right. Mary bound it tightly," she told him, keeping her voice steady. She even smiled. "In a few moments this will all be over."

"No," he told her. "It is only beginning."

Her first sight of Neall caused the moisture to dry up in her mouth. She could not swallow. How tall he looked, in his dark, formal suit, how imposing. His black eyes stared at her as if they could cut right into her. Neall was a tall man, his face craggy, his cheekbones jutting above hollow cheeks. His hair was black, his eyebrows so thick and dark that they nearly met over his nose, giving him a fierce look. The scar on his cheek was silver-pale. She stared at him, hoping to see some softness in him, some recognition.

His eyes flickered, once, and his lips twitched slightly, in a smile. She felt as if she were standing totally alone, the words of the marriage service only a buzz echoing against the vaulted walls of the cathedral. Alone except for Neall, his eyes boring into hers with a look of fierce possession. Yes, that was it, she thought quickly. Possession. He wanted to own her, to do—

She stopped the thought, licked her lips, tried to keep her eyes steadily ahead.

Somehow, without her understanding how it had happened, the ceremony was over. They drove back to Laughlan. While her belongings were loaded into the carriage, she dressed in the pale yellow silk gown with the satin weave, the plush bonnet trimmed with pearls, and the fur-trimmed sarcenet cloak. Then once more she sat in the carriage beside Neall, her cold fingers clasped in his own warm grip.

"Well, Brenna? And now we are married." Neall broke into a faintly crooked smile that showed his square, white teeth. It was one of the things about him she had liked.

"Yes." She steadied her voice, forced it to a normal tone. She might feel strange today, dreamlike and uncertain, but she certainly wasn't going to let him see that.

"I didn't have a chance to tell you," she added suddenly. "But my mare, Portia, fell and hurt her leg badly today. And I sprained my ankle."

He bent closer to her, patting her hand as if she were a fragile little girl. "Poor Brenna. Wasn't she the mare your father gave you for your birthday? That half-wild thing? She certainly wasn't any sort of beast for you to be riding. I'm amazed that your father allowed it."

Brenna tossed her head. "I'm a very capable horsewoman. Even my father admits that. I learned to handle her, and I tamed her."

"I don't want to hear another word about it. I may as well tell you, Brenna, that I will expect decent, ladylike behavior out of you from now on." He put up a hand to forestall the words about to burst out of her. "There's been some whispering about you, Brenna, some talk I didn't particularly like. Some say you go out on the hills at dawn wearing men's breeches instead of proper riding clothes. That you ride astride like a man, galloping like a wild thing. And they even whisper you've been seen swimming in the Liffey with your brother and his friends!"

"Is that what they say?" Two red spots of color had risen in her cheeks—she could feel them there, hot and hard.

"Yes, it's the talk. And I can tell you, it's not the kind of chatter that suits me."

"You heard such talk and still wanted to marry me?" She stared at him.

He drew in a sharp breath. "I heard the talk, but I discounted it as the gossip of dried-up old women with nothing better to occupy their hours." He hesitated. "Besides, you are so beautiful, Brenna, such a prize, with that peach-milky skin of yours, and those . . ."

His hand moved to her shoulder and then down the side of her body, brushing past the swell of her breast. A quiver ran through her, a strangely sweet shiver that started at her toes and went straight to her belly. She drew in air with a quick gasp.

"Sorry. I didn't mean to startle you, my dear. But you are my wife now. My wife." He covered her face with swift, dry kisses. The smell of him was in her nostrils, the smell of pomade and starch and soap.

"You are my wife," he murmured into her neck. "And God knows I've been waiting for this, to be the first one to—Brenna, if you only knew how I've been lying awake nights, thinking of the whiteness of you, the roundness and curves of you, your hair . . . God, I'd like to tumble it down around your bare shoulders, and bury my nose in the smell of it—"

She sat frozen beside him on the carriage seat, barely hearing the words that poured out of him. His hand was at her breast again, rubbing and caressing her nipples, sending spurts of fire pushing through her body, into her groin. Was this what it was like, this thing that men did to women? This liquid flame that raced through her, making her feel so soft and helpless? Dimly, she was glad that the coachman, up on his perch, could not know what was happening inside.

His hands explored the curve of her other breast, with an urgency that was almost frightening. "Wait until I get you home," he whispered.

"*Your* home," something made her say.

"Yours now, too. You are my wife now, don't forget."

Rounding a corner of the narrow, stone-walled road, they could see the house of Urquhart from the carriage window. Surrounded by magnificent formal gardens and sloping lawns, the dark stone manor house had two long wings, the left one incorporating an old tower.

It was not a welcoming house; its stones were too black and cold. But there were flowers in the main hall, freshly gathered from the gardens, and Neall's parents, coming directly from the wedding ceremony, were there to greet them along with the servants.

Brenna tried to smile at them, wondering if her cheeks were still flushed, and if they could guess that Neall's hands had sent fire through her only minutes before.

Neall's father was tall and spare-fleshed like his son, with fierce, hooded black eyes, although his skin held the pallor of ill health. He stepped forward to take her hand.

"Welcome to the family, my dear Brenna." It was the voice of a man accustomed to giving orders and being obeyed immediately, without question. Brenna shivered. Now she, too, would have to obey those orders. She tried to smile at him, conscious of the hard black eyes darting over her body, with almost the same look of possession his son had given her. She felt as if she were to be merely another family possession, like the heirloom tapestries and jewels, the horses and dogs.

"Thank you," she said.

"Yes, you are welcome here," added Neall's mother. She was standing slightly behind her husband, thin and dressed in black. Her eyes regarded Brenna, and Brenna faced her defiantly, knowing how she must look, her cheeks brightly flushed, her hair under the bonnet windblown from the carriage ride.

"I suppose you would like to freshen up," Lady Urquhart said. "We have set aside a very comfortable suite for you and Neall. I am sure you'll like it."

She turned to dismiss the servants, and Brenna stood looking around the high-ceilinged hall, with its huge fireplaces and faded, intricate tapestries. She shivered, longing for the cozy warmth of her own room at Laughlan,

with its sheepskin rugs and warm, quilted coverlet. Then
Neall's arm urged her toward the staircase and she followed numbly.

"Well, these are our rooms, Brenna. Do you like them?"
They were on an upper floor, smelling of soap and wax
and mildew. Neall had pulled open a door to reveal a sitting room furnished in dark, heavy furniture upholstered
in wine-red velvet. Turkish carpets covered the floor, and
an oil portrait, darkened and faded with time, hung over
the fireplace. Brenna caught her breath, thinking that she
would have to lighten the mood of these rooms or she
would never be able to live here.

Neall pulled her to the far corner of the sitting room,
where a pair of low, mullioned windows looked out on the
stiff formality of the gardens, with their yews clipped into
symmetrical shapes.

"During the day, when you're sitting here with your
sewing, you can look out onto the garden," he told her.
"And, of course, the hills. We're near the sea here, although we're too far away to hear it."

Brenna was silent, thinking of Portia, left behind in her
father's stables, and of herself, sitting in this ponderous
room with her needlepoint or embroidery.

"I've always hated sewing," she said suddenly, drawing
back from him.

Neall, however, continued to stare out the double windows as if she hadn't spoken. "It is a good thing that you
will be here with my family, since I will be making a trip
to New Orleans and Havana shortly. My father is very
anxious that I complete some business as soon as possible.
My mother will keep you company while I am gone."

"You're leaving?" She stared at him in surprise.

"You don't mind, do you?" He seemed pleased at the
thought that she might. "This trip will be purely business.
When I return, you and I will travel to Europe on a holiday
of our own. Meanwhile, my father is depending on me to
make sure our interests are looked after. He does not often
leave Ireland. He suffers from gout and shortness of
breath. Not only that, he gets seasick." Neall laughed dryly,
and reached for her. Again she felt the pressure of his body
against hers, the odor of soap and pomade. "But I'm not

traveling today," he murmured. "So we won't think of that just yet. Today is for other things. Isn't it, my sweet?"

His lips found her mouth, pressed against it urgently. Between kisses, his voice went on, the words falling over each other. "You are such an innocent, dear Brenna, with those big, shadowy eyes of yours, and that body, untaken by anyone . . ."

Inside her chest, Brenna's heart was beating in fast, uneven pumps. His moist tongue darted into her mouth. She didn't know what to do. She had never imagined anything like this, this hard and powerful male body moving against her with desire. She felt smothered, trapped in the hardness of his arms, the seeking of his kisses.

And yet a slow thrill of pleasure was rising in her, too. Her knees felt shaky, and her breath was quick in her throat. She was even perspiring inside the silk of her gown. Was this love, this feeling she had for a man who expected her to be a docile lady?

Then, almost as suddenly as he had clasped her, Neall released her.

"Much as I would like to . . . we had better wait until the evening. I will go to my old rooms down the corridor so that you can rest and freshen your toilette," he said reluctantly. "There is the pull-cord, if you wish to ring for one of the servants."

"Thank you. I think I . . . will probably just rest," she told him. "Or go for a walk."

"If you wish to walk, I will accompany you. There is much to see on the grounds. My father is thinking of installing a maze, planted all around with hedges, as they do in London. Perhaps you would like to see where we plan to put it."

He was gone. She sank down on one of the upholstered chairs, feeling the stiff texture of the fabric under her fingers. Here, in this room, she would be expected to sit and sew. Perhaps she would do some light reading, some china painting. In the evening, she would be asked to sing and play the pianoforte for the family and their guests. This, in fact, was the one ladylike thing she really enjoyed. Her voice was a clear, strong soprano, and could fill a room like a soaring bird, attracting more than just polite attention. At one time, Brenna had daydreamed of singing on the stage, but that, of course, was no occupation for a lady.

Lady, she thought rebelliously. She began to plan how she would persuade Neall to take her to America and New Orleans with him. It was New Orleans where, her father said, her mother's sister now lived.

It seemed a strange, tiring afternoon. There was the promised walk with Neall on the grounds, which left Brenna feeling restless, as if hemmed in by the sculptured formality of the hedges, the ordered rows of blossoms. Neall was attentive. His eyes rarely left her face. Yet she felt ill at ease with him. His attentions were to a Brenna who did not exist, except in his own mind; a Brenna whom she did not even know.

There was a formal supper with the senior Urquharts and a few guests, all of whom had attended the wedding, in the long, stone-flagged dining room. Brenna did not talk much. She felt dulled and dizzy by the glasses of wine which Neall kept pressing on her, only laughing when she protested she had had enough. Everyone seemed convivial, keyed-up, as if tonight were somehow extraordinary.

Neall and Brenna said good-night to the assembled company. She intercepted a brief look from Neall's mother —was it pity?—and then she climbed the stairs once again with Neall. She swayed dizzily, as if her feet did not quite know how to walk. Her twisted ankle was beginning to throb, and she stumbled, catching herself against Neall's arm.

"Don't fall, my darling. Not yet. Not yet." His voice was slightly slurred.

"You gave me too much wine!" she protested, hearing herself with astonishment. Was that loose, blurred voice really hers? Was all of this—the too-loud laughter coming from downstairs, Neall's arm about her—really happening?

"Too much wine? Don't be silly, my dear. On their wedding night, all brides are permitted a bit of wine. It has a mellowing effect." He laughed, pulling her against him.

"I'm not sure I want to be mellow. I don't like not knowing where my feet are."

"I'll see to it that your feet go where they're supposed to. You needn't worry about that!"

They entered their suite again, and this time Neall closed the door tightly behind him and locked it. He took off his coat and threw it over the back of one of the wine-red velvet chairs. Dusk came late to the countryside around Dublin, and a last shaft of sunlight picked out colored threads in the carpet. The rooms smelled fresh, as if the servants had aired them out while they were at table. In the shadowed light, Neall's shirt shone like an island of white.

"Brenna . . ." he whispered. "How shall I . . . I can't wait any longer. I must have you now—"

He picked her up, crushing her to him as he carried her through the rooms. She felt herself let down on soft eiderdown, saw the top of a four-poster over her, and knew that she was in bed. Their bed, the one they would share.

There was still enough light to show the outline of the bedroom, the mahogany furniture, the enormous carved wardrobe which seemed to loom at her. She fought off a feeling of panic, turning her head from side to side, trying to get her breath.

For one blurred instant, Neall stood above her, breathing hard. Then she felt his hand fumbling beneath her, pulling at the back of her gown, ripping at the buttons.

"I can't wait, darling. Oh, don't worry about the gown. I'll give you a thousand gowns, a thousand kisses, a thousand of anything you want, anything at all . . ." His words tumbled on, not making sense, as the buttons flew.

He pulled the dress to her waist, and tugged at the straps of her chemise. She sat up, hands covering her breast.

"What are you doing?" she managed. "What are you—"

"I'm only doing what all husbands must do, my darling. It won't be bad, I promise you. If you'll only just relax—"

Relax? She couldn't, not with him so close, with his mouth pressing on hers, his tongue seeking and darting, his hands dragging the dress and petticoats from her hips. She began struggling to pull away from him, frightened by his intensity.

She had not realized he could be so strong. His arms

pinned her against the eiderdown. She struggled against
him, but felt her strength waning, sapped by a strange
weakness which was spreading through her body.

"Plenty of fight, that's what you have, my golden young
virgin, but it won't be long now . . . I'll tame you . . ."
On and on his voice went in her ear. His mouth seemed
to find all the curves and secrets of her breasts. His tongue
flicked against the tips of her nipples, drawing from them
sensations she had never known.

Dimly she was aware that he was pulling off his own
clothes, that his hands were forcing her legs apart, that
something hard and throbbing was entering her.

She lay under him, feeling him move in her, his breath
hot against her shoulder, his body arching, heaving, at
last shuddering in spasm.

It was over. She felt like crying. Whatever she had expected, it certainly hadn't been this animal-like grappling
and forcing. She felt exhausted and soiled, as if her most
personal privacy had been violated.

Neall jerked away from her to the other side of the
bed, still breathing heavily.

"Well, Brenna, my fine young *virgin*. It seems that a
stallion has already gotten to this mare!"

"What do you mean?" For a moment she couldn't believe that she had heard him correctly. Automatically she
pulled the quilted coverlet over herself.

"I mean you were no virgin when I got to you! I had
expected—"

"Virgin? But of course I was one. I've never . . . done
this with any man before, ever. I never even knew what it
was like."

"I think you're a liar." It was as if Neall were not
the same person who had held her and whispered such
extravagant things to her. In one fierce motion, he rolled
off the bed and pulled on his pants. "Who was it? Did one
of the stable boys tumble you in the meadow when your
father wasn't looking? Or did one of your brother's friends
pull you onto the banks of the Liffey and get up your
skirts?"

She sat up in the bed, pulling the quilt over her breasts.
Anger pounded through her. "How dare you talk to me
like that? As if I were a . . . a common girl, a strumpet!"

"Aren't you?"

He paced the room, hands balled into fists, breath coming in deep, angry gasps. In the weak light, his facial scar glowed livid white.

"You were not a virgin when you came to me. That much is clear. Where was the bleeding? The pain, the difficulty in penetrating? Oh, you can't deceive me, you've had a man before. Haven't you?"

"No, I . . . I haven't. . . ."

To her amazement, he gripped her shoulders and shook her back and forth. An acrid smell of perspiration came from him, and she saw with horror that his bare chest was covered with black, tightly curled hair.

His fingers pressed painfully into her upper arms. She jerked away from him with all her strength, shoving at him with both hands. The quilt fell away, revealing her breasts and thighs, softly shadowed in the dusk.

Neall gasped as if he had been slapped. "Showing your breasts . . . you whore. Coming to marriage as a virgin . . . cheating me . . ." The torrent of words poured out, spoken so quickly that they barely made sense.

"I am not a whore," Brenna said coldly and clearly. "You are the one who ripped my clothing off me, ruining my gown and clawing at me like a beast. The one who—"

He slapped her, a resounding smack that threw her head to one side and sent pain flashing through her nose.

"Is this the way you treat your bride, Neall?" She moved back from him, managing to get her feet on the floor and her body standing upright. She clutched the quilt about her nakedness. "Force her, accuse her of being a whore, then hit her in the face for defending herself?" She rushed on. "I was a virgin, no matter what you might think. I fell from my horse once when I was twelve, and there was bleeding and pain. Maybe that took my virginity, I don't know. I only know that I have never lain with a man before this night, and I . . . I wish I'd never married you at all!"

His lips twisted. "But you are married to me, my dear Brenna." With a violent gesture he jerked at the quilt, tearing it from her. "Look!" he hissed, in a voice so full of venom that Brenna felt a thrill of horror. *Obsessed,* she thought wildly. *He is obsessed.*

"Look at that body of yours," Neall said. "What a fool I was to think you could be a virgin. Those breasts . . . too full for a girl of your years. And that belly, made to caress . . . what a fool I was to suppose the merchandise hadn't been handled." He paused, then spoke in a deeper tone. "Well, virgin or not, you are my wife now. No other man will have you now, not ever again. Only me."

"You talk as if you think I'm a . . . a . . . dog, or a horse, a possession," she said furiously.

"You're mine." He touched her cheek again, a soft slap just to show power. "And if I find that my dear little possession is slipping out to the fields with someone else, I will find a remedy, a remedy that you won't like!"

A coldness gathered in the pit of Brenna's stomach. She could not take her eyes away from that dueling scar. "You can't mean . . ." she whispered.

"I've disturbed you, haven't I? Frightened you. You aren't quite sure what I mean, and it worries you." With each word he twisted her arm, and pulled her closer to the window with its serene view of garden.

"No, please!" she gasped. "You're hurting my arm!" Resisting the vicious pain, she lost her footing on the loose Turkish rug. She fell heavily. Trying to catch his balance, Neall let go of her, his hands reaching in front of him, as if to catch hold of the window pane for support.

Except that the window, instead of supporting him, opened. His splayed-open hands pressed against the panes, pushing them wide. And with slow, horrid deliberation, his body followed those hands, and fell.

Brenna heard a choked cry, and he was gone. There were only the windows, swinging on their hinges.

She scrambled to her feet and looked out. Down below, like a huge, human-sized doll, lay Neall. His body was oddly twisted, his back bent at a terrifying angle. She could not tell if he was alive or dead.

She stood frozen at the window, her mouth so dry that she could not swallow or scream. The world seemed to stop around her, except for the sound of the night birds twittering in the hedges.

She had completely forgotten that she was naked.

❧ Chapter 1 ❧

April, 1820

WARM AND YELLOW AS BUTTER, the New Orleans sun slanted through the window and onto Brenna's dressing table, picking up russet glints in the tortoise-shell comb she had brought with her from Ireland.

Even the sunlight here was moist, she thought, picking up the comb and sweeping up her back hair in one long motion. Everything was wet in this city—the air, the opaque brown Mississippi, which insisted on flooding its banks just when it was most inconvenient for everyone; the cypress swamps, the torrential rains. Plants and flowers grew almost sinfully lush, twining luxuriantly everywhere. Even the weeds stood as tall as she, mockingly green.

She wore only a chemisette and drawers, for it was unseasonably hot for April, and every pore of her body screamed for coolness. It might be unladylike to sit this way, but it was cool. Besides, no one could see her here in the privacy of her bedroom, except Mary, and Mary didn't count.

She stared into the slightly wavy mirror. Her sleek, reddish-gold hair was parted in the middle, the back drawn up with a comb to fall at each side of her face in thick curls. She frowned at the curls, touched one, and let her hand fall to her lap. *Who cares about my hair?* she thought rebelliously. What did it matter how she looked tonight, or tomorrow, or any of the other days that stretched ahead in an endless row of parties. She felt listless, depressed, her energy sapped by the heat, and by the nightmares that had been haunting her sleep for ten months now, ever since they had left Ireland.

She shuddered, remembering how vivid those dreams were. Neall, sprawled on the ground, his back twisted grotesquely, his face bleached of color. How many times had she seen him exactly that way, sprawled and broken? And, in the eerie way of dreams, each night his face seemed to move closer to her, so that she could see the perspiration on his forehead, his mouth pulled apart in a terrible grimace. A snarl. And the snarl was directed at her, at her alone.

It was always then, with this realization, that she woke up. She would find herself sitting bolt upright in the netting draped bed, her heart pounding, her hands clenched into fists. Sometimes there would be a scream on her lips, and she would have to choke it back, so that Aunt Rowena or her cousin Arbutus would not come rushing into her room demanding to know what was wrong.

Each time, after the dream was over, she would have to get up, light a candle, and pace around the exquisitely wallpapered room which Aunt had given her. Up and down, forward and back, slapping at the mosquitoes, until she had walked far enough to tire herself, and could fall back asleep.

She would never forget the terrible events of what she still thought of as *that day*. Even now she could recall every detail of that nightmare moment when she had crouched at the double windows, staring down in horror at the body of her husband.

She never knew how long she had knelt there, conscious only of Neall lying twisted and broken. Then she had heard a shout. One of the servants had come running, his mouth slacked open with terror as he put his ear to Neall's chest. Then, as if tidying up, the servant had jerked at Neall, pulling him around so that his body lay straight. The servant crossed himself, muttered a prayer. Then he had looked up. The man's eyes had widened, and Brenna had remembered with a shock that her breasts were uncovered. Quickly she withdrew from the window.

Instinctively she had reached for her clothes, knowing that she must dress quickly, for people would soon be at the door of the suite, demanding to know what happened. To her dismay, she saw that her petticoat was ripped at the waistband. The gown, once the height of fashion, had lost most of its buttons and had been torn from the back placket nearly to her knees.

But she had needed to cover herself. So she stepped into the gown as best she could, pulling it over her body with shaking fingers. Two buttons, at the lower back, had been still intact, and she slipped them through the loops. Glimpsing herself in the ornate gilt mirror, she had been shocked at her appearance. Her hair, so lovingly prepared for the wedding, had straggled down her shoulders, snarled and fuzzy. There was a huge red welt on the side of her face where Neall had slapped her, and a trickle of blood from her nose. Her right eye had already started to swell.

All too soon there had been a rattling at the door of the suite. She hurried through the sitting room, clutching the back of her dress together with one hand. She found the key lying on a carved cabinet and opened the door. Lord Urquhart stood there, his face purplish-livid, his breathing rapid and stertorous.

"What happened up here? What did you do to my son?"

"I . . . I didn't—" She had stammered like a servant caught tippling the brandy. His eyes had raked over her, taking in the details of her appearance. Mercifully, anger began to harden in her.

"You wish to know what happened?" She turned so he could see the tatters of her gown. "I will tell you. Your son, Neall, tore off my gown, and then he . . . he ravished me—" She stopped, unable to go on.

"He did what?" Lord Urquhart's hand had shot out and gripped her upper arm like a claw of iron. The violent expression in his eyes was so like that of his son that Brenna felt a shiver run through her.

"I said he . . . he—"

"And what did *you* do to *him?*" Urquhart said hoarsely. "My son is lying in the garden, half-dead. His mother is

with him, weeping. I would like to know what happened
to him."

She felt the strength seep out of her. "He is alive,
then?" she whispered.

"Yes. Just barely, but he is alive. I have summoned
the doctor, and the servants are taking him on a litter into
the house. Were you hoping he was dead?"

"No! Oh, no, I . . . I didn't try to kill him, if that's
what you mean. It was an accident. He—he was twisting
my arm behind my back, and I slipped on the rug. He lost
his balance and tried to catch himself against the window.
It didn't hold. He fell."

"And why was he twisting your arm?"

"Because . . . why . . . because—" Her breath had
caught.

"Because you were no virgin," Lord Urquhart said in a
low, terrible voice. "Because you came to the marriage
soiled and under false pretenses. You see, he told me. He
whispered this to me while the servants were getting the
litter."

He had advanced toward her, and Brenna had stepped
backward, her heart pounding.

"What . . . what are you going to do?" she whispered.

"I don't know. Neall is my only living son. A thing like
this has never happened in our family. Neall—if he lives
—will be made the butt of a thousand laughs. To be pushed
out of the window on his wedding night! He will be called
a weakling, a buffoon, less than a man. This will injure
him deeply, in his pride. In his very manhood. And you
will have been the cause of his injury. You, a mere
woman." This last was spoken with deep contempt.

Brenna had felt the wall behind her and knew she could
back away no farther. She had no idea of what this man
would—or could—do to her. She only knew that she was
Neall's wife, and that she was in the Urquharts' complete
power. It was a frightening thought.

"*I* didn't cause his injury!" she had burst out. "He did!
If he had not been trying to twist my arm off, it wouldn't
have happened. I won't take the blame for something I
didn't bring about!"

"Enough of such talk. It is a woman's duty to submit
to her husband. To submit to whatever awaits her in the

marriage bed. It is monstrous to think that you . . . you would—"

Urquhart's fingers were biting into her arm. Again she was aware of the violence in him. She sensed that he was still too angry to think clearly. But later, when he had had time to think, his anger would turn cold and murderous. Someone would have to pay for what had happened to Neall, and it would be her.

There had been a shout from below the window. Urquhart turned involuntarily, his grip slackening. Seizing the opportunity, Brenna jerked her arm out of his grasp. Then, before he could react, she had pushed past him and was running down the corridor, her skirts lifted, needles of pain shooting through her ankle.

The passage ended in a back staircase, and she raced down it recklessly, hearing Urquhart's footsteps behind her. The stairs appeared to lead to the kitchen and scullery area, and she took them two at a time, holding her gown above her knees and thanking God she had had the wit to slip back into her shoes before answering the door.

An excited buzz of voices came from the scullery—the servants, she supposed, speculating about the accident, reveling in the change from their routine. Praying that none of them would see her, she darted out a side door and across the kitchen garden, hung with laundry, to a thicket that lay on the other side of the hedge. Darkness had finally settled on the land like a cape, turning trees and bushes into hooded shapes, blurring the clear outlines of objects. Thankfully, she had known that it would hide her, too.

It had been at least two hours later that she finally reached Laughlan, having run, walked and crawled the six miles of rough turf until she was at the point of collapse. She had tripped over rocks, skinned both knees until they bled, scratched her arm on a bush, and lost the remaining two buttons of her dress, so that her back was totally exposed to the chill of the night. With a sense of amazement she had seen Laughlan, crowning its hill like a palace, ablaze with yellow light. Home.

She had staggered across the grounds, dragged herself to the front door, and, with all her strength, pulled on the bell. Then she had collapsed.

Much later, in her bedroom, after she had been cried over, bathed and bandaged by Mary, Brenna told her father everything that had happened, even Neall's accusation that she had not been a virgin, although it had embarrassed her deeply to have to say such things to her father.

"And were you a virgin, Brenna?" Brendan Laughlan's face had been dark with pain.

"I was, Father, I was. I . . . I fell off my pony when I was twelve, and there was bleeding and pain. Mary will tell you that. It was not the kind of thing that I . . . that a girl would tell to her father, and only Mary knew. I swear to you, Father, I never slept with a man before tonight. I swear to you on my mother's grave."

"I believe you. You have always been an honest girl, Brenna, even if a bit headstrong. And it is true that you never did show much interest in having suitors like other girls of your age." He had paced the floor, like a weary lion outlining the limits of its cage. "But to think that Neall Urquhart would do this to my daughter . . ."

Brenna's face hardened. "Everything was fine until he decided that I was no virgin. Then it was as if he were not even the same man. As if—" She hesitated. "As if he were a devil."

"Devil is what he is, I'm afraid, dear Brenna. I see that now. I should have realized. . . . I wanted to see you married, I wanted to see you settled and happy, with a man who could give you everything you need. I let myself be carried away by contracts and money and promises, instead of—"

Brenna had put her hand over his. "It doesn't matter, Father. Really, it doesn't. I'm home now. The nightmare is over, and I'll take up my old life again, just as before. I . . . I don't care about marriage, Father. Neall wanted to keep me imprisoned in a sitting room, sewing and embroidering for the rest of my life. I don't think I want to go back to that. Not ever."

He looked at her with pity. "Brenna, I'm sorry. But your life here at Laughlan is over. You can't come back to it now."

"What do you mean? Surely you won't object if I come back to my old room again—"

"Of course I don't object. The Urquharts will. As Lord Urquhart told you, this has been a killing blow to their pride. It will be the talk of the county, at least for a while. Do you think they would stand for you living here, only six miles from their hall, riding out every morning on your mare as though nothing had happened? Do you think they would allow Neall's wife, whom they consider *their* property now, to get away from them as easily as all that? No, any minute now I expect to hear someone banging on the door, demanding that we give you back to them."

"I won't go back. I can't," she had whispered.

"You won't have to. I have no intention of giving my daughter up to them under these circumstances. It's obvious you've been beaten." He paused by the carved trunk where she kept her linens, his mouth grim. "If necessary, I will defend you with arms. However, I hope I won't have to. Your brother, I'm afraid, is not up to that sort of thing. It's not that he lacks the will, but there is no strength to him, no resilience such as you have, Brenna." He laughed dryly. "If only the situation had been reversed. Quentin with your spirit, you with his dreaminess and soft ways—"

"Are you saying that you might actually have to do battle over this?"

"I don't intend to. I've decided what we're going to do. You and Quentin and Mary are going to America, to New Orleans. Your mother's sister, Rowena, lives there, and I know she will be glad to take you in and look after you. I will tell her that I am very ill, that I have a tumor and haven't long to live, and that I don't want you here with me to see the final suffering. That I need a woman to give you the sort of social life that a sick man can't give you here in Dublin."

Brenna had shivered. "You dying, Father. What a terrible thing to think about."

"I must have some story to tell. Something to satisfy them. They must not know about this aborted marriage. Let this whole day be erased. I'll see to it that you're given . . . an annulment, or even a divorce, if I have to go to London and bribe the whole of Parliament. I'll manage it somehow. And you will go to America and start over again."

"But—"

"You are only eighteen, daughter. You have many years left to live. Thank God we are not Catholics or you would be tied to Neall until you were an old woman."

"But I don't want to leave Ireland!"

"You must. You have no other choice. And I want you to understand something. You are not to speak of this day again, to anyone, not even your aunt. I will swear Quentin and Mary to secrecy as well. As far as they are concerned in America, you are an unmarried girl. A virgin, if you will." He had stopped her protest. "If you are to have any chance at happiness, this day must be forgotten."

Brenna had slept only fitfully that night. The next morning Mary had told her that a servant from the Urquharts had brought a message. Neall Urquhart was still alive, but he had been permanently paralyzed from the waist down. He would never walk again, never make love to another woman as long as he lived.

That had been six months ago. She had arrived in New Orleans feeling uprooted and depressed, already haunted by the nightmares that were to plague her for months.

Her Aunt Rowena Butler's home was an impressive Greek-revival house on Prytania Street, in what their carriage driver had told them was the "American" sector of New Orleans. Americans were still considered upstarts in this old French city, Brenna had gathered, feeling bewildered by the new sights, sounds and smells that pressed in upon her.

Her uncle Amos had been at his office when they arrived, and they had been met by Aunt Rowena. Small, light-boned and auburn-haired, as Brenna's mother had been, that was where the resemblance ended. Where Brenna's mother had been soft and warm and full of smiles, Aunt Rowena was hard. There were frown lines in her forehead, and downward grooves running from her nose to the corners of her mouth. She had worn a dove-gray muslin housedress and white cap that day, looking immaculate despite the day's heat.

Rowena had welcomed them, taking the accompanying letter of introduction from Brenna's father and reading it

quickly. Had it been Brenna's imagination, or had her
face paled?

"I . . . I am sorry to hear that your father is ill," she
had said at last. "It has been many years since I last saw
him, but still—" Her lips had pressed together. "It is
strange that he would not want his children with him at
his bedside."

Brenna had flushed. "He insisted that we come."

"Still . . . Well, you are welcome here for as long as
you wish to stay. You will be company for my daughters,
Jessica and Arbutus. They are at the dressmaker's now,
but when they return, I am sure they will be delighted to
meet you." She had spoken in a dry, matter-of-fact tone
that did not convey a great deal of warmth. And her aunt
had looked sharply at Brenna, as if she did not entirely
like what she saw.

Still, in her efficient way, Aunt Rowena had soon settled them in their new residence. Brenna had been given
a bedroom delicately papered in a pattern of pink tea
roses, and Mary, after some deliberation by Aunt Rowena,
had been put in a small room on the top floor, away from
the slave quarters.

Quentin had quickly decided that he would rather take
bachelor quarters elsewhere in the city. "I would rather
not be sequestered in a house full of females," he had told
Aunt Rowena lightly. "So, for propriety's sake and everyone's peace of mind, since I sometimes keep late hours,
I think I will see what I can find."

True to his word, within a week Quentin had installed
himself in lodgings near Canal Street, where he engaged a
gens d'couleur, Etienne, to look after him and cook.

Brenna was not to have a child; that much had become
apparent during the crossing of the Atlantic. Mary had
given her an evil-tasting potion to drink, and her monthly
flux had appeared several days early, indisputable evidence. "Thank Jesus, Mary and Joseph," Mary had said,
hugging her, her gaunt face lit with joy. "It was the one
thing I was worried about, worried until I could hardly
sleep for thinking of it. Men and their ideas! What were
you to do if you arrived in New Orleans already starting

to swell with child? Your father didn't want it to happen, so it wouldn't happen. Pfah!"

Life in the Butler household was charming and smooth, if never-changing. Days were devoted to calls, correspondence, rides in the carriage, fittings for gowns, needlework, china painting, and music. Nearly everyone in the city played some sort of musical instrument, it seemed. Jessica played the pianoforte and the organ, and her sister Arbutus was an accomplished harpist.

Evenings were taken up with dinners, dances, the opera, parties and musicales; all undertaken with the sole aim, it appeared, of marrying off the two Butler girls. Jessica, the younger, was Brenna's age, a slim, small-boned girl like her mother, with the same beige skin and precise air. She was already starting to groove a frown line between her brows, and in ten more years would look exactly like her mother.

The elder daughter was named Arbutus, after the trailing, pink flower of Massachusetts, where her father, Amos, had been born. Arbutus was twenty, taller than her sister and even more slender, with big pansy eyes. Her delicate, fragile looks were in high fashion, but ill luck had worked against her. At seventeen, slipping and falling one afternoon on the damp brick sidewalk, she had broken her left leg in two places. It had not healed properly, had had to be rebroken, and had left her bedridden during the crucial year of her coming-out. Worse, it had left her with a pronounced limp. For these reasons, and because she was intensely shy around men, Arbutus had not married, although Brenna privately thought she was the most winsome of the two Butler girls.

The days in New Orleans passed quickly enough, yet they all seemed alike to Brenna. There were balls and gatherings, many taking place in weather so humid that she was soaked with perspiration under her layers of petticoats and gown. At night the mosquitoes were so thick Brenna had to crawl under the mosquito netting in order to undress. Often she longed for Ireland, for the cool, soft, green hills, and the clear air. But of Dublin only the nightmares remained to her now, and an occasional wistful letter from her father, enclosing funds to pay for her board and expenses.

Now she sat at her dressing table, pulling her hair this way and that, remembering dully that yet another musicale was to be held tonight, and that she would be expected to sing. Singing was the only part of the evening to which she looked forward. For a few moments, at the pianoforte, she could forget the memory of Neall's twisted and broken form.

There was a soft tapping at her door. Brenna quickly reached for the dressing gown draped over the back of her chair.

"Brenna, may I come in?"

"Of course."

It was Arbutus, in a lilac housedress which brought out the peculiar pansy-blue shade of her eyes. If it had not been for the ungainly limp, Arbutus would have been married by now, perhaps the mother of several babies. Why was it, Brenna wondered, that men could overlook a lovely, pale face and see only the physical handicap? Or place so much importance on virginity that they had no thoughts left for the girl herself?

"I've been practicing my harp until my fingers are nearly bleeding," Arbutus said. "I've just got to talk to someone for a while. I'm not interrupting you, am I?" Before Brenna could answer, she bubbled on, "Aren't you just sick of practicing? I think Jessica is the only one of us who really enjoys that! Although I suppose we must. All three of us are going to be on display like prize chickens, and we certainly don't want to hit a wrong note —that might horrify Mama into another week of her indigestion."

Brenna laughed.

"Well, it's good to see you laughing more often now, cousin," Arbutus said, going to the window seat and sitting down, managing to move with delicacy in spite of the limp. "I was beginning to wonder if you ever smiled."

"Me?" Brenna stared at her. "Me not smiling?"

"Yes, I'm afraid so! Oh, I suppose I shouldn't say this, but you have seemed so melancholy since you arrived here. I suppose it's your father, isn't it? Knowing he's so ill and not being able to be there with him, I imagine I'd feel unhappy, too."

Brenna felt herself turning red. She picked up the tortoise-shell comb and began turning it in her fingers, not knowing what to say. It had been difficult keeping her secret, especially in the face of Arbutus' friendliness.

"And I imagine you're homesick, too, aren't you?" her cousin went on. "You've talked so much about Ireland and that horse you used to have. I wonder if I would be homesick if I had to leave New Orleans. We've lived here nearly eight years now. That seems like a very long time, doesn't it?" Arbutus rose to look out the window at the courtyard below, which bloomed profusely with magnolia and Cape jasmine. "Oh! Did I tell you who is coming to the musicale tonight?"

"No, but Aunt Rowena has gone over the invitation list with me at least twice. There are the Rynne brothers, Ulrich and Toby, both of whom are very rich and influential and are looking for wives; a prominent judge, who is a widower and might be looking for a wife; and Monty Carlisle, a wealthy planter, who, by some strange coincidence, is also seeking a wife. Also—"

Arbutus giggled and made a face. "No, no, we've met all of them before, dozens of times at least. No, I'm talking about someone you haven't met, because he's just come back from China and Cuba and heaven knows where else. He is a *very* exciting man—at least, almost every girl in New Orleans is mad about him, and I think just about any of them would throw herself at his feet if he asked her to!"

"*I* wouldn't. I don't think I'll ever throw myself at any man's feet. In fact, I'm not sure I want to marry—" Brenna bit her lip, cutting off the last word of this sentence, which had been "again."

"You might change your mind when you see this man, Brenna! He's tall and light-haired, and . . . not that he would ever look at me, of course," Arbutus interrupted herself. "But, still, he's a member of one of Boston's oldest shipping families, and he came to New Orleans about two years ago to cash in on some of the shipping business here, Father says. He's made himself a million dollars! And he's not just some stuffy businessman—he's full of adventure. Mama calls him eccentric, but she always looks on the gloomy side of things. He actually sails his own ships, act-ing as captain. Says he can't stand to be tied to a high stool in an office, and wants to be out in the world where things can happen to him."

"I suppose he has been all over the world then," Brenna said half-enviously.

"Oh, yes. And women . . . there are rumors about him, Brenna, I suppose I should tell you so you'll be wary of him. His first wife died only a year after their marriage. They say he has had plenty of mistresses in New Orleans, and not just quadroon women but white women, too—the most beautiful white women in New Orleans! And not only that, they say he can make them do anything he wants them to!"

"Why, Arbutus." Brenna stared at her cousin in surprise. "It seems strange that Aunt would invite such a man to her home."

"Well, this is New Orleans," Arbutus said, shrugging, as if that explained everything. "Besides, I don't think Mama has heard all the rumors. Or, if she has, she's ignoring them. After all, many men here take quadroon or octoroon mistresses. It's something we whisper about and try to ignore, but it's true. If we were to exclude all the men who had brown-skinned mistresses . . ." Arbutus lifted her shoulders. "So, we shut our eyes to it, and pretend we don't know. It's easier. Besides, Kane Fairfield is very rich, much richer than Father, and I'm afraid Mama thinks of such things. It's only the Creoles who can afford to ignore the fact of money."

Brenna was about to ask another question, but just then Mary knocked on the door, ready to help her dress for the evening.

The Irishwoman shooed Arbutus out, promising to come to her room as soon as she was finished with Brenna. Mary, with her gift for arranging hair artistically, was in great demand in the Butler household. On party days, every minute of her time was spent adorning hair with flowers, ribbons, tortoise-shell combs, and fanciful curls.

"Are you ready to dress, now, Miss Brenna?" Without waiting for an answer, Mary took a pale green satin gown out of the wardrobe, along with its dark green, braid-trimmed silk spenser. The spenser, which fit over the dress like a short blouse, was a decorative detail much admired by the ladies in America, and Aunt had urged Brenna to go along with the fashion.

"I suppose I must dress now, then?" Brenna said wistfully.

"Enough of that sort of talk, Miss Brenna!" Mary smoothed out the folds of the gown, holding it up to stare at it critically. "You are a grown woman now, and your father sent you here to America to do this very thing—to go to parties and have fun and build a new life for yourself. And I'm going to see that that's exactly what you do. So step into this gown, my young lady. The color becomes you mightily."

"But I don't like attending parties and galas almost every evening!" protested Brenna. "I wish I could be back at Laughlan, riding Portia. I don't think I was ever meant to be a lady, Mary. I think God made a mistake when he made me. I should have been a . . . a . . . gypsy woman, or—" Brenna stopped, unable to think of an occupation adventurous enough.

"Sorry, miss, but you'll just have to endure it for a while longer—at least until you find a husband. I doubt if your Aunt Rowena is going to tolerate having an unmarried niece in her home for the rest of your life."

"Then I'll go back to Laughlan!"

"You can't, darling. Remember what waits for you there? Neall Urquhart, a man whose body is paralyzed and who will never walk again, and who blames you for it. Wurra! It makes me shudder just to think of the way that man must feel about you. You are far better off with an ocean between you and Neall Urquhart."

Brenna remembered the mad look in Neall's eyes as he had twisted her arm backward. "I don't care, Mary! It's all so unfair! Men can stay unmarried if they want to. Men can go sailing off to China, or go riding in the streets exactly as they please, without having to take Aunt along, or a maidservant!"

Mary's lips, in the gaunt, pock-marked face, tightened. "Who ever said it was fair, Miss Brenna? Life has always been like this. There's nothing new in it. One of these days you too will come to a man's bed, just like the rest of us."

"Not me." Brenna drew herself straight.

"You already have. Don't forget it, you married a man, and you shared his bed, and only a miracle of God prevented you from bearing his child. No, it will come to you again, and it will probably come soon." She put her hands on Brenna's shoulders and turned her to face the mirror. "Look at you, girl. You're ripe for the bedding. And any man seeing you will know it."

❧ *Chapter 2* ❧

AFTER MARY LEFT, Brenna stood at her bedroom window, looking down at the magnolia blossoming in the stone-flagged courtyard, with its tall, greenery-twined walls, water fountain and stone cupid. The cupid, recently installed by Uncle Amos despite the protests of Aunt Rowena, who thought it too frivolous, blew sprays of water through a ram's horn.

So often, these days, she thought about her mother, the lovely, auburn-haired Gwenyth Laughlan, who had met Brenna's father in New York, where she had lived with her family. Brendan had made an extended visit to the United States, and when he had finally returned home to Dublin, it had been as a married man.

Someday, my darling, you'll grow up and find a man as wonderful as your father, and he'll make everything worth-while. I promise you he will. Her mother had said that only weeks before she'd died in childbirth, delivering a small, stillborn brother.

Now, Brenna stared down at the cupid, thinking that her mother had been wrong. She hadn't found anyone wonderful. Instead, there'd been only Neall, and night-mare . . .

A sharp knock at the door scattered her thoughts.

"Brenna, are you ready yet? May I come in to see how you look?" Without waiting for a reply, Aunt Rowena pushed open the door and came in. Her aunt was sumptuously dressed in dark blue taffeta trimmed with satin ribbon. The gown hung slightly loosely, as if she had recently lost weight.

"Brenna, turn around, please. Let me see how that gown looks. I thought that last alteration made it a bit tight."

Obediently Brenna turned, hearing the swish of her pale green silk skirts.

"Yes. It's all right. That color suits you very well. Although I could wish the neckline didn't expose so much of your bosom. Still, I suppose we must go along with the fashion." Aunt Rowena sighed. "You look much as your mother did, although your hair is brighter." For a moment her aunt's expression clouded, as if she thought of unpleasant things. Then she went on, "Anyway, you had better hurry on downstairs. The guests are arriving."

"Yes, Aunt."

"Before you leave, bite your lips to redden them. There are going to be some important gentlemen here tonight."

"Yes, Aunt."

"Toby Rynne, especially, has been interested in you."

"Oh? I hadn't noticed." Toby Rynne, whom her uncle said was an important merchant in the city, was tall and thick-fleshed, rather like a giant bullfrog, Brenna thought uncharitably. He followed her about at most of the parties, as if fascinated by her.

"Perhaps you had better start noticing him, then," Aunt Rowena told her sharply. "You will be nineteen soon. And I am sure your father had someone like Toby Rynne in mind when he sent you to America, did he not?"

"Do you mean someone who is very wealthy and dull as a toad?" Brenna retorted. "I'm sure my father did not mean anyone like that!"

Two bright red spots appeared on Aunt Rowena's cheeks. "Am I mistaken, or are you being rude to me, Brenna Laughlan? After all I have done for you, providing you with a home and with a proper social life—I am extremely surprised that you would behave so."

"No, I'm not being rude, Aunt. I'm sorry if I offended you. It's just that . . . well, Toby Rynne does not appeal to me. He . . . He makes me think of—" Brenna stopped, unable to continue without adding further insult.

Aunt Rowena tightened her lips. "I don't think I want to hear what he reminds you of. Now, come along, Brenna. Please do. And remember, walk slowly down the stairs, with your back very straight and a slight smile on your lips. Do not lower your head and fuss with the folds of your gown, and do *not* bound downstairs as if you were a . . . a . . . jockey leaving for the races!"

Brenna grimaced. "Yes, Aunt."

In later months, she was to recall every detail of this night vividly, from the elegant gowns of the ladies, their white shoulders luminous in the candlelight, to the dull brown coat her Uncle Amos wore, precisely tailored to his stocky body. She hesitated for a moment at the top of the long, curving staircase. Then slowly, with her back proudly straight as her aunt had ordered, she descended the stairs.

The house was cool and airy tonight, its white paneled walls and crystal chandeliers gleaming. The turkey-red drapes had been freshly aired, the damask sofas carefully beaten until every speck of dust was gone. There was the smell of beeswax. Flowers, brought in from the garden, were everywhere, their fragrances mingling with the perfumes of the women in their full, high-waisted gowns.

Brenna looked about her. To her left, she glimpsed her cousin Jessica, in an Indian red satin, sitting on the piano bench, her face turned up to Ulrich Rynne, Toby's older, almost middle-aged brother, who leaned toward her attentively, one hand playing with his gold watch fob. If only her father could be here now, she thought. Perhaps then the oddly sad, regretful tone in his letters would cease.

She saw Toby Rynne headed toward her, large and imposing in his broad-collared green coat and long, tight trousers which clung to his heavy, muscular thighs. Although the younger of the two brothers, Toby seemed the dominant one, and Ulrich often deferred to him.

"Brenna! You are ravishing tonight." Toby took her arm, his hot, wet eyes dropping to her bosom.

Brenna found some light retort, trying to suppress a shudder. Toby Rynne was certainly not an unattractive man; there were many girls who gladly flirted with him, seemed pleased to dance with him, and clustered about him. But for Brenna there was something disgusting in the

thick body, well larded with fat and muscle. Toby had a
beefily good-looking face, with sideburns a shade too long
for fashion. His small blue eyes looked out from under un-
ruly eyebrows, and his lips were fractionally too red, as if
he bit or licked them often. At thirty, Toby already commanded great power in the city, according to Uncle Amos.
With hundreds of flatboats coming down the Mississippi
from the north each year, and steamboats regularly seen
on the river now, there were plenty of opportunities here
for the right sort of young men, as Amos said. No one
really knew a great deal about the Rynnes, other than that
they came from New York City, were wealthy, and had
been known to display hot tempers if crossed in any argu-
ment.

Toby propelled her into the dining room, nodding at
Jessica and Ulrich, who was less bulky than Toby but had
the same too-red lips. Ulrich was dressed in black and
fawn and wore a great deal of gold and diamond jewelry.
He had been paying attention to Jessica for several months
now, and Aunt Rowena fluttered about the possibility of a
romance between the two. From remarks Arbutus had
made, Brenna gathered that finances were not altogether
rosy in the Butler family; several of Amos' investments
had not done well. Otherwise, she was convinced, Aunt
Rowena would have been less warm toward the Rynnes.

"Will you have some punch, Brenna?" Toby managed
to make these words sound intimate. He led her to the
enormous table laden with wild turkey, shrimp, calves
feet *à la vinaigrette*, lobster salad and roast of sirloin.

"Just punch, I think, for now. I'm not very hungry."

For a few moments they stood sipping the punch, while
Toby told her of a steamboat he was planning to buy, to be
elegantly fitted out with plush and gilt, soft carpets, and
marble-topped bars of solid mahogany.

"And, of course, we'll serve nothing but vintage wines,
nothing but the best!" he boasted. "If you ask me, steamboats are going to be the coming thing on this river. In
twenty years, that's all you'll see."

He went on to talk further of business, of a large shipment of goods he was expecting, of a man he knew who
had arrived from Natchez last week with news of a steamboat boiler explosion there. Brenna only half listened. Her

mind was on Arbutus, who sat in a red damask chair at the far end of the room, looking unhappy. Arbutus, who bubbled with talk around women, could think of nothing to say to men. A few weeks previously, at an affair given by the Rydells for their five girls, Brenna had gone into the powder room to find Arbutus sobbing piteously, attended by a very annoyed Aunt Rowena.

However, that was evidently not to be the case tonight, for as she watched, Aunt Rowena collared a short, dark, wiry man and ushered him firmly toward her elder daughter, her expression saying that there was no possible escape.

Brenna smiled to herself, hearing the tail end of Toby's conversation. ". . . and so, she has been living in Natchez for some time with my stepmother, who has since remarried, and is now here in New Orleans for a visit. . . . Here she is now. Brenna, I would like you to meet my half-sister, Melissa Rynne."

Something dry in Toby's voice indicated that he did not altogether like the person.

She turned to see a girl of almost startling beauty. Blonde curls, artfully arranged, cascaded down around a perfect oval face. The girl had pale, cameo skin and slanting, catlike eyes that held a hint of mocking laughter. Her lips, a shade too full, were sensuous. A full, pale bosom rose above the bodice of her yellow satin gown. Her waist was so tiny it could have been spanned by a pair of hands.

For an awkward moment the two girls stared at each other. Dislike crackled between them, instinctive and sharp.

"Melissa is staying here for a month or so, at my lodgings," Toby said. "She is well-chaperoned, of course. I've seen to that."

"Oh?"

"Yes, there was someone here I came to see," the other girl said in a soft drawl.

"Well, I hope you will enjoy your stay here."

"Indeed I shall. There is much to keep me occupied here." Melissa's eyes sparkled with some joke which Brenna couldn't share.

As if to rescue Brenna, Aunt Rowena struck the Chi-

nese gong. It was a signal for the music to start. Laughing
and chattering, the guests began to gather in the drawing
room, where Arbutus already waited beside her harp,
white-faced and nervous.

She gave the first performance, playing with her eyes
lowered and her mouth grim, in spite of Aunt Rowena's
pantomimed gestures telling her to smile. Then Jessica, her
frown lines not in evidence tonight, played the pianoforte, receiving much applause, especially from Ulrich
Rynne.

Last on the program was Brenna, who sang a group of
old Irish love songs, many of them in Gaelic. It was the
best part of the evening for her; for a few moments she
could lose herself in the music's spell. As she sang, her
audience listened attentively, and even Melissa Rynne
seemed stilled by the soaring melodies, her slanted green
eyes enigmatic.

As she went into the last song, *Buachaillin Dhoun,* her
eyes caught a movement near the door, and she saw that
a man had entered late.

Her first impression was of a tall body as muscular and
graceful as a wild stallion's. He entered the room without
apology, all energy and pride. His hair, sunbleached to a
blonde-brown, was cropped fairly short, springing into
curls about his temples. His face was tanned a warm
brown, and seemed almost sculptured, so perfect were its
lines, marred only by the cleft in his chin and by two
deep-slashed dimples at the corners of his mouth. His
eyes were a clear blue, and they looked straight at Brenna.

She managed to continue to the end of the song, although her body seemed to flush alternately hot and cold.
She did not know what to do with her hands or eyes.
There was something almost physical in the way he looked
at her, as if his eyes actually touched her.

She was barely aware that the song was over, that she
curtsied to acknowledge the applause. She was only aware
that the man, whoever he was, was striding toward her,
wearing a dove-gray coat and trousers as if they were part
of his skin. Breathing quickly, she saw that his shoulders
were unusually broad, his waist narrow, and his thighs long
and muscular.

Then he stood beside her, taking her arm, as if he had come here especially to see her.

"And who might you be?" He spoke in a clear baritone with what she had learned was a Bostonian accent. "I thought I knew all the young ladies in New Orleans, but you're a new one, aren't you?"

"I . . . I'm Brenna Laughlan."

"Brenna Laughlan." He repeated the words slowly, as if savoring them.

"Yes, I'm Aunt Rowena's niece. . . . That is, I've come from Dublin, where I . . . where my father—"

"I haven't confused you, have I, by arriving so late?" His eyes laughed at her, as if he knew full well that she was turning warm and cool inside, that she didn't know whether to look at him or away. "If I'd known the singing was to be so glorious, I would have arrived much earlier, I can assure you."

"Thank you for the compliment," she told him coolly. "No, you haven't managed to confuse me. And by the way, who are you? I don't believe you introduced yourself."

"I'm Kane Fairfield, lately back from the splendors of the Orient." He bowed mockingly. "At your service, miss."

"Kane Fairfield! Then you're the one who—" She stopped, her cheeks flushing.

"The one they all gossip about? Ah, I see you have heard of me," he said, laughing. "It seems that a man like me is forever shocking the proper ladies in their proper drawing rooms, who think that their men must have lily-pale hands that never do any work. And yet—" He smiled down at her, overconfidently, she thought angrily. "And yet, if the truth were known, these very same ladies love a touch of adventure in their lives. They adore the faintly disreputable feeling that something unexpected might happen at any moment. . . ."

It was if he had looked inside her. She drew back. "You certainly have women figured out, don't you? Well, perhaps some women may react as you say, but not all of them."

He shrugged. "Perhaps. And perhaps not, my dear Brenna. We don't know each other yet, do we?"

"No, we don't, and I am not sure that we are going to!"

"Oh, yes, we will. I can tell that right now, Brenna
Laughlan. You and I are going to know each other very
well indeed." His eyes held hers with the hot blue of
flames. She felt like a rabbit, trapped by the burning stare
of a fox, unable to break and run. Anger began to pound
through her. How dare he look at her so confidently as if
she, too, were one of the women he could "make do anything he wanted," as Arbutus had said. Well, she, Brenna,
was not like other women! She was herself, and no man
was going to control her with nothing more than a blue-
eyed look, never!

For a long instant their glances held, until Brenna felt
her knees begin to waver under the layers of cambric and
silk.

"Someday, young woman—" he started to say in a low
voice meant only for her.

Then someone brushed past them, and the spell was
broken. Brenna heard Melissa Rynne's soft drawl.

"So there you are, Kane. I've been looking all over for
you! Why were you so late? You missed nearly all of the
music, and I was beginning to wonder . . ."

Her voice held honey mingled with a touch of tartness.
She slipped past Brenna, ignoring her, and touched Kane's
shoulder. She arched her head back gracefully to look into
his eyes.

Kane, without another glance for Brenna, bent his face
close to Melissa's, and whispered something in her ear,
something which made her color and grip his arm still
tighter. They were a fascinating couple, Brenna saw; both
of them light-haired, he tall and wild-animal graceful, she
small and perfect as a cameo.

"Excuse us, won't you, Brenna?" Kane bowed slightly.
"Again I must tell you how well you sang. Perhaps I shall
be lucky enough to hear you again."

The smile froze on Brenna's face as she watched them
walk arrogantly toward the punch bowl, as if it belonged
to them personally. In that moment, she did not know
which of them she hated more.

It seemed as if the party went on forever. First, there
was her brother Quentin, who came up to her a few

moments later, holding a nearly empty glass of punch. His
face was wet with perspiration.

"Lovely singing, sister, lovely. Took me right back to
dear old Ireland, it did. You have a voice like a bird."

"Quentin, what's the matter with you?" she demanded.
"You sound so . . . so strange."

"Do I? I feel just wonderful, sister." Quentin's handsome
features were blurred tonight, his mouth slack. "I saw you
and Toby Rynne together," he added. "He seemed very
attentive. Should make Father very happy, shouldn't it?
Rich man like that, known in all the right places—and a
few of the wrong ones, too."

"Oh, who cares about Toby? What about you, Quentin?
We've hardly seen you lately. And when we do, you always
get here late, or else you tell us you're coming and then
you never arrive. Aunt Rowena is getting very cross with
you."

"To hell with Aunt Rowena. She's too busy looking for
moneybags to marry her daughters." Quentin's voice defi-
nitely slurred. "Money, money, money, is that all there is?"

"Why, you've had too much to drink, haven't you,
Quentin? And you were so late coming; did you have
something before you arrived?" Brenna hated to see Quentin like this, so fuzzy and bitter. At Laughlan, she knew,
many times he had come home tipsy after an evening with
his friends. Yet Quentin could be winsome and generous.
Several of his sonnets had been published and someday he
could become a poet of note. But she wished her brother
did not enjoy the easy, pleasure-loving life of New Orleans quite so much.

"*Have* I drunk too much?" Quentin frowned elaborately.
"Well, maybe I did, just a bit. The climate here makes you
dry. They say here that a little fire on the inside lessens
the fire on the outside. I was with a . . . a friend, and
we were having a little wine, that's all, and she—we forgot
the time."

"Oh, Quentin! Maybe you had better go home, then.
Aunt Rowena would be upset if she could see you right
now. She'd say you were ruining her party."

"If I'm ruining it, I'm not the only one. There are other
gentlemen in this house who have had more than a bit.

Even that Toby Rynne of yours is well greased with liquor tonight, in case you hadn't noticed."

"He's not *my* Toby Rynne! And I think I'd better get one of the servants to take you home in the carriage. You're certainly not fit to walk."

"No ... no carriage. Fresh air will do me good." He slapped awkwardly at the back of his neck, where a mosquito was buzzing. Then he lurched out the front door to the broad, white-pillared porch.

"Go back in, Brenna, will you? I can get home in perfectly fine style. Etienne is waiting up for me. You go back inside and enjoy the party. Father wanted you to have fun." There was something leering and almost sarcastic in the way he said this.

"Fun? I'm not—"

But he had gone.

She went back into the house, passing Arbutus sitting on the sofa in the drawing room with the same short, wiry man. He was talking, while Arbutus stared downward into her lap, two red spots of color staining her cheeks.

"Brenna, Brenna, I was looking for you!" Toby Rynne pushed through the crowd toward her, carrying two plates piled with food. "Where have you been?" His eyes moved possessively over her.

He pulled her into an alcove draped with turkey-red damask. "Brenna, you are so beautiful tonight I can hardly keep my eyes off you. If you knew how much I think about you ..." He set the plate of food down on a marble-topped table and leaned toward her.

Brenna looked at him. In his eyes was the same possessive look of desire Neall's had held. She knew that if they were alone, Toby would attempt to kiss her, to press those full, red lips of his against her own. *No*, she told herself. It was not going to happen, no matter how much Aunt Rowena urged. Toby Rynne might be attractive to other girls, but not to her. She would not encourage him.

She pulled away from him and stood up. "I really must leave you now, Toby. Aunt Rowena has asked me to—"

"Oh, hang Aunt Rowena." Toby pulled her back down beside him with one quick move of his big hands. Brenna

gasped; she had not realized that he was so strong, or
that he would be so assertive.

"If I were not here among all these people, Brenna, I
think I would be kissing those lovely lips of yours. In
fact, were it not for politeness and convention, I would
do so right now—"

"Fortunately we are in the midst of a great many people. So you cannot kiss me. And even if we were alone,
I would not allow it. I'm not interested—"

"Not interested?" Toby grinned confidently, and again
Brenna felt a small shiver of surprise. "Brenna, my darling, you are an innocent. You have never been around a
real man before. You do not know what to expect, but I
would like to teach you. When we are married, I will teach
you to love as you have never loved before. . . ."

"Married?" She stared at him.

"Yes, of course. Why else do you think I have pursued
you these past weeks? Can't you see that you are a mania
with me, an obsession? I can't get enough of being near
you, of watching you, of listening to you speak or sing or
laugh. . . ." His hand clasped hers, in damp warmth, and
for a wild instant she knew what it would be like to share
a bed with this large, fleshy, muscular man. His kisses
would be strong and wet, and they would smother her. . . .

"No!" she cried. "No, Toby. I can't marry you. I . . . I
don't want to marry anyone."

Toby threw back his head and laughed, the muscles of
his throat working. "Of course you will marry, and I am
the man for you. Do you think that an exquisite creature
like yourself could remain a spinster? That any real man
would let you? It would be a crime against nature."

"Nevertheless, I don't wish to marry you, or anyone."

Toby's eyes narrowed. A slow, red, flush spread across
his features. "I believe you really mean that."

"Yes, I do."

He spoke slowly. "Well, I have a surprise for you,
Brenna Laughlan. I am not usually scorned by the women
I choose. I get what I want, Brenna, and you are what I
want. Don't think you can escape me that easily."

"But I—"

"I said, you are the thing I want. Don't make me
angry, dear Brenna, because I don't want to be angry with

you. But you had better remember this. . . . *I* am the man who will teach you what love is all about. Me, Toby Rynne."

Hot-faced, escaping from Toby at last, she hurried into the powder room. Could everyone see the anger and consternation on her face, the tears held back? If only the party were over, and she could go to her room and bury her face in her cool, goose-feather pillow!

"Miss Brenna? Anything I can help you with?" Hattie, a young slave, sat in the powder room with a stock of needles and thread, hairpins, combs, fans, smelling salts, and other necessities ladies might need. Hattie was about Brenna's own age, and was obviously enjoying herself watching the procession of ladies in their finery.

"No, thank you, that's all right. I'm fine. I just felt a . . . a bit tired, that's all."

She sat down on one of the dressing stools and stared at herself in the ornate, gilded mirror. Was this Brenna Laughlan, this flushed girl with the big, dreamy eyes? The pale green gown she wore brought out the green tones in her eyes and followed the curves of her body voluptuously. Why, Brenna wondered, hadn't she worn some other gown? Something which did not reveal her breasts so much, or show off the creamy texture of her skin?

"You look mighty fine, Miss Brenna. That green dress mighty pretty. All the ladies look so nice."

"Thank you, Hattie. But I wish I hadn't worn—" Brenna stopped, unable to squelch the eagerness in Hattie's eyes. She still felt uncomfortable with slaves. It seemed strange and wrong to her that another human being could be owned totally—body and soul. Didn't the slaves resent their masters? She had heard of slave rebellions, of course, yet Hattie seemed cheerful enough, as if she enjoyed her role in the powder room. Brenna could not understand it.

She picked up an ivory fan that lay on the dressing table and began to fan herself, hoping to cool the flush that still warmed her cheeks. If only it wasn't quite so moist and hot tonight . . . if only she hadn't seen that Kane Fairfield and gotten so confused. . . .

She was still fanning herself when Melissa Rynne swept into the room, her skirts rustling.

"I need a needle and thread right now," she said imperiously. "My petticoat has ripped and is trailing on the floor. Girl, can't you sew this up for me?" She turned and began preening herself in the mirror, studiously ignoring Brenna.

"Yes'm."

"And make it quick, will you? I'd like to get back to the party." Melissa lifted her hem to reveal a torn white cambric flounce.

"Yes'm." Hattie's dark hand found the white thread, and she threaded the needle deftly. Then, kneeling on the floor, she began to take careful stitches.

"Hurry it up, will you? You are the slowest, most butter-fingered—"

Hattie said nothing, but her lower lip quivered resentfully. Her eyes no longer shone with enthusiasm. Brenna could stand it no longer.

"She's doing the best she can!" she burst out. "It takes time to do a proper job of sewing, or it will only rip again as soon as you start walking."

"Is that so?" Melissa's voice was a dangerous drawl. She tossed her head so that the blonde ringlets bounced. "I don't recall asking for anyone's opinion."

"You got mine anyway." If Brenna had hated Melissa before, she loathed her doubly now. Brenna's father had always treated the servants with courtesy. It was the only way to get willing service, he said.

"Did you enjoy yourself with my brother?" Melissa asked. "Or were you two having a little lovers' spat? I saw how you got up suddenly and rushed in here." She laughed.

Brenna felt herself bristle. "Hardly a lovers' quarrel."

"No? My brother tells the story differently."

"He's wrong! I . . . I would never consider him as a . . . a lover! Why, he . . . he reminds me of nothing more than a big, fat, green bullfrog!"

Melissa's eyes narrowed. "My, that's an interesting way of describing my dear brother. I think he'll enjoy hearing it, don't you?" She gave an impatient tug at her skirt. "Hurry it up, will you, girl? Someone is waiting for me!"

❧ *Chapter 3* ❧

THE PARTY WAS OVER. The lobster salad and roast of sir-
loin had been demolished, the two punch bowls emptied.
A spilled drink marred one corner of the blue and red
Turkish carpet in the drawing room. The slaves worked
through the party debris, puffy-eyed with fatigue. As
Brenna turned to climb the stairs, she caught a glimpse of
Hattie, sighing and rubbing one knuckle against her eye as
she adjusted the cushion of a sofa.

Arbutus waited for her at the top of the stairs. "Brenna!
You're so slow about coming upstairs! Did you have a
good time? Your singing was beautiful. And did you see
the way Ulrich Rynne clapped and clapped for Jessica?
I thought his hands would actually fall off!"

It was as if her cousin had taken some rare, effervescent
drug. Brenna tried to smile. "And you, Arbutus? I see
you enjoyed yourself."

"Oh, yes! That is, I had a very good time. Monty was
telling me all about his plantation. It's called Carlisle Oaks,
you know, and is quite lovely. Did you know that his land
is flooded every single year by the Mississippi? He and
the other sugar planters have been building levees as fast
as they can, but the river always finds a way to get behind
them somehow, Monty says."

"Monty?" This time, Brenna's smile was genuine.

"Well, Mr. Carlisle, then. He said he felt as if he'd
known me for so long that we could be on a first-name

basis if that was all right with me. He said that in many ways I remind him of his first wife—in the way I laugh and speak, I mean."

Arbutus stopped her headlong flow of words to stare at Brenna. "Do you suppose that's a good sign? That I should remind him of his first wife? Would you want your looks to remind a man of some other woman, Brenna? Oh, do come," she said, pulling Brenna by the hand. "Come to my room and visit for a moment. Jessica has gone straight to bed. She says it's late and she's tired. But I can't be sensible tonight, can you, Brenna? Not with that moon outside so brilliant it lights the whole courtyard as if it were day!"

Brenna followed Arbutus to her small, white-paneled bedroom with its Rose of Sharon bed coverlet. She found herself thinking indignantly of the way Kane Fairfield had looked at her, as if his eyes actually touched her, as if he could see through her clothes to the intimacy of her body. And Toby Rynne. Toby, with his strangely worded proposal of marriage.

Well, somehow it would all work out, she told herself, as Arbutus began to chatter of the gowns the women had been wearing. The next time she saw Toby, she would discourage him firmly. She would tell him that she could not possibly think of him as a suitor.

Arbutus' room was rather like Arbutus herself—delicate and scented with dried lavender. On the chest of drawers sat two dolls with painted china heads, their dresses freshly starched. Brenna herself had played little with dolls, her favorite toys had been the small wooden horses Paddy had whittled for her.

"Brenna, did you know that Monty has a baby girl?" Arbutus asked. She had found a second candle and lit it from the one she was carrying. The flames seemed to leap across her face.

"A little girl?"

"Yes, his wife died last year of the fever. Monica is only fifteen months old, Monty says, with dark hair and eyes and two little dimples in her cheeks. . . ."

Another doll to play with, Brenna found herself thinking. She nodded and tried to smile over the dry feeling in her mouth. She had never seen Arbutus quite so glowing.

Yet there was a dull lump in her own chest which would not go away.

"Monica's cared for by a nursemaid at present, and in a few years there will be a governess, of course."

"And a mother?"

Arbutus blushed furiously. "Oh, Brenna, do you think . . . I know I've laughed at Mama, and I've hated all the parties, and a thousand times I've wished I could run away, or . . . or cut my wrists or something. And I've felt they were all laughing at me, at my leg. . . . Until now, Brenna. Now it all seems different."

She set the pewter candle holder down on the chest of drawers and limped to the mirror, where she stared at the wavering image of herself. "Do you suppose he liked me, Brenna? I know I'm not as beautiful as you are, or as some of the other girls, but—"

"You are lovely," Brenna said firmly. "I don't understand why some man hasn't snapped you up before now."

"You must be blind, then, cousin. You know it's my leg. It never healed properly. I'd hate to think of all the times Mama has thrown it up to me. She's afraid it's going to keep me an old maid forever."

"Don't listen to her. She doesn't know everything."

Arbutus bit her lip and turned away from the mirror, her high spirits quenched now. "And you, Brenna? Tell me if you had a good time. I saw you and Toby Rynne together—he leaning toward you and you moving backward ever so slightly, as if he were holding a snake in his hand."

Brenna laughed. "I wish he had been. Then I could have screamed and run away in good conscience."

"Don't you like him?"

"No! Ugh! He reminds me of a big, green bullfrog, all thick with meat and muscle. I know that isn't his fault, but still . . . well, I just don't like to be near him."

"I'm glad I don't feel that way about Monty. He may not be the most handsome man in the world, and I know he's too short and wiry. But, still, he has a nice face, and his eyes are the nicest shade of brown. They seem to smile right at you, as if you were the only person in the whole room."

"When I saw you, you weren't looking at him at all,"

Brenna teased. "You were staring straight down at your lap."

"Was I?" Arbutus giggled. "It seemed to me that I was looking at him all of the time."

"I suppose one look can last a lifetime, can't it?"

It was not a very funny remark, but Arbutus plopped down on the bed, pulling Brenna with her. And soon Brenna was laughing with her, the two of them rolling from side to side with helpless mirth. The more they laughed, the funnier it all seemed. At last Brenna sat up, rubbing her sides.

"Oh! I think I have a stitch in my si—" Arbutus began.

A sharp knocking at the door stopped her in mid-word. Wiping her eyes, Arbutus went to the door and opened it.

It was Aunt Rowena, wearing a long, white cotton apron tied over her taffeta dress. She looked tired, diminished somehow. Her eyes were puffy.

"Girls! Do you realize it is after midnight and Jessica is trying to sleep? You should be in bed, too."

"I'm sorry, Mama, if we were making too much noise," Arbutus said, beginning to giggle again. "It's just that Brenna said I wasn't looking at Monty, and I said—"

"I'm sure it was interesting, but we can hear about it in the morning. At this moment, I am preoccupied with cleaning up after the party. Also there is another matter ..." She hesitated. "I would like to ask Brenna to please come downstairs to Amos' study. There is something he would like to discuss with her."

"Me?" Brenna was bewildered.

"Yes, I am afraid so. A few minutes ago, a messenger arrived at the door, with a letter. . . . Well, Amos would like you to come down. He is waiting for you."

"Yes, Aunt." The laughter left Brenna abruptly. Now she felt only empty, cold with apprehension. A message, at this hour? What could it mean? She thought of her father, so far away near the soft green Irish hills and the sea. Suddenly her tongue was flannel in her mouth and she could not swallow.

"Brenna? Do you want me to come with you?" Arbutus touched her hand.

"That isn't necessary, daughter," Aunt Rowena said

dryly. "I suggest you retire now. It is much too late to be traipsing around and wasting candles."

"But, Mama—"

"That is quite enough, Arbutus. Get to bed. I am sure Brenna can discuss matters tomorrow with you if she wishes."

"Yes, Mama."

Brenna followed Aunt Rowena back downstairs. Her hands felt so cold that she buried them in the folds of her gown to warm them. At this hour, the house seemed an alien place, the carved neo-Grecian moldings casting strange shadows in the candlelight. It seemed to Brenna as if she could still hear crowds of people laughing, but it was only Hattie and Tiny joking among themselves as they tidied the dining room.

"I am surprised the slaves are still about at this hour," she heard herself say to Aunt Rowena.

"We must get the dishes cleared away tonight, Brenna. We fight a constant battle in this climate against insects and rodents, not to mention mildew. If we left things out overnight we would be very sorry. I can see, Brenna, that I have been remiss in my duties. You badly need training in the art of keeping house. Tomorrow or the next day, I will undertake your instruction. It is something that your father would have wanted, I am sure."

Would have wanted. The words sent a chill through Brenna. She clasped her hands together, trying to warm their iciness.

They found Uncle Amos in his study, seated at a large desk and writing with a quill pen. He was a squat, stocky man whose ruddy complexion was threaded with tiny red veins. He had a flowing brown moustache and small, prissy lips. His graying hair was combed carefully to cover a bald spot, and the tailoring of his brown waistcoat was impeccable; his white, starched shirt as fresh as it had appeared before the party. Yet there was a strong smell of whiskey in the room, and Brenna noticed that the hand holding the quill was unsteady.

"Ah, Brenna. Would you sit down?" Amos capped the inkwell, laid the pen down, and pursed his lips with a faint sucking noise. He motioned to his wife, who was hesitating at the door, to sit down as well. Rowena sighed, then reluctantly seated herself in one of the large, leather chairs.

Brenna also found a chair. There was bad news. She could tell by the way Uncle Amos would not look at her.

"Brenna," began Uncle Amos, clearing his throat. "A few moments ago a messenger came, bringing letters from Dublin. He had been instructed that you should receive the letters as soon as possible."

"A letter? From my father?" Brenna half rose in her chair.

"Well, yes. One of them was written by him."

"But may I see it, then? It has been more than a month since I heard from him last. I—" Something in the look on Amos' face caused her to stop.

"Brenna, my dear, your father is dead. He has been dead nearly three months now, evidently of the tumor mentioned in the letter you gave us."

"But ... a tumor ..." The room, paneled in cypress and lined with leatherbound books, began to whirl about Brenna. She had to sink back in her chair and clutch its arms for support. "But he ... he wasn't ..." She bit back the words. Her skin seemed to flash hot with perspiration, then turn clammy-cold.

Her father, dead. She shook her head, trying to absorb the news. So her father's story about a tumor had not been fiction but the literal truth. His sallow complexion, his weariness, the new, dark circles under his eyes—all the signs had been there, if she had only taken the trouble to look. But she had made herself blind. She had not wanted to see that her father was dying.

"There are two letters here," Uncle Amos said, his voice as distant as if it were coming from the depths of a well. "One of them is from a Sir Whitcomb Shawnessy, who states that he is a friend of your family. He informs me of your father's demise, and asks that you be acquainted with certain facts about your father's estate. The other letter is from your father, for you."

"My ... my father's letter. May I see it?"

"In a moment." Amos' eyes regarded her warily. "Are you quite in control of yourself, Brenna? If you wish, we can postpone the rest of this until morning. I am sure it can be faced better after a full night's sleep, don't you agree, Rowena?"

As her aunt nodded, Brenna rose. She could feel herself moving stiffly, like a puppet. Her chest felt swollen. Yet she could not cry, not here in this room with Uncle Amos shuffling the packet of letters as if it were a common business matter.

"I want to hear everything now," she said. "I . . . don't want to wait."

"Very well. The letter from Sir Whitcomb states a few rather unpleasant truths, my dear. The fact is that your father, at the time you left Dublin, was heavily in debt to a number of creditors, and had been forced to sell some of his land."

"Sell? But . . . I didn't know—"

"Never mind, dear. I'm sure he didn't want to bother your pretty head with such matters. Nevertheless, in the past months his fortunes had gone steadily downhill. Then another party managed to gain control of his land and certain other interests." Amos sighed, one hand caressing the tips of his moustache. "I am not certain just how it all happened. The point is that your father died virtually penniless, once the creditors were paid off."

"Penniless?" she gasped. "But . . . there was always plenty of money. There was what my mother left. And Quentin was to come into a trust fund at twenty-one. There was one for me as well."

"Not anymore. Your father died a pauper. And, in fact, his estate has been sold. I believe it was bought by a Neall Urquhart."

"Neall Urquhart!"

"Yes, do you know the man? At any rate, Brenna, your situation is a serious one, as I am sure you can see. You and your brother are both destitute and can no longer depend on receiving any support whatsoever from your father's estate."

Brenna moved to the window, which looked out on a huge live oak draped with Spanish moss, its bulky shadow almost menacing in the moonlight. She felt as if she were dreaming. Soon, she would turn over in bed. She would

look up to see the familiar white netting, and the shadow
of the moonlight across the wallpaper.

Amos' words whirled relentlessly in her head. *Your
father is dead . . . of a tumor . . . bought by Neall Urquhart . . .*

No, this wasn't happening, it couldn't be!

Yet, with cold clarity, one corner of her mind knew
that it had happened, and accepted the reality. Her father
had known he was dying. He had sent her away anyway,
knowing it was her only chance to lead a normal life, free
from the cruelty of the Urquharts. This, then, explained
the sadness in the letters she had received from him. He
had known he would never see her again.

Tears pricked the backs of her eyelids. She and Quentin
had escaped. But her father had not been so lucky. He had
stayed in Ireland. The ugly fact was that Neall Urquhart
and his father had deliberately ruined Brendan Laughlan.
She could see it now—the two had made it their business
to find out every detail of her father's affairs. Then they
had picked and chiseled away at his investments, corrupted
his managers, bought secretly, manipulated funds. Why
hadn't she seen this coming? Why hadn't she guessed that
her escape could not possibly have been so simple, that
somehow the Urquharts would exact their pound of flesh?

"Brenna, are you feeling quite well?" Aunt Rowena
was at her elbow, hovering close but not touching her.
Again Brenna was struck by the weariness in her aunt's
face.

"Perhaps you had better go to bed now, niece. You
look exhausted, and I am sure this has been a tremendous
shock to you," Rowena said. "There are many plans we
must make in the morning, and I know you will want to
be rested."

"Plans?"

"Yes, of course. What you will do now. You must, after
all, do something, mustn't you? Surely you must see that—"

"Later, Rowena," said Amos. "There is plenty of time
for all of this later."

Brenna felt her back stiffening. Plans? No one would
make plans for her, she wanted to shout. She would make
provisions for herself. Yet she could not say this. Her
uncle was staring at her, looking at her almost boldly.

And her aunt still hovered, as if she wished to give comfort but did not know how.

Again Amos cleared his throat. "Brenna, would you like to read the letter from your father? It has been sealed and marked for your eyes only."

"Yes. Yes." Numbly she took the letter from him, feeling the warm, moist touch of his fingers. Then she broke the seal and opened the paper with shaking hands.

Dearest Brenna, the letter began, in a handwriting more wavery than any she had ever seen.

> *When you read this, I will be gone. I wish that it could have been otherwise, that you and Quentin could have remained at Laughlan where you belong. Yet it was not to be. The Urquharts . . .*

here there was an inkblot and the sentence ended.

> *As you must know by now, I was not able to save the estate. I am sure that upon my death it will be sold to the highest bidder. Dear Brenna, I am sorry for what has happened. If I had not been so anxious to see you settled, you might be here in Dublin today, still riding your horse among the hills you loved.*
>
> *Please look after Quentin for me; there is goodness in him, but he is weak. I know you have the strength to help him, and to survive whatever else must come to you. Perhaps I myself did not have sufficient strength, or I could have fought back, could have done something before it was too late.*
>
> *One more thing: I did have certain matters taken care of. I was able to obtain an annulment of your marriage in London, although it cost me dearly in payments to the Urquharts and to certain Members of Parliament. Perhaps someday a divorce will not require an Act of Parliament. It is a necessary reform which I will never see enacted. At any rate, you are now free to marry as you will.*
>
> *With this letter I send much love and the wish that I could have seen your face one more time.*
>
> *Your loving father,*
> *Brendan Laughlan*

For a long moment Brenna stood holding the letter, staring at the faded whorls of ink, all that remained of her father. What was she to do now? What was to happen? With her father dead and Laughlan gone . . . Aunt Rowena was right, there were plans to make, but she did not want to make them. She wanted to go to her room and sink her hot face into her pillow. She wanted to scream and beat her fists against the mattress and smash her knuckles against the wall, and weep until her eyes were reddened and puffy.

"Brenna, you must come upstairs now," her aunt said. "I will fix you a sleeping draught."

"I don't want a sleeping draught. I . . . I want only to be left alone."

"But your brother must be told," Amos began.

"I will tell him in the morning."

"As his only male relative, I was planning to call him here and tell him myself, as is befitting," Amos said pompously.

"That won't be necessary. My father asked me to look after Quentin. I will tell him."

Then Brenna ran out of the study and up the stairs, before they could see her cry.

❧ *Chapter 4* ❧

SHE STOOD KNEE-DEEP in fog, in her dream, on top of a hill which rose above the gray folds of mist like an island. The sky was gun-barrel gray, and a cold wind fluttered the folds of her gown. She was completely alone, stranded there with only the wind for company.

Then, as she looked, a swag of mist lifted, and she was able to see that there were other hilltops, other islands rising out of the gray.

There was a hoarse outcry. Brenna gasped and turned to her left. On the island next to her, she could see two figures struggling in the fog, their bodies rolling in and out of the mist.

"Brenna! Help! Help me!" Was that her father's voice, high-pitched with desperation?

"Brenna, help me! Why did you leave me here?"

The fog twisted, coiled upon itself. One of the struggling figures raised its head, and, to her horror, Brenna saw the face of Neall Urquhart, mouth distorted, skin the color of bone. The form beneath, she realized, was her father.

"Brenna, why didn't you help me? Why did you leave me? Why?"

She woke up, shuddering. Moonlight streamed into the room, reflecting off the folds of her mosquito netting and pooling along the floor. She pushed back the muslin bed sheet and sat up, hearing the whine of mosquitoes beyond the netting.

The dream had been so vivid that her hands were icy-cold from fright. She tucked them under her armpits, and tried to stop her convulsive shaking.

It had been only a dream, she told herself. Yet guilt bored like an insect into her brain. If she hadn't left Ireland, perhaps none of this would have happened. Perhaps somehow her father could have died peacefully, knowing that both his children were secure. Perhaps. . . .

She lay back down, rubbing her burning eyes with her knuckles. She had cried in grief and anger. She had wept and slammed her fists into the soft feathers of her pillow. But nothing had relieved the hard lump inside her. Now, sighing and turning on her side, she cradled her cold hands. She slept.

In the morning, Aunt Rowena gave her permission to take the carriage to Quentin's lodgings. "I will be glad to accompany you," her aunt offered, in her dry, efficient voice.

"I . . . I think I would rather go alone."

"Well, you can't go alone, not here in New Orleans. Don't you realize what sort of ruffians roam the streets? Wild riverboat men who spend all their free time fighting and gambling and worse? Why, the militia patrol can't control them, and they don't even try."

"I don't care. I—"

"Whether you like it or not, young woman, Amos and I are responsible for you," Rowena said tartly. "You'll take Tiny, then. He is big enough to make any man think twice, and he's a good driver. And you will have to take Mary with you, too. I insist upon that."

As soon as breakfast was over, Brenna donned a straw bonnet and pulled a lace shawl over the shoulders of her dark green silk.

"Sure, and we're lucky not to be struggling along today in mud up to our boot tops," Mary said grimly as the carriage pulled out of the drive. She had heard of Brendan's death an hour ago, and her eyes were reddened and puffy. "I think the good Lord was thinking of us when he withheld the rain last week. Sometimes, Brenna, I wonder whether the mire and muck can ever be cleaned from the hem of your gowns. Oh, sometimes I do wish for the good, clean peat of Ireland!"

Brenna nodded. Often the unpaved streets, flooded with water that had nowhere to drain, were impassable. Those attending parties or the opera had to struggle on foot along the slippery plank or brick walks, or through the mud, carrying their shoes in their hands. When they reached their destinations, a servant cleaned their feet and helped them into their finery.

The two sat silently as the carriage rattled through the streets. The air was moist today, filled with a fine, soft haze. The heavy scents of magnolia and jasmine mingled with the odors of a poultry market, a perfume factory and the stench of the open gutters. In the Creole section, the houses were built of brick, covered with stucco, with over-hanging eaves and roofs sloping sharply to front and rear. As their carriage passed elaborately scrolled gateways, Brenna saw enclosed patios filled with banana and pome-granate trees, willows, palms and wisteria. The courtyards, so cool and lovely, made startling contrast with the stench of garbage and sewage in the streets.

"Wurra!" Mary said at last, wrinkling her nose. "You would think these people would worry about catching disease from all of this open water! I hear they have enough sickness here. Typhoid and yellow fever and Lord knows what else."

"There's nowhere for the water to drain," Brenna said. "That's why it's always so wet and swampy. They can't even dig graves here," she added, shuddering. "The water fills up the hole almost as fast as they can dig."

"I'd choose Ireland any day," Mary said with finality.

Feeling too heavyhearted to argue, Brenna sank back into silence. In a few moments, they reached Quentin's lodgings, a cream-colored stucco house with iron grillwork fashioned to look like a grape arbor.

As Tiny pulled the horses to a stop, they saw a girl leaving the house through the patio gate. She moved familiarly, as if she came here often. She was young, full-breasted; her skin so pale it was almost white, and she wore a deep yellow, ruffled dress. Her hair was wrapped in a white *tignon*, a cloth turban which all women of color wore.

The girl turned in the direction of the carriage, her hips swinging in an easy, indolent way. Then, startled, she looked up, her brown eyes widening, one hand flying to her mouth.

For an instant Brenna and she stared at each other. Then the other girl ran past them, her feet moving skillfully along the uneven bricks.

Brenna stared after her. *If we were to exclude all the men who had brown mistresses . . .* Arbutus had said. Was this Quentin's girl? But quickly she pushed the thought aside. The girl could be Etienne's lover, or even work in the house. Still, she found herself reluctant to get out of the carriage. Quentin had changed so much in the past months, become so broody and restless, that she no longer felt she knew him well.

"Wait here," she told Mary. "I think I should go in alone."

She found Quentin, in a gray morning coat, drinking a cup of thick chicory coffee. A half-eaten roll lay on a plate beside him. His skin looked puffy this morning, his eyes bloodshot.

"Sister, what are you doing here?" he asked. "I would have Etienne bring you a croissant, but he is out shopping, I think. To tell you the truth, my head is pounding so hard I didn't even hear him leave." He set the coffee cup down on a cabinet next to another, half-empty cup. "Well, don't stand there, sister. Come in."

The rooms, on the upper level, had a balcony that looked out onto an inner courtyard. The walls were of yellow-tinted plaster, and the chairs were upholstered in gold velvet. A small desk held Quentin's books and a few sheets of paper covered with inkblots and scribbling.

"There . . . there is something I wish to talk to you about," Brenna began.

"There is? Oh, sister, surely you don't mean to scold me for my behavior last night?" Quentin smiled and ran one hand through his auburn hair appealingly. "I wasn't really that bad, was I? At least, I know there were plenty of others who were far more under the influence than I was." He grinned at her. "Don't tell me Aunt Rowena is angry at me for that."

"No, no, she's not. It isn't that."

"Then what?" Quentin pulled open the wide French

doors and stepped out onto the balcony, breathing in deep draughts of the humid morning air. "Ah, Brenna! What wouldn't I give for a deep whiff of that Dublin air! To be there right after a rain, with the clouds piled up dark in the sky, and the rays of sun shining through—"

"Quentin . . ." Brenna clasped her hands tightly together under the folds of her lace shawl. "Quentin, there is something I have to tell you."

"What, sister?"

Brenna's mouth opened and closed. She did not know how to go on. But somehow the words came out. "Our father . . . he is dead."

"What?" Quentin had raised his arms in a dramatic gesture which took in the courtyard, the buildings beyond, and the whole sky. Now he stopped in mid-stretch, his body seeming to shrink. "What did you say, Brenna?"

"I said he is dead. Of a tumor. Uncle Amos received the news last night, from a messenger. Oh, Quentin, I think Father was already dying when we left Dublin."

There was a long silence, interrupted only by the sounds of birds in the courtyard, the distant shout of a fish vendor. Quentin seemed to sag in the doorway, his hands clutching the jamb for support. His lips were colorless, drained of blood. "I . . . I don't know what to say, sister."

"There is nothing to say. He is dead, and there is nothing we can do." Brenna shook her head. "But I am afraid there is more bad news, Quentin. You see, the Urquharts . . . well, they stripped him of Laughlan and of our whole estate. Somehow they managed to take it."

"You don't mean . . . Laughlan is gone?"

"Yes. Laughlan is in the hands of Neall Urquhart right now."

"Urquhart," Quentin repeated slowly. "I should have shot the man, Brenna. I should have killed him for what he did to you. But I didn't. Instead I allowed myself to be herded off to America like . . . like a milksop."

"Father asked us to go. We . . . you couldn't have known—"

"That doesn't change things! That doesn't bring Father back, or Laughlan either, does it?" Quentin walked past Brenna, and fumbled in a cherrywood cabinet for a bottle of whiskey and a glass. He poured himself an amber dose, then tipped up the glass and drank until his eyes watered. "God, I needed that, I'm ashamed to say. I am sorry to drink in front of you, sister, but it was necessary."

Brenna sank down in a chair. "You know, don't you, what all this means? It means that we are penniless . . . that we have no money of our own. Uncle Amos says we can't expect a penny from Father's estate, not a penny. Which means that these rooms of yours, my gowns . . . we can no longer afford such things."

"Penniless? Wiped out?" Quentin stared into the depths of his empty glass. Slowly his hand reached out for the bottle and poured another shot. "Surely, you can't mean that. There must be something left. Our trust funds—"

"No. The trust funds are gone. Everything is gone. We are poor, Quentin. We are dependent on the mercy of Aunt Rowena and Uncle Amos now."

"But I owe the rent on these lodgings, Brenna. It's almost two weeks overdue. And God knows why Etienne is still with me, I haven't paid him in a month. And my tailor bill . . . it's astronomical. My . . . my other bills are, too. Surely Uncle Amos must have made a mistake. It can't *all* be gone."

"It *is* gone. Quentin, the letter was from Sir Whitcomb Shawnessy. He was one of Father's close friends, and he wouldn't lie. There isn't any more money, Quentin. We have to face it."

"Gone," her brother repeated. "Do you know how much money I owe, Brenna? Do you have any idea what I am obligated to repay? Have you any notion at all?"

She watched him tilt back the glass, swallow noisily. "Do you owe money, Quentin?"

"I am afraid I do, sister. Afraid I do. Money!" He gestured with the glass. "Why are we so dependent on it, such slaves to it? Why does it have to be the most important thing in our lives?"

"Quentin, you'd better tell me. How much do you owe, and to whom?"

"You won't like this, but I owe ten thousand dollars, dear Brenna, and I owe it to Billy Love, of Love's Garden. I was in hope of recouping myself. My luck was changing. Just this past week, it was all going to the good again for the first time in months. I was going to get it all back—"

"Quentin!" Brenna could not conceal her shock. "What are you talking about? Who is this Billy Love?"

Quentin set down the glass on the paper-littered desk, his mouth quirking in a bitter smile. "Faro, Brenna, what else? On the riverboats they call this game 'the tiger.' But unlike the unsavory dens of the flatboat men, Billy Love's is a refined establishment. It is a fine place, Brenna. Many important men of New Orleans go there, and I am afraid more than a few have staked their land, and even their slaves, against the fickle heart of Lady Luck. I have even seen your fine Toby Rynne there, chancing a whole shipload of goods on the throw of the dice!"

"Do you mean, Quentin, that you have lost *ten thousand dollars* at this game of faro?"

Her brother had slumped into his chair, and was staring down at the gold seal ring on his left hand. "They say," he muttered, "that it does not go well for those who do not repay Billy Love. He is a big, red-headed man with a very quiet voice, Brenna. They say he has killed more than one man with the knife, and that he never forgives a man who does not pay his gambling debts."

Brenna listened with horror. One could not live in a city like New Orleans without being aware of the gambling mania which had swept the city, extending to every segment of the population. On Girod and Tchoupitoulas Streets, there were depraved and crooked gambling places for the riverboat men. But in other, more refined, establishments or coffeehouses a respectable man could go to play faro, roulette, vingt-et-un or écarté. And nearly every day, a body was found in the open drains or in a canal, shot, knifed or beaten to death. Whether these unfortunates had been set upon by criminals, or by personal enemies, no one ever knew. None of the murderers were ever found.

"Quentin!" Brenna breathed. "Do you think that this man . . . this . . . Mr. Love, would actually . . ."

"I don't know. All I know is that he has asked me about payment, in that quiet voice of his. More than once, Brenna, more than once. I told him my birthday was in five more months, I told him that I was expecting the trust fund . . . I thought I could get more funds from Father to tide me over . . ."

"There is no money now."

"I would hate to tell that to Billie Love. I would hate to."

"But, Quentin. He's bound to find out, isn't he? What will he do then?"

"I don't know, sister. I don't know."

She left the apartment, where Quentin sat with his face in his hands, and hurried out to the carriage, trying to swallow back her dismay. She had known, of course, that Quentin gambled occasionally. It was the pastime of most lighthearted young men of his group. But never, she was sure, had he gambled for such high stakes before, and never had a man like Billy Love been involved.

Brenna and Mary rode back through the city. Brenna was quiet, not wanting to burden Mary with this latest news. Mary had never liked New Orleans. She distrusted the black people and hated the swarming insects. Stoically she bore the heat and suffered the demands of Aunt Rowena, but it was clear to Brenna that she would much prefer to be back in Dublin. The Irish woman had seemed numbed by the news of Brendan Laughlan's death. Now, with Laughlan gone, there was no place for Mary to return to.

They arrived home to find the house quiet, baking in the midday sun. Hattie moved listlessly through the drawing room with a dust rag. She told Brenna that Uncle Amos was in court, Arbutus and Jessica were paying calls, and Aunt Rowena was confined to her room with indigestion.

Feeling restless, Brenna went to her room, deciding to change her gown and go for a walk in the courtyard, although she knew it would be breathlessly hot in the direct sun.

She had just pulled on the gown, an old russet calico that was too tight across the bosom, when there was a knock at her door. It was Hattie, panting from climbing the stairs.

"Miss Brenna, you've got someone here to see you.

I think it that Mr. Toby Rynne. Domo, he busy in the kitchen, so I answered the door." Hattie gestured excitedly.

Brenna tried to stifle the dread that seeped through her. "Very well. Thank you, Hattie. I'll be right down."

She waited by the mirror until the girl had left, staring at herself defiantly in the cloudy glass. Even though the gown was old, the russet brown picked up the gold glints of her hair and accentuated the rounded lines of her figure. Besides, why should she put on a new gown for Toby? She didn't care whether he liked her or not.

Toby was standing in the broad, parqueted entrance hall, his hands behind his back, his face a dull red.

"So there you are, Miss Brenna." He bowed to her exaggeratedly. "You are looking lovely this morning." Was there anger beneath the silken tone of his voice?

She decided to be blunt with him. "Nonsense. This is one of my oldest gowns. I was preparing to go for a walk in the garden when you arrived."

"A walk?" Again she sensed anger in him. "By all means, do not let me interrupt your plans. In fact, perhaps I will accompany you."

"That's not necessary. We can . . . talk here."

"But I enjoy walking, dear Brenna. It is something we have in common, isn't it?" Toby took her arm and Brenna felt the animal warmth of him, the beefy strength of the muscles beneath the dark green coat.

The courtyard was at the rear of the house, with the slave quarters on the left. At the center of the flagged enclosure was the fountain, flanked by the stone cupid. Honeysuckle grew profusely around the fountain, and vines climbed everywhere, twining and hanging and trailing. At the rear of the courtyard stood an enormous weeping willow tree, its branches drooping to the ground in thick swags.

Brenna felt uneasy in Toby's company. Had Melissa carried out her threat to tell him that Brenna had called him a bullfrog? That could explain his air of pent-up anger now.

"It's beautiful here in the courtyard, isn't it?" she commented, trying to fill the heavy silence between them.

"Beautiful. Yes. Like you, my dear."

"Although the heat is something one has to grow accustomed to, after the cool air of Ireland," Brenna heard herself chattering on.

He was silent. For a few moments they walked, their footsteps scraping on the loosely laid brick tiles. Then Toby's grip tightened on her arm and he drew her to a stop.

"The devil with silly talk about the climate! We have more important things to talk about."

She drew back. "Would you please release my arm, Toby? You are hurting me."

"I am hurting you? I am sorry, dear Brenna. I will release you at once." Ostentatiously he withdrew his hand, his eyes flashing at her.

"Toby, what is this all about? I did make my feelings clear to you last night, and surely I have every right to feel as I wish."

"Right?" He laughed harshly. "What right do you have to scorn me, a girl like you with a face and body made for only one thing. You do scorn me, don't you, Brenna? You laughed at me with my sister. You made fun of the love I offer you."

Brenna could not look at his small, angry eyes. "I did speak hastily to Melissa, I'll admit it. She and I . . . well, we didn't get along. I lost my temper. That was why I spoke as I did. I certainly didn't intend that your . . . your feelings should be hurt."

"My feelings are not easily hurt."

"But—"

"You will see, Brenna. You will see what it's like to deal with a real man. I told you, didn't I, that I get what I want? That I let nothing stand in the way of the goals I set for myself? Would you like to know something? I have not confided this to anyone in this city, but I will tell you. My father came to New York City from Germany. He was a tailor. He could not speak English and times were bad. My mother and brother and I nearly starved to death. Then my mother died of consumption from the poor food and from living in an unheated room. My father remarried . . . to a woman who had no use for two half-grown boys. She didn't want us to soil her precious little daughter! So we were on our own, then, and we survived somehow, even after my father died. No help from the widow we got! Do you know I pulled a junk wagon for a time? And a girl laughed at me once. A girl who looked much like you, all peaches and cream, a girl from a rich drawing room like your aunt's.

"I wonder if you can understand what it means. To fight your way out of a dirty slum that smells of dogs and vermin and children. I vowed that someday I'd lord it over a drawing room filled with carpets and chandeliers. I vowed I'd never be laughed at again. . ."

Toby continued in a low, monotonous voice, his eyes fastened on Brenna's face.

"I tell you, Brenna, a man has to take what he wants in his own two hands. If he doesn't, sure as the devil no other man's going to do it for him. No one ever did for me."

Toby looked so intense that Brenna could almost feel pity for the young boy pulling the junk wagon.

"I don't agree," she said. "Power has to be earned, not taken. My father always said—"

"Your father doesn't know anything. Some things can't be earned, not by men like me. No, Brenna, your father was very wrong. Some things are meant to be taken, even beg to be taken. You, for instance."

"Me?"

"You are a proud little beauty, but you can't hold out against the will of a strong man who knows what he wants. As I said, some things are best taken first, then argued about later."

Brenna stared at him. "Toby, I made my feelings very clear to you last night. I don't wish to marry. Not you, and not anybody."

He smiled. "You are only eighteen, still a child. You do not know what you want."

"That's nonsense," she told him. "I have always known what I wanted."

"And what is that?" His smile mocked her. He reached for a handful of honeysuckle, snapping the leaves and flowers off the stem in one pull.

"Why, I . . . I want to . . . to . . ." She heard herself stammering. She floundered on. "Why, I want adventure, and . . . seeing far places, and . . . and doing things. . . ."

He laughed, his head thrown back, his eyes slitted against the sun. "You're full of silly, childish dreams. You haven't the faintest idea of what it's like to want something and never stop wanting it until you get it. No matter what you have to do."

"I am *not* full of silly dreams! I—"

"You are. If you want adventure, I'll give it to you. If you want to do things, you can do them with me." He pulled her toward the heavy fronds of the weeping willow. "Look, Brenna. One of our magnificent American trees. Did you know that there is a secret room in this tree?"

Before she could protest, he had pulled her through the rough, hanging branches of the tree into a yellow-green, dappled enclosure. It was as if she had been pulled into another world, a world bounded by green. The house, with its white pillars and mellow plastered surfaces, could be seen only in fragments. The air was hot and close and full of sun.

Toby pushed her up against the rough trunk of the willow, and then she felt his mouth on hers. It was a strangely smothering kiss. Toby's lips were not soft, as she would have imagined, but hard and muscular. She felt her own lips forced apart and his tongue darting inside her mouth.

"No—" She tried to pull away. "No, Toby, please—"

But his arms only fastened about her body more tightly. "Brenna, why do you struggle? This was meant to be. In your soul, you know it."

"I don't know any such thing!" she gasped. "Will you please let me alone?"

"I do not intend to let you alone." To her shock, he picked her up, one hand under her knees, the other supporting her back.

"What ... what are you doing? Let me down! Let me down at once!"

The house, she thought quickly. People, the slaves, were nearby. If she called for help, someone would surely hear. Drawing breath, she tried to scream. But almost instantly Toby clapped his hand over her mouth. His hand was big and meaty. She could taste his perspiration.

"Stop that!" he commanded. "Screaming will get you

nowhere. When I'm finished, you'll have changed your mind about this, you know. You'll beg me for more!"

With all her strength she pulled her mouth free of his hand. "I'll never beg anything from you!"

"Oh, yes, you will."

It happened very quickly. With one powerful, twisting motion of his big hands, Toby ripped open the front of her gown from neck to waist. The russet gown was old, and had been washed many times. Its light fabric gave way easily to Toby's force.

Gasping, too frightened now to scream, Brenna tried to cover her breasts, but Toby forced her hands away, and lowered her to the ground. "No, do not cover yourself. You are mine, Brenna, mine!"

Afterward, she would never be able to remember these events clearly, but only as a blurred kaleidoscope. Toby's body covered hers, so heavy that she could not shove him away. His hands tugged at her skirts. Her thrashing legs met the resistance of his thighs, and his chest pressed against her own until she gasped for breath.

It is going to happen again, just as it did with Neall, came the thought, like a match touched to the tinder of her brain. *The same, the same . . .*

No! She screamed silently. No, she couldn't let it happen again. She couldn't! As if in release, rage began to pump through her veins. Sudden strength flowed into her muscles, and then, without thinking, she knew what to do.

She twisted her head slightly to the side, breaking the hold of Toby's lips on her mouth. Then she opened her jaws wide and bit down as hard as she could on Toby's lower lip, forcing her teeth through flesh.

The effect was instantaneous. Toby's body stiffened, and then he jerked away from her in surprise.

She saw the blood pouring down his lip, and tasted it, salty and bitter, on her own tongue.

"Why, you little—" Toby gave a choked cry of fury, half muffled by the flow of blood. He rose on one knee and reached for her again.

Brenna shoved at him with all her strength, toppling him backward. Then she jumped up and ran, through the willow fronds, barely feeling the branches snapping at her face and hair.

She started to run across the courtyard, stumbling on the uneven bricks, then paused in astonishment to see someone standing by the stone cupid. It was Mary, looking thin and tall in her plain gray dress. Her face twisted with surprise and horror.

"Sweet Mary in Heaven, what happened to you, child?" The Irish woman started toward Brenna. "I heard a noise in the courtyard, and ... why, there's blood on your mouth and on your gown. And it's ripped. . . ." And then she lowered her voice. "What happened?" she whispered.

"Toby. He . . . did this. He said some things are better if taken . . ." Brenna felt herself swaying. She drew in a painful gasp of air.

For an instant, Brenna saw Mary's eyes widen with shock. But quickly the Irish woman controlled herself, and took Brenna's arm. "Quick, child! You mustn't be seen like this. People will think the worst. It will destroy you. Here, put my shawl across your shoulders and wipe your mouth. Into the house with you, hurry! We'll go through the library entrance. Your uncle is still downtown and perhaps no one will see us. Hurry!"

"Yes." Brenna shook her head, feeling dazed.

"Hurry, child, hurry!"

"I . . . I'm coming." They moved quickly across the courtyard, Brenna, in her shocked state, clinging to Mary's arm.

"Is he still there?" Mary whispered, looking back. "Oh, Jesus and Mary, what was he thinkin' of? He has ruined you!" She gripped Brenna's hand firmly. "Hurry, now. He will leave by the back courtyard gate when we are gone. I am sure of it. We'll get you into another gown and no one will be the wiser. Oh, hurry, Brenna, do, before some-one sees us!"

They had almost reached the side entrance, when the paneled door was suddenly thrust open. In the doorway stood a small, neat, precise figure, white apron and cap immaculately starched and pressed.

"Aunt Rowena!" Brenna gasped. "What . . . what are you doing here?"

❧ Chapter 5 ❧

THEY STOOD AS IF FROZEN, staring at Aunt Rowena's form outlined in the doorway. From the courtyard came the heat-dazed sounds of afternoon: the drone of bees among the blossoms, the comfortable chirp of a bird in the wisteria. From a distance could be heard the deep, throaty laugh of one of the servants, the rhythmic squeak of the kitchen pump, the clatter of iron skillets.

But here was only silence. Aunt Rowena's short figure, raised several feet above them on the doorstep, intimidated them.

"What is the meaning of this scene? Would you please tell me?" Aunt Rowena's chest seemed to swell with anger. "I saw you from the window of my bedroom, you little slut! I saw what you did!"

"What *I* did?"

"You and Toby . . . I saw you walking together and then going beneath that willow tree. I saw your shadows, too, through the branches, lying upon the ground, embracing—"

"It's not as you think, Aunt Rowena." Brenna pulled open the shawl Mary had lent her to reveal the torn bodice of her gown, the white flesh of her bosom showing through the tear. She began to explain, but her aunt interrupted her.

"I know what I saw. Cozying up to that man, smiling

at him, letting him take your arm . . . now look where it's led you!"

Brenna stared at her aunt. "I did not . . . none of what you say is true. I did not want him, and I was only trying to tell him so when he pulled me beneath the tree and . . . and ripped my gown. He would have ravished me if I had not managed to get away from him."

Rowena looked at her in disbelief, two hectic circles of red staining her cheeks. "After all the kindness I have shown you, taking you in without question, giving you a social life, seeing to it that you were properly fed and cared for and chaperoned. Oh, for you to repay me thusly! I should have known this would happen. You are just like your mother!"

"Like . . . my mother?"

"Didn't you know? Your mother succumbed to your father before marriage. She was with child at her own wedding! It was the scandal of New York, her and her red hair and green eyes! Oh, she thought she was so clever, sneaking around behind my back, tempting Brendan Laughlan, smiling at him. He was the man *I* wanted, the man I was in love with. And he wanted me, too. Until she came back from school to steal him away from me!"

"But . . ." Brenna remembered the odd, half-resentful looks her aunt had given her from time to time. She had paled when she learned that Brendan Laughlan was ill, and had seemed upset by his death. Brenna started to protest. "I'm sure my mother would not—"

"She took him, all right, and I pretended I didn't mind. I acted as if everything were fine. I even served in the bridal party, calmly smiling as everyone congratulated *her*. And the way she looked up at Brendan as if he were the sun and moon and stars. And he! He only had eyes for her. How tenderly he treated her, how gently, as if she were so fragile she would shatter like crystal. But I knew how tough she was. How she could ride that horse of hers from dawn to dusk without even tiring, how she could ramble in the fields for hours, and then dance half the night—" Aunt Rowena swallowed, adding in a low whisper, "But I finally got my revenge, my justification. She died. Died in childbed, died in the bed of sin she had made for herself!"

"My mother did not die in . . . in *sin*. She was good!
I don't care what happened in her young days. She loved
her husband and her children. She—"

"And how would you know all this, miss? You were
only nine when she died," Rowena snapped. "In any case,
when you arrived, I did try to overlook the past, and let
bygones be bygones. However, when it comes to seducing
a man within the very walls of my home, besmirching
our name right in front of my very eyes! Well, history
repeats itself, and I cannot overlook the past any longer."

Before Brenna could reply, Mary spoke up indignantly.
"See here, ma'am, Miss Brenna is a good, virtuous girl.
Sure and she would never do such a thing as you're ac-
cusing her of."

"How dare you, only a servant, speak to me in that
manner?" Rowena demanded. "Especially when you are
dependent on my kindness for the very roof over your
head."

"But Miss Brenna did not—"

"I tell you to keep silent or I will have you thrown out
upon the streets within the hour!"

Mary, wincing as if she had been slapped, lowered her
eyes to the courtyard tiles. Her face was so white that
the pits from her smallpox stood out in dark relief. In
spite of her own agitation, Brenna felt a pang of pity for
the Irish woman. Her place of many years in Ireland was
gone. Now her position in New Orleans was threatened.

"As for you, you young slattern," Rowena turned back
to her niece. "I will deal with you later, after you have
gone to your room and removed that . . . that filthy, disgusting gown."

As Brenna hesitated, the sound of rustling branches came
from beneath the willow. Slowly the fronds were pushed
aside, and Toby Rynne emerged, his handkerchief pressed
to his bleeding lip. He smiled an ugly, crooked smile.

"You are right, Madame Butler," he said. "I was powerless against the wiles of this adept young witch. She can
tempt a man with but one look from her eyes." Toby's
own eyes glinted mockingly.

"No! That isn't true! You have no right to say such
things!" Brenna cried. But Aunt Rowena was nodding,
as if Toby had confirmed something.

"I thought so. Not that you are entirely without blame, Mr. Rynne. But still . . ." She turned to Brenna. "Go upstairs to your room instantly. To think that I allowed you to live in my home, allowed you to meet my friends and socialize with my daughters—"

Brenna shivered with fury. "Toby Rynne is lying, aunt! Take a good look at him, and you will see that I am telling the truth. Look at his bleeding lip. I bit it defending myself!"

Toby shook his head. "Nonsense. She's lying."

"*You* are lying, Mr. Rynne! You were trying to . . . to attack me, and you know it. Leave here at once! I find you utterly disgusting."

Toby bowed, elaborately. "Never fear. You won't be rid of me that easily, Miss Brenna Laughlan. Remember, there have been witnesses to what happened today, your aunt, your maidservant and . . ." He gestured toward the slave quarters where two or three black women clustered in a doorway. ". . . even the slaves, who will certainly tell the other servants what they saw. News like this travels quickly! Your reputation is ruined, my lovely young Brenna, much as I hate to say it. And I am the only one who can help you now."

"Help me! *You*, help me? You did not ruin me, no matter what wild tales you tell. I . . . I got away . . ."

Toby began to laugh, great peals of sound. "Tell that to them," he said, pointing toward the slave quarters. "They won't know that. They only know what they saw. No, you are ruined, Brenna, and only marriage can save you. If you marry me, the scandal will blow over in a month or so. People will chuckle and look kindly upon a couple so much in love they couldn't wait. Within a year it will all be forgotten. And you will be the wife of one of the richest and most powerful men in New Orleans."

"No! You can't mean that!" Brenna's voice filled with horror.

"But I do. I offer to save your very life and reputation, and you scorn me. Well, you had better consider my offer quickly, before I withdraw it. Remember, in a matter of hours, all of New Orleans will know what has happened here."

"But . . . we will beg the servants not to talk."

"Perhaps. But will you be able to stop *me* from talking?" With another laugh, Toby turned and lifted the latch of the back courtyard gate. He was gone.

The three women watched him leave. Aunt Rowena was the first to speak. "Well, Brenna? He is right, you know. You are totally ruined."

"But, aunt, didn't you hear what he said? Don't you realize what he is trying to do? Why he even told me that a man has to *take* what he wants. Can't you see how his mind runs? First he will ruin my good name. Then he will take over and 'save' me by making an honest woman of me!"

Rowena smiled coldly. "As your father did your mother? No, Brenna, the blame for this lies at your door. If you did not like Toby Rynne you should not have flirted with him, flaunted your body before him. Now it is too late. You must marry him to save your reputation."

"But I didn't flaunt myself! I don't intend—"

"Your *intentions*, my dear, make no difference." Aunt Rowena spoke precisely, and her eyes raked Brenna with hatred. "Now, please go at once to your room and take off that disgusting garment. Take the dress and burn it. Stay in your room until Amos and I send for you. And not a word of this to my daughters, do you understand?"

Somehow, Brenna managed to stumble up to her bedroom, Mary's arm about her for support. When they reached the room, Brenna flung herself on the bed and burst into wild weeping.

"Now, now, darling, it's all right," Mary crooned, taking her into her arms. "Mary's here. You're going to be all right. It's all right."

For a few minutes Brenna burrowed against Mary's breast, once again the distraught and bewildered little girl who had lost her mother. She clung to the Irishwoman, her body wracked with sobs. At last she sat up and began to wipe her eyes. Silently Mary handed her a handkerchief.

"Oh, Mary, what am I going to *do?* He . . . oh, it was wicked, what he did. He pulled me under that tree, Mary, and then he deliberately ripped open my bodice. He was going to . . ."

"Now, Miss Brenna, best calm yourself."

"But I can't be calm! Not when I think of those hands all over me, crawling on me . . . oh, Mary, his lips were on mine . . ."

"Get hold of yourself, Miss Brenna. You heard what your aunt said. You had better change your gown, since she is probably going to send for you soon. You want to be ready."

Brenna wiped her eyes, then flung the handkerchief down. "Is she? Well, let her then! I have no intention of . . . oh, Mary, imagine having to marry that awful man. Imagine those hands on your body every single night. Ugh!"

Mary hesitated. "Did he . . . touch you intimately, Brenna? With his private parts?"

"No, thank heavens. He did *not* manage to rape me, much to his great sorrow, I am sure." Brenna began peeling off the gown, in quick, angry motions, until she stood in her chemise and petticoats. Then she ripped the russet fabric, tearing at the cloth until she reduced the dress to a pile of red-brown strips. It was not nearly enough to express her deep anger, but it helped.

"There!" she cried. "There! Take it and throw it in the gutter or burn it. I never want to see that dress again. Oh, Mary, I feel so dirty. So . . . soiled."

"Child, child, you must calm yourself. I will refill your ewer and you must wash. Then lie on the bed and rest. Take a nap, if you can. Surely everything will seem rosier when you have had a chance to sleep for a few hours. You will be better able to accept your fate."

"What . . . what do you mean?" Brenna stared.

"Well, you know, Brenna," Mary said awkwardly, "you know, your aunt is probably right. Everyone will know what happened to you. You were nearly raped, your reputation is gone . . ."

"Why, Mary!" Brenna whispered.

"I'm sorry, Miss Brenna. But I'm the only one left around here who can give you good advice. And I can tell you that a girl with a tarnished name had better snatch at any chance for an honest marriage. Darling, you've been sheltered by your father all of your life. You don't know the cold hard facts of the real world at all.

Why, a young girl who is besmirched cannot get employment. She has no choice but to go to another city and become a . . . a kept woman, or a . . . a . . . whore, selling her body for money."

"I don't believe it. You, Mary, of all people! Saying such things."

"Darling Brenna, listen to me—"

But Brenna would not listen. She pulled away from Mary and stood trembling, her heart pounding in her ears. "Mary, would you please just go away and leave me alone?"

"But, Brenna, it's the truth I'm telling you. The truth, child!"

"Get out!" Brenna shouted. "Just get out!"

After Mary left, Brenna lay shivering on her bed, her eyes stinging with unshed tears. Yet she could not cry anymore. She could only creep beneath the covers to warm her cold body, cold in spite of the day's moist heat.

If she hadn't married Neall, she thought wildly, none of this would have happened. She wouldn't be huddled in this bed, still shuddering from the touch of Toby Rynne. And she wouldn't have been betrayed by Mary. How, she wondered, could Mary say such things? Mary, who had known her and loved her ever since she was a baby? Mary, who had been almost a mother to her?

She fell into a restless sleep, to be awakened only minutes later by the sound of a carriage passing by on the road outside. She got out of bed, pulled a dressing gown about her shoulders, and went to her window, to look into the courtyard below, at the willow tree shimmering in the afternoon sun. She rubbed her tear-swollen eyes tiredly. Somehow, she would have to make Aunt Rowena see that she was wrong.

Frowning, she opened her wardrobe and pulled out her somberest gown, a brown merino trimmed with heavy swags of green satin ribbon. The dress, purchased with funds she had brought from Ireland, was one that Aunt Rowena had selected, and Brenna had never cared for it. But its grimness would suit the occasion well. Slowly, Brenna pulled it on, managing the jet buttons at the back with some difficulty. Then she sat down to wait.

About an hour later, Hattie knocked on her door and told her that Master Amos wanted to see her downstairs in his study. Hattie's face, full of curiosity and subdued sympathy, told Brenna that the girl knew what had happened.

"I suppose you were one of the ones who saw Toby and me," Brenna blurted impulsively.

The black girl was silent.

"Hattie? Oh, Hattie, what did you see? He didn't rape me, you know," Brenna said quickly. "It didn't happen, because I fought him back, I bit his lip and pushed him away. I—"

"Yes'm." Hattie lowered her eyes, twisting her hands together in the folds of her white cotton apron. "Yes'm." She hurried away as if she were afraid Brenna might try to stop her.

"Wait!" Brenna called. "Hattie, I—"

But the girl was nearly at the end of the passageway and did not look back. With consternation Brenna watched her leave. So, even the slaves believed that Toby had raped her. All the servants gossiped among themselves, Brenna knew. It would not be long before the juicy news traveled all over the city, to be aired in kitchens, scullery rooms and even in drawing rooms.

Well, let it! she thought defiantly. She did not care what they said about her. She would face whatever gossip there was. As long as she did not have to marry Toby, she could bear anything.

On her way downstairs she caught a glimpse of herself in the mirror, her cheeks blazing and her eyes shining with a glittering fire. Very well, she thought. She would face her aunt and uncle proudly. She would not show them her hurt and bewilderment.

The confrontation came quickly. Brenna knocked at the door of Amos' study, trying to compose her features and appear calm and in command of herself.

"It's she," she heard her aunt say. Then Amos opened the door, his handsome Indian-red coat wrinkled from the day's work. His ruddy face looked even redder today, the small broken veins in his skin showing plainly. Again, there was the faint, fruity whiff of brandy in the air.

"Come in, then, Brenna," Amos said, looking at her

sharply. He settled himself behind his desk, but did not ask her to sit. Beside him, in a smaller chair, was Aunt Rowena, attired in her day garb of dark gray. Her hands, folded in her lap, were clasped so tightly that the knuckles showed white. The gray eyes stared at Brenna with contempt and anger.

"Well, miss," Amos began. "What have you to say for yourself?" His eyes roamed coolly up and down Brenna's figure as if searching for signs of damage.

"You will be glad to know, uncle, that I was not hurt by what happened to me this afternoon," Brenna said pointedly. "However, I must explain to you that all is not as it appears. Toby Rynne paid me an unexpected call this afternoon, just as I was preparing to go out in the courtyard for a walk. He . . . he insisted on coming along. He took my arm, and dragged me along with him. I had little choice but to accept his company."

"Don't believe her," Rowena said. "Toby Rynne is a perfectly respectable man, one of New Orleans' finest businessmen. He would never—"

"Are you quite sure he's so respectable?" Brenna flared. "Toby told me that he fought his way up from the tenements of New York, any way he could. And he also admitted that he intends to take what he wants, any way he can get it."

"Come, come, niece, let's get to the point of this," Amos put in impatiently. "I've just come back from my office, it was hotter than Hades there. I've had a miserable day, and the last thing I need . . . very well. Get on with it, would you?"

"I have just told you, uncle. Toby insisted on coming with me. Then he pulled me under that tree and attempted to . . . to attack me. He ripped open the front of my gown. Then he—"

"That will be quite enough, Brenna," Aunt Rowena said.

"But I am just trying to tell you what happened!"

Amos frowned and coughed, avoiding his wife's look. "Let her speak, Rowena."

Thus encouraged, Brenna went on to tell how she had tried to fight back, how she had bitten Toby's lip, and how she had escaped him. But before she could finish, Aunt Rowena interrupted, her voice low and shaking.

"Don't listen, Amos. That's *her* story. I saw the two of them last night, billing and cooing like a pair of doves. And today . . . well, it is plain to see what happened. She cast a spell on him, that's what she did! Ensnared him, so that he couldn't resist her. Just as her mother did twenty years ago—"

"Enough, Rowena! You are making yourself ridiculous with that kind of talk." Amos allowed his eyes to travel over Brenna's body again, this time more lingeringly. "Whether Brenna was really raped or not is something that only God, Toby Rynne and—perhaps—time can tell." Amos' full, prissy lips smiled slightly.

"But—" His wife began.

"It doesn't matter, Rowena. Can't you understand that? The point is not whether or not the act actually happened, but the fact that the girl's reputation is ruined. Raped or not, no honorable man will want to marry her now. Possibly she is no longer a virgin. For all we know she may even be carrying Rynne's child."

Toby's child! Brenna shuddered with disgust. "You don't have to worry. I'm not having anyone's baby!" she retorted angrily.

"Hush, miss," Rowena said. "Amos is speaking."

"So," Amos went on, "our problem is simply this: what are we going to do about this . . . this assault on our family honor? Am I to challenge Rynne to a duel? Me, a man of more than fifty years, and in uncertain health?" Amos leaned back in his chair, one plump hand playing idly with the inkwell.

Rowena's face reddened. "Of course you can't engage in a duel! For her? No. You are much too old to face a man in his early thirties, a good pistol shot to boot. No, Toby must marry Brenna, at once! What other solution is there? Once the two are wed, talk will die down quickly. Within months, it will all be forgotten. And we will be free of financial responsibility for her."

Marry Toby? Brenna felt a wave of nausea wash over her. Allow him to touch her body, her most intimate parts, with those large, hamlike hands? No, she couldn't! She could never bring herself to do such a thing. The very thought made her feel sick.

"I am sorry, aunt and uncle," she said. "But, as I have already told you, I cannot marry Toby Rynne."

"Cannot!" Aunt Rowena kneaded her temples with her fingertips, as if her head ached. "Whatever are you talking about, girl? Do you think you have any other alternative? Do you think we can keep you in this house forever, with no funds to pay for your food and clothing, or for your servant's keep? We are not rich, you know! Besides, I am not sure I want you to stay here, and tar my daughters with your brush of ill fame!"

"What ill fame, aunt? No one knows about this save for Mary, and a few slaves. Mary will not talk, and I am sure we could ask the servants not to discuss it. If we do nothing, if we act as if this had not happened—"

"Impossible!" Rowena cried.

"Rowena is right. The slaves mingle in the streets. Naturally, they talk. You must resign yourself to marrying Toby as soon as possible. I understand that he is willing to do so, that he is totally enamored of you." Amos' eyes again raked up and down the length of her body, and for the first time Brenna was fully conscious of the lust glowing in them. *He too,* she thought in despair. He, too, wants me and would press his body against mine, if Aunt Rowena were not here to stop him.

"But I don't love Toby," she said clearly.

"Love!" Aunt Rowena made a dismissing gesture. "What is love at a time like this? Do you realize how many well-bred young women enter marriages completely arranged for them? Consider yourself lucky that you have at least met your husband-to-be."

But you loved someone, Brenna wanted to shout. She tried to swallow, but her tongue was dry and thick, like cotton in her mouth.

"You seem to forget, niece," Amos added, "that I am your guardian, since your brother is not yet legally of age. I will decide what is best for you. And, under the circumstances, I feel you have little choice but to accept the marriage that Toby Rynne offers."

"No! Never! I'll never marry him!" Brenna shouted. She faced them, trembling. Their faces looked back at her, Amos' red and perspiring, Rowena's tight-lipped.

Then Brenna turned, gathered up her skirts, and fled from the room.

She ran down the corridor and up the staircase as if a demon were after her. Toby Rynne! That muscular body, those small eyes. . . . No! Marriage to him was impossible and horrifying, at least for her. They couldn't possibly *force* her to marry such a man, could they?

But they could. Dread filled her as she realized that she and Quentin were now penniless, and without protection. Her brother was not an assertive person, and he had trouble of his own. No, she could not depend on Quentin for help. Save for Arbutus, she had no friends, only the few people she had met casually through her aunt's social circle. They would not help her. What was she to do?

She had nearly reached the haven of her own room when she met Jessica and Arbutus in the upstairs corridor. Brenna had not breakfasted with the family, and had seen neither of her cousins during the day. She supposed they had been told of her father's death; surely Aunt Rowena would have mentioned it to them.

Instead of offering sympathy, however, Jessica only nodded indifferently and passed by Brenna with her skirts rustling, as if she preferred not to recognize her at all. Although she and Brenna were closest in age, the two had never taken to each other. Jessica's personality was cold, too much like Rowena's, and she had always seemed to resent Brenna's presence.

Her sister disappeared into her own bedroom, but Arbutus remained behind, and made a face at Jessica's retreating back. She looked pink-cheeked and glowing this morning, her eyes full of sparkle.

"Why, cousin, whatever is wrong?" Arbutus asked. "I didn't see you at breakfast this morning, and then Mama made Jessica and me pay a call on that fat old Mrs. Chisholm. Ugh, what a boring time we had! With Mama in a pet today. . . . Oh! Your letter, last night, Brenna! Mama said you had received some bad news, but she wouldn't tell me what it was. Surely it can't be your. . . . Oh!" Arbutus put her hand to her mouth.

"Yes, I am afraid it was my father."

Arbutus was instantly sympathetic, and Brenna found

herself led to her cousin's room, cossetted and petted. Yet there was something in the high, hectic glow of Arbutus' cheeks that made Brenna hesitate to tell her cousin the full extent of her problems. In many ways, Arbutus seemed very young, even younger than her years. Was it because the damaged leg had confined her so long? Whatever the reason, sometimes it seemed as if Arbutus drifted along in a gay, flower-scented, lighthearted world entirely her own.

She compromised by telling Arbutus of her father's death, but glossing over the worst parts of Toby's attack on her, and leaving out Quentin's debts and the fact that she and her brother were now penniless. There would be time enough later to tell her about that. And perhaps by then Brenna would have decided what to do.

When she had finished, Arbutus looked shaken. "Oh, Brenna, how terrible! You were so fond of your father . . . and not to be with him when he died!" She put her arms around Brenna. "But don't worry, cousin, you will have a home with us just as long as you want one. As for Toby, I am sure that will all blow over shortly. Mama often loses her temper. You'll see!"

"I am not sure, Arbutus. I think your mother is really angry. And I think they are going to try to force me to marry Toby, in order to save my reputation."

"Oh, no! I am sure they wouldn't really do such a thing," Arbutus gasped, but she looked worried.

"Wedding bells will be ringing soon in this house, I am afraid, if aunt has her way," Brenna said. She left Arbutus and went to her own room, feeling heartsick.

In her absence, Mary had been in the room, laying out her clothes for dinner and tidying up. A tin bathtub stood before the fireplace, waiting to be filled with warm bath water. At the sight, Brenna's eyes filled with tears. Since her babyhood, Mary had always been there, to hold her when she cried, to laugh with her at the antics of a colt or puppy. Mary was a last link with her childhood, with the golden days when there had been only the hills and the sea and the pungent grasses and her father's arms around her.

And now even Mary had abandoned her.

Brenna sat down upon the edge of her bed and let the tears roll down her cheeks.

❧ Chapter 6 ❧

IT RAINED DURING THE NIGHT, a soft onslaught of water which made cozy, tapping sounds on Brenna's bedroom windows. She got up, pulled aside the mosquito netting, and went to the window, to gaze out at the ghostly, wet, almost opalescent gray world. The trees and shrubs in the courtyard bowed beneath the flow of water. Looking at the gray-shrouded form of the willow, Brenna found it hard to believe that Toby Rynne had pulled her beneath that very tree.

But he had. And now, inexorably, she was being pushed into marriage with him. A marriage which filled her with physical disgust. Oh, it wasn't going to happen! It couldn't!

She knelt at the window for at least an hour, watching the gusting wind toss the branches of the willow like a giant feather duster. At last her eyelids grew heavy and she stumbled back to bed.

By morning, the rain had stopped. The sun rose, and drew water up from the ground in a damp mist. Brenna got up, dashed water on her face from the plain white ewer on her chest of drawers, and pulled on a light blue day gown. Then she went downstairs.

It was still early. Only the servants were about, clattering pots and pans in the kitchen as they prepared breakfast amid the yeasty odor of baking bread. Brenna begged a croissant from the plump, perspiring cook, and then slipped out of the side door into the courtyard.

Outside, she drew a deep breath. The air was new-washed, still wet. From somewhere came the smell of sweet olive, like ripe apricots. A soft breeze lifted the strands of hair which escaped the pins at the back of her neck.

For months her only exercise had been an occasional chaperoned stroll with Arbutus or Mary, and they had never ventured far from their own neighborhood. But today her muscles screamed out for activity, for hard use. She had to get away from this house in order to think.

As she left the courtyard, she felt freer than she had in months. The city had been drenched by the rain. Water still clung in huge droplets to the foliage and weeds along the road. The unpaved street was muddy, the brick side-walks slippery. Streams of water sluiced through the ditches that ran alongside the roadway. Brenna wrinkled her nose and hurried on, lifting the hem of her skirt to avoid the worst of the mud. Her shoes would probably be ruined, she knew, but at this moment she didn't care.

As she walked, munching her croissant, she could feel her muscles beginning to stretch and relax. It felt so good to be out, with no company but her own thoughts.

At first, as she pushed on quickly through the streets, she was still in what was beginning to be called the "garden district" because of the profusion of flowers, trees and shrubs surrounding the mansions. At each house, she saw signs of life: slaves pumping water from the courtyard or garden well; other servants beginning to hang laundry, beat rugs, tend gardens, mind children. At several sites, homes were under construction, plasterers and carpenters swarming about before the heat of the day became too intense.

Several workmen turned to stare curiously at Brenna as she hurried past, but no one said anything to her. She was barely aware of them, so intent was she upon her own thoughts. Her father, Mary, Toby, Quentin. Their faces seemed to whirl in front of her.

But it was Quentin who was uppermost in her mind. *"They say it does not go well with those who do not pay Billy Love."* Her brother's words kept running through her head, worrying at her. She had awakened once during the night with the frightening dream that Quentin's body, riddled with knife wounds, had been found in one of the sewage ditches along Rampart Street. Surely, she thought, Quentin had exaggerated about this man. And yet, there had been genuine terror in her brother's eyes.

She could imagine a group of river thugs, accosting him. She shuddered, picturing the brutality of such a scene.

Well, it wasn't going to happen, she told herself. Quentin was overexcited, that was all. He spent too many hours at his desk with his poetry, and had a vivid imagination. That was all there was to it.

She came to a lower-class section of the city, where the homes were of wood, with shingled roofs, some of them built on posts eight to fifteen feet above the ground. Here men, dressed in rough clothes, were leaving for work. Their wives, clad in plain gowns, emptied slops into the ditches, tended gardens or swept off steps. One girl, just Brenna's age but enormously pregnant, stared dreamily off into the distance, as if to savor the brief beauty of the morning.

Gradually Brenna found herself turning toward the river again. Was it her imagination, or did the streets seem muddier, the passersby more disreputable? Some of the men were shirtless, clad only in coarse trousers of linsey-woolsey and brogans studded with spikes. One man, with a barrellike chest and stubbled cheeks, a red scarf tied around his head, stared in Brenna's direction, and called to her in a sing-song voice. She lifted her skirts and hurried on.

If she had not known she was nearing the river, her nose would have told her. Rising above the odor of the ditches was the tangy smell of rotting sea-things. The sharp odor of rope, tar and mahogany logs mingled with the smells of roasting coffee, fish, spoiled fruit and stagnant water. From a distance she could hear the tumult of men shouting, dray-wheels squeaking, and the blast of a ship's whistle.

Slowly she became aware that she had walked farther than she had intended. She was now in an area of ramshackle shacks, built of rough cypress planks or with what appeared to be lumber from torn-up boats. Covered with crude gable roofs, many of the structures had red curtains hung at the windows, a curious note of finery. Peering inside one establishment, the front door of which sagged wide open, Brenna saw crude furniture, and a bar of rough boards supported by two kegs. Cursing, quarreling voices sounded from the back of the shack.

Brenna hurried on, frightened. She wished that she hadn't come so far. Should she turn right or left at the next corner? If only she had watched where she was going!

"Where you goin', miss? If you're lookin' for business, I'm lookin' for a little fun." A man lounged against one of the rough-hewn buildings in front of her, dressed in seaman's clothes. His face was unshaven, and a plug of chewing tobacco bulged out one cheek. His nose was oddly bent, and one ear had been partly torn off, its edge white with scar tissue. She gasped, and the man grinned at her, exposing a black gap in his mouth where his front teeth had been.

"Ugly sight, ain't I, honey? Got tore up fighting. Mixed me up with an harpy named Annie Christmas, and she damn near tore me to pieces—left her teeth marks in me to prove she was all woman!" The man's eyes lit up proudly, as if his scars were badges of honor.

"Do . . . do you know the way back to the Butlers'? It's on Prytania Street." She tried to keep her voice level, although her heart was pounding.

"Prytania Street? Why, no, miss, I don't." The man spat out a brown stream of tobacco juice into the mud. As Brenna jumped back, he laughed. "Don't give me no never-mind, dearie. I tastes a lot better than I looks."

He cackled loudly, and Brenna saw that a knife was thrust through his crude canvas belt.

"Well, thank you . . . I think I'll ask directions elsewhere." She started to move on, but he stepped in front of her, his gap-toothed grin menacing.

"Say. Ain't you from Mama Abilene's? Damn if she don't run the best damn house on Basin Street. Nothin' but girls of *su*preme quality."

"M-Mama Abilene's?"

"Sure, dearie. You looks the type, all red and peaches and cream, you is. I'd pay a lot, I would, if I hadn't lost

ever damn picayune I owned at roulette last night. And
got rolled for what was left this morning, too, damme."

The man eyed her speculatively. Then suddenly his hand
shot out and gripped her upper arm.

"Please . . ." She tried to pull back. "Please, I'm trying
to find my way home. Would you let me pass?"

"You can find your way right to my door, little honey.
I may be damn ugly, but I got something you would like
a lot, I does. I can give it to you right."

"Please . . ."

"Just what I needs this morning. Take my mind off my
aching head . . ." He pulled at her, one hand roughly
caressing her left breast. "I got a place where we can go,
dearie. Ain't much, but it'll do for what we want . . ."

To her dismay, he pulled her toward a narrow alley
that ran between two saloons. It was filled with trash, old
kegs and crates of empty whiskey bottles. At the far end
of the alley a man lay sprawled in sodden sleep, a rat
gnawing at garbage only inches away from his outstretched
hand.

"No! Please!" Brenna tried to pull out of the man's
surprisingly strong grip. "Please, I'm not one of those
women. I—" Desperately, she started to scream.

"What in hell—" someone shouted.

Suddenly another man was in the alley. Quick as a
cat's spring, he flung himself upon her molester. They
struggled wildly. Standing paralyzed against the wall,
Brenna could only see the newcomer from behind, but he
was certainly no riverboat man. He was lean, his back
lithely muscled beneath his well-tailored blue coat.

Quickly he forced the gap-toothed man to the ground,
and threw him a final punishing blow. The man gave a
surprised outcry, then fell unconscious in the mud, his head
lolling.

The newcomer stood up, wiping his hands on his mud-
spattered trousers. With one swift gesture, he bent and
removed the knife from the riverboat man's belt, then
flung it far down the alley into a tangle of waist-high
weeds.

"There," he said. "One less knife for one less footpad
to do his dirty business with."

He turned, revealing a suntanned face with slashed dimples, a cleft chin, and blonde-brown hair curling about his temples.

"Kane Fairfield!" Brenna gasped.

"My God!" Kane stared back at her, his eyes widening to match her own surprise. "You can't be . . . Miss Brenna Laughlan, is it?" He laughed harshly. "And here I thought I was helping some lady of the night in a bit of trouble on the streets!"

Firmly he took her elbow and propelled her out of the alley and onto the street. "Girl, what in the world are you doing on a street like this? And all alone to boot? Do you realize where you are?"

"Why, I'm near the docks somewhere," Brenna stammered, feeling flustered by Kane's anger.

"You're on Girod Street, in the toughest, most vicious area in the entire city! They call this district the Swamp, and the only law known here is the law of the knife and the pistol and the bludgeon."

"But I got lost. I didn't know—"

"You are a fool, then. A fool. The only thing that saved you at all was the early hour of the morning. Most of the swamp rats are still sleeping it off from last night . . . the ones who lived through the night, that is. Six murders a week they get down here sometimes, and God knows how many battered faces and bloodied noses. What kind of a trick were you trying to pull, anyway? Why, down here you're a newborn porpoise venturing into a school of sharks!"

Brenna was piqued by his scolding. "You may let go of my arm now, sir," she said tartly. "I'd like to thank you for what you did. If it hadn't been for you. . . . However, I might ask what *you* are doing here. If the Swamp is dangerous for me, it must be hazardous for you, too. Dressed like a gentleman, as you are."

Kane looked at her sharply, and again Brenna noticed the clear, intense blue of his eyes.

"I carry a pistol," he said. "And what's more, I can use it. For your information, I was trying to round up Scroggins, my first mate who, the last time I saw him, announced he was going to set a record for the longest drunk in the history of this fine city. A record, I might add, that it will be very difficult to break." Kane's smile revealed very white teeth.

"Your first mate?"

"Yes. I'll be setting back to sea in a few days, as soon as I get some other business cleared away. There's a certain matter of ... well, never mind. Come along, Brenna. I'll escort you home, a place that only a fool would have left without proper protection and chaperonage."

He steered her back down the muddy road the way she had come.

"Please, must we go so fast?" she protested angrily. "I can barely keep up with you!"

"Yes, we must. I'd like to get you safely away from here."

"Well, goodness knows you're succeeding in that!" she snapped. "I feel like a naughty child, hustled off to the nursery for a spanking!"

"An excellent idea." He grinned.

She walked along for a few minutes in angry silence. "I understand that you actually act as captain of your own vessel," she said tartly. "Don't most wealthy *gentlemen* stay home and let others do the physical labor?"

"I am sure they do. In fact, my own father does exactly that. He sits in his dry little office in Boston looking over bills of lading and shipping orders and counting the money in his safe, smoking his pipe. But me, I'm different. I've known it since the day I was twelve and stowed away on one of my father's ships bound for France."

In spite of her pique, Brenna laughed. "What happened?"

"The captain was terrified when he found me. He recognized me right away and wanted to turn the ship around and sail straight for home."

"And did he?"

"No. I was a fast talker for a twelve-year-old. I persuaded him that my father would be even more furious with him if he lost valuable sailing time, and that he should keep right on going. And I would be his cabin boy, and shoulder any blame myself. Oh, I was a persuasive child," Kane said, grinning. "I begged and I pleaded and I promised, and then I threatened. I had poor Captain

Armitage so confused he didn't know one end of the compass from the other."

"So he really let you sail."

"The entire way. Didn't know what had hit him. I told him that my father would want me to learn all there was to know about ship handling, and by God, the man taught me. Taught me all about the sea, and there was never a better teacher, once he got over his bewilderment at being stuck with me."

Brenna laughed. "And after all that, I hope you found that you liked sailing."

"Like? I'm not sure that's the word for it. I became part of it, you could say. It grew around me, and I grew around it. There is always something different happening at sea. There are calms, and terrific storms. We see whales sometimes, spouting and rolling through the water in play. There is nothing like it. The ports, swarming with seamen and women in strange clothing, teeming with smells and odd sights. Cargo piled up to be loaded . . ."

"But what happened when you got home? When your father discovered what you'd done, I mean?" Brenna asked.

"Why, he whipped me, of course. What else would any self-respecting father do? But I'd known it was coming, and I endured it. It was small price to pay, after all, for the glory I'd seen."

"But what about Captain Armitage? Did your father fire him?"

"No. Men like Armitage aren't easily replaced." Kane was thoughtful for a moment. "I . . . I wanted to be like him. A few years later my father tried to send me to Harvard College. I ran away. Told him if he didn't give me a ship I would sail out as a common seaman. The sea was in my blood, and no one was going to stop me."

Then Kane's expression changed. "But all of this is getting away from the subject at hand, which is why you were roaming these dangerous streets by yourself?"

"I . . . I had to get out. To get away for a while."

Kane's eyes flared with anger. "Hasn't your aunt told you not to go out unescorted? Hasn't she told you what some of the districts of this city are like?"

Brenna flushed. "Yes, aunt has been very insistent on

chaperoning me at all times. But so much has happened
... I had to get away so I could think."

"And what have you to think about, my lovely? What
to wear to the opera? Whom to flirt with at the next
soirée? The latest fashions from Paris?"

"I am not, as you seem to think, some little ninny with
a head stuffed with goose feathers!" Brenna cried. How
arrogant this man was, how full of male superiority! "Just
because I am a woman does not mean that I mightn't have
serious problems to trouble me ... something more important to think about than clothes and bonnets and dressmakers!"

"Really?" Kane grinned at her infuriatingly. "And what
could that be?"

Brenna felt the furious blood pounding through her.
"Nothing *significant,* of course," she said. "Merely the fact
that my father has died, leaving my brother and me penniless. Merely the fact that my brother, Quentin, owes ten
thousand dollars in gambling debts, and is under the impression that some horrible person named Billy Love is
going to hurt him if he doesn't pay up. Finally, the fact
that my uncle and aunt are forcing me into marriage with
a man who makes my very flesh crawl!"

Brenna was amazed to see Kane tilt back his head and
laugh heartily.

"How dare you laugh at me?" she stormed. "I suppose
you think all of these things are humorous, don't you?
That my father's death is ... is laughable, that Quentin's
debts are ... are just good, pleasant fun—" Her voice
caught.

"Hardly. It's just that if you could only see your own
face, so lovely, and so clouded over with righteous indignation ..."

"I don't think you're funny."

"Perhaps I am not." For an instant the creases on
Kane's cheeks deepened, and she sensed he was holding
back another smile.

They picked their way along a partially split section of
walk, slippery with splashed mud and water. "Do you
know who this Billy Love is?" Brenna asked.

"Of course."

"Then tell me! Quentin says that Billy Love gets very angry at those who don't pay their debts. He seems to think the man will do something terrible to him."

"He might."

"What? Are you serious?" Brenna stopped walking, and stared in horror at Kane.

"Of course. No one knows where he came from, or whether Billy Love is his right name, but the man has been in New Orleans about two years, and is well on his way to becoming wealthy. Some say he carries a knife with a blade at both ends, so that he can cut into a person from whichever angle he chooses, at his own convenience. I would say this is purely rumor. But, nonetheless, he knows how to use a knife, and has done so many times in the past, if street talk be any judge."

"Oh! How horrible!" Brenna could not repress a shudder.

"For the past year, the man has been operating a gambling house frequented by young blades like your brother and also by respectable businessmen. Quite an establishment, Billy Love's. The floors are covered with fine carpeting, and he serves sumptuous buffet suppers. There are private gambling rooms for the aristocrats and for those city officials who refuse to gamble with the masses. Vast sums are won and lost at Love's. In fact, some men become paupers overnight."

"I ... I suppose you've been there, and know all of this firsthand."

"Naturally."

"And I suppose *you* won."

"Of course."

"But, it is all just rumor, isn't it? This man wouldn't really ... knife Quentin, would he?"

"My dear Brenna, nothing about New Orleans surprises me anymore. If such rumors are circulating about Billy Love, then there is probably truth in them. Remember, any man who lives by his wits, as this man does, is certainly no fool."

With sinking heart, Brenna thought of Toby. He, too, by his own admission, had lived by his wits in New York. Did Toby also carry a knife or pistol? Were there other things about him—dark and secret things—about which she knew nothing?

She walked on, so absorbed in her own thoughts that Kane had to speak twice to her.

"I say, what is this about your being forced into marriage with someone who makes your skin crawl?" His blue eyes sparkled with a teasing light.

"The situation is *not* funny!" she flared. "At least, not to me. It seems that an ... an incident happened that my aunt felt was ... compromising to me," she explained with difficulty. "Now Toby Rynne thinks it gives him every right to propose marriage to me, and he does not care that the very thought makes me shudder."

"Did you say Toby Rynne?" Kane's eyes suddenly narrowed. For an instant she was aware of the violence in this man, of swift, powerful muscles beneath the elegant clothing.

"Yes, my aunt introduced us. His brother, Ulrich, is courting my cousin, Jessica."

"I would advise you not to associate with the Rynnes too closely, Brenna. There are certain things which can't be proven yet, but—" Kane hesitated. "Take my word for it, and leave them alone."

"But they are accepted in society, they—"

"Society? You mean money-grubbers like your Aunt Rowena?" Kane gave a short, hard laugh. "People like your aunt and uncle are genteel opportunists. They'll grab any social opportunity, and follow the lead of anyone who appears to have money or power. They would never be accepted in Boston. Only here, where the city is growing so quickly, can people like your aunt get a toehold."

"Why do you come to her parties, then?"

Again Kane laughed, his eyes closed to narrow slits. "Why shouldn't I, if I wish? *I* don't have to be a slave to social convention. I go where I wish, and see whom I wish."

"I am sure of *that!*" Brenna said in exasperation, remembering what Arbutus had told her about him.

"Are you, my dear? Are you so sure about me?" Kane had stopped in the street, half-smiling. Her heart pounding, Brenna was aware of his closeness, of his clean male scent. Her breathing quickened, and, although she wanted to make a sharp retort, her mouth would not open. She was caught and held in the look from his eyes.

Then his lips were on hers, soft and sweetly warm. A thrill of pleasure surged through her body. Almost without conscious will, her arms crept about his neck.

It was as if all her senses had come totally alive. She drowned in the feel and smell of him, the curly texture of the hair at the back of his neck, his clean, slightly salty body odor. His arms pulled her so close that she could sense the strong pumping of his heart against her own. His body pressed against hers, urging her.

Then, like a dash of morning-cold water, it was over. He released her, and stood looking down at her with a small, crooked smile.

"See, Brenna? Don't ever be sure of Kane Fairfield. No one predicts my actions, or ever will. Especially no woman. I tried marriage and domesticity once, but never again. Remember that."

Marriage! Domesticity! Oh, the arrogance of him. As if she were thinking of marrying him!

"I will keep that in mind, Mr. Fairfield," she said, her voice shaking.

"Please do."

When they reached her aunt and uncle's house, she barely spoke to him, bidding him farewell as curtly as she could. Only after he had turned and was walking down the street did she realize she had never asked him about Toby Rynne. Why had he told her to leave the Rynnes alone? And what should she do about Quentin?

The rest of the day, hot and steamy, passed in agonizing slowness. Brenna, pleading a headache, asked for and received her luncheon on a tray. In the early afternoon, her aunt left to pay calls, taking Jessica and Arbutus with her. Brenna peered out of the upper hall window to watch them leaving, all three dressed in watered silk gowns, hems held fastidiously out of the mud. Ribbons and flowers bedecked their hair, finery that must have taken Mary all morning to concoct. Perhaps, she thought, Aunt Rowena had decided to squelch any rumors about the Toby Rynne matter. Or, maybe she planned to spread them still further, she added to herself wryly.

Well, she didn't care. No matter what people whispered

about her, she didn't want to marry Toby and didn't plan to.

She sighed and, finding a volume of Washington Irving's *Sketch Book*, loaned her by Arbutus, she sat down to read, opening the book with trembling hands. Perhaps it would take her mind off her father.

But within only a few minutes, she let the book fall from her fingers. Kane's kiss filled her mind. The audacity of the man, she thought crossly. First he held and kissed her on a public street, in full view of any passersby. Then he implied that she might be thinking of marriage with him!

Well, she just would not think about Kane Fairfield anymore. She would pretend he didn't exist. It was the sort of treatment the man deserved.

After dinner, an awkward meal, Arbutus came to Brenna's room, where she had retired immediately after eating.

"Oh, Brenna, I hate to tell you this, but Toby Rynne is here in the house," Arbutus said. "He has been closeted in the study with my father ever since dinner."

"Here? Again?" Brenna felt her face pale.

"Yes, and I wonder what on earth they can be saying in there. I must admit I made an excuse to go by the study door, but I did not hear anything at all. Other than the two of them laughing together like a couple of conspirators! What do you suppose it all means?"

"I don't know," Brenna said soberly. "But I am afraid I can guess."

❧ *Chapter 7* ❧

THE HAND-CARVED WOODEN FAN, suspended over the table and pulled back and forth by a small boy with a cord, creaked monotonously.

"Brenna, you are barely touching your gumbo. Are you ill, or merely putting on airs?" Her aunt's voice was sharp, her eyes glittering at Brenna.

Brenna looked down at her plate, heaped with the filé-flavored rice dish, slices of pink ham, lobster salad. Whatever dislike her aunt felt for her, she reflected to herself wryly, it did not include starving her. The only trouble was, she couldn't eat anything. Her stomach was too churned up with anxiety.

"No, aunt, I'm fine. I'm just not very hungry tonight."

"But you will waste away to nothing if you don't eat. Then your admirers will not think you pretty!" Rowena laughed harshly, hiding her mouth behind her hand.

It was the following night. The family was at supper with their guests the Chisholms, planters who lived a few miles out of the city near the levee. After the meal, they would hear a light French opera at the Saint Philip Theater. Brenna, too, was expected to attend. Aunt Rowena had made that plain.

"Mourning faces are not for girls who must marry in order to save their reputations," she had told Brenna privately. "You will join us tonight, niece, and you will pretend you are happy about the plans for your wedding.

No one has to know just yet that your father is dead. There will be plenty of time later for mourning."

The meal had passed pleasantly enough, livened by the plump Eulie Chisholm, whose bulging torso was laced almost to the point of breathlessness. Eulie was speaking about voodooism among the slaves, a practice brought to New Orleans from the French colonies of Martinique, Guadeloupe and Santo Domingo.

"They *say*," Eulie whispered dramatically, "that many white women consult these voodoo queens about their love affairs and other matters. And some of the advice they are given . . . why, improper is hardly the way to describe it! . . . My goodness, what has got into me?" she said suddenly. "I clean forgot to tell you all. I heard this afternoon that a duel was fought this morning by none other than Ulrich Rynne! Wasn't he attending your Jessica at the soirée the other night?"

Eulie paused for effect.

"Yes, he was," Jessica said, tensing. "Do go on, Mrs. Chisholm. Who was the other man? What happened?"

Eulie dabbed at her upper lip with her napkin, her small eyes shining like marbles. "Now, what *was* his name? Oh, yes, I remember now! It was that young man from Boston with the fleet of ships . . . Kane Fairfield. I believe Mr. Fairfield called Mr. Rynne a pirate, or something else equally fantastic. Of course Ulrich couldn't let that stand . . . what man of honor would?"

The reaction to this news was all Eulie could have hoped for. Brenna could not conceal her surprised gasp, while Uncle Amos released a low grunt, as if someone had kicked him in his portly stomach. Jessica leaned forward, her hands gripping the edge of the table, as if to keep herself from falling.

"Are you *sure* Ulrich Rynne fought the duel, and not his brother Toby?" she asked.

"As sure as grass grows up. My cousin, Matthew Watson, was one of Ulrich's seconds, and that's how I got the news. He called this afternoon, just as I started to dress. My goodness, Matt had the strangest look on his face when he told me, so white and perspiring, as if he'd seen the very Devil himself!"

"Devil? What do you mean?" Brenna's hands were suddenly icy cold. Duels were common here, she knew. The Creoles usually fought with swords, and often a token blood-drawing would end with the two participants clapping each other on the back and going out together for a drink. But the Americans were different. Americans often chose pistols, and shot to kill.

"Why, that devil, Fairfield, of course!" Eulie sniffed. "Matthew told us that Mr. Fairfield fired before Mr. Rynne had finished turning. That's what he said . . . and I declare, I've never seen a man so upset. Ulrich Rynne has a bullet wound in his side, and Doctor Bradley says it will take a miracle to pull him through."

"What?" Jessica half-rose from her chair. "There must be a mistake. Ulrich cannot be wounded. He is a top shot, he cannot be the one . . ."

"Oh, yes, he's badly wounded, and people are already starting to talk. Why, the whole thing is most shocking. I declare, these duels do have a tendency to get out of hand, and ought to be stopped!"

"But Kane . . . he is all right, isn't he?" Brenna whispered.

"Oh, my, yes, hale and hearty as can be. That sort always is. Like cats, they always land with their feet on the ground."

"But I can't believe—" faltered Jessica.

"My dear Jessica, Cousin Matthew Watson saw the whole thing," Eulie said with relish. "And is prepared to swear to it as well. There were four other witnesses, he says, and each one of them is prepared to swear that Kane Fairfield fired early. Why, the man is no better than a murderer!"

"Murderer! Why, Mrs. Chisholm, you must be exaggerating, surely," Brenna began.

"My dear, you are new to our country, and can be forgiven your ignorance in such matters. But to deliberately flout the rules of the duel . . . why, it's a most serious offense, tantamount to cold-blooded murder. He left Mr. Rynne with no chance at all. It was a monstrous thing!"

"But Mr. Fairfield did not seem to me to be the kind who could—"

"You would hardly be in a position to know, Brenna," Eulie said dryly. She related further details of the duel, while Brenna sat, shocked, trying to reconcile this story with the man who had leaped into the alley to save her. Surely, Eulie Chisholm must be wrong. She must have gotten her story garbled somehow. Kane Fairfield would not need to fire early, already having the advantage of his lightning-quick coordination.

A few minutes later the meal was over, and the ladies retired upstairs to freshen up for the theater. Following the other women up the staircase, Brenna heard Jessica and her mother arguing in low, intense voices.

"But, Mama," Jessica was saying. "I want to go to him. Perhaps I could help him, or nurse him."

"Nurse him? What could *you* do?" Rowena said scornfully. "You have never been near a sick person in your life."

"But I could be with him. I could—"

"You are not leaving this house, Jessica Butler. Do you think I want people laughing at you? You are not even affianced to him, you little fool! What do you think it would look like, you trotting over there like a . . . a . . ."

"But, Mama . . ."

"No. I have had entirely too much from you girls recently. I do not want to hear any more about this, Jessica. Do you hear me?"

Jessica paused on the stairs, and her eyes met her mother's. Then, slowly, her glance went to the floor. "Very well, Mama. As you wish."

The streets were greasy and slippery with black mud, and the party was obliged to make their way to the theater on foot. They made an uncertain procession, Tiny in front bearing a lantern, followed by Amos with another lantern, and then the women, carrying their shoes, the two Chisholm girls giggling as they slipped and slid in the muck. Kendall Chisholm and another slave brought up the rear. But the theater was worth the trip. It had been built in 1808, Arbutus told Brenna proudly, and could seat seven hundred persons. It had two tiers of boxes and the main floor was, from time to time, used for dancing.

They arrived to find most of the audience already there,

the women gaily attired in bright silks, embroidered cloths
and rare laces. Brenna found the Creole women especially
beautiful, with their masses of dark hair, soft dark eyes,
and animated expressions.

Already seated in the front row of boxes was a young
blonde woman in rose silk who, from a distance, looked
like Melissa Rynne. But when the girl turned to speak to
her escort, Brenna saw that she was not Melissa at all.
Of course, she told herself. Melissa would probably be at
her half-brother's bedside. Especially if he were as badly
injured as Eulie said.

She gazed around at the crowd, hearing scraps of conversation, most of it about the duel. "Young ruffian!" one
short, fat man was expounding, thumping one fist into the
other. "Ought to be drummed out of town!"

Murderer . . . killer . . . other words rose out of the
press of people, until Brenna wanted to cover her ears.
Much as she disliked Kane, she couldn't believe he would
murder. Not a man who had held her close, until she could
actually feel the beat of his heart . . .

"Oh, Brenna, what do you think about Eulie's news?"
She felt Arbutus touching her hand. Her cousin's cheeks
were pink. "Isn't it terrible that Kane Fairfield should turn
out to be a killer?"

"But Ulrich Rynne is not even dead. Arbutus, you don't
really believe such a thing, do you?"

"Why, it's the truth, isn't it? To fire early in a duel is
the same thing as attempted murder. It's very serious."

"Arbutus, I can't believe Kane would do such a thing. I
know the man."

"Know him?" Arbutus looked bewildered. "How could
you? Brenna, you only just met him the other night!"

"I . . . I saw him yesterday while I was out walking.
I just don't think he's the kind of person to cheat at a
duel."

Jessica, wearing a wine-red taffeta, suddenly spoke up.
"There are witnesses to the thing, *dear* cousin! Five men
saw what happened, including Doctor Raoul Frontenac,
whom Mama knows well. And all of them say Kane Fairfield is a cold-blooded murderer."

"Then all of them are wrong."

Jessica's eyes flashed. "A man is lying ill, perhaps dying. Don't you care about that, cousin? Don't you care about the brother of the man you are to marry?"

"Of course I am sorry that a man has been hurt. But I don't think the duel was unfair. I can't believe that."

"Then you actually defend a killer!"

"I'm not defending a killer, as you put it. Ulrich is still alive, isn't he? Why does everyone say the word murder when—"

Brenna stopped. The short, fat man she had seen earlier was pushing his way through the crowd toward Uncle Amos, his cheeks puffed out with self-importance. He spoke intently to Amos. When the man left, Amos came over to them, pulling out a large, white handkerchief and mopping his forehead copiously.

"Well, it's happened," he said. "Ulrich Rynne lost so much blood that he died about an hour ago. They say he died cursing Kane Fairfield."

Aunt Rowena caught and supported Jessica, who was swaying on her feet.

"Get a fan!" Rowena ordered. "We must find a chair for Jessica, she is feeling faint!"

"Dead . . ." the girl muttered. "And you wouldn't let me go to him, Mama."

"It wouldn't have done you any good. He had a doctor, didn't he? What more could you have done, or anyone?"

Jessica's eyes closed, her face strangely slack. Then she opened her eyes, staring straight at Brenna. She spoke in a monotone. "Get her away from me. She defends a killer. I don't want her near me."

The first act of the opera passed in a blur. Brenna was dimly conscious of the music, of the high, lilting tones of the French soprano. At intermission she left their box, wanting only to escape Jessica's hostility.

The front doors of the theater were propped open to let in the heavily scented night air. Groups of men stood in the street smoking. Suddenly Brenna felt a hand touch her shoulder. She whirled about.

"Oh, Quentin, it's you," she said with relief. "Where have you been? You were to join us, and now you've missed the entire first act!"

"I don't care about that. I wouldn't have come at all if

I hadn't had to talk to you." In only two days, Quentin's appearance had deteriorated alarmingly. His dark green coat was rumpled, his fawn vest stained, and both hung loosely on him. His eyes were puffy and his cheeks more hollow than Brenna remembered.

"Oh, Quentin, what's happened? Is anything wrong?"

"It's Billy Love."

"What do you mean?" She was jostled by a group of men going outdoors to smoke, and had to clutch Quentin's arm to keep from being knocked over. Under the fabric of his coat sleeve, she could feel him trembling.

"He is stalking me, Brenna. Like a tomcat who knows he's spotted a juicy mouse, and intends to have a little fun before he settles down to eat."

"But, Quentin, a man in your position—a respectable person—surely he can't do anything to you?" Brenna's voice faltered as she remembered what Kane had said about Billy Love and the knife he carried.

"He can do anything he wants, sister. He's made that very plain. He came to my rooms this afternoon, he and a couple of his . . . friends, or whatever they are. All of them dressed in the height of fashion. Billy Love was wearing at least three diamond rings, Brenna. I confess I was so agitated that I could not count them."

"But what did those men do? What did they say?"

Quentin was perspiring. "They stayed about twenty minutes. First the talk was all casual . . . who'd been having a big winning streak, who'd lost everything. Then Billy Love—oh, he's a big man, Brenna—began telling about a body they'd found in the alley across from his establishment. Knifed, the man was, with at least forty wounds in him. They told me this dead man had been gambling at Billy Love's, and had owed Billy Love money."

"Oh." It was all Brenna could say. She swallowed hard.

"Brenna, you've got to help me."

"But, what can I do? I don't have any money," she said frantically. "What little father sent is gone. I could sell my jewelry, I suppose—mother's brooch. But what I have isn't worth all that much, certainly not ten thousand dollars! Of course, my gowns, maybe they would bring something . . ."

She babbled on, driven by frantic fear. *Take care of*

Quentin, her father had said in his letter. But how? What could she possibly do?

"No, that won't be enough." Quentin was eyeing her speculatively. "But there is something you could do, Brenna. Something that would help me."

"What? Please tell me!"

Intermission was over, and people began to stream back to their seats. The crowd around the door thinned, and Quentin seemed to draw himself apart from them, his body swaying slightly, the sweetish smell of whiskey on his breath.

"Marry Toby Rynne, Brenna. That's what you could do."

"You can't mean that!"

"Sister, sister, something has got to be done, or I'm going to be lying in some alley bleeding out my life! It's going to happen, I know it, I swear it, unless you do something to help me. And I can only think of Rynne. He's rich, Brenna, so rich he probably doesn't even know how much money he has. He's a big man here in New Orleans, with a lot of big warehouses and God knows what kind of secret dealings among the merchants and the shippers. I've heard some things . . . well, I know he's got the money. He'd barely miss it. And I'm sure he would do it for you."

"But . . . to marry him . . ."

"Why not? You've got to marry someone, haven't you? And I've seen the way he looks at you. He wants you, I'm sure of it."

"Yes," she said dully. "He wants me."

"Then what's stopping you? The sooner you are married, the safer we both will be. Don't forget your little trouble in Ireland. So far no one here has heard of it. You've been lucky." He took both her hands in his, eyes pleading with her. "Brenna, please, it's my life. Do you think I would ask you if there was any other way, if there was any other solution I could think of? You are my only hope!"

Brenna stood, stunned, on the steps of the theater, watching Quentin leave. He disappeared into the darkness where someone, probably Etienne, waited for him, holding a lantern.

She hurried back into the theater, reaching the Butler box late, and out of breath. But Aunt Rowena, surprisingly, said nothing, and Brenna watched the rest of the performance without seeing it, her stomach churning with so much nausea she feared she would be ill.

At last the opera, and its numerous curtain calls, was over. They left the theater.

A knot of men, shouting and gesticulating angrily, stood on the brick sidewalk across from them. Some held lanterns, brought to light their trip home.

"Murderer!" someone shouted.

"Young swine," another man yelled. "Coming here with your fancy ideas . . ."

"Brenna Laughlan, how dare you pause to watch such a thing?" Aunt Rowena hissed, pinching Brenna's arm. "Tiny is here, with the lanterns. Come along at once. No proper lady would stay to see such goings-on."

Other men were running to join the group, and Brenna noticed the short, fat man who had spread the news about Ulrich's death. And, yes, there was even Kendall Chisholm, Eulie's husband, his Adam's apple bobbing, his brows set in a scowl. Yellow lanterns swam in the dark, and the shouts grew louder and more menacing.

Pulling away from Aunt Rowena's grasp, Brenna ran into the street, and pushed into the edges of the mob. There was someone in the middle who held their attention. She had to see who that person was.

She pushed herself closer, slipping between the tall men.

"Miss, what are you doing here? Get back!" someone said. She felt a hand on her arm. Quickly she shook it off. She had to see . . .

They had left a circle of empty space around him, as a circle of wolves would leave space around dangerous prey. Kane Fairfield stood on a raised section of the sidewalk, his eyes almost yellow in the glow of the lanterns that surrounded him. His face was coated with a sheen of perspiration, his lips thinned and grim. He did not look frightened. On the contrary, a raw energy crackled from him, so that the men at the front of the crowd shifted uneasily.

"Gentlemen, you have been lied to!" Kane shouted.

"The contest I fought with Ulrich Rynne was fair and honest in every way."

"Fair! Honest!" A hoarse shout rang out from the back of the mob. "Gunning down a man in cold blood? You call that fair?"

The crowd began to shout, but fell silent when Kane stepped forward, one hand poised near the pistol at his hip. "The witnesses lied. I will find out why. And when I do, someone will suffer for it."

"Five men? How could they all lie?" The same voice rang out again, and Kane whirled in its direction with a quick, feral motion.

"I don't know how five men could lie . . . six if you count Rynne himself. But they are all lying, every damned one of them. And I intend to prove it. No one brands me a murderer. I will not stand for it."

Kane's hand still hovered near his pistol, and his eyes, shining yellow in the lantern light, roved among the crowd, searching out individuals. For an instant, the men stood muttering, their feet shifting uneasily. Then, slowly, those at the front began to leave, shoving the others farther back so that they, too, had to disperse. Kane waited impassively.

At last most of the crowd had become dark shapes along the streets, their lanterns yellow circles of light. Men rejoined their families, and sought out carriages.

Turning, Kane, saw her. For a long moment their glances held, until Brenna had to lower her eyes, frightened somehow by the power she sensed in him, held tightly in check like a coiled spring. The pulse pounded hard in her throat.

"So, Brenna, it's you," he said at last. "And again you're where you shouldn't be. Go home, Brenna. Go home."

Then he turned, striding off down the sidewalk, and was swallowed up by the darkness.

❧ Chapter 8 ❧

"No . . . NO, PLEASE. *Don't hurt him. Don't hurt my brother. Please—*"

In her dream, she was screaming. She lay beneath her mosquito netting, her body tossing from side to side, perspiration soaking her nightgown.

"Brenna! Wake up!" Arbutus pulled aside the mosquito net and shook Brenna. "Cousin, are you all right?"

Brenna groped her way through the fog of nightmare and struggled to sit up. "Arbutus, is that you? Oh . . ."

"You were screaming, cousin. I could hear you from my own room. It's a wonder you didn't wake Mama, too. Oh, Brenna, what's wrong?"

"Nothing . . . just a frightening dream, that's all."

"But dreams usually have a reason, don't they? You haven't been the same since . . . since Toby Rynne was here."

Moonlight flooded the room, revealing Arbutus clearly, her soft, fine hair streaming about her shoulders. She wore a dressing gown carelessly buttoned, and looked worried.

"Well," Brenna admitted. "I suppose you are right. There is something." Reluctantly she told Arbutus about Quentin's debt, and about Billy Love.

"Oh!" Arbutus' hand flew to her mouth, her eyes widening like a child's. "Oh, cousin! What will Mama say when she hears this? She will be so angry. She hates gambling. She even made Papa fire his law clerk for gambling."

"Is there any chance that uncle might help Quentin?"

"I don't think so. I overheard Papa and Mama arguing yesterday. I think my father has made some poor investments and Mama is very angry at him. Oh, Brenna, I am so sorry . . ." Arbutus touched Brenna's hand. "As much as I love you, there is nothing I can do . . ."

"Yes." Brenna tried to smile, not wanting Arbutus to see how weary and depressed she felt. *So Amos needs money*, the cold thought ran in her. Was that why he had been talking with Toby like a co-conspirator?

"Well," she said. "I suppose I should try to go back to sleep."

Arbutus threw her arms around her cousin. "If I had any money of my own, I would give it all to you, Brenna, I swear it."

"I know, Arbutus, I know."

After her cousin left, Brenna was seized with an overwhelming feeling of sadness. Life was reaching out long, strong fingers to touch all of them. Jessica had fallen in love with Ulrich Rynne, only to lose him before they could even become engaged. Arbutus had a serious suitor, and would probably be married soon, acquiring a ready-made daughter. And she herself was caught in the ugly net of her uncle's, Toby's, and Quentin's needs. Somehow, some way, she must find a way to escape that net . . .

The morning dawned windy. There was the threat of rain, a smell of moisture on the heavy air. Brenna peered out of her bedroom window, to see the bushes and trees in the courtyard buffeted by the wind, white blossoms flying in the air.

Quickly she dressed. It was a day that appealed to her. The wind seemed to hint of the power of the hurricanes that occasionally blasted the area, flooding the city and flattening buildings with their awesome strength. The wind, strong and insistent, seemed to fit with her mood.

Breakfast was uncomfortable. Jessica remained in her room, and Aunt Rowena and Uncle Amos were sharp with each other. After the meal, Brenna wanted to walk, feeling that she must escape the oppressive atmosphere of the house. Arbutus, however, had an appointment with her music instructor, and Mary was to wash and dress Rowena's hair that morning. Well, she would have to go out alone then, Brenna decided. But this time she would stay within the Garden District, where no harm could come to her.

She threw a lace shawl about her shoulders and stepped outdoors. The moment she stepped off the porch, the wind caught at her skirts, frothing them about her feet. Even her hair flew quickly out of its pins, long strands of it blowing. She walked quickly, feeling oddly exhilarated. Today made her think of mornings in Ireland, when she would ride out along the cliffs by the sea, then climb above the water to watch the surf crash in great, curling rolls on the huge, giant-tumbled rocks.

She had just turned a corner when she saw a man striding rapidly toward her, his heavy arms swinging from his shoulders in a familiar way. Toby!

She stopped in dismay. He was headed for her uncle's house, probably to confer with Amos again about her marriage.

Without stopping to think, she reversed her steps and began to hurry in the opposite direction, hoping he would not recognize her. As the wind buffeted her from a new direction, she tried to smooth the telltale strands of her reddish-gold hair beneath her bonnet. If he recognized her . . . well, she just had to hope he wouldn't.

"Brenna!" She turned to see that he had almost caught up with her. His face was flushed from running.

She continued to hurry on, but the wind, with another strong gust, whipped the folds of her skirt between her legs, and she stumbled. Then she felt his hand catching her.

"Toby, what are you doing here!" she cried angrily. "I was planning to walk by myself. I didn't invite you to accompany me, and I certainly don't want to see you, not today and not ever."

Toby stiffened, his small eyes glaring at her. "So . . . you don't like me. Is that what you are trying to say, my lovely Brenna?"

"I. . . . No, I don't like you.'

"Are you sure? I wouldn't have thought it the other day. You pushed your body into mine as if you enjoyed every minute of it." Toby smiled insinuatingly.

"I . . . I did what?" She attempted to pull away from him, but his hand gripped her arm.

"I said you liked it. You liked everything I did to you. Oh, you're a wild one, but I'm going to tame you. What's more, after we're married, there won't be any more of this fighting and struggling nonsense. You'll have to submit, because you'll be legally my wife and you won't have any choice."

Toby smiled again, and Brenna felt horror choking her throat as he added, "Of course, then things will be different. You will like what I do to you. You will like what a real man can do for you."

"You . . . you're no gentleman to speak to me like that!" she flared. "If Aunt Rowena had even an inkling of the kind of things you are saying to me, she—"

"Of course I'm no gentleman. You and I both know it."

"But . . . I don't want to marry you," she whispered.

"That's because you are young, and don't know what is good for you. A prim and proper 'society' gentleman is no good for a woman. No, you will come to enjoy being my wife, I promise you that." Toby scowled. "Of course, now that my brother is dead we should postpone our plans, but I'm not sure I want to do that. I don't want you slipping through my hands like a fish through a net."

"If I were a fish that's exactly what I'd do!" she cried. "Toby, you . . . you have never stopped to consider that I might have wishes and feelings and emotions of my own. You act as if I were some sort of *thing* . . . some possession."

"But you are a beautiful thing. Something I have dreamed about ever since the afternoon I first saw you, driving in the carriage with your aunt and cousins. Dressed in pale yellow, you were, with a white lace shawl on your shoulders. You were beautiful, but haughty, with your lovely little nose in the air, not seeing me or anyone . . ."

Toby clenched her arm harder, not seeming to realize what he was doing. "There was a girl once . . . she was like that. Like you. I'll never be able to possess that girl, my dear. But I'll possess you."

Brenna wanted to shrink away from his intensity. "Please, take me home, Toby."

"But I am enjoying our walk. Aren't you?"

"I said, please, Toby, take me home, or I will . . . I'll start screaming. People will come running out of their homes to see what is happening. They'll all stare at us."

Toby laughed. "After what I've already done, do you think that makes any difference to me? I'll explain away your screaming as the vapors, or a fit of temper. That would be truth enough, wouldn't it?"

Brenna could not hold back her fury. "Why, you're no better than those men who prowl the alleys down in the Swamp, are you? Only your clothes are expensive and fashionable, that's the only difference! I hate you, Toby Rynne. Do you hear me? I would not marry you if . . . if Uncle Amos were to hold a loaded pistol to my head!"

Toby's eyes glinted. "We shall see about that, Brenna Laughlan. We shall see."

The enforced walk lasted ten more minutes, while Brenna fumed and tried to control her growing rage. How dare Toby do this to her? Yet he refused to release his grip on her arm, and, in spite of her threat, she dared not attract attention by screaming. It would only add more fuel to Aunt Rowena's contention that her reputation was ruined.

Toby seemed to enjoy the farce, posturing and bowing as if they were two genteel lovers out for a stroll. If she married this man, would the rest of her life be like this?

"You'll have to submit," he had said. Apprehension caught in her throat. Yes, once married to Toby, she would be at his mercy. Her body would be his plaything, her intimate privacy violated by him every day for the rest of her life.

When they finally arrived back at her uncle's house, she pulled away from Toby and ran inside, barely managing to conceal her tears from Tiny, who was waiting in front with the carriage.

She ran upstairs.

"Brenna? Child, is that you? Is anything wrong?" Mary came out of Aunt Rowena's room, wearing her usual plain gray house gown, and carrying a basket of curl rags, hair tongs, combs and pins. Her tired, bony face looked so

familiar that Brenna wanted to run and throw herself
into Mary's arms. But she stopped herself. Mary had betrayed her and wanted her to marry Toby. She would
never feel the same about Mary again. That security of
her childhood was gone.

"You look so white and sad, child," the Irishwoman persisted.

"I'm fine, Mary, really."

"Would you like me to do your hair this afternoon?
You'll want to look fine for . . ." Mary stopped, biting her
lip.

"For Toby Rynne? Never! I will do my hair myself,
and I don't need to look fine for anyone!"

Hurt spread over Mary's face. Brenna hurried into her
room and closed the door.

She stood for a moment, her body shaking uncontroll-
ably, hearing the sound of Mary's steps passing down the
corridor to the stairs at the far end, which led to the
servants' loft. Then she flung herself on her bed, heedless
of the neat, quilted covering, and buried her face in her
pillow, her body wracked with sobs.

She was not sure how long she lay there, but at last she
sat up, pushed back her tangled hair, and wiped her swollen eyes. She felt dry, empty, all her tears cried away.

Restlessly she got up, went to the mirror, and began to
brush the snarls out of her hair. She barely glanced at her
reflection in the glass. Her skin was blotchy, her eyes
puffy. At this moment she did not look in the least pretty
and she did not want to see herself.

For a long time, as she brushed, her thoughts remained
blank. But gradually she began to think about the previous
evening at the opera. *Quentin*—If Billy Love's threats
could be taken seriously, her brother's life was in real danger. If she did not get the money, he might soon be killed,
his bleeding body tossed into an alley as ugly as the one
she had seen in the Swamp.

The Swamp. She thought of Kane Fairfield, and of his
lithe quickness as he had sprung upon her attacker. He had
kissed her, exciting her mind and senses in a way she had
never felt before. His arms had held her, strongly and
firmly.

Kane Fairfield had given her a long, intimate look last night, his eyes seeming to burn into hers. And he had spoken her name softly, with a kind of rough tenderness.

For a long time she sat at her dressing table, brushing her hair until the long, reddish strands crackled with electricity. Kane Fairfield was wealthy, Arbutus had said. Wasn't he the son of a great Boston shipping family, and didn't he himself own a whole fleet of ships? Had he not kissed her, rescued her from a dockman? And, last of all, no matter how many mistresses he had, wasn't he now a widower, owned by no other woman?

Brenna's brush paused midway through a strand of hair. *Well, why not?* she thought defiantly. Surely it would not hurt to see him again, to talk with him once more.

Filled with sudden energy, she flung down the hairbrush and went over to the washstand. She rinsed her face in the tepid water, hoping to take away some of the swelling and blotches.

For long minutes she rubbed her face briskly with a towel, until she could feel her skin tingling. Then she stripped off her clothing and, standing naked, began to wash her body, savoring the cool, clean feeling of water on her skin. As she dried herself, she caught a glimpse of herself in the mirror. Her skin was peach-smooth, she saw, her breasts lush, full, and pink-tipped. Beneath the swell of bosom, her belly was flat, and her dainty waist curved out to form the rich line of her hips.

She allowed herself no time to think. Quickly she rummaged in her chest of drawers, finding clean underthings, petticoats, corset cover, corset. She must feel her best today, even in the garments that did not show.

At last she went to her wardrobe and pulled out a light blue silk with a low, lace-trimmed neckline which exposed her bosom as fully as fashion allowed. The dress was her most daring, and the color would set off her eyes and skin. Hastily she pulled on the gown, reaching awkwardly around her back to struggle with the button loops.

She picked up her brush in despair. Why had she told Mary she did not want her hair done? Mary's gifted fingers could work miracles with hair—cause curls to fall in lus-

trous ringlets, pouf back hair to just the right shining fullness.

But she could not ask Mary's help without telling her of
her plans. So she took the brush and began drawing it
through her hair, frowning in concentration. Judiciously
she pulled the curls to the back of her neck in a thick,
red-gold knot, securing it with pins. A few strands fell at
her ears, and these she twisted about her little finger, to
make the curls tighter. Then she gave herself one last, critical look.

The blotches were gone. Her eyes were deep and glowing, shining with suppressed excitement. Her hair was
drawn back simply from her face, a few wispy curls falling on each cheek. Framed in the blue neckline of her
dress, her bosom swelled enticingly.

Yes, she thought. She would do.

She started to leave the room, then ran back for a small,
cameo brooch to pin upon the dress. She also grabbed a
light, embroidered mantelet. She did not want to appear too
conspicuous on the streets.

She went downstairs. At the front door she hesitated,
her heart beginning to beat quickly. Where, exactly, would
she find Kane? To her dismay she realized that she did
not know. Except, she supposed, that he must be somewhere by the docks.

She was nearly ready to cry with frustration when she
spotted Tiny in the drive, bringing the carriage back from
his errand. The big, muscular young man was singing to
himself, some rhythmic tune in a language Brenna did not
understand.

"Tiny! Oh, Tiny!" She ran out onto the drive, waving at
him frantically.

"Yes'm?" He stopped the horses and looked down at her
from his perch in surprise.

"Tiny, could you . . . I need to go somewhere very
badly. Could you possibly drive me to the dock area? I
have to . . . find someone."

Tiny's broad, dark face clouded. He was not accustomed
to being spoken to in such a pleading manner. Also, he
had received instructions from Aunt Rowena.

"But, Miss Rowena, she say—"

"Please, Tiny! We'll be back quickly, before Aunt Rowena will need you. I promise you that. Only I need help in getting to Kane's office, or ship, or wherever he is. . . . Please, Tiny. Look, I'll give you this. It's a cameo. Don't you think it's beautiful?"

The boy—in spite of Tiny's size, he was only about seventeen years old—stared down at the brooch covetously, as if visualizing it on someone else.

Brenna pressed her advantage. "If you have a special girl, Tiny, this brooch would look just wonderful on her. And I'll give it to you if you'll only take me to the docks!"

Tiny licked his lips. "Sure, Miss Brenna. Get in and tell me where you wants to go. I takes you."

They were on their way, taking a circuitous route because mud had made some of the streets impassable to carriages. Tiny began to sing again, his voice a rich baritone. Once a tall, black girl came through French doors, carrying a bucket, her head swathed in a clean, white *tignon*. Tiny bowed to her, his gesture an imitation of Uncle Amos' best, and the girl smiled back delightedly.

Soon they smelled the river, rich with the scent of rotting things and stagnant water. Tiny stopped to ask directions from a man selling ginger beer and small cakes from a tray supported around his neck.

"He have the office by the levee," Tiny said, coming back. "You want me to take you there?"

"Yes . . . yes."

"It not a good place for a lady," he said dubiously. "There not many gentlemen from the riverboats, they fighting and drinking all the time, and when they see a lady like you—"

"I don't care, Tiny. I have to see him. You can wait nearby with the carriage, can't you? I'll be all right."

The riverfront area was full of noise and confusion, crowded with men, carriages, horses, goods, and boats of every description, from the canoelike *pirogues*, to the flatboats that actually had people living on them, their laundry drying in the wind, their looms and spinning wheels riding precariously on the crude roofs.

Kane's office was in a brick and stucco building a block from the docks. Brenna instructed Tiny to wait with the carriage, and under no circumstances to leave until she appeared.

"I be here, Miss Brenna, don't you worry none," he told her, his teeth showing in a wide grin. "Take a wild alligator to drive me offa my perch here," he boasted, like the seventeen-year-old he was, and Brenna found herself smiling back.

"I'll hurry, Tiny," she promised. "Remember, don't go away until I come."

Inside the building were several offices, each opening onto a central corridor. On one door, in small, elegant black letters, was written the name KANE FAIRFIELD AND CO., SHIPPING. For the first time, Brenna hesitated. Would his clerks stare at her? Would Kane even consent to see her?

She did not have time to wonder, for suddenly the door burst open, and Kane himself appeared, shoving her with such force that Brenna staggered backward and had to catch herself against the wall. As she righted herself, the mantelet slipped from her shoulders, revealing the bare flesh of her bosom, creamy-pale in the subdued light.

"My God, it's Miss Brenna Laughlan again!" Kane looked annoyed. "Are you my nemesis, following me everywhere I go?" He steadied her with one hand. "Tell me. Are you planning to faint upon my doorstep?"

"Faint? I've never fainted in my life!"

"I thought that was all the fashion." His irritation had passed, and Kane leaned casually against the wall, his eyes inspecting her until she felt her cheeks burn. He was wearing a dark blue coat over a gray brocaded vest, and the snowy-white shirt contrasted with his darkly tanned face and neck.

"Perhaps," she retorted. "But *I* wasn't brought up to have graceful vapors. My mother didn't believe in such things, and neither did my father. They encouraged me to learn to ride and hunt, and I daresay I'm every bit as good on a horse as you are."

"Really?"

What had made her say that? Was he laughing at her? Brenna lowered her eyes, feeling foolish and angry. If only her heart would quit hammering, if only she could have a chance to think and compose herself.

"Yes, I rode astride, too," she babbled. "Although all the old women in Dublin gossiped about me."

Kane smiled, the corners of his eyes crinkling into a fanlike network. "Very interesting. I must say you are right. I don't ride very well. Never had much interest in it, and I certainly haven't indulged since I've been here in New Orleans. Haven't had time."

"Neither have I," she said regretfully. "My uncle doesn't keep riding horses."

He took her arm. "Come on. There's a small courtyard at the back of the building. We can talk privately there."

Obediently, she followed him. The courtyard was tiny. High brick walls shielded it from the street, where, on the other side of the wall, Brenna could hear a dray driver shouting obscenities at his horses. One banana tree grew in a corner, and there were two wrought iron benches facing each other. Kane motioned her to sit beside him.

"Very well, Brenna. What was your purpose in coming here? Surely you're not lost again."

She flushed. "No, no, I'm not lost. Tiny drove me here in the carriage. He is waiting outside for me."

"Tiny? Isn't he that monstrously big slave your aunt keeps? Magnificent-looking specimen. He would fetch a high price at sale, I'd wager."

"Tiny is not a *specimen*, as you call him. He is a human being," she said icily.

"Here in New Orleans he's a slave. You're living in the southern United States and you'd better accept our realities, my dear." Kane studied her until she wanted to squirm. "Well?" he added. "Why are you here? You still haven't told me."

A seagull soared overhead, crying raucously. Brenna sat twisting her hands in her lap, wishing she hadn't come. This had all seemed so easy, back in her bedroom. But now, with Kane beside her, it was difficult to speak.

"It's my brother, Quentin," she said at last. "That . . . that Love man has been threatening him."

"I wouldn't doubt it."

"How can you be so cool? This is my brother we're talking about! My father told me to take care of him, he's always needed managing. He—"

"Calm yourself, Brenna. I am sure your brother will find a way out of his dilemma. His sort usually does."

"How? He's not suited for heavy work, and even if he were, how could he get ten thousand dollars? My uncle certainly won't help him. My aunt hates gambling, and besides, Uncle Amos has financial trouble of his own." Brenna wiped angrily at her eyes. The last thing she wanted was to cry in front of this arrogantly confident man, lounging so easily beside her.

"Is this why you're here, Brenna?" he asked slowly.

"Yes. I . . . my uncle wants me to marry Toby Rynne, as I told you. But I . . . I can't do that. Toby reminds me of a big, disgusting frog or insect or—"

Kane put up a hand, laughing. "Come, come. Other girls have found Toby Rynne desirable. Plenty of them."

Brenna shuddered. "Ugh! *I* never could! He is repulsive to me. And he . . ." She thought of Toby's gloating expression as he told her she would have to submit to him after marriage. "Oh, I just can't. I think I would rather die first."

"Then don't marry him."

"But I . . . I must. I need the money for Quentin. If I don't marry someone . . ." She stopped, feeling his eyes on her. Badly, she wished she'd never come. Why had she? But now she was here, and she forced herself to continue. "The reason I'm here . . . I am offering myself in marriage to you, if you will pay Quentin's debts."

"You are *what?*" Kane's face was unreadable.

"I am offering myself to you. You find me desirable, don't you? I assure you I will make a very good wife. I—"

She would have continued, but her words were drowned out by Kane's mocking laughter. "So, marriage is what you want! Marriage to the famous—or infamous, I should say—Kane Fairfield. Well, well."

She looked at him angrily, the blood burning in her face. "What is so wrong about my asking you? If marriages can be arranged by fathers and uncles and anyone else who happens to have financial interests to consider, why can't they be arranged by the girl herself? I assure you, there is no one to look after my brother's and my interests except myself."

"So that's why you are wearing that evening dress in the middle of the day. You thought to seduce me, to attract me with your charms."

"It ... it's only a ruse any woman might employ," she said defiantly.

"Yes." For a long second, he gazed at her. "Well, it's effective." Suddenly he reached for her, and she was swept up in the strength of his arms. His lips devoured hers. His hand probed inside the neck of her gown, warm against the flesh of her breast, his fingers seeking her nipples.

Dimly she was aware that her heart pounded slowly and deeply, that she ached to be closer to him.

Then, roughly, he pushed her away.

"Kane ..." She could not believe it was over. She wanted him near her. She had wanted the kiss never to stop.

"You are desirable, you little bitch. God knows you are. God knows a man could ... but you have much to learn, Brenna. I told you never to predict me, never to anticipate what I would do or say. And no woman can walk up to me and blandly assume that I will succumb to her charms and marry her."

"But ..." *You kissed me!* she wanted to scream at him. But she was stopped by his twisted scowl.

"No, Brenna, I will never marry again. I love my freedom far too much for that. I don't want to be smothered with hugs and kisses and pleadings! Of course, I do enjoy women. They are useful in their own way, pleasant company, a way for a man to relax—"

"A pleasant way to relax! Is that all women are to you?" Brenna asked furiously. She sat bolt upright on the bench, her fists clenched at her sides. She wanted to slap him, to smack the palm of her hand against his smug face. It was with great effort that she controlled herself.

"Why not? It's what women were made for, isn't it? To provide pleasure for men? To warm a man's bed and see to it that his needs are met?" His eyes glinted. Was he laughing at her?

"Oh! You!"

"Of course, some girls would jump at the chance to become my mistress. I could offer a woman a very enjoyable experience. She'd lack for nothing ..."

"You are asking me to become your mistress?"

"Would that be so unpleasant?"

"But I am not that kind of girl! I was not brought up to ... to ..." she sputtered.

"Not even if I give you the funds you need?"

She stared at him. "But that would be—as Mary said—selling myself ..."

"Is that not what you are doing when you offer yourself in marriage?"

Before she could even think, her hand shot out and slapped Kane across the face. It was a hard crack that left her palm stinging.

For an instant the two of them stared at each other, Kane speechless with anger, Brenna paralyzed by the enormity of what she had done.

Then Kane recovered himself. Fury seemed to crackle from him, his dimples cleaved into bitter lines.

"So, my little wildcat! So this is what you are like! Well, I have come to a decision. You will get no money from me, and neither will you get an offer of marriage. And I would prefer a woman with a milder disposition as my mistress."

Brenna glared back at him. "Well, whoever your mistress is, I pity her!"

"Do you?" Abruptly Kane rose. "You'd better leave, my young shewolf. Go back to your uncle's house, where you belong. I might have offered you my protection, but I see that you are well able to defend yourself!"

As Brenna hesitated, he added, "Well, what are you waiting for? Go! Go!"

Blindly she found the door to the building, and ran outside, stifling angry sobs.

"Home, Tiny!" she cried. "Just as fast as you can. I don't like this place. There's a stench here that fills me with disgust."

Sitting in the carriage she was glad that she faced Tiny's back, and that he could not see the tears which filled her eyes and dampened the embroidered folds of her mantelet.

❧ *Chapter 9* ❧

IT WAS TO BE a double wedding—Brenna and Toby, Arbutus and Monty.

Numbly, Brenna had agreed to all the plans. Nothing seemed quite real to her, and certainly not a marriage to Toby Rynne. But she had tried to hide her feelings from Arbutus, who was genuinely happy at the prospect of becoming Mrs. Monty Carlisle, and who had insisted on having the wedding as soon as possible, since Monty's little girl needed a mother.

Once Kane had refused her, things had happened quickly. Brenna had come home, and had braved her aunt in her sitting room.

"Well, niece?" Rowena had looked up from her needlepoint, her mouth curved in a small, precise smile of satisfaction, as if she had already known what Brenna planned to say.

"I ... I have decided to marry Toby." The words seemed to have come from someone else.

"Oh?" Aunt Rowena cut off a thread. She held the canvas up to the light and looked at it critically. "So you have decided to cooperate."

"Yes. I really did not have any other choice, did I?"

"No, you didn't. As it is, people are already beginning to talk about you and Toby. I can sense it. They are whispering behind their fans, calling you a strumpet—"

"I don't believe that."

"It's true. You wouldn't know, you are not acquainted with these people as I am."

"But ..." Anger had swelled through Brenna, and she had felt the wild urge to strike out at her aunt. "Is it not correct," she had continued rashly, "that Uncle Amos is selling me to Toby like a slave?"

"Selling you?" Her aunt looked quickly away. "Why, what nonsense!"

"I don't think it's nonsense at all. I think that is exactly what is happening. I think Uncle Amos and Toby have hatched out a nice little plan. Amos gets a large sum of money, and Toby gets ... me!"

Aunt Rowena's tongue darted out quickly to moisten her lips. "That is a lie, of course. But why talk of it now? The thing is done. You have agreed to marry Toby. When you are his wife, all the gossip will stop. That is the important thing, is it not?"

"Yes. I will marry him." Brenna had felt as if she could not breathe enough air. "But I'm doing it only because of my brother. Do not think I am doing it for you, or to save my reputation, because I'm not!"

She gathered her skirts and swept out of the room, trying to control her tears of despair.

The scene with Toby had been another nightmare. After making her decision, Brenna had sent a note with Tiny, asking Toby to call on her at her convenience. Within the hour, Toby had arrived.

Brenna had received him in the drawing room. At the far end of the room, the pianoforte and Arbutus' harp stood mutely, and Brenna had been forced to remember the night of the gala, when she had first met Kane Fairfield, and when Toby had first made clear his desire for her. How long ago that had seemed!

"Well, my dear. So you wanted to see me," Toby said gloatingly. His red tongue touched his lips.

"Yes, I did. I wanted to tell you ..." She paused, unable to continue.

"Go on." His small eyes were already beginning to light with triumph.

"Well, under certain ... conditions, I might possibly consent to ..." She swallowed. She could not bring herself to say the word *marriage*. "... to an alliance between us. But here is the problem." Quickly she outlined Quentin's situation and the threats made on his life. Toby listened, his lips pursed, one finger playing with an enormous seal ring on his left hand.

"I need at least ten thousand dollars. And probably more. I want Quentin to be able to pay off his debts in their entirety. And ..." She drew a deep breath. "I want the fare to send my maid, Mary, back to Ireland if she wishes to go. Quentin, too. I think he would be better off away from this city."

For a long moment Toby had stared at her. "So. You would like to strike a bargain."

"Yes." Brenna had flushed deeply, remembering Kane's taunt about selling herself. But quickly she pushed this to the back of her mind. She had decided to sort out the rights and wrongs of it later, in the privacy of her own room. For the moment, she had Toby to deal with.

"Then a bargain it will be."

She began to thank him, but he put up a hand to stop her. "Not so fast. There is one thing we haven't discussed yet."

"What ... what is that?" She swallowed, feeling her tongue as dry as cloth.

"Why, *your* part of the bargain. Do you really think that just marrying me will be enough? That you can wear my wedding ring and spend my money without giving anything in return?"

"Of course, I ... I know that—"

"You do not know anything! But if we marry, you are going to learn. Do you understand me?" She felt his fingers biting into her upper arm. "I expect to enjoy all the pleasures of marriage ... *all* of them. I am a very sensual man, Brenna, as you will learn. I will expect you to be in my bed, waiting for me, whenever I feel desire for you."

He leaned closer to her, his voice thickened. "What's more, I expect you to go along with my wishes, no matter how strange or different they may seem to you."

"What do you mean?"

"Why, there are certain things that I like ... that give me pleasure ..."

"Oh ..." Brenna tried to pull away from him, sickened, but he refused to release her. His face was so close to hers that she could smell his breath.

"And there are times when I desire to watch a woman making love to another man, his hands upon her body, caressing her—"

"You can't mean that!" Brenna's lips were stiff with shock.

Toby laughed loudly. "Ah, you don't believe me. Well, you have consented to marry me, and you must take the good with the evil, mustn't you, my dear?" He let go of her arm so suddenly that she staggered. "It's settled, then. The bargain? I pay off Quentin's debts and send the two back to Ireland. You ... give yourself. Fair enough?"

"I ..."

No, I can't! she had wanted to scream. *I'd die first, before I'd let your hands touch me.*

But the words clogged in her throat. She was barely aware that Toby was calling to Aunt Rowena, that her uncle and aunt had appeared in the drawing room, their faces alight with expectation.

"She has finally agreed," Toby had told them.

"Good. Then it's settled," Amos had said with obvious relief.

"However, I would like to get it done quickly. You can understand why."

"Yes, yes ..."

"The wedding will be in five days," Toby said. "You had better start preparing for it, for there is much to do."

"Yes, of course," said Aunt Rowena. "Of course."

I desire to watch a woman making love to another man. . . . Those words haunted Brenna's thoughts, ringing in her brain over and over. Sometimes she was not sure if she had heard them. No, she told herself, she couldn't have. A husband watching his wife in bed with another man? She had never heard of such a thing.

She had no one she could talk to about it. Everyone was immersed in plans for the double wedding, which was to be held in the house. There were flower arrangements to plan, silver to polish, linens to press, trousseaux to sew. The entire house must be polished from top to bottom, floors waxed to a brilliant shine. Dressmakers must be engaged, hair arrangements debated and argued over. Aunt Rowena took pains with the guest list which, she told

Brenna, included "the richest Americans in the city." And everything was being done in a tremendous rush. Dressmakers worked overtime. Extra slaves were borrowed from neighbors.

No, there was no one in whom she could confide. Mary was busy with the responsibility of supervising the two trousseaux and dressing the hair of all the women in the household. Arbutus was absorbed in her own happiness, and in the thousand chores she felt must be done before she could become the mistress of a busy plantation.

As for Jessica, she had withdrawn into a sullen shell, and spoke little, coming downstairs only for the main meal shortly after noon. When Brenna met her on the stairs, Jessica drew her skirts to one side, as if afraid Brenna might contaminate her. But in a way, Brenna could not not blame Jessica. It was as if life had reached out malevolent fingers to touch them both.

Brenna sent Quentin a message informing him of her wedding plans, and inviting him to attend. However, she was deeply worried about him, and three days before the wedding, went to see him. She and Arbutus were returning from a fitting of their wedding dresses, and, as the carriage pulled up in front of Quentin's building, Brenna asked Arbutus if she would mind waiting outside in the coach.

"But, cousin . . ." Arbutus was bewildered.

"I know it is very rude of me, but I want to speak with my brother alone. About the . . . the problem he has."

"Oh. Of course, Brenna. How silly of me to forget. I declare, I am so taken up with my own thoughts that I forget the rest of the world is going on as usual."

Brenna squeezed her cousin's hand. "Don't blame yourself for that, dear Arbutus. You have every right to be happy. And I love you for it."

It took a long time for her brother to respond to her knock. When he finally opened the door, she gasped with shock, for Quentin had deteriorated further. Today he was even thinner. His clothing was disheveled, his shirttail hanging out of his trousers. He reeked of whiskey. He stood unsteadily, staring at her as if he did not recognize her.

"Quentin! Quentin, it's me! Are you all right? What's happened to you?"

"Nothing, sister." His words were slurred. "C'mon in. Place is messy, got to admit that. But it's home. As much home as anything can be here in America."

She followed him inside, looking about her with dismay. Whiskey bottles and dirty dishes were everywhere. Soiled clothing hung over the furniture. The desk, where Quentin wrote his poetry, was littered with papers, and a pool of spilled coffee seeped slowly into a stack of books. Mercifully, the door to Quentin's bedroom was closed, but she could imagine what that room must look like.

She turned to him. "Quentin, where is Etienne? He should have cleaned this up."

Her brother shrugged. "Etienne is no more, dear Brenna. I couldn't pay him, so he left yesterday morning. I don't need him, though. I can get along without him."

"I see that." Brenna made a face. "Let me help you. At least I can help you straighten this mess." She began stacking his papers in order.

For a moment Quentin watched her, then he sank limply into one of the chairs. "Brenna ... are you getting the money?"

"Yes. Toby promised it after the wedding. And he has also promised to give me your fare back to Ireland. You certainly can't stay here any longer. This city is ruining you." She slapped the books into a stack.

Quentin sucked in his cheeks. "How much is he giving you?"

"Why, more than ten thousand dollars, I suppose. I told him you had a few other debts ... I want them all paid, Quentin. I want everything finished here, so I don't have to worry about you anymore."

Something about his expression caused her to look sharply at him. "Quentin? Have you gambled more than that?"

He said nothing. He stared at the rug, one hand plucking at the velvet upholstery of his chair.

"You have, haven't you? Haven't you?" Her voice rose. She grasped the edge of his desk, her fingernails digging into the polished finish. She wanted to grab him and shake him. She could feel herself trembling.

"Well, I had to do something, didn't I?" His voice was almost a whine.

"But to go out and gamble further! When Billy Love has actually threatened you, and you are in danger of losing your life!"

"I know that, I know that, sister, but I told them you were getting me the money. I told them that in a few days all my debts would be paid. They didn't mind. They ... they often give credit to men who—"

"*They*? Who are *they*? Are you speaking of Billy Love?"

"Why, no. I went somewhere else this time. To another establishment. I don't recall the name right now, but I am sure I'll think of it. I won last night, Brenna. I won fifty dollars, not enough to pay my debts, but it's a good sign. My luck is changing for the better. I—"

"Quentin! Do you think that I can keep on getting money for you indefinitely? Do you think I can work miracles?" She had never before spoken to her brother like this. Since childhood she had looked up to him, had followed him about and tried to be like him. But now things had changed. Now she seemed the older one, he the younger.

"No, sister, of course not ..." He squirmed in his chair, not looking at her. "Where is the bottle?" he muttered. "Thirsty ..."

"You've had enough! Quentin, I don't understand it. What has happened to you?"

"Nothing has happened. It's just that it's hard, knowing they might come ... I mean, am I supposed to sit here in these rooms, just *waiting?*" His eyes pleaded with her. "I can't ... can't just sit here. Had to have something to do, something to occupy my mind. Even Lucille is angry with me. She ... she's afraid, too."

Lucille? For an instant Brenna could not think who this might be. Then she remembered the lovely octoroon girl she had seen leaving Quentin's apartment at her last visit. Quentin's mistress. A month ago, this information would have shocked her, but today she heard it without a tremor. For the first time she saw the true extent of Quentin's weakness.

"What about your poetry? And your books?" she asked harshly. "Can't you occupy your mind with them?"

"I have tried ... but it isn't enough." Perspiration clung in large beads to Quentin's forehead.

"Well, you are going to have to find something. I am not sure I can get you any more money. I am not even sure I can bear to go through with the wedding. I just don't know what's going to happen, Quentin!"

For a moment he stared at her. Then his face was in his hands, his body shaking with sobs. She crouched and put her arms around him and held him.

It seemed hours later that she finally returned to the carriage. She found her cousin sitting inside fanning herself and gazing out of the side window.

"I have been watching the most interesting sights," Arbutus announced. "Two of quite the loveliest quadroon women were walking together, and, I declare, they were as ladylike as you or I, with their fine muslin dresses and scarves—" She paused. "Cousin? Are you quite all right? You look as if you have been crying."

"Nonsense," Brenna said. "I'm fine. Truly I am."

As they drove through the streets, Brenna forced herself to talk about wedding plans, to smile, to ask questions. Her cousin wore her happiness like a shining shield. Brenna could not spoil it.

They had not gone more than two blocks, however, when Arbutus turned to stare intently out of the carriage window. "Why, isn't that Mr. Fairfield?"

Brenna looked. He was walking along the sidewalk in loose, athletic strides. His face looked hard and angry.

"My goodness," Arbutus said. "When he has that expression on his face, he looks like the very Devil, doesn't he? I am certainly glad I never had to fight a duel with him!"

As they passed, Kane looked up. His eyes, fiercely blue, met Brenna's. A warm weakness spread through her. Helplessly, she remembered the kiss he had given her, the way their bodies had melted together. But he had refused her, she told herself. He had laughed at her, scorned her. Left her to Toby.

"He's looking right at you," giggled Arbutus. "Shall we nod to him?"

"Certainly not!" Brenna snapped. "I wouldn't dream of recognizing such a person!"

❧ *Chapter 10* ❧

THE MORNING SUN lay across the sheets in a warm, bright band. Brenna stirred and threw one hand across her eyes. Then still half asleep, she stretched in the bed like a cat. An odd feeling of excitement began to vibrate in her. Something was going to happen today. Something . . .

Then, as if a shadow had suddenly fallen across her bed, she remembered. Today was her wedding day. Today she would become Toby's wife.

She turned on her stomach and buried her face in the pillow.

"Miss Brenna? Are you awake yet?" There was a knock on her door and Mary entered. Brenna heard the rattle of a breakfast tray, and then the soft sound of the mosquito netting being drawn back.

"Your breakfast looks tasty this morning," Mary continued. "There's ham, and raspberry jam, and toast, and eggs like you like them . . ."

"Ugh." Brenna turned over to see the Irishwoman dressed in her best gray linen housegown, her cap freshly starched. "I'm not hungry."

"You? Not hungry? I'd like to see that day!" Mary hovered purposefully near the bed with the tray. "Now, do sit up, and I'll prop the tray on your knees. Hurry, darling, before your egg gets cold. I have to leave you soon, as there's much to do downstairs, with the chairs to be set up in the drawing room. And then I have to come back up and do your hair and Arbutus', and help you both dress."

"I can't eat anything," Brenna insisted.

"Of course you can! It's going to be a very long day, young woman, what with the wedding, and the trip Toby's planned to Lake Pontchartrain, and ... and all else," Mary finished lamely. "You'll need your nourishment."

"Nourishment for the night with Toby?" Brenna laughed bitterly. "I am afraid, Mary, that if more brides knew what lay in store for them, as I do, there would be far fewer weddings."

"You don't really mean that. You know Toby will be a good husband to you. You know you did the only sensible thing in accepting him. You'll never lack for anything, never be hungry or have to go without, never—"

"Never be fully alive again." Brenna gave Mary a quick, despairing look. "Oh, Mary. To spend the rest of my life with him ..."

"You must, child."

Why must I? Brenna wanted to scream. But she couldn't. She had promised her father to take care of Quentin ...

Silently she sat up and reached for the breakfast tray, spread jam on a piece of toast, took a bite. She was surprised to discover she was hungry, after all.

"That's right, child. Eat hearty. You'll need all the strength you can muster for tonight." Mary added in a lower voice, "There are some things I've been meaning to tell you. Some things you must do."

Brenna finished one slice of toast and reached for another. She swallowed the food without tasting it. "What do you mean?"

Mary hesitated. "You have no mother to advise you. No one to tell you these things save me. And tell you I must, lest the same dreadful thing happen to you twice ..."

Brenna stopped eating. She thought of Neall Urquhart, his face distorted with anger. *You were no virgin when I got to you ... you slut ...*

"You must do three things," Mary said. "When he starts to enter you, you must tense all your muscles against him. You must cry out in pain. And," she said, pulling a small knife out of her apron pocket, "after he is asleep you must take this knife and open up a very small cut on your leg, just enough to bleed slightly. Let it stain the sheets where you have been lying. By morning, the cut will not be noticeable."

Brenna stared at the Irishwoman, sickened. But Mary was not finished. "You must act shy and reluctant at first, as if you don't understand what is happening. Believe me, it will be easy. He will be so intent on his own pleasure that he won't even think of you."

There seemed nothing more to say. Brenna sat huddled over the remains of her breakfast tray, her appetite genuinely gone now. All she could think of was Toby's body over hers, his meaty hands touching her. How was she going to stand it? What would she do?

She was relieved when Mary took the breakfast tray and left. It had been a long week, the whole household simmering in a state of pre-wedding tension. Nerves were short, tempers sharp. In one way, she wished that it were all over with. Perhaps, she told herself valiantly, the waiting was actually worse than the reality.

She slid out of bed and went to the window. She leaned out, gazing at the clear blue sky, tufted with clouds so downy white and pure they made her heart ache. It was a beautiful day to be married, she thought suddenly. Only not to Toby . . .

A few moments later, Arbutus burst into her room without knocking. Her cousin clutched a pink dressing gown about her slim body, her hands mottled white with nervousness.

"I . . . had to come and talk," Arbutus said. "It seems I've barely seen you this week, I've been so busy with everything. I . . . oh, Brenna, I'm so excited and mixed-up inside. Sometimes I wonder if I'm doing the right thing after all. I was so happy when Monty asked me to marry him, and now . . ."

In spite of herself, Brenna laughed.

"Well, it is a big step," Arbutus said defensively.

"Yes. Of course it is."

"And there's this, too." Arbutus twisted her fingers together. "I don't know what's going to *happen*."

"Of course you do, silly. You and Monty will be as happy as two fleas in a pocket. You'll raise his little girl, and have about two dozen children of your own, and take care of the plantation, and you and Monty will love each other the way married people do . . ."

"That's just what I'm talking about," Arbutus whispered. "How do married people love each other? What do they do?"

"You mean you don't know?" Brenna regarded her cousin with surprise. Although she was fairly innocent herself, she had grown up around horses, sheep and other farmyard animals.

"Well," Brenna said slowly. "The man, naturally, has an organ . . ."

Carefully she led Arbutus through the story of procreation as she knew it. Her cousin listened in shock, two red circles staining her cheeks.

"So!" Arbutus gasped at last. "So that's it . . ." Her fingers twisted about each other until the knuckles showed white. "I wondered . . ."

"Are you very surprised?"

"No. It's just that I can't imagine it, not really. It seems rather like an ugly little story someone would tell to frighten children." Arbutus giggled nervously.

"Don't worry about it, cousin." Brenna touched Arbutus' hand. "I am sure you will be fine. After all, how many thousands of women have gone before us? They managed to get through it, didn't they?"

"Yes." Arbutus brightened. "Perhaps it won't be bad. And Monty does seem kind. I suppose that is something."

"Of course it is." Brenna thought of Toby. Toby wasn't kind at all. And the things he would do to her would not be at all like what would happen between Arbutus and Monty.

Ruthlessly, the minutes ticked by, forcing her toward what lay ahead. Within a short time, Mary was back with her basket of curling irons, combs and curl rags. She began to dress both girls' hair, her fingers moving quickly at her work.

"I can't believe it," Arbutus sighed, submitting meekly to the curling iron. "Tomorrow at this time I'll be a married woman with a child to take care of."

On quick heartbeats, time passed. Mary fussed and tugged at their hair, at last pronouncing them finished.

Arbutus looked oddly stiff and imposing, her hair piled high on her head to cascade down the back of her neck in a torrent of thick curls threaded artfully with white satin ribbons.

"Very fine, if I do say so," Mary said. "Aren't you going to look in the mirror?"

Obediently Brenna went to peer at her reflection. Her hair shone with a russet luster. Delicate curls wisped over her ears, and a fuller mass of curls were arranged to fall at the back.

"It's lovely . . ."

"Yes, isn't it? And now, Arbutus, if you would go to your room I will come and help you dress, as soon as I've finished with Miss Brenna."

Obediently Arbutus left, and Mary went to the wardrobe and pulled the stiff satin gown from its tissue padding. The gown was fashionably tight-waisted, with a full bell skirt heavily festooned with French lace and white satin bows.

"Beautiful!" Mary said. "You will look lovely in this."

It did not seem quite real. Numbly Brenna suffered the tight lacing of her corset. Then she stepped into the embroidered cambric petticoats, stepped into the gown itself, felt the buttons being fastened at her back.

"There! Didn't I tell you? You're a vision, Brenna, a perfect vision. Look at yourself."

She looked. Looked at the girl in the glass, that young woman with the dreamy gray-green eyes faintly smudged with shadow. The dress fit her perfectly, revealing the full swell of her breasts. The gown itself, with its white swatches of lace and ruffles and ribbons, was a fairy tale concoction, a little girl's dream. Brenna had seen the fabric before it was cut, had sat through four fittings, but today the dress seemed different, as if it had a personality of its own.

Mary left to dress Arbutus, and Brenna found herself drawn to the window. She stared out at the willow tree where Toby had attacked her. A flash of movement caught her eye; was there a carriage parked at the back gate? She saw Hattie running across the flagstones, her skirts flying.

She waited tensely at the window, although she was not

quite sure why. And when the knock came at her door, her heart gave a small jump.

"Yes? Who is it?" she called.

"Miss Brenna? Miss Brenna? It's me. Hattie."

Brenna hurried to the door and opened it. Hattie was breathless and panting, a sheen of perspiration moistening her face. Her eyes widened as she saw Brenna's gown.

"Miss Brenna, they's a man out there by the back of the courtyard, and he told me to come and tell you he was here. He even give me a dollar, he did!" The girl's eyes were shining, fairly dancing with excitement.

"Who's out there? What man?"

"I don't know he name. But he out there, and he give me a dollar."

Brenna's heart was beginning to pump absurdly fast. Who could the man be? Toby? But surely Toby wouldn't be at the back gate—of all places—on his wedding morning.

Then who could it be?

"He say you come down," Hattie insisted. "He say I should wait and bring you down there."

"But I'm in my wedding dress. I can't go out there in the courtyard!" But even as she protested, Brenna reached into the wardrobe for a dark cloak to pull over her gown.

"Hurry, Miss Brenna," urged Hattie. "He say hurry, he say he can't stay there long."

A huge, painful excitement was bursting in Brenna's chest. She followed Hattie out into the corridor and to the back staircase. A gust of baking smells rose up to meet them. These steps led directly to the kitchen and were seldom used by the family. She lifted the hem of her gown and hurried after Hattie, hoping that the servants would be out of sight in the kitchen or drawing room.

They didn't meet anyone. When they reached the bottom of the staircase Hattie led her down a narrow hall that opened onto the courtyard. Then they were out in the sun, the heat beating down on their shoulders. Brenna pulled the cloak tightly about her. Her feet flew across the flagstones toward the back gate, her curls bouncing as she ran.

"So you decided to come." He stood on the other side of the wall, out of sight of the house. His body was trim in a closely fitting dark green coat and tan vest, the sun glinting on his blonde-brown hair. He was smiling impishly at her.

"Kane!" Brenna's hand flew to her mouth. She could feel her heart pounding in long, slow thumps.

"Surprised to see me?"

"Yes! Yes, I . . . I didn't think . . ." she stammered. Waves of hot and cold shivered through her body.

"You make a breathtaking bride, my dear. Virginal white becomes you quite nicely."

Was he mocking her? She was sure there was a wicked sparkle in his eyes. She stepped backward uncertainly. Behind Kane was his carriage, a fine large one trimmed with black leather and brass studs, pulled by two matched blood bays. A young quadroon coachman sat on his perch staring off politely into the distance.

"You don't need to make fun of me," she said in a low voice.

"I am not making fun of you."

"Then why are you . . . I didn't plan for things to happen this way. I didn't—"

"I know what you planned." Kane was openly laughing now.

"I'll thank you to leave right now, before uncle or Toby sees you!" she cried. "Do you realize what they would do if they knew you were here, talking to me on my wedding morning? Toby would probably kill you!"

Kane's face changed. One minute he was smiling, and the next his expression was arrogant, his eyes cold.

"No. Toby will not kill me. He has already challenged me to revenge his brother's death, but I will not meet with such scum. I refused him."

Brenna was shocked. "You refused his challenge? But Arbutus said . . . isn't that the worst possible insult you can give a man?"

"It is."

"Then why? Toby will be livid with fury. He will be beside himself!" She shivered, thinking what a dangerous enemy Toby Rynne would make.

"Let the man rant and rave. It doesn't matter to me." Kane's mouth twisted. "He's no gentleman. In fact, I suspect he's even lower than that river rat you met the other day. I wouldn't dirty my hands dueling scum like that."

"But Toby can't be dismissed so easily. He holds grudges. I know he does. He will be your enemy for the rest of his life."

"Let him."

"But . . ."

Kane turned and spoke to Hattie, who had remained at a distance. She nodded, looking frightened.

"Well? Aren't you coming?" he said to Brenna when he had finished.

"Coming?" She looked at him.

"Yes, of course," he said. "Unless you want to stay here and use that fancy white dress."

"Use . . . the dress?" She had a sudden vision of Toby's hands on the wedding dress, his fingers ripping at the buttons, tearing the cloth away from her breasts.

"You know what I'm saying, Brenna. I'm asking you to come with me. Drop it all . . . drop Toby and just come with me."

"But . . ." There was nothing in the world but herself and Kane. Her eyes were caught in his gaze and she couldn't look away if she had wanted to.

"Just forget the wedding, forget Toby. I drive a good bargain, too."

A pain was pressing at her chest, and she felt as if she would choke. "My brother . . ." she whispered.

"I'll take care of him, I promise. Just hurry, will you? We've got to be away from here." With a lithe movement, Kane swung himself up into the carriage and looked down at her. "Well?"

She did not know quite how it happened. But suddenly she laughed, deep in her throat, and all the pain left her chest. She felt as if she could get in the carriage with Kane and fly across the countryside with him, forever and ever.

"Yes," she said. "Yes, I'll go with you."

She swung herself up beside him, heedless of the hem of her white dress as it swept against the carriage wheel. She felt his hand clasping hers. Then the driver whipped up the horses and they galloped down the alley. And she was laughing inside herself for sheer joy because she was free.

❦ Chapter 11 ❧

As long as she lived, she would never forget that carriage ride, the coach alternately bouncing over hardened ruts and straining through soft mud. Each time the carriage jolted she was thrown against Kane and she shivered, feeling the animal vitality of him even through the folds of her cloak.

Everything seemed heightened. The brilliance of the flowers crowding along the wrought iron fences, the full blue of the sky with its white clouds. The pungent odor of the streets mingling with the perfume of jasmine and wisteria, the smell of the river. All blended together to assail her senses.

They did not speak, and Brenna was content merely to ride, savoring each moment as it came. She was free. She did not have to marry Toby. That was all that mattered. And perhaps—she shot a sidelong look at Kane—perhaps Kane would make her a good husband. For, although he hadn't mentioned marriage, that was what he had meant, wasn't it? She, after all, had made her feelings very clear on becoming his mistress.

A small pang of doubt stabbed her as she remembered Kane saying *I drive a good bargain, too.* But in her relief to be finished with Toby, she pushed this thought aside. She was free, the day was beautiful, Kane was beside her. Surely nothing could go wrong.

They were in the Creole section of the city now, and

Brenna gazed about her, entranced by the scrolled-iron fences, the glimpses of green, secret patios.

"Where are we going?" she asked at last.

"I know a place where you'll be safe enough."

"Safe?"

"Surely you don't think that we can ride away from a wedding, just like that? Toby Rynne will be like a maddened bear who's just lost a big pot of his favorite honey." Kane laughed dryly.

She frowned. Suddenly the day seemed clouded over, the city less charming. She had been so eager to escape her uncle's house that she hadn't given anything else a thought. Of course Toby would be angry, she thought with a shiver. She remembered what he had said: *What's mine, I keep, no matter what I have to do!*

"Do you think . . . Toby will realize it's you I ran away with?" she asked in a low voice.

"He'll find out. I told that little slave girl of yours to keep her mouth shut. But eventually they'll get it out of her. She doesn't know my name, but she'll be able to describe me. He'll know."

Brenna thought of Hattie—Uncle Amos and Toby shouting at her. Hattie in tears. Yes, they'd get Hattie to talk.

"I . . . I hope they don't hurt her. I didn't know . . . I didn't realize . . ."

"Don't worry. That girl is smart. She'll tell them what they want to know quickly enough. But it'll give us a head start." Kane's mouth twitched grimly.

Brenna was silent for a moment. Then she said, "Well, I'm glad we're going to a safe place. I suppose we can stay there for a while and then get married when everything has settled down."

She could sense Kane's body tensing. "Marry?"

"Why, yes. We're getting married, aren't we? You did come back, and I thought you meant . . ." Her voice trailed off. She swallowed painfully.

Of course, she thought dully. He wasn't planning to marry her at all. She'd been so eager to get away that she had jumped to conclusions. Or rather, hadn't made any conclusions, but had gone with him without asking a single question.

"I thought . . ." she whispered.

Kane was staring at her. "Is that why you came with me? You thought I was going to take you up on your proposal of marriage?" A smile twisted his lips. "I was married once, to a girl who wanted nothing more than a convenient man at her beck and call. But never again. I never want to be tied down to a set of petticoats and a little fire on the hearth. That isn't for me and it never will be. I told you that."

She felt like crying. She felt like burying her face in her hands and letting the sobs pour out of her in torrents. She had thought . . . oh, she had thought . . . but it wasn't to be. Kane only wanted to use her body, as Neall Urquhart had, and as Toby Rynne had wanted to. What had she been thinking of?

Suddenly, instead of crying, she wanted to slap him, to feel the flat smack of her palm across his face. Slowly, burstingly, the anger grew in her.

"How . . . how dare you do this to me?" she cried. "You! Why, you're as bad as all of them. You want to use me for nothing more than your own pleasure!"

Kane's lips pulled back from his teeth. She felt a spurt of fear, but was too angry to back down. "You knew I'd think you meant marriage, didn't you? In your arrogance, you knew I'd come away with you. You knew I'd—"

"I knew you needed to use me as much as I need to use you!" His voice cracked out like a whip. The words seemed to echo in the close air of the carriage, to ring in Brenna's ears. *You needed to use me as much as I need to use you.*

"What? What are you talking—" she began.

But he did not let her finish. "Don't come off so high and mighty with me, young woman. You know very well that you don't give a damn for anything but money! You'd wed anything in pants just to get a chance for that blasted brother of yours! Now, wouldn't you?"

Brenna sat paralyzed, hearing the sneer in Kane's words.

"You hate Toby Rynne," he went on. "But you'd marry him, wouldn't you, for money? Then when I came along, you'd go with me, too, wouldn't you—as long as I promised funds for Quentin? 'My brother,' you whispered. Remember? And you accuse me of using you. I would say that you, my fine friend, are using me!"

Brenna gasped. She could feel the blood burning in

every vein in her body. She did not know where to look, or what to do with her hands. She wanted to weep, to throw herself out of the carriage, to die.

"But they will kill Quentin if I don't get the money," she said through dry lips.

"Perhaps they will. But you, my beautiful young trollop, will forestall that. You will sell yourself and get the money for him, won't you?"

"It wasn't like that!"

"Wasn't it? Face reality, Brenna. By marrying a man and making him promise to help Quentin, you're selling yourself just as surely as if you had gone out on the streets and bartered your body to every flatboat man who walked past."

"And you're willing to buy," she accused him.

For a minute she thought he was going to hit her. "Why not?" he asked through tight lips. "The merchandise is there, why shouldn't I have it? Especially when, by taking it, I can run a needle under Rynne's skin. Quite a bargain for me, eh? With an amount of money I won't even miss, I can get myself the most beautiful mistress in the city, and at the same time revenge myself upon my enemy in a particularly delightful way."

"Oh . . . oh, I hate you. You are the most . . . the most contemptible man I have ever met. If you think I am going to be your mistress—"

"You will be."

"I won't! I'll never give you that satisfaction. I wouldn't let you touch me if . . . if . . ." She was stammering. Her head was beginning to ache with the pumping of her blood.

"Ah, but you will let me touch you. And what's more, you'll probably like it, too, once you get used to me. You see, my little wildcat, you don't realize it yet, but, like the Roman generals, you have burned your bridges behind you."

"Burned . . . my bridges?"

"Of course. You see, by coming with me, you have thrown Toby Rynne away. Do you think he would have you now? After the humiliation you have heaped upon him? Do you think he would pay good money to help your gambler brother now? Not a chance!" Kane's eyes flashed with bitter humor. "So, you have only one resource left. Namely, me. If you don't want your brother butchered in some alley, you've got to take the only offer you have. It may not be quite what you wanted, but what in life ever is?"

"I will not—"

"You will, because you have to. Remember, you need me just as much as I need you."

"Oh . . . you are hateful! I . . . I wish I were dead!" she cried despairingly.

Kane smiled, the white of his teeth flashing against his tanned skin. "That is another of your illusions, my innocent. You see, you love life, Brenna. You love everything about it. It's written all over you—in the way you laugh, in the way you move. You don't want to die at all. On the contrary, you'll do everything in your power to remain alive."

He touched her shoulder, then let his hand move down her side to cover her breast. His warm palm seemed to burn through the fabric of her gown.

"As a matter of fact," Kane said, "I think you're going to enjoy being alive. I think you're going to enjoy it very much, in spite of yourself."

"Never!"

They rode the rest of the way through the streets in silence, until the carriage finally came to a stop.

It was a three-story house, stucco over brick, embellished with iron scrollwork along the balconies. At each end of the balcony was a fan-shaped *garde-de-frise,* a spiked barrier to prevent thieves entering from an adjoining balcony. On the ground floor, a dark young girl of about twelve was sweeping indolently with a large broom, as if she had all the time in the world.

"What place is this?" Brenna asked.

"A friend of mine lives here. She owes me a favor. She'll take us in, I'm sure of it. You wait here in the carriage while I go inside and talk to her."

Before Brenna could protest, he had jumped out of the coach and was striding toward the house. He walked with an easy swing, a very slight roll, as if he were on the deck of a ship.

Brenna waited, feeling more uncertain by the minute. What was she doing here with this arrogant, impossible man? If it had not been for Quentin, she would have jumped down from the coach and run away.

Just as she was considering this, a drunken boatman came staggering past the coach. Twice he nearly fell. Brenna watched him with a sinking heart. *Oh, Quentin,* she thought in despair. Without the money, would he end like this? Or, worse, would he finish as a sodden corpse in one of the city's water-filled ditches?

Kane was back, grinning at her. "It's all right. She's got a very nice back room for us. No one will ever dream of looking for us here!"

"But . . . who owns this house?"

Kane hesitated. "A very fine woman named Maud Sweet. She and I are old friends. She'll look after us, and be glad to do it, too."

However, when Kane attempted to help her out of the carriage, Brenna resisted. "I'm not sure I want to go with you! I think I would rather—"

"Die first?" Kane showed his teeth in a crooked grin. "It's too late for such thoughts now. As I told you, you've burned your bridges behind you. Now, hurry, will you? We haven't time to spend chatting in the street, someone might see us. If you won't come willingly, I'm going to drag you in there kicking and screaming!"

She felt his hands close firmly about her upper arms. Then he lifted her out of the carriage.

"What are you doing!" she cried angrily. "Set me down at once! I demand to be set down!" She tried to swing her arms to beat at him with her fists, but he held her too tightly.

"Let me go! Let me go!"

He put her down on the wooden sidewalk so hard that she felt her teeth rattle. But before she could cry out, he clamped one hand across her mouth.

"Listen. You made a bargain, and both you and I know what it was. I expect you to hold to it. And if you don't, I won't honor my part of the agreement. Then where will your brother be?"

She shoved his hand away. "You . . . you're wicked!"

He smiled. "It may please you to think that."

He dragged her toward the veranda of the big house. "Walk properly, or I'm going to pick you up, throw you over my shoulder and carry you in with your hindquarters wagging in the air like a trussed pig."

The mental picture this brought was a humiliating one. Brenna straightened her spine indignantly. "You wouldn't!"

"I would. And what's more, you know I would."

The young girl on the veranda had stopped her sweeping to stare at them in amusement and curiosity. Brenna, her face hot, followed Kane up the wooden walk. To her surprise, he did not knock again upon the door, but proceeded inside. Hesitating, she entered also.

She had never seen anything like the interior of this house. There was a parqueted entrance foyer, with several paneled portals giving onto other rooms. Each doorway was adorned with a pair of naked marble cherubs holding unlit wax tapers. Through the doors, Brenna glimpsed rooms, full of crystal chandeliers and gilt. There was black walnut woodwork, a huge, gilt-embellished grand piano, and pale blue upholstered furniture covered with tassels. Oriental rugs covered the floors almost too thickly, extending to the carved marble fireplaces, over which hung large, dark oil paintings. Mirrors were everywhere, reflecting the lush surfaces of the rooms over and over.

For a moment, she thought she could hear a woman laughing. Then the sound ceased, and the house seemed oppressively empty. There should at least be someone to play the piano, she thought uneasily. Someone to make the mirrors come alive with movement.

"Well, well. So this is the girl. Lovely, isn't she?" The voice came from Brenna's left. She turned, startled, to see an imposing woman coming toward them, clad in a pale blue brocade gown that almost matched the shade of the upholstered furniture. She had an enormous jutting bosom swooping down to a waist so tiny that Kane's hands could have spanned it. She was in her early thirties, with blonde hair piled on her head in a cascade of curls, and a round face with the suggestion of a double chin. The blue eyes inspected Brenna frankly.

"Yes, indeed. This girl could go far if she wanted to. Yes, sir."

"I beg your pardon!" Brenna drew a deep breath, offended by the intimate way this woman looked her over.

"Brenna, may I present Mrs. Sweet?"

"I'm very pleased to meet you, I'm sure," Brenna said stonily.

"I'm sure you are." The woman twisted her full pink lips into a smirk. Brenna pulled the folds of her cloak more tightly about herself.

"Well, then. About the room," Kane was saying. "You say it is at the back, away from the noise?"

"A very quiet room, on a separate corridor. Very private." The woman put one powdered arm on Kane's shoulder. Her hand caressed his face. "For you, anything."

Brenna watched in amazement as the pink-skinned woman fondled the back of Kane's neck, her fingers touching the place where his hair was downy-fine and soft. And Kane, Brenna saw with indignation, was enjoying these attentions. He seemed to preen under the woman's fingers like a dog being petted.

"Very well, then." Maud Sweet at once was all business. She pulled a pale blue tasseled cord that hung on the wall. "I will have Arcadia show you to your room. Arcadia is a very intelligent girl, and I am sure she can help your young lady find the new clothing she will need. It's quite obvious that she does not have any baggage."

Brenna flushed. Maud Sweet could see that the gown she wore was her wedding dress. What must she think? What on earth had Kane told her?

She spent an uncomfortable few minutes while Kane chatted idly with the woman about a recent steamboat boiler explosion in Natchez in which, Kane said, five crewmen had been scalded to death.

Maud Sweet shrugged her shoulders and shuddered. "Ah, well," she said. "It's what will happen when they race each other. I, for one, do not place much stock in gambling. I would much prefer to bet on a sure thing."

"You are not a gambler, then?" Kane smiled easily at the woman, his eyes looking into hers, until Brenna wanted to tear the two apart.

"Never! Why should I give up what I have worked so hard to earn? Gambling is for fools and men!" Maud Sweet threw back her head and laughed heartily, her laugh surprisingly harsh. "Ah," she added. "Here is Arcadia. She will show you the way."

A young dark-haired girl hurried down the staircase, her eyes still faintly puffy, as if she might have just gotten out of bed. She was dressed in a simple cream linen gown which clung to her figure and showed off the lines of her exquisite bust and small waist. Her face was heart-shaped, and her large brown eyes stared curiously at Brenna.

"Arcadia, this couple are friends of mine, and they are going to share that big, back bedroom—you know the one I mean, don't you?"

The girl nodded.

"They will be borrowing the room for a few nights, and I want them to have absolute privacy, do you understand? Furthermore, no one must know they are here. No one." Maud Sweet's voice lowered. "I don't want you to talk to *anyone* about this, do you understand? Anyone at all, including those in this house. Because if I hear that you have been talking . . ."

A shudder seemed to pass through the girl's slim body. "Yes'm." She nodded to Brenna. "Come with me."

She led them up a wide, dark walnut staircase, and then down a long corridor that seemed to extend the full length of the house. There were many rooms along the passage, but no sounds came from behind their doors.

"It's . . . so quiet here," Brenna whispered nervously.

Arcadia gestured toward one of the shut doors. "They are all asleep. They won't wake up for another hour or so. Then it will be lively enough."

"They? Who—"

But Kane said, "Keep still, you little fool! Do you want the entire world to know we are here?"

"Oh. I'm sorry. I—"

"Just be still, will you?"

There was a bend in the corridor and a narrow staircase going up another floor. This passage, lit by a window at the far end, was also lined with doors. Their footsteps echoed on the polished wooden floor. Even their breathing seemed to beat against the plastered walls.

At last Arcadia pulled open a door and motioned for Brenna to enter, Kane behind her.

She saw an entire room decorated in pink—from thick carpets to brocade upholstery, to flowered wallpaper. The pink was a pale, bon-bon shade, reminding her of the soft, pink arms and throat of Maud Sweet. There was a cloying perfume smell. And everywhere were mirrors, reflecting the pale pink roses of the wallpaper, echoing the opulence of this strange room.

"Do you like it?" Arcadia exuded pride. "It's one of the loveliest rooms in the house, I think. The bathroom is down the hall and to your left. And, of course, the . . . convenience is there, behind that screen." Arcadia pointed to a delicate bamboo screen in one corner of the room. "And there is the pull-cord." She pointed out a pink velvet tasseled cord hanging on the wall. "If you pull that, I will come and bring you food—whatever you want."

"Very good," Kane said. "Now, if you would just leave us alone for now. There is much we have to discuss. The young lady can send for fresh clothing later. I assume you'll have it ready."

"Of course." Arcadia backed out of the room, her bright eyes veiled behind thick lashes. "I'll be back with it as soon as I can."

"Don't hurry," Kane said. But the girl was gone.

As soon as Arcadia left, Brenna walked to the window which looked out upon a small courtyard, overgrown with trees and greenery. She stood clutching the folds of her cloak about herself, her body trembling.

"Why don't you take that clumsy cloak off?" Kane said. "God knows you must be hot, all bundled up as if you expected to go out in a Boston winter."

She whirled around. "All I have to wear is my wedding dress," she snapped. "I feel like a fool in it."

"You don't look like a fool. You look very lovely, especially with the red heat of anger in your cheeks." Kane reached out and removed the cloak from her shoulders. It was a sensual gesture. She felt his hand against the back of her neck, the slow slide of the fabric off her back. She stood very still.

Kane tossed the cloak over a pink chair. "Sit down, why don't you? And relax. We're going to be here for some days."

"Relax! I . . . I can't! I don't like this place. Something about it is . . ." She struggled for words. "Too sickly and cloying. I wish we didn't have to stay here."

His eyes held a glint of laughter. "We must, though."

She turned to look again out of the window. Two girls had just entered the minuscule courtyard, sauntering and lazy. One of them was yawning.

"Strange . . . all I have seen in this place are women," she said suddenly.

"So?"

"No men, not even any men servants. Just women. Is Mrs. Sweet a widow? Is this some sort of girls' school?"

Kane stared at her for a few seconds. Then he began to laugh, clapping one hand on his thigh. "You mean you don't know?" he gasped. "You really, seriously, don't know?"

She was angry. "Know what? All I know is that in a rash moment I jumped into your carriage and now you have brought me to this big, incredible house filled with . . . with mirrors and gilt and . . . and women . . ."

Kane stopped laughing. "You're beginning to understand?"

She put one shaking hand to her mouth. "No!"

"Yes, indeed. You and I, my sweet Brenna, are ensconced in the best room of the fanciest brothel in New Orleans."

❧ Chapter 12 ❧

"A BROTHEL? You can't be serious."

"Of course I'm serious. What better place to hide us? Who would look for us here? Believe me, Maud Sweet will make sure our secret is kept. She owes me a favor. You see, I saved her life a few months ago when one of her fine gentleman customers suddenly went berserk and started swinging a cutlass in the house with serious intent—"

"Do you mean he would have killed her?"

"He did slash one of the girls badly. It was most unpleasant. And he was headed straight for Maud with the blade of his knife still red when I got to him. It was a very close call for Maud and she hasn't forgotten it. Or me," he added complacently.

Two near-murders within the silken and brocaded luxury of this opulent house. Brenna felt as if her head were whirling. She sat numbly while Kane told her that he was going to leave her here in the room for a few hours while he went to take care of some business.

"But I don't want to stay here by myself!" she pleaded.

"Nonsense. You'll be fine."

"But—"

"I said you'll be fine. Surely you're not afraid, are you? Nobody's going to mistake you for one of the residents, not if you stay inside this room with the bolt locked." Kane laughed.

"Of course I'm not afraid! I wasn't thinking that at all. I . . . I was just wondering where you were going," she said awkwardly.

"I'm going out to track down a few lies, that's all. Your fine friend Toby Rynne has managed to convince the entire city of New Orleans that I'm worse than the lowest murderer. But he's not going to get away with it. I'm not a murderer. I can prove it and I *will* prove it."

"Can you?" something made her say. She was not prepared for the feral way he turned on her, his face twisted frighteningly.

"You defend that blackguard? Perhaps I should have left you to his mercies."

"No, no," she said quickly. "It's just that he . . . he frightens me."

"As well he should." Kane's expression was unreadable. A few minutes later, he left. Brenna shot the bolt, and then she was alone in the lush pink room, with no company but her reflection in the mirrors. Restlessly she began to pace back and forth, watching the white-gowned girl in the glass perform the same action.

There was a knock on the door.

"Who is it?" Brenna called.

"It's me. Arcadia."

"Very well." Brenna released the bolt and opened the door to admit the dark-haired girl, who was laden with yards of silk and cambric spilling from her arms.

"I have brought you some clothing, miss." Arcadia looked at Brenna's wedding gown matter-of-factly, as if a young girl in bridal apparel in a brothel were something quite ordinary. "Of course, it is not new, since we had such short notice. But it is nearly new, and it is quite clean. Mrs. Sweet always keeps some nice dresses on hand for new girls."

"I . . . don't think . . ." she began.

"It's clean," Arcadia reassured her. "Come, do take that gown off and try some of these." Before Brenna could object further, Arcadia had begun to unfasten the satin loops at the back of Brenna's gown. "This is a wonderful dress," the girl added admiringly. "Perhaps you could dye it and wear it again."

"Ugh." Brenna shuddered. "I couldn't."

"Then perhaps you would permit me to have the dress. I am very good with the needle. I could alter it quite nicely."

"Go ahead, if you want it," Brenna said. "I never want to look at it again."

She was soon standing in her petticoats and chemisette, watching while Arcadia riffled through the pile of folded clothing with obvious pleasure. The girl finally extracted a sea-green silk gown and held it up. "Yes, this will fit."

Brenna stepped into the gown, and felt the buttons being fastened at her back. Arcadia pulled her over to one of the wall mirrors and Brenna stared at her reflection, repeated from all angles in the multiple mirrors.

She looked . . . sensual. Worldly. The neckline of the green gown was cut lower than anything she had ever worn, revealing the pale tops of her breasts and inches of cleavage. The thin, irridescent fabric clung to the lines of her body, revealing every detail.

"Very nice," Arcadia said.

"But I can't wear this. It's much too revealing."

Arcadia looked bewildered. "Why not? Men like to see a woman in a dress like this. Surely you want to please your man?"

"No, I . . . no, I don't."

"But all women wish to please their men. Isn't that what women are made to do?"

"No!" Brenna sank into one of the soft, upholstered chairs and put her face in her hands. Her body shook with suppressed sobs. "I . . . I don't know what I was made for, but it certainly can't be for *that* . . . to be pawed over, to have the man ripping at your gown, tearing away the buttons . . . no!"

She did not know how long she sat and cried. But at some point she became aware that Arcadia had slipped out of the room, leaving the folded pile of clothing behind.

An hour passed, and Kane did not come back. She washed her face with water from a pink china ewer she found on the dressing table, and dried herself on a soft linen towel. Then, for something to do, she began to look through the used gowns and petticoats, hoping to find something more modest. But there were only more evening dresses with revealing necklines, dresses that would cling to her figure, exposing even the outline of her nipples. She couldn't wear these!

But she had to. At least until she could get more suitable clothing. Going through the pile again, she discovered a light evening shawl. If she draped this about her shoulders, and folded it over her front . . . and, of course, there was her cloak. She could wear that on the streets.

Restlessly she prowled about the room, stopping to gaze down on the courtyard again. This time she saw six young women sitting and chatting on benches, all dressed in daring evening gowns. As one of the girls looked up, Brenna stepped hastily back into the shadows. They mustn't see her, she realized. Or they would talk. And that would make Kane angry.

Where was Kane? What was he doing? And how long did he expect her to wait for him, with nothing to occupy her time? Even needlework, she thought ruefully, would be better than simply pacing the thick carpet, back and forth.

Dusk began to settle. The girls left the courtyard, and through her opened window Brenna could hear piano music from the front drawing room. There was another knock at her door, and Arcadia came in with a lighted candle and a tray laden with food. There was heavily spiced shrimp gumbo, red beans and rice, and crusty French bread. Brenna ate hungrily.

Arcadia waited until she finished her meal. Then the girl said, "*He* is not back yet, is he?"

"No . . ."

"Then I have something I want to show you. Something you said this afternoon . . . I want you to see that it isn't as you said. Not at all . . ."

As Brenna watched, Arcadia went to the corner of the room and pulled aside the bamboo screen. Behind the screen was a small, miniature painting, hung at eye level. Carefully Arcadia lifted this from the wall, to reveal a small pane of glass.

"They will not be able to see us," she whispered. "Our

window has been carefully hidden." She motioned for Brenna to step forward. "Come and look."

As Brenna hesitated, Arcadia took her hand and pulled her forward with a strength surprising in a girl so small. "There! You see? There is a woman pleasing a man, and see how she enjoys it? See how excited and happy it makes her?"

The view through the pane of glass was an extraordinary one. It revealed another room similar to the one they were in, lit only by flickering candles hung in sconces along the wall. But the center of the scene was the bed. A man and a woman were lying there naked, their bodies glowing creamy white in the candlelight. The woman lay languorously against the satin sheets, her back arched, her mouth slightly open. And the man bent over her, his mouth on her breasts in a long, tonguing kiss . . .

Brenna drew in a quick breath. There was something dreamlike about the scene, something in the candlelight wavering on white bodies that made it seem unreal. But it was real, she told herself. In the very next room, separated from her only by a wall, a man and a woman were—

"No!" She pulled back, her heart beating oddly fast.

"But you haven't seen—"

"I have seen all I want to see," Brenna said firmly.

"Later you may want to see more. The peephole will still be there, and you may use it anytime you like."

Brenna shivered. She looked at the other girl, at her small, catlike smile. "You like living here, don't you, Arcadia?"

For an instant the girl looked angry. "Yes. And what is wrong with that? I came from Natchez, from a family with thirteen children, and I was the twelfth. We were always poor, often we starved. I was raped when I was fourteen and my baby died at birth. I . . . I had to leave home then. My mother was sick, and I came here . . . and found Mrs. Sweet. She can be tough, but there is plenty of food here, and pretty clothes. I like pretty clothes . . ."

Arcadia's voice was high and soft like a child's. "I have five gowns," she said. "Five beautiful, silken gowns. And . . . I have men to hold me and love me, give me good feelings . . ."

"How long have you been here?"

"Two years. Since I was fifteen."

So this girl was only seventeen, two years younger than herself. Brenna did not know what to say. "I . . . I think I wish to go to sleep now," she managed. To her relief, Arcadia nodded and smiled, then left.

Brenna lay down on the bed and tried not to hear the noises from other parts of the house—raucous laughter, the tinkle of the piano, someone shouting. She thought about the peephole. Was there another piece of window glass set up to spy on her room as well? Could there be someone watching her right now? Quickly she got up and searched the room, finding nothing. Or was the peephole merely too well hidden?

She did not know how long she waited for Kane, alternately waking and dozing. But at last he was there, shaking her shoulder roughly.

"Wake up! We've things to do. We've got to go out."

"Out?" She woke up fuzzily. "But you said we were going to remain hidden."

"We will. That's why I want to go out now, while it's dark, and no one will see us."

"But where are we going?" She sat up, digging at her eyes with her knuckles. Her body ached, and she felt so tired. She felt as if she could crawl between the satin bed sheets and sleep for a week.

Kane pulled at her shoulder. "Don't fall asleep again. I want to go and see your brother."

"Tonight? But—" She struggled to come fully awake. Then terror struck her. "Is anything wrong? Has anything happened to him? Is he—"

"No, no, it's nothing like that. I just want you to see for yourself that I am carrying out my part of the bargain."

"An excellent idea," she heard herself say coldly.

In the flickering half-darkness of the room, she saw Kane's face twist. "You don't trust me? Well, I don't trust you, either. That's why I'm going to make this agreement in two parts. I will pay your brother's current gambling debt—the money he owes Billy Love. I will give him a monthly allowance for the rest, to cease immediately if you and I should have a falling-out. Is that agreeable?"

"But I don't want Quentin to stay here in the city," she protested. "He cannot stand this way of life. I want to send him home to Ireland. He and Mary as well."

Kane's eyes glittered. She felt caught in their depths, like a mouse mesmerized by one of Louisiana's deadly snakes. "Perhaps Quentin will return to Ireland . . . perhaps. *If* you and I get along. Fair enough? Of course, one day I will tire of you. Then I will pay you off and send you packing fast enough . . ."

"Pay me off! Send me packing!" Brenna almost sputtered in her indignation. "What do you think I am, a household servant? Someone you can summon on the slightest whim and get rid of just as easily? Someone like Arcadia, who'll take whatever you choose to give her and consider herself lucky to get it? Well, I'm not such a person! And don't think you can treat me as one!"

Kane's lips tightened. "We'll see about that." He pulled her roughly to her feet. "Now, come along. Joachim is waiting outside for us."

As Brenna stood up, she was conscious that a great deal of her bosom showed above the low neckline of her dress. However, although Kane's eyes lingered appreciatively, he made no comment other than a harsh, "Wear your cloak." She flung it about her angrily, pulling it close.

He led her out of the room to a narrow back stairway, which he maneuvered without a falter, even though the candle he carried barely illuminated its dark corners.

"You are so familiar with this staircase, it would seem that you have used it before," Brenna said tartly. Anger simmered in her. Never had she disliked anyone so much before. Even Toby Rynne, with his thick hands and lustful eyes, had not roused her fury like this man.

"I've used it many times," Kane said, grasping her arm as they turned a corner at a dark landing. "This, of course, is the staircase that many of New Orleans' wealthiest gentlemen use when they wish to remain discreet. It opens onto a small, narrow alley with just enough room for a carriage to wait."

"Very handy."

Kane refused to be disturbed by her sarcasm. "Yes, indeed."

The night was cool and moist, with a wet breeze coming in off the river. Brenna drew a deep breath of air, thinking how good it felt. She had been cooped up in that terrible bedroom for most of the afternoon. Even if she had to be with Kane, it was still a relief to breathe some fresh air.

It was a short ride to Quentin's rooms, and neither of them spoke during the time it took to get there. When the carriage pulled up in front of Quentin's building, they saw a light glowing in the window of his bedroom.

Kane looked about the street cautiously, then jumped out of the carriage. "Get out," he ordered. "No one seems to be around, but we might as well move quickly. There's no sense risking being seen."

They had to knock at Quentin's door for a long time before they heard any response.

"I hope he hasn't passed out," Kane commented casually, as they waited.

"Passed out?"

"It's common knowledge that your brother cannot hold his liquor."

"Oh, that's not true at all! Quentin does drink a bit too much. It's a weakness of his. But he holds his whiskey like a gentleman."

"Does he?"

Just as Brenna, forcing back doubts, was about to defend her brother furiously, the door swung open to reveal Quentin.

For a moment brother and sister stared at each other. It is as if Quentin were a stranger, came Brenna's first, half-hysterical thought. The person he reminded her of most strongly was the drunk she had seen staggering down the street outside Maud Sweet's. His face was blurred and flabby, his eyes bloodshot. He had not shaved, and there was a raw, swollen cut on his lip. His hair hung in dirty, oily strands nearly to his shoulders. And, worst of all, her brother's right hand kept picking at the filthy folds of his shirt, in a repetitive, unconscious gesture.

"Oh, Quentin. Quentin . . ."

"Let's go inside, Brenna. We can't talk to him out here." Kane ushered her into the room, his hand firm on her arm. She stopped short just inside the door. A sour smell permeated the rooms, although it was obvious that someone had tried to clean up the mess.

Quentin was clutching her. "My God, sister, what happened to you? You were to marry Toby, it was all planned. You promised . . ." He pressed her hand like a supplicating beggar.

She could not help herself. She moved away from him, toward the shelter of Kane. "Is that all you can think of, Quentin? The money? The everlasting money?"

"But you promised."

"That's right, I did promise. And I will give you the money. I—"

But his anxiety was such that he could not let her finish. "I've got to have it sister, I've got to!" he gabbled "It isn't often that I've asked you something, but now there isn't any choice. B-Billy Love was here just an hour ago. He did this to my lip. And he hit me in the stomach. I . . . I can barely walk." Quentin's lips quivered. "I . . . I begged, sister. I pleaded. I made a fool of myself. I told him there was some mistake, there had to be. I told him you'd get the funds somehow, that you had another source." The sound of Quentin's swallowing was loud in the room. "He's coming back in another hour."

"Don't worry," Brenna said at last. "I . . . we do have the money for you tonight. That's why we're here. To give it to you. So you can pay your debts and take care of yourself."

She nodded at Kane, who began counting out bills.

"This is to go to Love," Kane said shortly. "Not for whiskey and not for more gambling. Do you understand?"

"Yes, yes. Oh, yes." Quentin's hands shook violently as he took the money. It was a sight almost obscene.

And he is not yet twenty-one, Brenna thought.

"Further, thanks only to your sister, there will be more money each month, *if* you behave yourself, and if she behaves as well."

Quentin stood clutching the money, his eyes moving quickly from Kane to Brenna, as if he had grasped the situation for the first time. "Oh, yes," he babbled. "Yes, she'll behave herself. She'll be good to you, she'll do anything you ask—"

Brenna's hand shot out and she slapped her brother's face.

The sound echoed in the room. Quentin seemed to wobble on his feet, and he reached up to touch the reddened imprint of Brenna's hand.

"How dare you speak of me that way!" she cried. "If it were left to you, you'd sell my body on the streets, wouldn't you? Toby Rynne or Kane Fairfield—you don't care who I get that money from, or how. Just as long as your own precious hide is saved. Well, I got it for you. You'll never know at what cost, but I got it. And now I'm beginning to see that I did it all for nothing. For nothing, do you hear? You are the reason I sold myself? *You?*"

Furious tears were running down her cheeks. Angrily she dashed them off with her fist. "Father asked me to look after you. So I did. Well, Father was wrong. He was so very, very wrong. You aren't worth looking after. I should have let Billy Love have you!"

"Sister . . ." Quentin stretched out his hand to her.

But Brenna turned and ran out onto the upper veranda, her cloak flying behind her, tears streaming down her face.

❧ *Chapter 13* ❧

HOURS LATER, Brenna lay bolt awake in the bed at Maud Sweet's, her heart still pounding from her sudden awakening. Had there been a noise? She didn't know what had jolted her out of heavy sleep so quickly.

She lay, listening to the sounds around her. Kane's breathing came irregularly from the upholstered couch at the other end of the room. There was a thump as he turned over and his feet hit the end of the couch, which was far too short for him. She heard a burst of drunken laughter coming from her opened window, sporadic off-key notes on the piano. It must be very late, she thought wearily. Did the amusements in this house keep going until dawn?

Her body stiffened as Kane caught his breath in a half-moan. It was a vulnerable sound of deep sleep, and made him seem less hard and arrogant, more human.

Not that he had been unkind to her this night, she thought slowly. They had left Quentin's apartments with herself huddled on the carriage seat beside him, her body shaking with sobs. She had been unable to stop crying. Even knowing the contempt Kane must have felt for her could not make her stop gulping and weeping, her voice so ragged that she had barely recognized it as her own.

"Brenna, he isn't worth those tears," Kane had said.

"I know. B-but he's my brother."

"True, but he's not worth crying over. You've done

what you can for him. Now forget him. What will happen
to him will happen, regardless of what you do."

Heartsick, she had continued to weep. "But I could have
done more. I should have helped him more . . ."

"What could you have done? You did more than most
sisters would have. Now at least he doesn't have to worry
about Billy Love. The rest is his problem. A man has to
fight his own battles, you know. He can't let a woman do
it for him."

"But Quentin is weak, he needs someone to look after
him . . ."

"And you would do that, wouldn't you? No matter how
contemptible he is . . ." Kane's voice continued, and in her
weariness Brenna had begun to slump against him. It had
been a long day, and her limbs were twitching with exhaustion. She had let her head rest on Kane's shoulder, and for
a few moments, she had felt a piercing contentment.

Then, as if someone had tossed a pitcher of iced lemon-
ade in her face, Kane was shaking her roughly awake.

"Hurry, Brenna. People are starting to leave Maud's
now, and I don't want to be seen. Wake up now!" He
had half-lifted her from the carriage.

"Come on, walk, can't you? Walk, or I'm going to drag
you."

Wearily she placed one foot in front of the other, and
managed to follow Kane up the narrow back staircase.
At the first landing they heard someone coming downstairs. Kane had whirled her around and pulled her back
down the steps and into a dark corner. They stood in the
shadows until the man had lurched past. In a few minutes
they had heard him shouting in a slurred voice for his
servant.

"Upstairs now, and hurry, before someone else comes
blundering along," Kane whispered, pulling her after him.

They reached the room and Kane lit one candle. "You
take the bed, and I'll make do with this ridiculous short
couch," he had said, giving her a push. "Go on, will you?
Before I regret what I've said. And you can take that gown
off, too," he added, as she stumbled toward the bed fully
clad. "You'll crumple it."

"But I can't undress with you here . . ." If she hadn't

been so tired and so numb, she would have exploded with anger. But her lips felt stiff, and her anger had been buried under an overwhelming blanket of exhaustion.

She had felt his hands at her back. "Turn around, will you? And stand still. I can't manage these damned tiny buttons with you tossing about like a mare settling down for the night."

"A mare? I'm not . . ." But her words trailed off, and numbly she suffered the feel of his fingers at her back, releasing the buttons.

"Now step out of this thing."

Like an automaton, she had obeyed. She stood swaying in her chemisette and petticoats, the night air cool on her skin.

He had given her a light shove. "Now, get into bed, will you? Before I—" His breath had caught. "I'll drape the netting for you. Go on."

She half-fell across the bed and had been instantly unconscious. But that had been hours ago, she was sure. Now, only seconds ago, something had awakened her. A hoot of laughter, an unfamiliar creak in the solid old house? But whatever it was, she had sprung from deep sleep to complete awareness.

Then she heard it again. A hoarse, ragged moan.

She lay tensely. It was Kane.

He moaned again, and this time his voice was louder, and there were words mixed with it. "No . . . no. . . . They're tying him up. . . . My God! My God! Chop his knees . . . chop his knees—"

The voice grew louder, almost a hoarse scream now, terrifying in its nightmare intensity. "No . . . all of them . . ." She heard violent sounds and knew that he was thrashing about on the small couch. "Kill them! My God, kill them for what they're doing! Get them—"

Brenna could stand it no longer. Shoving aside the mosquito netting, she jumped out of bed and ran across the carpet. She knelt on the floor beside the couch, and, pushing Kane's shoulders, tried to make him lie down again.

But he shook her loose as if she had been a mosquito. "No!" he screamed. "No . . . my God . . . get the blood . . . get the blood out. . . . No!"

"Kane, Kane, it's a nightmare," she pleaded. "Please wake up. You're only dreaming, and it's all right."

He thrashed convulsively, then fell back on the couch. She stroked his forehead gently. An odd feeling pressed at her chest. How damp his face was. Were those tears wetting his cheeks?

"No . . . God . . ." He turned on his side and moaned into the pillow, his body rigid.

"Kane, you must wake up. You're having a bad dream. Please."

He awoke so quickly that she wasn't prepared for it. In a flash he sat up, and stared at her.

"What are you doing?" he demanded coldly.

"Why, I . . . you were shouting in your sleep. You were having a nightmare. I was just trying to wake you so you'd—"

"It's none of your business to flutter over me! Understand this, will you? I will not be fussed over, and I will not be taken care of. If I'm having a nightmare, just let me alone. Don't interfere!"

"Interfere! Why, I was just trying to help you! You were screaming and moaning about killing, and blood, and—"

"Be quiet!" His voice cracked out like a pistol shot. "Go back to bed and mind your own business. When I want your help, I'll ask for it. Is that perfectly clear?"

"Oh, yes! Perfectly!" Her voice shook. Her knees trembled as she crawled back into the bed and rearranged the mosquito net. Never had she hated him so much, she decided. He was a cold, arrogant man, and she loathed him! Tomorrow she would . . . tomorrow she would . . .

She slept.

Morning seemed to come almost instantly. One moment she was lying wide-eyed and fuming in the dark, and the next minute soft sunlight was streaming across her bed, little motes of dust dancing in the yellow.

Someone rapped at the door. Brenna stirred and sat up, noticing that Kane was gone. "Who is it?" she called.

"It's just me, Arcadia, with your breakfast." Brenna got up and opened the door to admit the dark-haired girl, who carried a tray laden with coffee, croissants, eggs, toast and jam. Arcadia's hair was tied back with a satin ribbon, and her eyes looked heavy and satisfied. Unwillingly, Brenna remembered the sounds she had heard the previous night, the full, low laughs of women.

The tray was set for one, and Arcadia cheerfully explained that Kane had left half an hour ago, leaving a message that he would be back in a few hours.

So she would have to spend another day in this pink room with the mirrors. Brenna frowned, remembering her angry thoughts of the previous night. If only she could run away! But to where, she wondered. Certainly not back to her aunt and uncle's—they would only force her to marry Toby, she was sure.

Arcadia left, and Brenna finished her breakfast without tasting it. When she had eaten, she put aside her tray and saw that the girl had left a marked piece of linen on the dressing table, along with needle, yarn and hoop. Brenna smiled ruefully to herself. Once she would have bridled at the very thought of sitting with a needle and thread, and would have tossed the embroidery to the floor and run outdoors. But here at Maud Sweet's she couldn't go outside. And today the needlework was a godsend, something to keep her hands busy and her mind occupied.

Slowly she selected a skein of yellow yarn for the daisies in the pattern. Then she threaded the needle and began to take slow, awkward stitches, trying to make her mind a blank. She didn't want to think at all.

Kane reappeared in the late afternoon. He looked hot, tired and irritable, and came slamming into the room as if he didn't care whom he awakened.

"Well, it's you." She looked up coolly from her embroidery. She had made progress, and had even remembered some of the stitches Mary had taught her. She had spent the day *not* thinking of Kane, erasing him from her thoughts as if he had never existed.

"Yes, it's me."

"Where have you been, might I ask?"

"Where do you think?" Kane's brows drew together in a scowl as he took off his waistcoat and tossed it onto a chair.

"I'm sure I wouldn't know. Since you choose not to confide in me."

"Well, if you want to know, I've been out tracking

down lies! I don't understand how Rynne did it, but he's managed it somehow. Every damned one of those men swears he saw me shoot Ulrich Rynne in cold blood. Their stories are so convincing that I'm beginning to wonder myself if I really did it." Kane slumped onto the couch and sat staring at the floor. "If I could only get my hands on them. . . . Ah, maybe they're right. Maybe I really am a murderer."

"Perhaps you are."

For an instant there was silence. Then Kane looked at her, his complexion darkening. "It isn't true! If you weren't a woman, I'd fight you for saying that."

"Or challenge me to a duel? In any case, I'm glad I am a woman," she said calmly, although her heart was thumping. "Does this have anything to do with your nightmare of last night? All that jumbled talk about blood and killing?"

"All right." Kane got up and began to pace the room furiously. "Since you're so persistent, I'll tell you. Rynne has gotten to the men who witnessed that duel. Suddenly, when I try to find them to question their stories, they're gone, wisped away like smoke. Arthur Costigan, Ulrich Rynne's best friend, is suddenly gone to Havana, with 'important' business there, his wife swore to me. What's more, damn their hides, Doctor Rene Perrier and Raoul Frontenac are in Havana with him. Perrier was the physician Ulrich Rynne had engaged."

"Oh—"

"And then, of course, there's Matthew Watson, the broker. He left just this morning on a steamboat upriver, taking his family with him, I've been told. As for Raleigh Cardell, my own second, he's completely disappeared into thin air. I went to his rooms, but no one there knew where he'd gone or what had happened to him. All they knew was that he'd left a signed statement, implicating me in the death of Ulrich Rynne . . ." Kane slammed one fist into the other, his face twisted. "Lies! All of it! Damned, outright lies!"

"Do you think, then, that you will be tried for murder?" Brenna asked.

"Let them attempt it!"

"But—"

"The authorities are slow. They'll have to catch me first. And no one will catch me until I've located those five witnesses myself and forced them to tell the truth."

"But will they tell the truth? If Toby Rynne has them that terrified—"

"They'll tell. Never you fear about that." Kane's mouth hardened, and his eyes were cold blue stones, with a pinpoint of light at their core. Brenna felt a chill. Perhaps, she thought uneasily, Kane really had murdered in cold blood. Certainly he looked ruthless enough at this moment.

"What . . . what are your plans?" she asked at last.

"My plans are simple. I'm going to track down those liars and make them tell the truth and exonerate me, if it takes me months to do it. What's more, I'm going to expose Toby Rynne for what he is, a cheating, conniving sea slug with his fingers in every evil pie that's ever been served here in New Orleans."

"What do you mean by that?"

"Why, piracy, for one thing. Surely you don't think that the Rynne brothers came by their money honestly, do you? You've heard of Jean Lafitte, the pirate, have you not? Some years ago, Lafitte and his bunch organized the rabble of pirates and privateers on Grande Terre Island. They financed pirates on the high seas, and then collected the loot and sold it to God-fearing New Orleans merchants, who made a pretty penny off the blood of their fellowmen. Some of these merchants would actually go to Grande Terre to do their buying."

Brenna stared at him. "Do you mean that pirates actually kill people? I've heard stories, of course, but I thought they . . . just robbed them."

Kane laughed derisively. "Where have you been, Brenna Laughlan? You've lived here in New Orleans all these months without hearing about the bloodier pirate exploits?"

"I have heard that pirates are a great danger, that a ship is hardly safe along these coasts, that they even sail up the Mississippi, attacking boats on the river. But I didn't think . . . I didn't realize—"

"You romanticizing drawing room fools! I suppose you ladies think pirates are vaguely daring and swashbuckling and even rather attractive. Well, I have news. If pirates take over a ship, you can expect wholesale murder of the entire crew. Beatings, garrotings, stabbings, heads sliced off. One captain I know was tied to the mast and his legs were sliced off at the knees, one at a time. Then they started on his arms . . ."

Brenna remembered Kane's nightmare, and the horrid recurring phrase, *Chop his knees*. She swallowed back a surge of nausea.

"The only ones they let live are the slaves aboard, and any young and pretty women. These they hold for ransom, raping them in the meantime as much as they please. Some of the women get thrown to the crew, who abuse them worse than the lowest animals. These women are lucky when they finally die . . ."

"But Toby Rynne wouldn't do such things," she faltered. "He may be a . . . a disgusting person, but surely he would not murder, or do such hideous things. I think you're mistaken."

"Mistaken! Brenna, I'm convinced that Rynne has taken over where Lafitte left off. Not on such a grand scale, certainly. Public opinion is too much against it. But still, he does finance pirate ships. And he does receive stolen goods and sell them to businessmen here in New Orleans. Goods stained with the blood of murdered men."

As Brenna started to protest, Kane went on, "Just because your fine friend does not personally wield a cutlass, don't make the mistake of thinking he's innocent. He knows what's happening. He even goes to the big contraband slave auctions the pirates have. Sometimes he buys a young and comely girl for himself, I've heard. And the things he does with her are not always pleasant."

Brenna felt physically ill. "But why? Why do the merchants buy from him? They must know what's happening."

"Some people can close their eyes to anything. If the goods are available, at good prices, why shouldn't they buy? After all, *they* aren't murderers, are they? *They* are are only buying liquor or pewter."

Brenna closed her eyes, remembering her uncle's alliance with Toby. Did her uncle know what business Toby was in? Know, and still urge her marriage?

"I've lost two ships this year to those damned murdering

renegades. I've concealed my sailing dates, I've varied my routes, and I've kept my destinations secret. But still it happens. Dead men . . . sometimes I see dead men in my sleep. Corpses floating in the water, their faces down, their bodies drained of blood . . ." Kane's fists kept clenching and unclenching, as if only the greatest effort kept him from pounding them into someone.

"Well, I'm going to stop him," he said. "Somehow, I'll do it. And I'm going to start by sailing to Havana, where three of the witnesses to the duel are. They won't get away from me as easily as they think."

"Havana?" Brenna stammered. "But what about me?"

"You?" Kane shook his head as if to clear it. "Why, you'll come with me. Why not? We can turn our journey into a pleasure trip."

But the smile he gave her promised anything but pleasure. Brenna shivered with foreboding.

Kane went out, and returned after dark to tell her that his ship *Sea Otter* was nearly ready. They would sail as soon as she had been fully loaded and provisioned.

Brenna, thinking of her makeshift wardrobe, was dismayed. "But my clothes!" she protested. "Surely you don't expect me to go aboard in this!" She indicated the low-cut, sensuous green gown.

"Why not? You look fine to me."

"Fine? I look like a . . . a slattern, that's what I look like! Which isn't surprising, considering where this dress came from."

"Nonsense. What is wrong with a lovely woman showing off her charms?" Kane smiled at her teasingly, in one more aspect of his swiftly changing moods. "Anyway, think of me. I don't dare go back to my lodgings just yet, so I must go out and see if I can buy some second-hand clothing. I've told my crew, incidentally, that my wife will be sailing with me."

"Your wife!"

"Do you object?" His voice was abruptly sharp. "Be thankful, at least, that you don't have to travel in your wedding dress."

"I'm not sure I want to travel at all. How dare you ask me to travel as your *wife*, when you have refused to marry me! I . . . I'm not sure I can go through with this charade. Suppose I tell you I want out of it? Suppose I tell you that I want—"

"Do you think you can get out of it as easily as that?" The teasing look had left Kane's face. She felt his hands pressing into her upper arms. "You and I made an agreement. I intend to hold you to it. You're my mistress now, whether you like it or not. You're coming aboard the ship with me, if I have to tie you up and drag you."

"You wouldn't dare!" she gasped. "I'll scream!"

"You'll do no such thing. If you try, I'll gag you. If necessary, I'll stuff you into my traveling trunk. How would you like that, you little wildcat?"

Brenna felt a wild desire to laugh. "You don't even have a trunk, and you told me yourself you can't go back to your lodgings just yet."

"Don't think I can't get one. And don't think I wouldn't hesitate to stuff you in it. After all, if you'd consent to marry that blackguard, Toby Rynne, what is so different about coming along with me? Do you find me all that repulsive?" His eyes burned like two blue coals.

"Yes!" she screamed. "Yes, I do find you repulsive! As for me and Toby Rynne, what about that half-sister of his, Melissa? What about her? You say Toby is a sea slug who is involved with pirates and murder and God knows what else. Well, what about Melissa? Isn't she involved, too?"

For a moment Kane seemed taken aback. A whiteness appeared about his upper lip, and Brenna was afraid she had gone too far.

"Melissa knows nothing of this," he said stiffly. "She and her brother are not on the best of terms."

"Oh? Are you sure?"

"Yes. I am sure. And I don't want to hear you mention her name again. What she and I have—or have had—is nothing to do with you."

"Nothing?"

"That's right. My affairs are none of your business. After all, you are only my . . ."

"Your mistress," she finished bitterly. "Your possession, your chattel. Well, I hate belonging to you. I hate it!"

"You'll come to like it well enough, I'll wager."

"I won't! I'll never like it! Oh, I know why you are so eager to have me. You told me yourself. You want to spite Toby Rynne. Like a malicious little boy stealing another's marble, you just want to take something he wants!"

"Does it concern you so much? You are a desirable woman. Why shouldn't I want you?"

She remembered the way Melissa Rynne, with her perfect, cameo face, had smiled up at Kane. "Yes," she said. "I'm sure you've had most of the desirable women in the city. But I don't want to be among them."

"Then I think it's time I changed your mind."

Suddenly Kane's hand slid to the back of her gown. With one strong arm he pinned her to his chest so that, try as she might, she could not push him away. He deftly unfastened the buttons of her gown, as if he had had long practice in performing such actions.

"What are you doing? I am not one of your strumpets! How dare you . . ." Summoning all her strength, she shoved him. But he was almost immovable. He scooped her up, flung her on the feather mattress, and pinned her body with his own.

"Don't try to scream," he warned her. "That won't do you any good here, at Maud's. Do you think they would even listen, my foolish, foolish Brenna?"

"Oh! Oh! I hate you! I—"

In one pull, he stripped the layers of petticoats from her. Then he tugged at her chemisette and she felt the fabric tear, exposing her breasts.

She arched her head into the mattress, turning it from side to side in shame and fury. She felt her pantalets being pulled off. Then she was naked, exposed to the gaze of this arrogant and hateful man.

"You . . . you are a beast!" she sobbed.

"Not a beast. An admirer. Oh, you are so much more beautiful than I had imagined. Such a lovely little devil . . ."

His hand stroked her inner thigh, sending cascading delicious sensations through her. She became vaguely aware that he was divesting himself of his own clothes, that his maleness was exposed before her, huge and hard and throbbing. She fought in real panic now, her hands pushing and scratching at Kane's bare chest, her teeth sinking into his arm as he struggled to subdue her.

Fiercely she kicked, no longer caring that each kick exposed her nakedness, knowing only that she had to get away from him. Her thighs, hardened by years of horseback riding and hiking, were strong. Thrusting out, she managed to send him reeling backward.

Instantly she sprang up. She was almost off the bed when he caught her, bringing her down on the mattress with sheer force of body weight. Now he lay on top of her, pinning her down, his weight so heavy that she wanted to sob with tiredness and pain. Slowly his smooth, iron-hard thighs began forcing her legs apart.

She fought against him, panting and gasping for air, her heart flailing inside her chest. She could feel the beat of his heart, too, quick and strong and powerful. Inch by inch he spread her legs wider apart, until her entire body trembled from the effort of resisting him.

She felt a throbbing hardness as he entered her. Slowly, deliberately, he began to move in her. Each stroke brought a weakness to her. She couldn't struggle anymore. There was only a pulsating sensation within her, plunging to the deepest core of her, building and growing.

She lost track of time and space. She was immersed in a whirlwind she was powerless to control. The whirlwind grew and grew, arching and cresting. She screamed with the sweetness and pain of it.

It was over. Kane lay beside her, one arm flung across her, his nude body covered with a sheen of perspiration. She felt drained, weak, as if she could drift away. She felt like crying, except that she was too weak to cry.

"I'm sorry," Kane said after a moment. "I suppose I shouldn't have done that. But you were asking for it. You wanted it, and you enjoyed every second of it."

"I didn't!"

"Didn't ask for it, or didn't enjoy it?" Kane laughed comfortably. She felt his hand caressing her belly, moving into the soft nest of her pubic hair. She lay still, letting his hand move where it would. She felt too tired, too delicious to move. . . .

Kane brought his hand up to cup her chin. Then he
kissed her gently, his lips soft against her own. "You were
like a little wild animal, fighting me, weren't you? Ah,
well, let's go to sleep. I can go out and buy those clothes
tomorrow . . ."

She heard his voice drift off. Then she was sleeping beside him, and did not awake until several hours later, when
she discovered that she had thrown her bare leg across
Kane's body. His arm lay across her breasts, his fingers
tangled in her hair.

❧ Chapter 14 ❧

"Miss Brenna, would you like hot chocolate this morning?"

The voice intruded on Brenna's dream.

"Miss Brenna, wake up. It's nearly ten o'clock."

"What? Morning?" Brenna's eyelids fluttered, and then she opened them on the glare of morning. Sun streamed through the heavy curtains.

"You slept a long time, didn't you?" The voice belonged to Arcadia, dressed in an elaborately ruffled blue dress which accented the hazy shadows under her eyes. She regarded Brenna curiously.

Brenna sat up, pulling on a dressing gown, blinking the sleep from her eyes and stretching contentedly until she felt the pull in every muscle.

They would stay at Maud's a day or so, Kane had said, until he got his ship fitted and provisioned for the trip to Havana. He must have gone out early to take care of all the arrangements.

With Arcadia's help, Brenna settled the breakfast tray on her knees and bit into a croissant, still warm from the bake oven. She chewed slowly, savoring its flavor. Arcadia turned to leave, saying, "I'll be back to get your tray."

Brenna nodded, glad to be left with her own thoughts. She felt confused. She hated Kane, yet last night she had actually enjoyed what he did to her.

She decided to have a bath, and asked Arcadia, when

she returned. The bath, a hand-painted tin tub which Arcadia filled with water from tin canisters, was almost luxuriously refreshing. Soaking in the warm water, Brenna let the exhaustion and confusion seep out of her pores.

She had finished bathing and, in her dressing gown, was leaning over the tub to wash her hair, when Kane returned.

"Well, I see you are feeling much better this morning."

She straightened up, blinking her eyes against the soapy water that ran down her face and stung her eyes.

"Yes." She swallowed hard, feeling his glance rake over her, the silken wrapper clinging to the lines of her breasts.

"Well, enjoy your freshwater bath as long as you can. The tide's right, and we're setting sail in a few hours."

"Today? But I thought you said you had to provision your ship and get your crew . . ."

"And so I must. But my first mate will manage the details. My job is to dig him out of whatever saloon he's holed up in. Scroggins is all right aboard ship, but goes on binges ashore."

"But I don't have any decent clothes," she reminded him.

"We'll send Arcadia out to buy some second-hand things, since we haven't time for a dressmaker. You won't need much but, despite my teasing, your dress should be rather sober. We don't want any of my crew to get ideas."

"Ideas?" Her eyes widened.

"You needn't worry about that. I'll whip anyone who dares touch you." Kane's face held menace, and Brenna felt a chill run lightly across the nape of her neck. She knew he would do exactly as he had said.

Kane and Brenna rode to the docks early that afternoon in a rented carriage, hats pulled down to disguise their faces. Brenna wore a shapeless dark brown dress, ugly but modest. Several more such dresses were packed in the bag at her feet. Suddenly, rounding a corner on their way, they met another carriage, all gilt and polish and matched horses. Arbutus was inside, with her new husband, Monty.

"Arbutus!" Brenna half-rose from her seat, intending to call out to her cousin, who had not yet seen them.

"No!" She felt Kane's palm over her mouth. "Are you

a fool? Do you want the entire world to know of our plans?" He held her firmly gagged until the other carriage had passed.

As soon as Kane had removed his hand from her mouth, Brenna stiffened her back indignantly. "What were you doing?" she cried. "Why did you stop me from calling out? What harm would it do? My cousin wouldn't tell anyone where I am . . . she loves me. I am her friend."

"Perhaps. But your friend's husband has no such obligations to you, does he?"

Brenna slumped down, her eyes miserably on the toes of her slippers. "But I . . . I wanted to see her," she said slowly. "I . . . I ruined her wedding by running away as I did. I hope she isn't too angry with me. I wonder if she hates me now."

"Don't be silly. You did what you had to do, and your cousin is doing what she has to do, you may be sure of that."

Something in his voice made her turn quickly. "What do you mean? Didn't you see how happy she looked? Arbutus couldn't wait to start mothering that little girl of his."

"Children will help, I suppose."

"What sort of remark is that? Of course Arbutus plans on having a large family. What do you mean by saying that will 'help'?"

"By taking her mind off her problems."

"What problems? My goodness, but you don't make sense to me. I've never seen Arbutus look happier. What problems could she possibly have?"

"You don't know, then?" Kane pressed his lips together. "No, I suppose you wouldn't. You New Orleans ladies manage to close your eyes to a lot of things you'd rather not know about."

"What are you trying to say? That Arbutus has problems she doesn't know about? If you ask me, Kane Fairfield, I think you're talking nonsense."

Kane's lips curved sardonically. "Not nonsense, but truth. You see, without realizing it Arbutus has already acquired a very formidable rival for the affections of her husband."

"Rival?"

"Her name is Yvette, and she's one of the loveliest quadroon women in the city. I know, because I've seen her myself. For the past eight years Monty Carlisle has kept her in a house on Rampart Street. I think she's given him two children—or is it three? Anyway, his union with Yvette predated his first marriage, and is of long standing. Perhaps even for life."

"But there must . . . must be some mistake." Brenna's lips were suddenly dry. "Not Monty. Monty wouldn't do that. He has been so good to Arbutus . . ."

"He was good to his first wife, too. That has nothing to do with it."

Brenna felt sickened. She thought of the light-skinned girl she had seen leave Quentin's apartments. The clear, honey-colored skin, the swaying, lissome walk. "No, it can't be . . ."

"It is. Your pretty little cousin is going to have to contend with her husband's mistress for the rest of her life, whether she knows it or not."

For the rest of her life. Brenna thought of Arbutus, so innocently bubbling with plans for the child, for the plantation, the other children she would have. Children! That was why he had married her, Brenna thought angrily. So he could have white sons to carry on the plantation.

"It's not fair!" she burst out.

"What isn't fair? After all, Arbutus is getting something, too. She'll be the chatelaine of a large sugar plantation, instead of an unwanted old maid in her father's house. And soon there will be children. That will be enough for her."

"Always, always, it's a bargain, isn't it?" The words seemed to choke in Brenna's throat. "Arbutus, too. Only she didn't know she made a bargain. She thought she was marrying a man who would love her, who would cherish her."

"And who says he won't cherish her? If she's fertile and has many children, she'll be a very valuable property for him." Was there a teasing glint in Kane's eye?

"Property! Is that all the world is to you? Bargains, and property, and . . . oh, Kane Fairfield, you make me sick. Don't talk to me anymore for a while."

But Brenna's mood changed as they neared the crowded docks, and soon Arbutus was forgotten amid the sights, sounds and smells of the booming place. Drays clattered, boat owners scurried, dockmen staggered under heavy barrels and crates, and all the men, it seemed, cursed and shouted at each other. Caught in the exhilaration of it, Brenna leaned out of the carriage window, gazing eagerly at the long dock crammed with hundreds of ships and small boats.

"Which is the *Sea Otter?*" she asked.

"There she is. That one." Kane pointed to a rather rakish ship with two masts, its sails still furled. Her hull was painted black, with a line of gold trim at the rails, and four mounted guns, two on each side. The name *Sea Otter* was painted near her bow.

Brenna bit her lip with dismay. She had made the trip from Dublin in a four-masted square-rigger with a crew of one hundred. "She's rather small, isn't she? I had thought—"

"You expected a five-master? Ah, I have larger ships in my fleet, boats that can sail around the Horn, but they are all at sea just now. Besides, we are not going far, only to Havana. The *Sea Otter* is small and fast, which is what I'm interested in at the moment. If we have good wind and better luck, the trip shouldn't take long."

A few minutes later they boarded the ship and stood on the main deck, which was scrubbed and swept and swaying gently in the current. Brenna looked above her at the seemingly incomprehensible tangle of ropes, rigging, wires and stays that stretched to the tops of the two masts, swaying and creaking in the wind. Near the top of one of the varnished masts, in a web of rigging, perched a young boy of about fourteen, his fair hair blowing.

She heard an odd, clucking noise and looked toward the stern, where there were some wooden crates, the slats set an inch or so apart.

"Chickens?" She laughed incredulously.

"Chicken dinner," Kane corrected. "If we want fresh meat, we have to carry it live. On the China run, we carry pigs and sheep, too."

Brenna looked about her with excitement. "I never can

understand how sailors can figure out all the sails and rigging. It all looks so very complicated."

"It isn't. Not when you've grown up on a ship, as most of these men have. When sailing is your life, you know how everything works the same way you know how to put your pants on. If it were the wildest, blackest night, these men would still know where everything is and how it works," Kane said proudly. "But enough of that. I want to show you my cabin. You can stow your gear there."

The master's cabin seemed small to Brenna, but Kane assured her that it was a kingly size for ships of this type. The cabin itself was appealing enough, with rosewood and mahogany paneling, polished brasswork fittings, and dark red cushions on built-in seats. There was a built-in dresser where everything could be neatly stowed away, and even the bunk, built into the wall, had storage space beneath.

"This is charming, Kane," she exclaimed. "And so neat! Why, there's not a thing out of place."

"Neatness is a seaman's way of life, Brenna. And I'm glad you like this cabin, for you'll see precious little else. Other than the saloon next door, of course, where we'll eat our meals."

"What do you mean?" she demanded. "Do you mean that I am not to go on deck? That I must stay in this cabin where I can't even look at the sea?" To her consternation, her voice cracked.

"I mean just what I said. I am the master of this ship, which means I am in sole command of the lives of all aboard. And the last thing my men need is the distraction of a girl as lovely and provocative as you are. And the only woman aboard to boot. There could be trouble."

She stared at him. "I don't believe you. Don't some captains take their wives with them on voyages?"

"A few. But the women are *wives*. And they are usually old and plain, not like you. Do you realize, Brenna, just what a temptation you present?"

She drew in a hard breath. "Well, I'm not interested in what your men think of me. I will die if I have to stay cooped up in a tiny room for days and days. I either have the run of the main deck, or I don't sail!"

He hesitated. "Very well. Just be careful, that's all I

ask. If any one of them steps out of line, the man gets
whipped, and you will be required to watch."

Brenna turned to stare out of the small porthole, ringed
with brasswork, her heart slamming. There was a new,
authoritative ring to Kane's voice. And the officers and
seamen all treated him with such deference, she thought
rebelliously—as if he were supreme in authority next to
God himself.

Kane's voice went on. "And now, Brenna, if you will
step aside, I will dispose of this money." He produced a
leather sack and a chisel.

"Money?"

"Gold. As long as we're in Havana, I plan to make a
few purchases, and this will cover them. There's no sense
in wasting the trip." He knelt, and lifted a corner of the
deep red carpet that covered the cabin floor. Then he pried
up one of the floorboards near the bunk and hid the sack
in the space beneath.

"You're putting your gold *there?*"

"Best place for it," Kane said. "You and Jemmy, my
cabin boy, who's like a son to me, are the only persons
who know where I keep my money. And since you'll be
in the cabin much of the time, there'll be someone to see
to its safety."

"I suppose you are thinking of pirates."

"Perhaps." Kane shrugged. "But I don't intend to welcome any aboard the *Sea Otter*. Not if I can help it. That's
why we're carrying the guns. I've also got a store of
weapons locked in the hold if the need arises, not to mention the pair of pistols I carry myself. Come to think of it,
I might teach you to use them. Would you like that?"

"Yes . . ." Brenna hesitated doubtfully. "Yes, I . . .
I'll learn."

Within half an hour, the *Sea Otter* was underway, the
wind catching and ballooning her sails, the white canvas
glaring brilliantly in the late sun. Kane took her on a tour
of the fo'c'sle, where the men slept, and the main deck.
He told her the names of the various sails and how they
were raised and furled. She squinted about her, eyes narrowed against the sun, fascinated by what Kane called

the "ratlines," a rope network to which sailors were expected to cling like spiders in a web.

"Who was the boy I saw when we first came aboard, climbing up there without a thought? Isn't it dangerous? There would be nothing at all to break his fall."

"That was Jemmy and, yes, it's dangerous enough. Sailors do fall off the rigging, and sometimes the sea is so high that a ship can't turn around to pick up the fellow. But Jemmy doesn't mind. In fact, he doesn't even think of the danger. His father was master of the *Aphrodite,* which was lost off Cape Horn three years ago. I'm giving Jemmy his training. He's a quick learner, and trustworthy. He'll do all right."

She stared up at the taut network of ropes, shrouds and battens. "But how does he ever do it? It looks so difficult!"

Kane grinned. "I did it myself plenty of times, and it's not so bad if you don't let yourself think about what you're doing. You climb the weather side, so that the wind blows you onto the rigging. And you don't let go of one rope until you've got a good grip on another. 'One hand for the man and one for the ship,' as the saying goes."

Kane introduced her to the first mate, Andrew Scroggins, a burly man in his thirties with a flowing brown moustache, gold front teeth, and a prominent nose. He was dressed in sober blue, and when introduced, nodded at Brenna, his eyes reserving judgment. Was this the man, she wondered, who had had to be scoured out of the saloons so the ship could get going? He seemed sober enough now, except for slightly reddened eyes.

"I think Scroggins can smell his way through the fog with that whiskey nose of his," Kane told her after leaving him. "He's one of the best officers I've ever had. He can get that little 'extra' out of the men that sometimes means the difference between foundering and surviving. He got those gold teeth in New York harbor, defending the crew in a brawl."

They went by another man, kneeling on the deck splicing ropes. As they passed, the man looked up at them, and Brenna saw a half-shaven face and dark eyes that fastened on her like a pair of leeches. A soiled red scarf wrapped around the man's head like a turban accented his strangeness.

"Who was that?" she whispered to Kane when they were safely out of earshot.

"Phelan. He's our ship's carpenter. He's rough enough . . . came from the slums of Liverpool, and has knocked around the world ever since. But he can work like hell when he has to."

"He . . . he stared at me."

"Of course he did. You're the first woman I've brought aboard, and the crew may not really believe you're my wife. That's why I want you to keep to the cabin."

They stood at the stern of the ship, watching the green shoreline recede into the distance, while the wake of the ship fanned out behind them, flecked with white curls of foam. Brenna, turning around, saw that Phelan was still watching her.

After supper, which consisted of fresh beef and fruit—the last beef, Kane said, that they would see for a while—Brenna had to admit that she was not feeling at all well. Even in the cabin, she felt the ceaseless rolling of the ship.

After Jemmy had cleared away their meal, Brenna excused herself and went to lie on the bunk. The bunk itself seemed to sway and swoop beneath her, while overhead she could hear the slap and thump of feet as the sailors went about their work. Each time the boat rolled, a wave of nausea swept over her, subsiding, then growing again.

When Kane came in an hour later, he found her lying limp and white. She had been sick several times in the chamber pot, which she'd managed to find just at the crucial moment.

"*You*, seasick?" Kane's laugh held amused superiority.

"I think I am," she had to admit. "I suffered from it on our voyage from Dublin. But don't worry, I'll be over it soon."

"You'd better be." He was still amused. "I don't fancy spending the entire journey cooped up with a case of *mal de mer*."

Anger sparked through her. "Don't concern yourself

about it!" Another rush of nausea possessed her, and she groped blindly for the chamber pot. "Go!" she choked. "I . . . I don't want you to see me sick."

"Nonsense." Before she could protest, he was holding the pot for her. Then, while she lay back, weak and dizzy, he took the pot away and sponged her forehead with cool water.

The night passed in a long round of retching and nausea. Never had she felt so sick. Once she would have shuddered at the intimate acts Kane was performing for her. He even helped her out of her dress and into a cool night gown. But she couldn't care about anything. She was only glad that there was someone to help.

At some point during the long night hours she woke to see another face beside her bed.

"Is it . . . Jemmy?" She peered into the darkness.

"Yes, miss. The master went on deck for his watch, and he told me to come and see to you. Would you like me to light the lamp?"

"Yes, please."

The boy busied himself with the oil lamp, and when it was lit Brenna saw how young he was, his skin just beginning to roughen with a beard. There was a gentle look to him; she wondered how he liked shipboard life.

"Are you better, miss?" He brought her a pan of cold water and a cloth to mop her face again.

"I . . . I think so." She said this more to please him than because it was the truth.

"We don't often have passengers on the *Sea Otter*," Jemmy said. "Is it true you come from Ireland?"

"Yes. My home was just outside Dublin."

Jemmy seemed interested, so she told him something of Ireland, even about her horse, Portia, for whom she still felt painful spasms of longing. But Ireland seemed so far away now. Had she really been married for a brief day to Neall Urquhart? Had she really fought off Toby Rynne under the willow tree? All of it seemed shadowy and unreal. The only reality was here, in this compact cabin, with the creaking noises of the ship's timbers and the sound of the sea only a few boards away.

She and Jemmy talked a few moments longer, and she

learned that Jemmy was excited, even enthusiastic, about being at sea. He thought Captain Fairfield was "the finest man I ever saw."

"Why do you say that, Jemmy?"

"Dunno. Except that he makes you feel . . . important, I guess. Oh, he's a hard one, and he makes you work until sometimes you want to hate him. But he makes us keep the crew's quarters clean, and he don't cheat none on the rations. With good rations, miss, you can put up with a bit of knocking about from the sea and still not mind."

Somewhere in the middle of this speech, Brenna drifted off to sleep. She awoke to the sound of bells ringing, and stirred sleepily in the bunk. To her surprise, she felt better. If she was not hungry for breakfast, at least the thought of food did not make her sick.

"Well? How is my little wildcat this morning?" Kane asked cheerfully, coming in from the adjoining saloon, his hair windblown.

"I think I'll live. On the trip from Dublin, I had only one day of seasickness, then I felt fine." She sat up, covering herself with the quilt. "What time is it? And where did you sleep last night? Certainly not here in this bunk with me!"

Kane smiled, the creases in his cheeks dimpling. "Eight bells, my dear, which means eight o'clock and breakfast time for the crew. They've been up since five."

"Yes, I remember from my other voyage."

"As for me, I slung a hammock there in the saloon. It's not a bad way to sleep. In fact, on hot nights I often take a hammock up on deck."

"Oh. It was gallant of you to give up your bed for me." Brenna was surprised to hear sarcasm creeping into her words. "I would thank you, except that I didn't ask to come along in the first place, did I?"

Kane's smile disappeared. "You made a bargain with me. What did you expect? Now you must live with your agreement."

She pressed her lips together. Her good mood had evaporated abruptly. Her mouth tasted sour, her body felt sticky, and her cotton gown was damp with perspiration.

"If you don't mind, I would like a bath," she said. "Could you have Jemmy bring me some bath water, please?"

"It'll have to be saltwater. Our tank isn't big enough for personal bathing. Well, I have work to busy me. Jemmy will bring you your bath, and your breakfast when you want it. Just remember to stay here in the cabin, if you know what's good for you."

She did not reply but sat stiffly, the coverlet pulled about her shoulders, until he had left.

Later Jemmy and another boy lugged in a hip-bath sloshing with water, and set it down on the floor. Jemmy, she noticed, was flushed-looking, his eyes heavily shadowed, and he shook his head once as if he were feeling dizzy.

"Jemmy? Are you sure you're all right?"

"Yes'm. I'm fine." She thought she saw fright in his eyes. "I've some sunburn, is all."

"Well, you shouldn't be climbing in the rigging until you feel better."

"Yes'm."

After the two boys left, Brenna prepared for her bath. Slipping out of her nightgown, she noticed how weak and shaky her legs still felt. Food would bring up her strength, she decided. If she could eat it.

She tested the water, found it lukewarm, and settled in the tub for a long soak. Drowsily, she sat enjoying the peace, only distantly hearing the background noises of the ship—the shouts of the mates, the pounding of feet, the creaking of the timbers and the occasional flapping of the sails. But none of these noises disturbed her lazy somnolence.

Then there was a slight sound behind her.

Sudden, absurd panic swept through her. She jerked around in the cramped tub to see Kane standing near the door of the saloon. A half-smile was on his lips.

"You are very beautiful. Did you know that?"

"What . . . how long have you been watching me?" She crossed her hands over her breasts, feeling a flush spreading over her whole body.

"Not long." He sauntered over to the bunk and sat down on its edge, moving with the powerful, effortless grace of a big cat. His brownish-gold hair shone in a shaft of sunlight from the porthole. He had changed to a well-cut blue coat with big pearl buttons, and wore a brocaded vest with a white cravat. His light gray pants were so tight that she could see the bulge of his masculinity.

She huddled farther down in the tub. "Would you please leave the cabin while I am bathing? I . . . I'm not accustomed to taking my bath before an audience."

"Surely you would not deny me such a simple pleasure? After I nursed you so faithfully last night?"

Was he mocking her? She felt her hands curling into fists. If it were not for her modesty, she would jump out of the tub and slap him.

"I didn't ask you to nurse me! I didn't ask you to bring me along on this . . . this wild goose chase of a voyage! And now I'm not asking you to stand there staring at me as if I were an actress on the stage for men to goggle at!"

He settled himself more comfortably on the bunk. Then he took a large cigar out of his vest pocket, tamped the end, and leisurely lit it, puffing out rings of smoke. "Go ahead, Brenna. Finish bathing yourself. I have all the time in the world."

"You . . . you . . ." She glared at him, so angry that she could not speak.

"Why should such loveliness, such perfection, be hidden from someone who would enjoy it as much as I? Especially when I have paid so well for the privilege."

"I hate you, Kane Fairfield. You are the most despicable man I have ever met."

"Perhaps." He crossed his legs and puffed out another smoke ring. His eyes raked her body. "Would you like me to scrub your back? I'm told that I'm very good at that sort of thing."

"Oh, you've been told, have you? By whom? Melissa Rynne? Maud Sweet? Or one of the hundreds of other women you've probably had?"

He smiled again, but the smile did not touch his eyes. "By no one you know. Nonetheless, the offer still stands."

"No! No, I don't want you to scrub my back! I don't want you to do anything except get out of here at once! How dare you stand there—" She stopped, sputtering in her fury.

"Come, Brenna. Yours is a most lovely and healthy body, and you shouldn't be ashamed of it. It was made for pleasure, after all, wasn't it? Pleasure for both of us."

"No . . . no, I . . ." Stammering, she clasped her arms about her breasts tighter. If only he would quit staring at her! If only he would leave!

"Very well." He stood up and stubbed out the cigar in an iron spitoon near the bunk. He came closer to her. "You must learn, then."

"Learn what?" She cowered from him on the other side of the small tub. She knew she looked ridiculous, but she was powerless to do otherwise. Her only alternative was to leap, naked, from the tub, but she could not bring herself to leave its protection.

"Why, learn once and for all what your body is for. You're a cold little thing! Not in your body, perhaps, but in your mind. Your mind has been well-trained to think some things are 'proper,' while others are not."

Kane stripped off the patent leather Wellington boots that he wore. "But all things are proper, Brenna, if they give pleasure to both participants and hurt no one."

She could not believe her eyes. Kane was pulling off his clothes in front of her, one garment at a time. His blue coat, his brocaded vest, his white ruffled shirt and pants—one by one, all went into a heap on the floor.

She could not help herself. She had to look. His bare chest was broad and brown and covered with curls of blonde hair. Ridges of muscle, marred by a long, white scar, rippled on his midriff, which narrowed to a small, tight waist. Oddly, the skin below his waist was very white. His legs, too, were muscular, coated with a fuzz of light hair.

But it was his sex, erect and throbbing, rising out of a nest of crisp hair, to which Brenna's eyes were drawn.

His laughter broke her horrified silence. "Well? Do you like it?"

"I . . . I've never—"

"Never seen anything like it? I wouldn't wonder. The way girls are reared, like flowers under glass. You don't even know what a man is. Such ignorance!"

"Ignorance! I'm not ignorant! I can read and write and

sing and do mathematics, and I speak French and Gaelic—"

His teeth showed white. "That's not what I mean. Now,
relax. I promise you, I won't hurt you."

Her heart jerked wildly as he knelt beside the tub and
picked up the cake of soap which she had let fall upon
the floor. Weakness spread through her. She felt as if she
could faint. His bare chest, with its fascinating matting of
hair, was so close. She closed her eyes.

His fingers, moist and slippery from the soap, touched
her arm. Slowly, delicately, he lathered her skin. His hands
moved to her armpits, to her breasts. His touch was as
soft and silky as water.

She heard soft moaning—was it herself?—but she did
not open her eyes. There were only those soft hands, gently
stroking her skin, probing every crevice of her body. His
hand moved between her legs, parting them, caressing,
drawing out of her a sweetness she hadn't known existed.

She arched her back, moaning again and again in pleasure as his hands searched her. He lifted her out of the tub
and carried her to the bunk. Then his body was against
hers, the moisture of the bath water oiling both of them.

She felt his mouth on hers, his tongue probing, then
thrusting inside her mouth. At last she relaxed fully and
let her body accept the full throbbing completion of him.
She let herself move with the joy of him in her, move
arrowing to a sweet, shuddering explosion that seemed to
go on and on. . . .

❧ *Chapter 15* ❧

THE SUN WAS STRONG and yellow. It glittered off the flat swells and bounced, blinding white, off the empty sails. In the middle of one night, the wind had deserted them. For days, they had sat on an endless flat expanse of water, scraps of seaweed floating listlessly on its surface.

Brenna stood at the stern, staring out to sea. Perspiration covered her forehead and ran in rivulets down her sides beneath the ugly brown merino dress Arcadia had bought for her.

If only the wind would come, she thought. If only it would fill the sails again and ease her burning face.

"I can't understand it. We should hit the trade winds soon, yet we're just ghosting along," Kane had said that morning with a scowl. "There's nothing a sailor hates worse than no wind. It's maddening—and dangerous, too. We sit here roasting in the sun and using up our supplies to no good. No wonder the crew is in a foul humor. I feel the same myself."

Neither of them had mentioned their love-making in the bath again. But Brenna could not stop thinking about it. She brushed a strand of damp hair away from her forehead, remembering the swift explosion of feeling he had drawn from her. Physically, she was helpless against him, she knew. Anytime he wanted her body he could have it. Yet, she thought with pain, to what purpose was their love-making? He did not love her. He had made it plain that he would never marry her. She was no more to him than a cheap mistress, someone whom he could use and quickly forget.

Depression seeped through her. What should she do? What *could* she do? Here on the *Sea Otter*, sharing the close quarters of Kane's cabin, there was no way she could run from him, no way to save herself from hurt. Anytime he reached for her, her traitorous body would respond.

Immersed in her thoughts, she was only half-aware of the activity going on a few yards behind her, where three crewmen were resentfully holystoning the deck. Phelan, the carpenter, was in charge of them, and occasionally his voice rose, hoarse and gravelly. Once, turning, she caught him staring hungrily at her, as if she were food and he starving. Probably she should have stayed in the cabin, she thought uneasily. But today the cabin was like an oven. She would have baked there. Even Kane couldn't force her to stay below on a hot, windless day like today.

"You had better beware of sunburn, Brenna." Kane appeared at her elbow, his dark blue coat with its brass buttons stained under the arms with moisture. He carried the ship's logbook, and looked distracted. "You're not even wearing a bonnet."

"A bonnet? But it's too hot for one," she protested.

"If you don't wear something, your face is going to be so badly burned and blistered that you'll be in misery. Sunburn can be torture aboard ship. Go get something to shield yourself at once."

"Very well, then." She sighed, thinking of the hot, still air of the cabin.

"What are you waiting for? Go get your bonnet."

"Yes, *sir*." Face hot, she scurried past him to the companionway, conscious of the crewmen staring at her. Had they overheard? She bit her lip in humiliation. The windless spell affected everyone, she told herself. The crew complained about their water ration and moved reluctantly about their work. Even Kane had snapped at the cook for burning the noon stew.

Below, the heat from the cabin hit her in the face like a blast from an opened oven door. She hurried in and began fumbling through the drawer that Kane had allotted to her. The bonnet, purchased by Arcadia second-hand, was obviously the discarded finery of some plantation owner's wife. Made of white straw, encrusted with lace, ribbons and feathers, it was ridiculously ornate for a woman on board ship. She grabbed it and stuffed it on her head without looking. There was no large mirror, and besides, it was just too hot to linger.

She emerged into the corridor still fastening the bonnet. To her surprise, there was someone coming down the companionway. She had to back down until the other person had finished his descent.

"Well, if it ain't the captain's fine lady." It was Phelan, the ship's carpenter, his wide, barrel chest blocking her way. Beads of sweat glittered among the stubbly whiskers of his face, and his nankeen shirt was soaking wet, exuding a sour, gamy odor.

"Please, would you let me pass?"

"Now, why should I do that?" When he smiled, she saw that most of his back teeth were missing. His mouth looked like a dark cavern.

"Because I request it." She tried to make her voice firm.

But Phelan only grinned, exposing the black cavity. "And what part of the docks did you come from, honey?"

"I didn't come from the docks! How dare you suggest such a thing? And would you please move so that I can use the companion ladder?"

"Seems like I seen you somewheres before, little lady."

"Well, you haven't."

"I never forgets a face. Especially one like yours, all milk and honey. You I'd never forget seeing." He moved closer to her, his sharp body smell hanging about him like a cloud. "Now, let's see. Seems like I remembers a street by the docks. And a little whore in a blue dress hurrying along, looking about her like she was afraid, see? Wouldn't even speak kindly when a friendly word was offered her."

"No, no! You've never seén me before," she insisted. Yet she felt herself shrinking inside. Hadn't she worn a light blue dress that day she'd wandered into the Swamp? Could Phelan have seen her there?

She pressed herself against the opposite bulkhead. "Please, I . . ."

"Pretty uppity, aren't you, for a floozy who earns her living on her back? Where'd the master get ahold of you, anyway?"

"He did not 'get ahold' of me, as you say. And I'm not a . . . not one of those women!"

"You coulda fooled me, little lady. With them big boosums of yours, it's no wonder the master can't keep his hands off'n you. I'd be the same myself, I would."

She could see a web of spittle shining on his lip. He was so close that his smell nearly made her gag. She could not press herself any farther back against the bulkhead.

Suddenly she pushed him with all her strength. As he staggered backward, she ran past him and up the ladder to the deck.

Brenna hurried to stand beside Kane, trying to control her trembling legs.

"What have you been up to?" he asked coldly. "You look about to faint."

"Nothing," she stammered. "It's just . . . some of the men look at me so strangely. It frightens me."

"And what do you expect, the way you've been flaunting yourself in front of them. Has one of them touched you?"

"No . . . no . . ." she stammered. Phelan had frightened her badly, but she could not bear to see him flogged.

"So now you're protecting someone, you bitch." Never had Brenna seen Kane so angry. His skin was white, his lips curled back in a dangerous little smile. "From now on, you'll stay below in the cabin, no matter how hot it is. Maybe that will convince you to take my advice seriously."

Before Brenna could protest, Kane turned his back to her. She stood frozen. Did he really believe that she flaunted herself in front of the men? She thought of the cold emptiness of his eyes, the little smile which had twisted his lips, the same smile he probably had worn when killing Ulrich Rynne.

She drew a deep, convulsive breath and hurried below.

"Here it is, sir. The supper." Jemmy stumbled into the saloon, carrying a tray laden with yams, pea soup, stewed chicken, tea and cake, his narrow body looking even smaller than usual, his face still flushed.

"That's fine," Kane said.

"Cook says he . . . he's sorry he burned the food this noon, sir. He hopes you'll like this better."

"I'm sure he does."

Jemmy nodded uncertainly, then left the saloon. Another time, Brenna might have been amused, but now she felt only exhaustion. She had spent hours lying on the bunk in the cabin. For a while she had cried, but then she lay, dry-eyed, staring up at the ceiling, reliving it all.

For what it was worth, she had saved Phelan. But he wasn't the reason her heart ached. It was Kane, and the cold enmity that blazed from his eyes. He believed she was a bitch, and hated her for it.

Although the food was well-cooked, she couldn't eat. She put down an untasted forkful of chicken and looked at Kane, who sat brooding on the other side of the small mahogany table. He hadn't spoken to her since ordering her to the cabin.

"I have to say this," she said. "You're wrong if you think I . . . I tempted any man. One of them did try to accost me, but nothing happened—nothing!"

"I told you it was best to stay in the cabin."

"But it was so hot that I couldn't! I didn't tempt him, can't you see that?"

Kane's laugh was bitter. "I wonder which of my crew you find to your liking. Perhaps Big Bart or Bates or even Scroggins—"

She jumped up, knocking over her coffee cup and splashing dark liquid onto the table. "Don't you dare ever talk to me like that again!" she cried wildly. "If you do, I . . . I'll jump overboard! I'm not a strumpet, and I'm not one of the residents of Maud Sweet's, either. I don't go running after every man who comes near me. I don't care about them, I don't care about any of them, none of them matter to me but—"

She had almost said *but you*. She stopped, horrified. Kane was staring at her, a strange, soft expression on his face. For the first time since that afternoon, his features relaxed.

"Sit down, Brenna. Eat your meal," he said quietly.

"I'm not hungry."

"Eat. After your bout with seasickness, you've got to

build up your strength again. You'll grow too thin and then you won't appeal to me." Now his lips were actually twitching in a smile.

Flushing angrily, she picked up her fork and pushed the chicken around on her plate. "What does it matter if I appeal to you or not? As you've made plain, you'll soon grow tired of me anyway."

"Perhaps. But at this moment you appeal to me very much. Do you know how lovely you were this afternoon with that breathtaking red-gold hair of yours flying out of its knot, your face pale and upset, and your chest heaving? It was easy to see why any man would want you."

His eyes covered her with a warmth that penetrated through the fabric of her gown. "I am ashamed of it, but I felt like killing someone this afternoon, even if he had only looked at you. And I hated you for it. I hated you for making me want you so much that I would kill any other man who touched you."

In one swift movement Kane stood up, and took her hand. "Let the meal stay where it is. Neither of us is hungry anyway. Except for each other. Are you hungry, my Brenna? Are you as hungry for me as I am for you?"

To her surprise, she discovered that she was. She loved the feel of hands stripping her of her gown and caressing her bare flesh. The two of them locked together on the narrow bunk as if time and the ship had all disappeared, as if there were nothing else in the world but the two of them and their sweat-moist bodies, moving in each other and with each other.

❧ *Chapter 16* ❧

THE NEXT DAY passed slowly, each half-hour marked off by the ever-present bells. Although she was not directly a part of it, Brenna felt herself settling into the ship's routine. The day began with the first light. The hands turned to at five a.m., at that time receiving their drinking water ration. At six-thirty, their voices echoed in the clear morning air as they washed down the decks and lashed and stowed their sleeping hammocks away. At eight o'clock there was breakfast, the crew's meal consisting of salt pork, oatmeal, and hard bread, washed down with strong coffee sweetened with molasses. Brenna and Kane also added tart oranges and honey.

On Wednesdays and Saturdays the decks were holy-stoned, she learned, and on Fridays the crew washed their clothes in buckets. The daytime hours were devoted to maintaining and repairing the complex, heavy sails and the fathoms of valuable rope.

Permeating all hours of her life were the inconveniences of shipboard living. Sometimes she felt as if she had always lived this way, drinking dank and brackish water, trying not to waste a drop in case the calm spell lasted too long and their supply ran out. Just the thought of limited water made her thirstier. She could spend hours daydreaming about water, cool and pale in a crystal goblet, beads of moisture running down the outside of the glass.

There was the sun, too, burning down on her skin until her face felt raw and throbbing. A short hour on deck could redden her cheeks, and she found herself grateful for even the hated bonnet, for anything that could give her respite from the worst of the glare. When she undressed at night, she found a red line at her neck and wrists. What would Aunt Rowena think of her complexion now? She smiled to herself. If Rowena were aboard, she would undoubtedly throw up her hands in despair.

Noise, too, was a part of life aboard the *Sea Otter*. It followed her wherever she went, even intruding into her dreams, until it seemed that she had always slept with the hundreds of creaks, rattles, squeaks and bangs that crept like ghosts through the ship's timbers. There were the officers shouting out orders to the crew. There were the curiously stirring sounds of the sea chanteys the men sang, as if this music were the only pleasure allowed them. There was the thunderous flapping of sails and blocks as the ship made new tacks to catch any possible breath of wind. The sea itself made constant sounds; ripples and lappings, the swirl and slap of water against the sides of the ship.

Late the following afternoon she stood at the helm with Kane while he stood watch. Since they had made love last night she felt more relaxed around him, more at ease. He had thought of her. He had been hungry for her. The fact filled her with happiness. She watched his hands on the tiller, the long, strong fingers sprinkled with light hair that shone in the sun.

"Tell me about the China trade," she said. "Is it as exciting as I've heard?"

"It's like nothing else. Nothing else I've ever done, or will do."

"Did you pass around Cape Horn?"

"We certainly did, and it's like sailing into hell itself. A bitter cold hell, and full of fog. The seas are frighteningly high, the waves actually looming taller than the ship. They come rolling across the deck from rail to rail, and the spray freezes to the decks and spars until your fingers turn icy too . . ."

Men, he told her, were sometimes swept overboard. "I know of ships where one whole watch—that's half the crew—were swept over within minutes, just like that." He snapped his fingers. He told her about the China trade, and she listened avidly.

"Tea, silk, lichee nuts, kumquats—oh, it sounds almost like poetry," she sighed. "Someday I'd like to see Canton and eat plover's eggs, and . . . and do it all! It seems as if there's a hunger in me."

Kane looked at her sharply, then laughed. "Yes, I've felt that way too, ever since I stowed away as a boy. There's something about the sea. It gets into your blood and your bones and then you can't leave it."

He began reminiscing about his days as a cabin boy, telling her of Captain Armitage, who had taught him navigation, drilling him on winds and currents and all the parts of a square-rigger until he could have named them in his sleep, and, he had been informed by other crew members, often had. Scrambling up the rigging, hauling the braces, scrubbing the deck—there was no job on the ship he hadn't done himself as a boy.

"Armitage had his lighthearted moments, however," Kane said. "One day I felt rather lethargic. Perhaps it was a touch of the grippe, or just laziness, I don't know. But I went to him and told him I felt sick. 'How do you feel sick?' he asked and I answered 'Sick all over, sir.' 'Well, I have just the cure for you,' Armitage told me. 'We'll give you a good cleaning out. Run along to the galley and have the cook heat up some hot water for you.' I did as he asked, feeling a bit puzzled, but innocently looking forward to the day of loafing and rest in my hammock.

"When I returned with the water, I found Captain Armitage attaching a piece of rope to a bristly wire brush used to clean out bottles. I stared at it in dismay. At last I got up my courage and asked him what he was going to do with it.

" 'Why,' he said, 'I'm going to clean you out fore and aft. I'll reeve the forepart down your throat and the cook will haul the afterpart out through your stern. It'll do you a world of good!' "

"Needless to say, I was out of that cabin like a shot and up the foremasthead, and I didn't come down until night!"

Brenna laughed uproariously. "Oh! I know I shouldn't laugh, but I've never heard anything so funny!"

Kane made a wry face, his eyebrows drawing together. "It was not all funny, God knows. But I hated leaving the sea to go back home. Captain Armitage is dead now. His ship disappeared off Charleston. They said it was privateers. I don't know; I've often thought of him since."

Kane fell into a moody silence, while Brenna stood looking out at the sea, caught in her own gloomy thoughts. After the noon meal she had seen Phelan loitering outside the captain's cabin, as if wondering whether he could get inside. "Well, miss," he had said to her. "And what have you got inside that cabin that's so precious? Eh? You?" Then he had laughed deep in his throat.

She had hurried into the cabin, slammed the door, and bolted it. For the first time, she remembered the gold hidden under the floorboards. Could Phelan possibly suspect its presence? Was this the reason he had been near the cabin yesterday, too? But if she told Kane of her suspicions, the man would get a whipping, or worse. She didn't think she could bear to watch such punishment.

"Privateers," Kane was saying thoughtfully. "Perhaps today might be a good day to begin your pistol instructions. It can't hurt, and will at least give you something to occupy your time."

"Yes," she said. "Although the sea is so empty. It doesn't seem possible that anyone could find us, let alone pirates."

"Don't let that faraway horizon fool you. Those cutthroats can navigate by the seat of their breeches. Their ships are so small and light—they're mostly sail—that they can skim over the water like a leaf. The kind of loot they're interested in doesn't require a lot of cargo space. What they do need, though, is a big crew—enough men to overpower a merchant ship."

As he fell silent, a picture came into Brenna's mind of a shipload of brown rats, eyes and teeth gleaming. But she tried to smile. "They don't sound like the sort of guests we'd like to invite aboard."

"No, indeed. So you'd better learn your pistol well, my little wildcat. Not that I expect any trouble. But just in case."

"You show a surprising aptitude for shooting," he told her two hours later, as they sipped strong coffee brought them by the burly cook. Jemmy, who had been set to scraping the loose varnish from the foremast, was perched far above them near the topgallant, his hand moving reluctantly, as if there were other things he would rather be doing. The regular sound of his scraping added to the flow of ship's sounds, blending with them.

"Do I?" She tried to smile. She had hidden her revulsion for the heavy pistol with its long barrel and awkward ball, powder and percussion cap ammunition, and had tried to do her best, conscious of his critical eyes on her. But the thought of really killing a man made her feel sick. Never, never did she want to kill any living thing.

"You're not afraid to touch a pistol, like most women," Kane told her with satisfaction. "Your grip is firm and your stance is like a man's. When the time comes, you'll do all right, I'll wager."

"I . . . I'm not so sure."

"Pirates are not human, Brenna, not as we think of humanity. They are animals. Worse than animals, for at least the beasts don't butcher their own kind for the sheer pleasure of it." Kane looked down at the pistol he held, touching its surface, scrolled with gold. "Unless you're afraid. Is that it?"

"No. I don't think I'm afraid, or at least not much." She groped for words. "But . . . to see a man die, and know that you caused it. That you ended the only life he could ever have—"

"Listen to me." He pulled her around to face him. She could smell the clean scent of him. "Pirates in these seas have been responsible for the deaths of hundreds of men. Hundreds! And these were hideous deaths, many of them filled with unnecessary torture and agony."

"But—"

"Don't you see? A pirate is *not human.* Having murdered in cold blood, he's lost his humanity, he's lost his right to have his own life considered. Don't turn soft on me, girl! Haven't you learned yet that the world isn't a sweet children's story, all full of goodness and honor? There's death, evil and violence. If we let ourselves give in to it . . ." Kane's shrug was eloquent.

"I suppose you are right. But I don't want the world to be that way. I don't want to see things like that."

"Who does? But life favors the strong. It's the strong and quick who'll do the surviving, not the weakling who stands with both hands sweating on the butt of his pistol, wondering whether or not he has the nerve to kill."

Brenna pulled away from him. She looked out at the water, where a thousand shades of green and blue mingled ceaselessly, and a school of porpoises leaped.

The nerve to kill. The words seemed to ring inside her head. Oh, she was so confused. She couldn't think straight anymore. She only knew that when she talked with Kane, his face convinced her, his touch sent warmth through her, warmth and faith. He couldn't be a murderer. It was only later, when she was by herself, that doubt nudged at her, spoiling everything.

"You'd better go to the cabin now," she heard Kane say. "Your face is already too red, and by nightfall you'll be miserable with sunburn."

Unreasoning anger swept through her. She thought of the small, cramped, overheated cabin waiting for her.

"No, I'll stay on deck for a while, where it's cooler."

"You've never had a real burn. You don't even know what you're saying."

She felt like a small child being banished to the nursery. "What you mean is that you've given me the pistol lesson, and now you're through with me, so I can go. I can be stowed away like your other gear, until you need me again. Is that it?" She jerked at the ribbons of her bonnet, feeling her fingers shake. "Well, I'm not a piece of sail, to be stored away and taken out only when wanted."

He regarded her as if she were an insect crawling on the canvas. "Brenna, what is it about you? If you were one of my crew, I would have you put on short rations for insolence. You just won't follow orders, will you? Even when those orders are issued for your own good."

Her tongue seemed to have a life of its own as words popped out of her mouth. "Perhaps I don't wish to follow orders issued by an accused murderer. A man who has just told me that it's the strong who survive and that he intends to be among them."

Did his face whiten? "You still believe I'm a killer, don't you? That I kill for pleasure, or for no reason at all. Well, go ahead, if that's what you want to think. But it won't make much difference when we get to that cabin alone, will it? You like a strong man well enough then."

Angrily she turned and was about to walk away across the deck, when a sudden clatter caught her attention. She looked down and saw Jemmy's wire brush lying on the deck. She knew that Kane saw it too.

They looked up into the network of rigging, narrowing their eyes against the sunglare. Jemmy was a dark form perched above, near the mast, swaying slightly, his hands clutching at the shrouds.

"Jemmy!" Kane shouted. "Hang on, you young fool!" Brenna saw that Kane had completely forgotten her, his attention solely on the boy swaying in the rigging like a treed cat.

"I can't—"

The ship pitched and perilously Jemmy tilted, his hands slipping along the ropes.

"Kane, he's going to fall! He was dizzy yesterday, and I told him he shouldn't go into the rigging."

But Kane was already stripping off his fashionable blue coat. "Hold on just a bit longer, Jemmy," he shouted. "I'm coming up to get you."

Kane began clambering up the ropes, hand over hand, as sure as if he were still a boy himself. But with dismay Brenna saw that he was not going to be fast enough. Already Jemmy's grip was slackening, his torso sliding to the right. And there was nothing beneath him to break his fall but the hard planks of the deck.

"Hurry, Kane, hurry!" He did not seem to hear her, but continued upward, placing each foot and hand with care. She could hear him telling Jemmy to hang on, not to let go.

But there was no reply from the boy, nothing to indicate he had heard. Like a rag doll, Jemmy began to sag farther to the right, with only his left foot, tangled in a network of ropes, to prevent him from plunging.

Then, just as the boy was about to topple, Kane reached him. He grabbed him roughly, almost losing his balance himself. From her position below, Brenna could only sense the struggle that was going on. But she knew that, young as he was, Jemmy's limp form was disastrously heavy to be handling on such a high perch.

The muscles bulged and strained in Kane's back as he attempted to haul the boy upward so he could rest him across the yardarm. For one horrid moment, Kane seemed to waver, as if the weight of Jemmy's unconscious body were pulling him down.

"Kane—please be careful!" She was hardly aware that she was calling out to him. Her hands clenched together with anxiety. If the *Sea Otter* happened to lurch again in another swell . . .

But that didn't happen. Kane took a firm grip on the boy again, and, inch by inch, pulled him up and balanced him across the timber, face down, arms and legs dangling.

"Get me some help!" he called to her. "I can't handle him alone. Where is—"

For the first time she became aware of the presence of other crewmen. Big Bart was running toward them with a coil of rope.

Slowly, painstakingly, they lowered Jemmy by rope, until he lay in a tumble of arms and legs on the deck, looking pathetically small and helpless. His cheeks were flushed bright red. And was it only Brenna's imagination, or did his forehead, where it wasn't flushed with the fever, seem tinged with yellow?

"Kane, he must be ill. I thought he didn't look well yesterday."

"A bit of the ague, I'll wager." Kane pressed his lips together grimly. "We'll take him into the mates' cabin. Jemmy's father was my friend, and I can't just send him back to the fo'cs'le. The officers will have to string hammocks on deck for a night or two."

They lifted Jemmy, Kane taking him under the armpits and Bart under the knees.

"Do you think he'll be all right?" Brenna persisted, walking along beside him. She noticed that Big Bart, too, was waiting to hear Kane's answer.

"Of course. It's only an ague. A day of rest and he'll be back in the rigging again, clambering about like a monkey. Careful now," he added, "we don't want to bang him about." They maneuvered the companionway with a good deal of difficulty. "Brenna, go to the cabin now. You've seen this through, and Jemmy's going to be fine."

"But I want to help with him."

"I asked you to go to the cabin. Can't you follow orders just one time without arguing?"

"You are a . . . a fool, Kane Fairfield!" she burst out, forgetting Bart's presence. "I've been a useless and unnecessary fixture on this ship, going on deck when told, staying in my cabin when told, not contributing anything. But now there is something I can do. Jemmy needs a nurse, and I happen to be quite able to nurse him. Besides, I . . . I like Jemmy."

"No. I don't want you doing it."

They were in the mates' cabin now, small and painfully neat, with dark paneled bulkheads and narrow bunks, one atop the other. An oil lamp and a stack of leather-bound books showed that one of the occupants was a reader.

Carefully Bart and Kane lowered Jemmy to the bottom bunk. As they laid him down, he stirred and moaned something unintelligible, his arms thrashing.

"And why can't I help?" She was indignant. "It's the one thing I might do to be useful, and you forbid it. Are you afraid I might soil my dainty hands? Are you afraid it isn't ladylike? Well, I have no intention of ever being a lady. I want to help!"

Kane's boots scraped on the polished floorboards as he came toward her. Behind him she could see Big Bart, his eyes focused on Jemmy with apprehension.

"I tell you, Jemmy's not that sick. A day of rest is all he needs. That's all for now, Bart," he added. "Get someone else to take over Jemmy's job. And tell the crew that he's going to be fine."

"Aye, sir." The man touched his knit cap in rough salute and then scuttled out of the cabin, the look of fear still in his eyes.

"*He* doesn't seem to think Jemmy's going to be all right," Brenna said.

Kane hesitated. He looked down at the figure of the cabin boy, who was beginning to tremble violently, as if chilled, in spite of the heat in the cabin. "I don't know," he said. "But I don't like this. I don't like it at all."

"What do you mean? You said yourself that he just has the ague. That a day or so of rest ought to put him right again."

"Perhaps. Perhaps it *is* just the ague. Or even influenza or the grippe. I'm not sure." Kane touched Jemmy's forehead, frowning. "I do know he's burning up with fever.

If he grows delirious, we're going to have to strap him into the bunk. Do you think you'll be up to doing that?"

"Of course I can." She bent over the boy, loosening the collar of his frayed linen shirt and trying to make him more comfortable. "Would you send down to the galley for some water? I'm sure he's thirsty, and we're going to have to sponge him off until the fever breaks. Go now, please hurry." She gave him an urgent push.

"His fever is too high. I don't like it."

"High or not, he needs caring for. We don't want to let him die, do we?"

"That's just what I'm afraid of," Kane said.

Through most of the night she stayed with Jemmy, sponging his slight body, stripped down to rough cotton pantaloons, the ribs showing on his chest as if he had not eaten for several days. He was very sick, she was certain. When she tried to take his pulse, it seemed slow and erratic. He fell in and out of consciousness, his eyes rolling in his head, bloodshot and frantic. His flushed, dry skin seemed to radiate heat like an oven.

"Water," he would croak. Pityingly, Brenna would lift his head and help him to drink, precious water spilling to the bunk as Jemmy struggled and thrashed.

"Mama!" he cried out once in a cracked voice, babbling on about "Papa on the big ship" and "my little toy horse" until it was clear to Brenna that Jemmy, in his mind, was a little boy again, reliving his Boston childhood. Her heart ached for him. Over and over she moistened his forehead with a cool cloth, trying to tell him—and herself—that everything would be all right.

As the hours passed, his thrashing became more violent. When she approached him to sponge his face, he pushed her away, his arm frighteningly strong.

"Jemmy, please, I'm only trying to help you," she pleaded. "I only want to make you feel cooler."

"No—no—no—no—" he muttered thickly. "Let me alone. Leave me be. I don't want—don't want to tell. Leave me be." He struggled to sit up and banged his head against the wooden framework of the upper bunk, leaving a red gash on his forehead. Even by the flickering light of the oil lamp, Brenna could tell that his face had grown darker. Small drops of blood were oozing from his lips, gums and nose.

"No!" Jemmy screamed again. "Leave me be!" Blood trickled down his forehead from the cut. His fist flew out and smacked against the paneling, his back arching convulsively, in the midst of a seizure.

Brenna was so frightened, and so sorry for the boy, that she wanted to cry. Kane had been right; Jemmy would have to be strapped down. If they didn't do it, he would injure himself further. But she would need help. Young and small as he was, in this delirious state Jemmy had the strength of an adult male. Perhaps even two men would be needed to help tie him down.

Closing the door firmly behind her, she ran to the main deck. After searching for a few moments, she almost collided with Kane, who was emerging from the fo'cs'le, his eyes hard, his lips pressed into a grim line.

"What are you doing here?" he demanded.

"Jemmy needs strapping after all. He . . . he hurt his forehead. I think he's having convulsions, too."

"*No.*" The word was a protest, coming from some deep, unprotected part of Kane. But he quickly hid his emotion. "Very well. I'll come myself."

"Yourself? But he's in a very bad state. We might need someone else to help."

"I don't want anyone else involved in this. Now, come along, will you?" He took her arm and pulled her toward the companionway so quickly that she nearly stumbled.

"Please," she protested. "I can't walk so fast . . ."

When they reached the mates' cabin, they found the door standing ajar.

"The door," Brenna whispered. "I didn't leave it like that."

"He must have gotten out. God only knows where he is now."

"But how could he? He was so sick—" In her worry, she pushed ahead of Kane and into the room, only to step backward, gasping with dismay. For Phelan stood at the foot of the bunk. The crewman was looking down at Jemmy's prostrate body, rigid in the bed, the blanket spotted with blood and a strange, black substance.

Phelan! What was he doing here? And what was the black matter on the blanket near Jemmy's mouth? A strange, tight feeling filled Brenna's throat.

Phelan smiled. He licked his lips and scraped his feet in a servile way. "Don't pay me no mind," he said. "I was just payin' a visit to our young friend here. Big Bart told me he was sick. Jest wanted to see it for myself, that's all."

"And now you've seen." Kane's voice was cold. She could sense his hand moving toward his pistol.

"No, Kane!" She stepped between them, trying to conquer her fright and disgust. "I'm sure Phelan meant well. He . . . he only wanted to see how Jemmy was. There's no harm in that, is there?"

"Harm? No, none at all, miss!" Phelan threw his head back and released a peal of ugly laughter through the black gap in his teeth. "No harm in the entire ship's knowin' we got another passenger along—a passenger named Bronze John."

Kane stiffened. "What did you say?"

"I said Bronze John. I seen it often enough in New Orleans. Look . . . looka there! If that ain't the black vomit, I'm a Chinee."

Kane drew his pistol. "Get out of here. And don't say a word of this to the crew or I'm going to have you wrapped in irons and dropped overboard, do you hear?"

Phelan's head jerked defiantly. "Maybe that's a better fate than I'll have if I stay aboard," he muttered. He turned to leave. "Maybe it is at that."

The door slammed behind him. Brenna approached the bunk, where Jemmy was starting to thrash and struggle again, his tongue trying to moisten his lips. Her heart hurt for him, yet somehow she did not dare to touch him either.

"Black vomit?" she whispered. "What is it, Kane?"

For a moment he did not speak. Then he said, "It's the fever. We've got yellow fever aboard. Some call it Yellow Jack, but whatever the name, one of the other crewmen has it, too. That's why I was in the fo'cs'le."

"Does . . . does that mean Jemmy is going to die?"

"Probably. And we'll be lucky if half the ship doesn't go with him."

❧ *Chapter 17* ❧

BRENNA FELT THE BLOOD leaving her face and neck. "I remember my Aunt Rowena talking about the fever," she said slowly. "She said most people left the city in midsummer and went to Lake Pontchartrain to avoid catching it. But I . . . I didn't really think much about it. I'd arrived there after that time, and—" She stopped, shaking her head. "It's something like the plague, isn't it?"

She remembered what her father had told her of the plague in London, the bodies carted away from homes daily, or just left where they fell in the streets. She remembered the fright during her childhood when smallpox had swept through Dublin.

"It is bad," he agreed. "It's odd, though, that not everyone dies from the fever. And the ones who live through it never seem to get it again. I had fever in Havana last year, and recovered soon enough."

The labored sounds of Jemmy's breathing became more tortured. Kane walked to the porthole and stared out at the clear blue sky, the mild sea.

"But Kane, we've got to do something for him—we can't just stand here and watch him!" *Watch him die,* she had meant. But she couldn't say it.

"We can pray. Give him water. Keep him restrained so he doesn't hurt himself any worse than he already has." Perspiration had appeared on Kane's forehead and upper lip. He spread his hands helplessly. "No one knows what causes this damned sickness, or what to do for it. People try all sorts of remedies, from putting onions in their shoes to taking quinine. If we had some opium we could give him that. At least he wouldn't have so much pain. If we had some cups, or some leeches, we could bleed him. Dammit, Brenna, what can I say? The ship's captain is supposed to doctor the crew. Set their broken bones and bandage up their crushed skulls. I can do that, always have. But this . . ."

The set of Kane's shoulders was bitter. He was fond of Jemmy, Brenna knew; had treated him like a son, confided in him. A man could fight something physical. But a disease—that was something else.

"Something else is bothering you, however, besides Jemmy," she said suddenly.

"Yes. It's the crew. They're bound to find out about this. If Phelan doesn't tell them, they'll learn the facts soon enough from the sick man in the fo'cs'le." Abruptly, as if shaking off some dread malaise, Kane was all action again. "I want you to start carrying a pistol," he told her. "I'll get one for you. Keep it near you. And stay here in this cabin with Jemmy until—" He stopped.

He reached into a sea chest and pulled out a coarse cotton sheet, which he began ripping into wide strips. "Come, we'll bind these about the poor lad. It's about all we can do for him."

On the bed, Jemmy was jerking again in convulsions, his back almost arching off the bed. Brenna was ashamed for the feeling of revulsion that ran through her. *Bronze John.* What if she caught it from Jemmy? What if she should die, too?

"I wouldn't worry," Kane added, almost as if he had read her thoughts. "The cards are already played. If you're going to get it, you've already been exposed. So don't think about it. And help me get him tied down. Poor little wretch, dying here without even his family to be with him."

It was a struggle, for the two of them, to get Jemmy safely bound to the framework of the bunk. He thrashed and kicked against them, shouting hoarsely.

"Oh, Kane. To die like this, bound hand and foot—"

"The straps are flat. They can't hurt him. And it's got to be done, so don't think about it."

But she did think about it. When they had finished, Kane went off to see to the ship while she sat with Jemmy, listening to the creak and bang of the ship's timbers, and summoning up all the prayers she knew.

Near dawn, Jemmy died. Brenna woke from a half-doze and immediately sensed that something was wrong. She jumped out of her chair and rushed to the bunk, where she found the boy lying waxy and still. His body seemed to have shrunk within the canvas that lashed him to the bunk.

"Jemmy!" she cried, blinking back tears. "Jemmy!"

But he did not stir. Slowly, with fumbling fingers, she untied the canvas bonds. *He's a quick learner, is Jemmy. He'll do all right,* Kane had said. She buried her face in her hands.

She found Kane and gave him the news, which he took without comment, narrowing his eyes and staring out to sea as if searching for something there.

"Well?" she demanded. "Aren't you going to say anything? Jemmy's dead. He was only fourteen years old." She felt an odd, bleak anger.

"The wind's picking up. We're nearing the west coast of Florida."

"Is that all you can say?" Exhaustion made her voice tremble. "Don't you care?"

"Yes, I care. More than you know. But life has to go on. I have other things to think about. For instance, Jemmy's burial. Ordinarily, we would hold an auction of his effects, but this time I'm going to have them thrown overboard with him. We'll have his burial, such as it is, in fifteen minutes."

"Fifteen minutes?"

"Why not? It's as good a time as any."

"But he's not even cold yet!"

"He's cold enough. Dead is dead, Brenna. I said fifteen minutes. The mates and I will take care of it. You don't have to attend if you don't wish to."

"Oh, but I do wish it! Of course I will come."

The ceremony was short and bleak. Both mates wore pistols, she noticed. It was the first time she had seen them armed.

The crewmen, clad in their assortment of cotton pants, rough shirts, and knit caps or head-rags, muttered among themselves as Jemmy's body was carried up, hastily wrapped in an old, patched square of canvas. She saw Phelan among them, his mouth moving rapidly, his hands gesturing. What was he telling them? About Bronze John, probably. But there was nothing anyone could do.

Kane read briefly from a small, black Bible, his voice stern. Phrases seemed to echo and sink in Brenna's mind. *Yea, though I walk through the valley of the shadow of death . . . For there is hope of a tree, if it be cut down, that it will sprout again . . .*

The crewmen coughed, shuffled their feet, stared at the deck. Then, before Brenna could take in what was happening, Bates and Scroggins had picked up the body and had tossed it overboard, following it almost at once with the small duffel bag containing Jemmy's clothes and personal effects. Only white splashes of froth marked the places where they had entered the sea. Brenna stood shaking, and Kane had to lead her back to the cabin, his arm firm about her.

"Get some rest," he told her. "You were up all night with him."

"Yes . . ." She felt dazed. Her head throbbed with pain, weariness grinding through her. She was so tired. All of this seemed so unreal. Surely any minute now, Jemmy would be coming with breakfast.

"Just two splashes," she muttered. "Two splashes and he was gone. As if he'd never been here at all."

"These things happen," Kane said. "The men know what sort of risks they take."

"Do they? Did Jemmy? When would a fourteen-year-old boy ever have time to think about death?"

"Jemmy did. He lost his father, remember?" They were in the cabin. She felt Kane slipping off her clothes, pulling the loose folds of a cotton wrapper over her. "Rest now. I'm going into the saloon and write a letter to Jemmy's mother. Then I have the ship to see to."

"Yes . . ."

Brenna lay down on the bunk. Above her head she could hear Scroggins shouting at the crew, his voice harsh. But almost instantly she fell asleep, her heavy slumber shot through with fragments of dreams. Jemmy, reaching his hands to her, begging her to help him. Kane and Jemmy, struggling together in the rigging.

It was hours later. Brenna neared the surface of sleep, and was dreaming. A hot, jerky, disorganized dream that skipped rapidly from place to place, making her head whirl.

The deck of the *Sea Otter* was painted a blinding white. She stood at the rail, the sun hanging over her head like a ball of molten iron. It beat down on her like an angry god.

"So? You think you have him, do you? You think you love him." From behind her came Melissa Rynne's voice, slow and mocking. She turned to see Melissa, dressed in a low-cut white gown, looped with yard after yard of expensive lace and flounces. In it Melissa looked like a white, swaying flower, the perfection of her bosom swelling out of the bodice. Even her face was like a flower. Small, oval, and perfect.

"I . . . I . . ." Brenna stammered.

But Melissa was smiling, her look condescending. "Well, you are wrong, Brenna. You don't have him at all. *I* have him. I and all the other women he's known. *We* are the ones who hold his real interest and his love. *We* . . ."

Nightmarelike, the scene shifted. Now she stood in the over-decorated plush bedroom at Maud Sweet's where she and Kane had stayed. Arcadia was with her, and they were standing behind the screen, at the peephole.

"Go ahead and look," Arcadia said. "You know you want to."

"No! No, I don't!" Panic swirled through her. "I don't want to see!"

"But you will see." She felt Arcadia's fingers cutting into her arm, strong as manacles, forcing her in the direction of the small, malignant square of glass.

"No!" she screamed. "No! I won't look! I won't!"

"You will." Inexorably, Arcadia pulled her toward the glass, pushed her face into it. She tried to screw her eyes shut but Arcadia forced them open with gold toothpicks—

Kane was on the other side of the glass. Kane and

Melissa. They were lying naked on a bed covered with pink satin sheets. Kane was caressing Melissa's soft, white body. Melissa arched her head back against the satin pillow, moaning softly. As she moaned, her face changed into the exquisite features of a stranger, a redhead—a woman Brenna had never seen before.

Now the body of Melissa was changing, too, becoming longer and leaner, more sharply curved. Kane moved on top of the woman to cover her body with his . . .

No . . . oh, God, no. . . . No. . . .

She woke to feel Kane's hand across her mouth, tasting faintly salty. "What in the hell do you think you're doing, screaming like that?" he said angrily. "You'll wake up the entire ship. After what they've been through today the last thing I want is for them to hear your screaming!"

"Screaming?" She struggled up dazedly, putting one hand to her head. "Oh, my head . . . I think there is a drum in it, beating on my brain—"

"What are you talking about? Do you have a headache?" He put a hand on her forehead. "My God, Brenna, you're burning up!"

"Burning . . . burning . . . the sun . . ." The room began to whirl about her. She fell back on the bunk and watched the ceiling swoop toward her and then away. Again and again she watched it, dizziness whirling through her in waves. Nausea pushed inside her throat. She felt as if she might be about to be sick—

Kane touched her forehead again, then felt her arms, her chest. "Your entire body is burning with fever. Don't tell me you've—"

He stopped, as if he did not want to go on. But it didn't matter. His voice was only a blur to her, a drone like the humming of a thousand bees. Nausea swelled in her like a hard bubble, growing larger every second. And no wonder, she thought confusedly, for wasn't Toby Rynne trying to kiss her, his thick, wet, red lips lingering on her mouth? Wasn't he pulling at her gown, pushing at her with his greedy fingers, breathing toward her with his pork chop breath? Their wedding, that was it. He wanted to consummate their wedding.

She pushed at Toby, pushed and kicked at him with all

of her strength, screaming at him to get away from her.
Oh, she couldn't stand it; his hands on her like vile insects—

"Brenna, Brenna, don't push me away. I'm only trying to
help you. I'm just trying to take off your wrapper. I'm going to sponge you, it'll help your fever." From somewhere
far away the voice came. But it didn't seem to have any
meaning. It was just words, buzzing and roaring like bees.

"No, Toby," she moaned. "I don't want you . . . don't
want you watching me. . . . Hate you . . ." The sun was
burning her, burning away all her flesh, but she summoned
the strength to kick at him.

"Brenna, if you keep on struggling and thrashing like
that, I'm going to have to restrain you, can't you see that?
Oh, darling, I don't want you to be like Jemmy . . . and
by God, you're not going to be. You're not going to be.
I'll see to that."

Again that strange, echoing voice. Restrain her . . . had
she heard that? What was happening to her?

She felt liquid being forced into her mouth. Tart, sharp,
limey liquid that puckered her tongue and made her want
to spit it out. She did. Why was Toby doing this to her?
Why was he torturing her? Was he trying to get her to
submit to him? Well, she never would. Not as long as she
lived. She didn't belong to Toby. She belonged to—

To whom? To that distant voice that shouted at her,
that begged and pleaded with her, saying the most extraordinary things? *Live. Live, Brenna. Please, please live.
Fight against it. That's it, don't give in. Don't let Bronze
John get you.*

"Bronze John?" she muttered. She tossed and turned,
shoving away the hands that attempted to put something
wet on her face. "Who's he? Someone I met at Aunt
Rowena's? At a party? I hate parties! I'm never going to
another one again. Not with you, Toby, not with you!"

"I'm not Toby. As God is my witness, I'm not Toby.
I'm Kane. Kane. Don't you understand?"

"No . . ."

"I wouldn't . . . I'd never hurt you. I'm only trying to
help you. To take care of you so you won't die. Please,
Brenna, try to fight it. Don't give in to it, don't die like
Jemmy."

Jemmy? Who was that? She was high in the rigging of the ship, clinging like a monkey, the sun licking at her with a tongue of flame. And when she looked down at her arms, she saw that they were nothing but white bones, that the sun had baked all of the flesh off her body. She was nothing but a skeleton, dressed in a brown merino dress and an ornate bonnet.

"No!" she screamed at the huge, bronze ball of fire. "Give me back my skin! Give me back my body! I won't let you take them, I won't!"

The ropes of the rigging were slapping at her body, each stroke a raw slash of pain. For a long time she hung there, hurting. If she let go of the ropes, she would fall. Yet below her was the sea, infinitely cool and green. . . .

"Water!" she heard herself croak. "Water!"

"Here it is, here." She felt the cool tin of a cup against her chin and drank thirstily. Who was giving it to her? She didn't know, couldn't see. Everything was a yellow-white blur, blinding her.

"Sponging didn't help," the voice said. "You're still burning up. My God, will nothing help? Water, that's it. I'll give her water, I'll soak her in it. Soak her. Why not? What else is there to do?"

She was naked. She was plunged into the sea, her body spiraling down to meet the jaws of the sharks that swam beneath. The shock of the water was icy. It screamed against her hot bones, a collision almost beyond bearing.

"No!" she screamed. "No! You can't do this!"

"But I've got to. You're going to stay here in this tub until your fever goes down if I have to strap you in. Dammit, Brenna, I don't care how much you scream, I don't care how much you suffer, you're going to live! I won't let you go with Jemmy, I won't!"

"But why?" she wept. "Why are you doing this to me? Oh, it hurts so!"

But his reply was muffled, lost in the blinding white glare that concealed him from her.

Never had she been so cold. It was as if her very bones had turned to shards of ice. She lay shivering, her body shaking convulsively, her teeth chattering. Weakly her hands reached for the blanket, tried to pull it closer about her chin. Dimly she realized that the oil lamp was flickering, sending long shadows up the bulkheads. Beside the bunk was the tin bathtub, partly filled with water, the carpet stained dark about it.

Kane was in the cabin. "Your fever's gone down," he said. "I nearly killed you to get it down, but I did it."

"Fever down . . ." she repeated. "I'm . . . cold. So cold."

"Cold?" Kane wiped perspiration from his own forehead. "God, you can't be. It's hotter than Hades in here."

"But I am cold," she heard herself whimper. "I'm f-freezing."

"Very well, darling, if you say so." He pulled the blanket to her chin, tucked it in, put another one on top of that. She huddled under the warmth.

"Do you want more water?"

"Yes . . . yes."

She felt her head being lifted and there was the tin cup again. She drank greedily. The water tasted stale and metallic but infinitely delicious. "I never thought water could taste so good," she said at last. "Could I please have some more?"

Again she drank, emptying the cup two more times. Then she sank back on the pillow, exhausted. Half-remembered dreams ran disturbingly through her mind. Melissa Rynne. Toby, with his red, wet lips . . .

She shook her head painfully. There was something that Melissa had said . . . but she didn't want to think about it. Not now, while she was so weak.

"Of course, it's too early to say, but I think you're getting better," Kane told her, putting away the tin cup. He, too, looked exhausted, with puffy shadows about his eyes. The pants and thin singlet he wore were stained and rumpled, as if he had slept in them. "Anyway, your fever is down and you're talking rationally."

"Rationally." She spoke the word with care, letting it rest on her tongue. "What is wrong with me? I remember such crazy dreams. You screaming at me. Oh, it's all such a blur."

"You are ill."

"I have yellow fever, don't I?"

"Yes," he said reluctantly. "You do. But you're not as

sick as you were. Remember, I told you that some people make it through Bronze John and live. I think you're one of them."

"But you took care of me, you exposed yourself." She sat up, frightened.

He was smiling at her. "I've had the fever, don't you recall? So don't worry. Don't worry about anything."

During the next two days she drifted in and out of sleep, waking periodically to find Kane beside the bunk with food, or another cup of water, or the scorching hot tea that the cook brewed in huge quantities for her. Kane, in his faded trousers and singlet, was a far different sight from the fashionably attired captain who had begun the voyage. He had not shaved in days and his beard was growing in darker than his hair, giving him an oddly disreputable look.

On the second day she roused herself enough to ask what was going on with the rest of the ship.

"We've two more men down, Bates and a man named Cartle, but I think that's the last of it. I've been giving them cold baths in seawater. Bates is improving, but I think Cartle is going to go. He's a scrawny thing, is Cartle, without much fat on his bones. I don't think he had much strength to begin with."

"But the crew, aren't they frightened?"

"They are. You'll notice I'm still going around with two pistols. But since you've begun to improve, they take it as a good luck sign. A sign that our troubles are over. Fortunately, we should reach Cuba soon. They'll be on dry land again, and presumably safe.

"Also, I got rid of Phelan, who was urging mutiny to the crew. Put him to sea in the ship's boat, with a store of food and water. He'll probably make it to the coast."

"Kane, you put him to sea in that tiny boat?" Brenna gasped. "Even if he does make it, there are Indians and pirates . . . he will starve to death in the swamps!"

"I would have been within my rights to execute him. A mutineer is the most dangerous sort of beast to have aboard ship; Phelan could have infected my whole crew with his panic. But cold-blooded execution rather turns my stomach, so I just put him over the side. It's what he wanted in the first place."

"But . . ." Brenna was too weak to think anymore. She drifted into sleep again.

It was during Brenna's period of recuperation that Kane told her about Edith, his wife. He had been brushing Brenna's hair for her, pulling the brush through the long, red-gold strands until they crackled with electricity.

"Your hair," he said softly. "When it's down around your shoulders like this it reminds me of—" He stopped.

"I hope it doesn't remind you of some other girl," she said, trying to laugh.

"As a matter of fact, it does."

"Your wife?" Brenna's heart seemed to stop.

He had been twenty-two, he told her, newly back from the China run and full of cocky self-confidence because of the things he'd done and seen. Edith Emory was a girl he'd known from childhood. Her family was one of the old Boston families, her father a wealthy banker. As a little girl, Edith had been a quiet, shy creature with red-gold hair and huge, brown eyes—the sort of child barely noticed by an active boy.

But now she was eighteen, tall and softly curved, her body as proud as a ship's figurehead, her brown eyes fringed by long, incredibly thick lashes. She was lovely, and she listened wide-eyed to the stories he told her.

Two months later they were married. And before the honeymoon ended, the quarrels began. Why didn't he plan to stay home now, and be a proper husband to her, instead of wandering all over the world like a nomad? He was rich, he didn't have to earn his living, he could stay at home, where a married man belonged. Then they could keep a good house in town, with the proper number of servants, and all the civilized amenities.

As for bed, she didn't enjoy that part of marriage at all. It wasn't proper for a woman to appear naked in front of a man, even her husband, she told him, horrified. There were marital duties, and she submitted rigidly to them. Only a wanton could *enjoy* the disgusting things he tried to do to her!

Supporting Edith in most of her opinions was her mother, a tall, embittered woman who had borne nine children, only two of whom had survived to adulthood. Every day Kane could see Edith, pinched with displeasure over the turn their lives had taken, becoming more and more like Mrs. Emory.

"So one day I just put out to sea again," Kane said. "I wanted to think. Perhaps I thought she'd be more agreeable when I returned, I don't know." His fists were clenched together, the knuckles showing white. "Eight months later, when I came back to Boston, I learned that she had been pregnant when I left, and had died from hemorrhaging after a miscarriage. And her mother blamed me for it."

"It wasn't your fault—"

"Perhaps not. But I can still see the way that woman glared at me, her nostrils flaring, as if I were some sort of carrion found beside the road. And God help me, when I looked at her, I could see Edith the way she would have been in twenty more years. A nag and a shrew, pinning her husband down until he had scarcely an opinion of his own. Until he couldn't even breathe.

"So I left Boston, I had to get away. Eventually I bought out part of my father's interests and went to New Orleans."

"I'm sorry," Brenna said at last.

"Sorry? For what? It's too bad Edith's dead—certainly I wouldn't have wished that on her. But she would have smothered me, Brenna. Would have killed something in me. I couldn't have lived that way, shackled to her pinched, narrow ideas of how my life should be run. Perhaps I'm bad luck for women, perhaps Edith's mother was right when she said I'd killed her daughter. I don't know. But I do know I'll never let it happen again. I'm not the marrying sort, and I know it."

❧ *Chapter 18* ❧

By the time they approached the channel leading to Havana harbor, Brenna was up and about, although she still felt weak, more than willing to rest in the chair which Kane had brought up on deck for her. The dresses that she had brought on board now hung loosely on her ribs, and would need altering as soon as she could find a seamstress.

"And perhaps I could find someone to make me a new gown," she said wistfully to Kane as the ship tacked along the beautiful green island set in the blue sea like a jewel, its white sand beaches distantly visible. "I am so tired of the grays and browns I brought aboard with me. I do long for color!"

"Well, maybe that can be arranged. If you will promise to eat and gain back the weight you have lost. I have no intentions of making love to a scrawny chicken." Kane's dimples flashed.

"Oh?" Ordinarily she would have bristled at this comment. But today, with the sun on her shoulders, she felt languid, almost happy. As happy as she had been in months. For she had come through Bronze John with her life; Kane had taken care of her with all the fierce attentiveness anyone could have wished. Almost as if he were really fond of her. Even his disturbing story about Edith Emory couldn't bother her today.

The rest of the ship seemed to have caught her good

mood as well. Kane, who had shaved off his beard, was in voluble high spirits. Even the crew could be heard raising their voices again in the sing-song chants they loved. It was as if the long, green island had beguiled them all.

Havana harbor itself was lovely. Brenna stood at the bow, entranced, as the *Sea Otter* entered the narrow channel, guarded by two brooding stone fortresses, high on the precipices to either side. One, a curiously menacing structure, was called Morro Castle. It was a prison, Kane said, with many grim dungeons and stone chutes, cut out of solid rock, leading down to the sea.

"Convenient apertures for disposal of their enemies," Kane added with a quick grin. "In fact, they may still be used, for all I know."

"Disposal?" She was puzzled.

"Of course. Any recalcitrant prisoners were dumped down the chutes and into the water. I understand that sharks used to gather below the castle, waiting for any tidbits that might be thrown their way."

"Oh, no!" she exclaimed. They had been in the habit of throwing garbage off the ship, and the picture of sharks was vivid in her mind. Quickly she looked down at the water swirling past the bow. A clear, limpid blue-green in color, it was so transparent that she could see far into its depths, even glimpse the forms of fish swimming below. Perhaps some of them were sharks . . .

No. She couldn't let herself think of that. She lifted her eyes to the other sights, the long stretch of seawall, the thickly grouped masts of the shipping area, the corrugated red tile roofs of the city.

"Where will we be staying?" she asked after a moment.

"A friend of mine owns a hotel here, one of the better ones. I am sure he will have accommodations for us."

"Very well. How will you introduce me to him? As your . . . mistress?"

Kane frowned. "No. Havana is a Spanish city. You will be my wife."

"Your wife. 'Mrs. Fairfield.'" She could not keep the sarcasm from her voice. She had begun to forget the conflict that raged between them, the hated bargain. Now he made her remember it.

"Can't you just relax and accept the way things are?" he demanded. "The way things must be?"

"Accept!" She was so angry that she stared unseeing at the splendors of Havana, the tall spires of a cathedral, a belfry silhouetted against blue sky. "Accept the fact that you practically kidnapped me? That you carried me across the sea like a . . . a . . . piece of baggage? That you force me to pose as your wife, to live the most ugly and sordid of lies? That I mean nothing to you but . . . but pleasure in bed?"

She was shaking, perspiration on her forehead, clammy and wet. At the stern they could hear Scroggins shouting at the crew, who were preparing to drop the enormous iron anchor.

"What's wrong with you?" asked Kane.

She stared at him, her head throbbing. She had an overwhelming desire to break into wild weeping.

"You . . . you don't understand, do you? You just don't understand."

"Understand what? I understand the need a man and a woman have for each other, the need to blend and share their bodies. Isn't that enough?"

"Is it enough?" she asked. "Is it?"

"Sit down, Brenna. You are upsetting yourself, and it can't be good for you. I don't want you to have a relapse."

"I don't care if I do have one," she said dully.

"Perhaps I was wrong then. Perhaps I never should have taken you away from your uncle's house."

"Yes. Maybe you were wrong." Tears streamed down her cheeks. If he had not taken her away, she would be Toby Rynne's wife at this very moment, and forced to lie under his fleshy body. A pang twisted through her. "Well, what's done is done, isn't it?" she cried. "I can hardly back out of the bargain now, can I? I'm thoroughly trapped!"

Before Kane could reply, she jumped out of her chair and ran toward the companionway, holding her skirts high so that she would not trip and fall, and be humiliated even further.

The hotel was on a main road near the harbor. Flowering vines twined over its pale yellow stucco in a riot of purple and red. The rooms would be small and not very elegant, Kane warned her, but there was a handsome restaurant on the ground floor.

The main room of the hotel was huge, empty and echoing, with a marble floor and a few groupings of cane furniture. The owner, Señor Tranquilo, came scurrying out to meet them. He was short, plump and red-faced, with black handlebar moustaches that twitched as he talked. He puffed incessantly at a fat brown cigar, and paid Brenna profuse compliments.

"Ah, the señora is lovely indeed, with hair like the setting sun. Truly we are honored to have such a beautiful lady among us."

He kissed her hand, the moustache tickling her fingers. In spite of her anger at Kane, she had to fight the urge to giggle. But Señor Tranquilo himself acted with the utmost seriousness, behaving as if she were a fragile jewel.

He gave them two small, adjoining rooms on the second floor, reached by an outside veranda. After the opulence of New Orleans the rooms seemed oddly bare, with no carpets or curtains. The windows had tall iron bars to keep out intruders, but no glass. The bedsteads were iron, with plain bedding, and were draped with the familiar mosquito netting.

Restlessly Brenna went to the window, which looked down on the cobblestoned street. What would Señor Tranquilo say if he knew she wasn't Kane's wife, but his mistress? Strumpet. That's what she really was. And no polite introductions or lavish compliments could change it. Unseeing, Brenna gazed down at a crude oxcart lumbering by, a heavy wooden yoke lying across the horns of the two oxen.

Kane was behind her. "I'd like to warn you about something," he said. "Don't go about barefoot in the room."

"Whyever not?"

"There is a small insect that can burrow its way under the skin of your foot. It's most uncomfortable, and can fester. And another thing: you can't go out alone. It just isn't done here. Only slave women walk alone on the streets."

"But—"

"You are in Cuba now, which is ruled by Spain. You will follow their customs precisely. I don't want to have to worry about you, is that clear?"

"Very clear indeed."

"Put aside the clothing that needs to be washed," he added. "Señor Tranquilo has a slave girl he bought from an Irish family. She can speak some English, so you'll be able to talk to her."

"Yes, of course," she said listlessly.

A noise from the street below caught her attention. She saw a ragged procession of black men, with irons around their ankles, wrists and waists. Chains linked them together in line, and with each step the chains clanked. The chained men seemed to move to some gloomy rhythm of their own.

"Kane!" she called. "Come and look. Who are those men?"

"That's a chain gang from the prison. Some are criminals, others are probably escaped slaves. They do heavy labor, like repairing roads." Brenna stared at him. "Don't look so horrified," he said. "Chain gangs—and slavery—are facts of life in Cuba."

"I don't care," she said stubbornly. "I'd rather not see such horrible things."

"Then don't look. You may not like it, my dear, but slavery has existed for thousands of years. Cubans accept it as perfectly normal and natural. You would, too, if you lived here and depended on sugar or tobacco for your living."

"I'm not so sure I would," she said slowly. "At least Aunt Rowena's slaves seemed happy enough. But those poor men in chains . . ."

Kane looked at her, his blue eyes distant. "Well, I hope you can come to accept these facts, because we are going to take some slaves back to New Orleans."

"We are?"

"Yes, I plan to buy some high quality slaves to sell in New Orleans. Since I have taken the trouble to come here, I should take back a paying cargo."

Brenna knew that Congress had decreed it illegal to import slaves, and was about to protest, but Kane silenced her. "I don't want to hear anything more about it."

"But—"

"I said that finishes the discussion. Now, please gather our soiled laundry so the girl can wash it."

Face burning, Brenna opened their trunk. A few moments later the maid arrived, a small, pretty girl with skin the color of *café au lait*. She wore a plain cotton dress, and her belly bulged in unmistakable pregnancy.

"You want your clothes done?" Her eyes inspected Brenna curiously, then slid over to Kane.

"Yes, I want them washed and pressed nicely, and do be careful not to scorch them."

"Yes'm." When the girl left the room, her hips swung back and forth provocatively, a fact not missed by Kane, who watched her, smiling.

"Did you notice she is pregnant?" Brenna asked irritably.

"Yes, she certainly seems to be."

Brenna thought of Señor Tranquilo, his shoe-button eyes looking at her with open admiration, his extravagant compliments. Could he be the father? She turned away from Kane and looked out the window again, her back stiff. She would never understand slavery, she would never understand Kane, and she wished she had never come to Havana at all.

It was time for the midafternoon siesta, but Kane declined to nap, saying that he had urgent business. He left, and a few moments later she heard a carriage clattering off down the street. She supposed he would look for some of the witnesses to the duel—were they Costigan, Perrier and Frontenac? Well, whatever their names, right now she didn't care. She felt too tired. Her very bones seemed to ache with exhaustion.

Her nap was a restless one, constantly interrupted by church bells chiming out the quarter-hours. She tossed and turned, her body soaked with perspiration. Again the cameo face of Melissa Rynne came to haunt her dream. *I'll clap you in chains,* she heard Melissa scream. *Clap you in chains . . .*

Brenna awoke to see the long afternoon shadows creeping into the room. She stretched and yawned, feeling un-

accountably better, as if the tropical air itself had powers
to refresh. From the street came the liquid cry of a vendor
shouting out his wares. She got out of bed and looked
down to see a black man balancing on his head a wicker
basket stuffed with long upright loaves of bread.

She made her toilette as best she could, combing her
hair high in back and allowing the side curls to fall irregularly at her ears. There was a small mirror in the
room, bordered with dark, carved wood, and she inspected
her face searchingly. She was thinner. Her cheekbones
were more prominent, her gray-green eyes large and
shadowed. But her cheeks, flushed with sun, were the color
of a ripe peach. No, she had not lost her looks, not yet.
And if she were careful to rest . . .

But she didn't want to rest, she decided, tossing her head
with sudden impatience. Whether she liked this city of
Havana or not, she wanted to see it, all of it. She had no
intention of spending all her hours in a hotel room!

Just then she heard footsteps on the veranda and Kane
burst into the room. His face was dark with temper. He
had not been able to locate Perrier or the other two men,
he told her. Perhaps they were in Havana under assumed
names. Or were in one of the other cities of the island.
Or, through some mishap, had not yet arrived.

"I'm sorry," she murmured. It had been many days since
she had seen him like this, with pent-up anger in him
perilously near explosion.

"You're sorry? Why should *you* be sorry? You're half-
convinced I'm a cold-blooded killer anyway. Why should
it matter to you whether or not I vindicate myself?"

She drew a deep breath. "You don't have to take out
your temper on me just because you've hit a snag in your
plans. You can't expect those men to be where you want
them, just at the moment you want them there. Even I
know that life doesn't work out that neatly."

"*Touché.*" He bowed mockingly. Some of the flush
gradually left his face.

"You'll find them," she added. "It will just take some
time, that's all."

"I know it. And when I do . . ." He did not finish his

sentence, but Brenna saw his eyes flicker and she suppressed a shiver.

"Well, enough of that," Kane said more calmly. "If we expect to eat today, we had better order some food. I'll go down and see if I can get something sent up."

The meal consisted of a chicken dish served with saffron-flavored rice, an omelette, a light-colored squash and a mixture of strange fruits, most of which Brenna had never seen before. The coffee was strong and dark.

Cubans, Kane said, spent their evenings shopping and calling on their friends. There was a band concert every night in the main square, and fashionable people drove their carriages leisurely around and around the square, greeting friends, flirting, the fine ladies receiving compliments from their admirers.

"Are these Spanish women very beautiful?" Brenna asked.

"Extremely so—some of them, anyway. They have dark hair and eyes, and pale, languid skin. And of course there are other women in Havana, too—many Americans and even some Irish. But none, naturally, are lovelier than you."

Was his compliment only perfunctory? As they left the room, Brenna stole another glance at herself in the mirror. If only she could wear something other than this loose brown merino dress!

At the door of the hotel, for a sight-seeing drive, Kane hired an odd-looking carriage that he called a *volante*. Built for two or three occupants, it had two huge wheels and was pulled by a horse with a braided tail. A black coachman rode in front, and a small coach boy clung to the back.

Later, Brenna would never be able to think of Havana without seeing color. The houses were pale blue and yellow and ochre, with dull-red tiled roofs, all twined with flowers of red, blue, purple, yellow. Scarlet poinsettias flamed in great bushes; the palms and mangoes were deep green. Over it all floated the clear, cloudless, shimmering blue of the sky.

She was entranced by the city, by the narrow cobbled streets barely wide enough for one carriage to pass, with narrow sidewalks along the sides and a gutter down the center for rain and refuse. Pedestrians thronged along the narrow streets, poorly dressed dark people in rumpled clothing mingling with fruit vendors, laden donkeys and crude oxcarts.

They passed an old monastery with a three-story look-out tower built to give warning against pirates. Brenna saw cafes with tables and chairs set out on the sidewalk, and homes with iron-barred windows, and doors wide enough to drive a carriage through. She saw the cathedral, with its two great square towers capped with moss-grown belfries.

The Castello de Atarés, however, cast a pall on the afternoon. A massive structure built of age-mottled stones, Atarés had been built on the summit of a conical hill overlooking the countryside and the harbor. It had, Kane told her, thirty eight-inch cannon and a subterranean vault full of torture instruments.

"No!"

"Oh, yes, I'm afraid so. They say there is an iron ring hung twelve feet above the floor, from which people were suspended until they died, a ladder upon which naked prisoners were stretched upside down and flogged, and, of course, the chair with the iron collar. Some of the instruments no one can remember how to use today."

"I'm sure it's just as well." Brenna tried to swallow.

"And there," Kane said, pointing to an area covered with a white, powderlike substance, "that is the death hole. That white material is quicklime."

"Stop!" She clapped her hands over her ears. "I don't want to hear it. Torture, slavery, chains, people being thrown to the sharks—I've had enough of it for one day."

"These facts exist, whether you like them or not. But if you wish, I'll take you away from Atarés. We'll go to the concert in the square, hear some music, and watch the promenade. Would you like that?"

He said something in Spanish to the driver, and they drove back through the narrow, cobbled streets.

Suddenly, rounding a corner, they found themselves confronted by another *volante* trying to go in the opposite direction. The two drivers stood up and began shouting at each other in Spanish, gesturing threateningly.

"Kane . . . oh, Kane . . ." Out of the confusion, a young woman's voice floated from the other carriage, sounding throaty and sensual, filled with pleased surprise.

The other *volante* moved slightly, and Brenna was able to see the two occupants. One was an elderly woman in a black dress, obviously a chaperone. The second passenger was a young woman with red hair piled elaborately on her head and dressed with flowers and jeweled pins. Her muslin dress was daringly décolleté, displaying full, pointed breasts.

"Coleen, it's you!" Kane leaned forward to smile at her. It was the slow, crinkling, easy smile which he seldom showed Brenna.

"Why didn't you write me you were coming?" the girl asked excitedly. "I didn't expect you! You could have stayed with us!"

Almost reluctantly, Kane turned to Brenna. "Pardon me, Coleen, but I would like you to meet my . . . my wife, Brenna. Brenna, this is Coleen O'Reilly. Her husband is a sugar planter here, and they have a lovely house in town as well."

Did Coleen flinch at the news that Kane was married? She regarded Brenna coldly. "I am pleased to meet you, I am sure. The lady beside me is Señora Elenora Rodriguez, my chaperone, but I am afraid she speaks only Spanish."

Brenna nodded and smiled at the older woman, who inclined her head briefly.

"How is Patrick?" Kane asked.

Coleen's eyes were fixed on Kane as if Brenna did not exist. "He has been so ill—I'm afraid he has consumption. The doctor says he can recommend nothing for him except a change of air, and of course, Patrick won't hear of that."

Brenna sat listening as the two talked. On the surface, their words were circumspect enough. But there was something about the tense way Coleen O'Reilly watched Kane, as if she would like to jump out of the *volante* and throw her arms around him.

"You must come and see us," Coleen said at last, her tongue coming out to moisten her full, red lips. "Perhaps you can cheer Patrick up. God knows he needs it."

To Brenna's dismay, Kane accepted the invitation, setting a time. A few minutes later, the two coachmen settled matters, and, with a great deal of arguing and jostling, maneuvered the two vehicles so they could pass.

They clattered away. But Brenna sat stiffly, her hands clenched in her lap. She remembered the voice she heard in her dreams. *I have him . . . I and all the other women he's known.*

❧ *Chapter 19* ❧

DUSK HAD FALLEN. The stars appeared, as large and numerous as berries, and so deceptively close that Brenna thought she could almost reach up and pick one. The military band, in their seersucker uniforms, started to disperse, and the gathered carriages drove away leisurely, as if the whole evening lay ahead, still to be enjoyed.

"The concert was lovely," Brenna sighed. They had driven around the promenade to listen, and once Kane had reached over to hold her hand. She had almost been able to forget Coleen, and the disturbingly possessive way she had looked at Kane.

"I'm glad you liked it. Perhaps we can do some shopping now. I did promise you a new gown, didn't I?"

"But . . . at nine o'clock?"

"This is Havana. The shops will still be open."

A few moments later, they found a shop that sold dry goods, its enormous marble-floored salon displaying bolt after bolt of muslin, silk and cambric in an almost intimidating display of luxury. To her delight, Kane bought fabric enough for two gowns, a creamy jaconet muslin, and a pale yellow organdie. Kane arranged for a dressmaker to come to the hotel, take Brenna's measurements, and begin work on the dresses.

As they emerged from the shop, Brenna looked idly about her. On the corner, a watchman called out the half-hour, holding a long pike in one hand and a lantern in the other. To her left, a large, black, English-style brougham slowed down in the heavy traffic. Its occupants, two men in black coats and hats, were talking together.

She stared at the carriage. One of the men, his face turned partly away from her, seemed somehow familiar. There was something about the way he held his head proudly back, his high cheekbones curving into the lean line of his jaw. It was as if she had seen or known him before.

She felt a chill run through her. Who was the man? And why did the sight of him make her heart beat in such quick, desperate thumps?

"Come on, what are you staring at?" Kane asked sharply.

"N-Nothing," she managed. The black carriage had gone.

Kane spoke to the waiting *volante* driver, who, as seemed to be customary here, did not turn around or acknowledge that he had heard his instructions.

"Where are we going?" she asked.

"Back to the hotel. You are to get your rest, Brenna. I want you to regain your strength before we return to New Orleans."

"And you?"

"I am going to make the rounds of the cafes. Perhaps I can pick up some news about Frontenac and the others."

"Very well, then," she said reluctantly.

Because of her long afternoon siesta, she found it difficult to sleep. She lay on the coarse linen sheets beneath her tent of mosquito netting, twisting and turning from side to side. Her throat felt thick with tension. What was wrong with her? Kane meeting a red-haired woman he knew should not make her so restless. Or was it perhaps the oddly familiar man she had seen? At last she fell into a heavy, dreamless sleep.

When she awoke, it was morning. From behind the drawn shutters she could hear strange birds singing, the ringing of church bells, laughter, the sounds of pottery clattering in a kitchen somewhere. She rolled onto her back and stretched, as sensuous as a cat. Energy surged through her. She sat up quickly, pushing aside the mosquito netting and remembering to slip on her shoes before going to the other room to see if Kane was up.

His shutters had not been closed; the room was flooded with sunlight. And the bed had not been slept in.

She paced up and down the two rooms, frightened and angry, her nightgown swirling behind her. Where was he? Why hadn't he come back? Had there been an accident? Nervously she stared out of the barred window to the street below, where a *volante* was passing full of veiled women on their way to early mass. Cathedral bells pealed forth in a ringing explosion of sound.

Brenna stood with her hands clenched into fists. Perhaps Kane hadn't gone to the cafes at all. Perhaps he had gone directly to Coleen's. Surely one sick husband wouldn't be difficult to evade. Maybe at this very moment he was lying in bed with Coleen, his hand casually flung across her naked breast.

The thought sent an ache through her.

She felt tears pricking her eyes, and blinked them grimly back. She wouldn't cry, she told herself; not if she could help it. After all, they had made a bargain. Nothing had been said about Kane's being faithful to her. If he was with another woman, it was none of her concern. She was not his wife, and had no right to tell him what to do.

She wished she could die.

The morning passed slowly. There was no pull-cord or bell in the rooms, so she had to call from the veranda to ask for breakfast. The maid brought oranges and coffee to her room. Slowly Brenna began to eat one of the oranges, tasting its acid-sweet tang. But she was not hungry. The pulp seemed to stick in her throat like dry bread crumbs.

There was nothing to do in the room. Despondently she dressed in one of her newly clean gowns, and listlessly combed her hair. Even the arrival of the French seamstress could not cheer her. However, she forced herself to describe the gowns she wanted. If Coleen O'Reilly could have tempting décolletage, then so could Brenna Laughlan. She, too, could be sensually appealing. If lovely gowns and a curving body could ensnare Kane, then why not use them herself?

When the dressmaker left, Brenna sank into one of the cane chairs and stared unseeing at the rough wall. By the sound of the church bells, she knew it was noon. Carriages rattled over the cobblestones as people streamed home from mass. Anxiety flooded through her. Was it possible that Kane really was hurt? A carriage accident, a runaway horse, a fight?

She rose decisively. She would go down to the main salon and see if she could find Señor Tranquilo. Perhaps he would know of any accidents.

She entered the main salon of the hotel, but when Señor Tranquilo himself came hurrying across the marble floor, she could not bring herself to ask about Kane. In a low, shamed voice, she asked him how to find the patio. She wished to take some fresh air, she told him.

The patio was overgrown with weeds, but lovely with a rose trellis, a central fountain and a large mango tree. Morning glories and other flowering vines climbed over the yellow stucco walls. Near one wall stood a row of large red clay pots, each big enough to hold a man.

"In case you are wondering, the pots are used to store water," Señor Tranquilo said behind her.

"I . . . I didn't know," she managed. She felt her cheeks reddening.

"Yes, we have some natural springs near the city, but each home customarily collects as much rainwater as it can." His eyes lingered on her breasts.

"I am sure," she replied coldly. "Now, if you will please excuse me, I have a headache. I think I will return to my room. The sun is very bright here."

"So soon? But you have just arrived, my lovely Mrs. Fairfield." He moved closer to her, and she could smell the sweetish odor of some scent he wore.

She evaded him and left the patio, hurrying back up to their rooms and locking the door behind her. *Kane*, she thought despairingly. *What has happened to you?*

It was two o'clock by the time Kane appeared. She let him in with shaking fingers.

"Where have you been?" she whispered.

He regarded her defiantly. His elegantly cut blue coat was freshly pressed, his shirt clean, his cravat immaculate. "I don't believe it's your business to ask me that."

"What? Not my business! When I have sat here all morning wondering where you were! Whether you had been in some accident . . ."

"I am here now, aren't I?"

"You were with that woman, weren't you?" Her voice rose stridently. She was ashamed of losing control, but could not help herself. He calmly reached into his vest pocket for a cigar, lit it, and took a puff with slow ease.

"What woman?" he asked.

"You know who. That . . . that red-haired creature we met last night. I saw the way she looked at you. You knew her before, didn't you? She's one of your women, isn't she?"

"Perhaps she is. Perhaps she isn't. But whatever I might feel for her has nothing to do with what I feel for you. Your anger is completely unjustified. I warned you that I am not the sort of man to be meekly content with one woman. I won't be tied down, and I won't be forced into explanations. Lovely and delicious as you are, you are not my wife. You never will be. Have I made that fact plain enough to you?"

"Very plain. Oh, very plain indeed!" Her chest heaved up and down with quick, angry breaths. She wanted to smack his face. She wanted to dig her nails into his skin and rake bleeding scratches across his chest. She turned away from him with an effort, and stood at the window, her back to him, ramrod straight.

"*Why?*" she whispered. "Why did you take me away with you? Why? When it can never . . . when we can never . . ."

There was silence. She turned to look at him, but he had left the room.

Brenna pushed at the seafood and rice mixture on her plate with her fork. "I'm not hungry," she said dully.

"Of course you are. Please eat," Kane ordered. They were in the hotel restaurant, an impressive room with a cool marble floor and ceilings twenty-four feet high. The great windows were open to the floor. Rows of small tables were covered with white cloths, each with a bright pyramid of oranges in the center.

After leaving her alone for more than half an hour, Kane had returned to tell her that it was time for dinner. People would ask questions if they did not go to the restaurant.

He had ignored her protests and pulled her along with him, and now they sat in the half-filled room. Most of the patrons were men, talking business. She heard scraps of conversation about sugar and rum.

After the white-clad waiter brought their soup and main course, Kane spoke to her in a low voice. "All right, Brenna. Enough of this nonsense. If you don't stop your pouting and tantrums, I will lock you up on the ship. You would hardly have a chance to wear your new gowns there, I am afraid."

She stared at him. "You wouldn't dare do that!"

"Wouldn't I? You don't know me very well if you think I wouldn't carry out any threat I made."

"You are despicable."

He inclined his head slowly, as if she had said something amusing. "That may be so. Nevertheless, please try to eat your food. Have you tried the fried plantains? They are surprisingly good. I learned to enjoy Cuban food when I made my last visit here. They have an astonishing variety of fruits."

But Brenna was not interested in talking about fruits. "Indeed? Is that when you came to know the O'Reillys?"

"No, I met them in Boston. O'Reilly and my father were once business associates. That was before Patrick decided to come to Cuba and make his fortune in sugar."

"And Coleen? Is she the one who nursed you through your fever?"

"No, she was frightened of it. But I did convalesce at their home for a few weeks. She felt it was the least she could do for me."

"I am sure of that." Brenna could picture it all; the tall, slender Coleen dressed in a white apron, lingering by Kane's chair to chat, making sure he observed the pointed perfection of her breasts, the creamy flush of her skin . . .

"You needn't wrinkle your nose when you speak of Coleen. She is a very bright and beautiful woman married to an older man. She hates living on this island of Cuba and is acutely homesick for Boston. As a fellow Bostonian, she was only too happy to see me. Can you blame her?"

Brenna bit her lip, choking back an acid comment. For a few short days on the *Sea Otter*, she had been almost happy. She had basked in the feeling that Kane cared for her. Now it was all spoiled.

"Are . . . are you in love with Coleen?" she heard herself ask.

"Love? Does anyone really know what that is? Is it need for a certain person, a desire to be with her? If that is the definition, then, yes, I was in love with Coleen. For a time I was entranced with her."

"I see," Brenna said flatly. She did not know what else to say. She toyed with her food.

"Will you stop looking at me that way?" Kane demanded. "Coleen is an old friend, can't you understand that? Her husband is dying of consumption, yet he refuses to leave Cuba. She's always been high-strung, and it's hard for her to cope. She has no one to turn to here. As for my not coming back last night, I can explain. You see, I—"

"You don't have to tell me anything more. As you so clearly pointed out, you don't owe me any explanations."

"Very well, then."

They continued with their meal. Kane had awkwardly begun to tell her about the rum-making process, and the sugar plantations, when two men entered the restaurant. One was pushing the other in a wooden wheeled chair, lifting the apparatus with difficulty over the marble threshold.

Brenna was not the only one in the restaurant who turned to stare at the man in the wheeled chair. He was a striking sight, with a tall torso and a hawklike face, but thin to the point of emaciation. His deep-set eyes roved around the room imperiously.

Shock pounded through her. She sat tensely, waiting for him to notice her. Surely this was the man she had seen yesterday in the carriage. The man who had looked so familiar. She gazed at him intently. Something in the arrogant set of his features made her think of Neall Urquhart. There was even a pale scar on his cheek. Yet this man was far thinner than Neall had ever been, and of course there was the chair—

Then she remembered. Neall had been paralyzed by his fall.

Neall Urquhart. It was as if a nightmare had begun to

unfold in this public place, with the sun shining through the large windows and the oranges bright spots of color on the white tables.

Neall looked at her, his eyes like two dark holes in his head. She felt a quiver run through her.

"Brenna? Are you chilly? Shall I get you a wrap?"

"No. No, I'm fine. I . . . I think someone must have walked over my grave, that's all. It's an odd feeling." She forced a laugh.

"But you look so white. Are you quite sure you're all right?"

She felt like laughing hysterically. In one moment, Kane could threaten to lock her aboard ship. In the next, he wanted to know why she looked so pale. Would she ever understand him?

To her vast relief, Neall and the other man passed by their table without speaking, and were seated at the far end of the room, by the large, iron-barred window.

Kane spoke suddenly. "I don't know who that pair are, but the one in the chair is an ugly one, isn't he? There's something about him I don't like. And he looked at you, Brenna. You would think he knew you."

"He doesn't!" She shifted her feet uncomfortably. "I think I saw him in a carriage last night, that's all."

"Really? Well, it doesn't matter. Havana is small, and since he seems to be staying here at the hotel, I suppose we shall run into him again."

Kane changed the subject, and devoted himself to the dessert—a dense, rich cake served in thin slices. When the meal was over, they went back upstairs to their own rooms. Kane locked the door and closed the shutters.

"Come here, darling." He began stripping off his coat and vest.

"But . . . the siesta . . ." she said weakly.

"What do you think the good Spanish are doing behind their closed shutters at this time of day, my dear? Come here, will you?"

He enfolded her in his arms, covering her face with soft, light kisses. Her heart pounded, her thoughts whirled in scattered confusion. Coleen . . . Neall Urquhart . . . But when Kane kissed her, she forgot everything. She was only aware of his hands, his mouth, his manhood pressing urgently against her.

"Brenna . . ." he whispered. "Do you really think that any other woman could compare to you in bed? Do you?"

She felt as if her heart were bursting. She tried to say something but he kissed her, melting his body into hers. He pulled off her gown. Feverishly, she helped him. She wanted to bare her body for him, and to be naked with him.

He carried her to the bed and laid her down. He kissed her breasts, his tongue touching her nipples, teasing them erect. His mouth moved to her belly. Slowly, deliberately, he kissed her. And when his mouth moved farther down, she was not surprised, but moaned softly as his tongue probed her, tingled her, unutterably sweet, until she wanted to scream aloud.

Then suddenly he embraced her again, and she felt him entering her, moving inside her, ever more intense, until at last there came the quick spurts of ecstasy, shuddering through her body and mind.

They lay together in the bed, sleepy, satiated. Kane's arm rested across Brenna's bare breast, and she stretched lazily, savoring the moment. Whatever had happened last night, whatever other women he had had, for the moment he belonged to her. Nothing could take that away from her.

"You know," Kane said suddenly, "when I'm with you, I forget that I've been accused of murder. I forget everything. It's as if the two of us have a small world of our own, where nothing else can get in. Do you feel that, too?"

"Yes," she whispered.

"Strange . . . you're the only one who—" He stopped, as if he had said too much. Then he rolled over, pulling her body, spoonlike, into his, cupping her breast with his hand. Gradually she felt his body relax. She knew he was asleep.

After the siesta, Kane left, and Brenna remained in the room, her warm mood gradually seeping away. They were to visit the O'Reillys tonight, Kane had told her. The thought filled her with dread. How could she face Coleen if Kane had spent last night with her?

If only her new gowns were ready! But they weren't, so she carefully went through her trunk, to select the most attractive dress she could find. At last she chose a sober dark green taffeta with embroidered lace inserts. Part of the lace was ripped, however, and she ventured out of the room to find one of the maids, and ask for a needle and thread.

An upper veranda ran around three sides of the hotel, overlooking the patio. Although she leaned over the rail and called, no servant appeared. She was about to go down the stairs when she heard a creaking noise behind her. She turned to see Neall Urquhart, wheeling his chair along the veranda. He looked more emaciated than ever, his cheekbones carved out into great hollows, his eyes sunken.

"So. It is you, Brenna." His eyes burned at her. "It's really you. I thought I saw you last night, but I told myself it couldn't possibly be you. There was one chance in a million that you would be here in Havana. Yet here you are."

Even his voice seemed drier, harder. It was difficult to realize that this was the same vigorous man she had married; the powerful man who had ripped the wedding dress from her body.

"Neall . . . you've changed so. I barely recognized you," she managed to say through stiff lips.

"Changed?" He threw back his head and laughed. "Of course I have changed. I am paralyzed from the waist down. I have lost forty pounds. I haven't had a woman since our wedding night. Being in my state does peculiar things to a man, wouldn't you agree?"

His eyes fixed hers. She felt like a rabbit, mesmerized by a hawk. She tried to back away along the rail of the veranda.

"No, don't leave, my pretty. We have much to talk about, do we not? After all, I owe my present condition to you."

"It was not my fault you went through that window! If you hadn't attacked me, you wouldn't have fallen!"

"You lie! You little . . . you, monstrous slut of a girl.

It's because of you that I am like this. Because of you that I can't make love to a woman. Because of you that I cannot ride a horse or walk or—"

A door slammed farther down the passage, and Neall stopped, his hands tightening on the wheels of the chair. "I came to Havana to see to the family's interests. We've invested in several sugar plantations and want to expand. Besides, my physician thought the sea air might be a tonic for me. A tonic! The best tonic I ever had is seeing you today, Brenna."

"What do you mean? Why do you say that?" She felt terrified.

"To see the woman who caused my present misery, yes, indeed, that is a sweet sight. After all the long hours and days and months I have spent thinking about you, thinking about what I would do if I ever saw you again."

Didn't you already do enough to my father? she wanted to scream. But his eyes were like dark pits, and she began inching away from him nervously. "I . . . I must go now," she said. "I must consult with Señor Tranquilo—"

"Are you staying here with your *husband?*"

"Yes, I . . . that is . . ."

"Does your husband know your past history? Does he know that you came to me as tainted goods? That you were a cheap, lying little slut? Did you even tell him of the marriage and the divorce? Did you?"

"No!" she gasped. "No, I didn't! He doesn't know anything about you. Please don't mention this to him. He . . . he wouldn't understand."

"Ah. Indeed. I'm sure he wouldn't."

"I . . . I must go now. Really, I must."

She turned and, lifting her skirts, she ran fast as she could around the corner to the passage where their rooms were. As she ran, she was conscious of his eyes behind her, black and envious.

Chapter 20

BRENNA SAT HUDDLED in the *volante* next to Kane, her body shivering convulsively. The night was warm and balmy, but she felt as if a bitter wind were raising goose bumps on her arms.

"What is wrong with you? You're quiet enough." Kane's voice was sharp.

"Nothing is wrong with me. Nothing at all."

"Didn't you enjoy seeing the O'Reillys' house? It is very typical of the Spanish homes here."

"I don't care how typical it was! I don't care! Did you think I enjoyed that . . . that travesty of a polite evening we had? With Coleen's poor husband, too ill to greet us, coughing and coughing from upstairs, as if he were about to die at any minute?"

To her dismay, she heard her voice rising bitterly.

"You step beyond yourself, Brenna. Be quiet. I don't want to hear any more about this," Kane said coldly. Brenna felt her cheeks turning crimson.

It had been a nightmare evening. Neither Kane nor Coleen had wanted her to be there; that had been plain to Brenna from the start. And even the O'Reillys' home had made her feel uncomfortable. Completely bare of carpets and curtains, its variegated marble floor was set with two rows of American rocking chairs facing each other grotesquely. Each corner of the big salon held a triangular claw-footed table, loaded with wooden saints, glass balls and china vases.

Coleen had greeted them effusively. She wore a watered silk gown of the palest green, cut so tightly that the curve of her bosom swelled above the neckline. Her fiery hair had been arranged in long ringlets, artfully held by jeweled pins. There were the faint traces of rice powder on her face.

"I suppose Brenna would like to see the house," she had said grudgingly, after a few moments. "I insisted on having kitchen cupboards—would you believe that the people here actually wash dishes outdoors in the servants' courtyard? Oh, I loathe this house. Patrick insisted upon it, though. He'd like nothing better than to be more Spanish than the Spaniards. Oh, what wouldn't I give to be able to go into my mother's parlor in Boston with its beautiful Brussels carpets and Chippendale furniture!"

She paced to the huge, barred window and stood for a moment, her shoulders slumping. "If it weren't for Patrick . . ." She turned to meet Kane's eyes. "If it weren't for Patrick, I would go home to Boston. Perhaps I might even sail along with you, Kane. Would you like that? Would you take me home?"

"Take you home? Why—"

But Brenna, her heart pounding, had broken in. "I am afraid it would be uncomfortable traveling, Coleen. Kane is buying some slaves to take back with us. And quarters will be cramped, since Kane and I are already occupying the captain's cabin."

Coleen's eyes narrowed. "Kane told me about your *marriage.*"

"Oh . . ." Brenna faltered. Hot color flooded her face.

Coleen laughed lightly, her mood mercurial. "Well, don't worry, my dear. I will keep your secret. It will be just between the three of us, won't it, Kane?" Possessively, she linked her arm through Kane's. "Although I don't see why you couldn't take me home with you," she pouted. "I am *so* lonely for Boston."

Brenna tried to recover her poise. "But of course you won't be coming back with us. How could you, with a husband to take care of?" As if on signal, a heavy, hacking cough sounded from the upper regions of the house.

A tense, nervous expression had passed over Coleen's face. "Oh, drat him! He refuses to die, and he refuses to return home, and he's too weak to see to the plantation here. . . . Oh, it's useless! Why shouldn't I run away? What is there for me here? Sugar! Tobacco! Pineapples! Bah!"

Kane had looked down at Coleen, his face troubled. "So you really want to come?"

"Yes! I . . . why not?"

Before Kane could reply, Brenna moved to his other side and took his arm with all the grace she could muster. She smiled her prettiest smile. "You realize, don't you, Coleen, that we had yellow fever aboard the ship when we arrived? Kane did tell you that, didn't he? Three of our crewmen died. Fortunately, I've had the disease, and so has Kane. Have you?"

Coleen paled visibly. "No . . . no, I've never had the fever."

"They say that even the doctors don't know how the fever comes. Clouds . . . bad air . . . a miasma . . . perhaps it is still lurking inside the ship, in the hold and in the dark corners." Brenna smiled innocently, enjoying herself.

She'd had the satisfaction of seeing Coleen nervously change the subject, and then the servant had entered with coffee and cakes. Shortly afterwards, they had left.

Now Brenna sat in the *volante,* remembering the evening with fury. "As for that . . . that woman suggesting that you take her aboard the *Sea Otter,* I hope you're not considering such a thing," she said. "You aren't going to Boston! And it would be a hideous thing to do to a sick man, a man who's supposed to be a friend of yours. *Two* of your mistresses aboard your ship—would that please you, Kane? Would you find that amusing?" She knew she was overstepping herself, but couldn't seem to stop.

Almost instantly she felt the sting of his palm across her cheek. The blow was not hard, but it was humiliating. Tears sprung to her eyes.

"In the first place, Brenna, you are taking great liberties if you think you can categorize Coleen's relationship with me that easily. The poor girl is alone, and needs a friend. Have you ever considered that? Besides, you have no claims on me, Brenna, none whatsoever. Anytime I decide to drop you, I can do it. I could even leave you here in Havana, would that suit you?"

"No . . ." she whispered, frightened.

"Well, I want you to know that I have no plans for taking Coleen O'Reilly aboard the *Sea Otter*, at least not this trip. You're right. She does owe something to her husband. And perhaps I owe him something, too."

The remainder of the ride home was a silent one. The streets, lit by a full moon, were serenely beautiful. Under other circumstances, Brenna would have been entranced, but now she could only think of sliding as far away from Kane as possible.

She hated Kane, she told herself. Hated him! For humiliating her in front of Coleen O'Reilly, for being so arrogant and difficult, for threatening to leave her in Havana. Oh, she loathed him as she had never hated anyone before, even Toby Rynne.

They pulled up in front of the hotel. Kane gave her the huge, ornate room key. "You go on up to the rooms," he told her coldly. "I will be up in a few minutes."

"Very well," she replied equally as coldly. She would have died before she asked what he was going to do. She didn't care. He could go anywhere, do anything, and she wouldn't care.

Stifling a sob, she found the main door of the hotel unlocked and slipped inside. The huge salon was filled now with long shadows, casting strange shapes upon the walls. As she walked across the marble, her footsteps echoed eerily.

She climbed the stairs as quickly as she could, thinking that she had had enough of Kane and his bargains. Kane and his women. She couldn't bear any more hurt.

The top of the stairs fronted on the open veranda. She glanced down into the patio, where the leaves of the banana and mango rustled in the steady night wind, and a strange insect chirped. The moon blurred the outline of the weeds, picking out the roses on the high trellis, so that they glowed silver. She turned left, toward their rooms.

She found their door and fumbled for the big key,

inserting it in the lock. To her surprise, the door did not open immediately, but required two more tries before she was able to push it open.

There was an oil lamp upon the table, but she decided not to light it, since the moonlight was so bright. Yellow light streamed through the large windows, lying in stripes along the floor. Or in bars, like a dungeon . . .

She shivered, walking over to the cane chair, where she took off her shawl and folded it neatly. She was fumbling with the buttons of her dress when she heard a slight noise from the second room. A creaking sound, as if someone had trod on one of the floorboards.

She stood frozen, holding her breath. A mouse? Or just the big building, settling itself? It couldn't have been anything else, she told herself, since the room had been locked.

Or had it? Had opening the door been difficult because it was already unlocked?

She heard another noise, a faint sibilance. Was it breathing? Then a clattering noise, and Neall Urquhart rolled himself in his wheeled chair into the room. A long dueling pistol gleamed in his lap.

Brenna screamed, and screamed. And then, for the first time in her life, she fainted dead away.

She was lying on the floor, on her back, the room spinning around her like one of the tops she had played with as a child. From a very long distance away, someone called out her name.

"Brenna! Brenna, for God's sake."

"No . . ." she mumbled.

"Brenna, what happened?"

She licked her dry lips.

"I heard you scream, and came running. What happened? Did someone hurt you? Did you see who it was?"

"No."

"What happened?"

She shook her head, suddenly seeing in her mind a picture of Neall Urquhart, his eyes dark pits of hate. *No, don't leave, my pretty. We have much to talk about, do we not?* He blamed her for his paralysis. Blamed her . . .

"This kind of thing doesn't happen without a reason," Kane persisted. "Are you sure you didn't recognize him? His face? His clothing?"

"No, no, I didn't. I didn't! How could I?"

"Brenna, you're lying." He gently lifted her onto the bed. She lay savoring the softness of the mattress. "I can see it in your eyes. You know who the man was, don't you?"

"No! I don't know anyone in Havana, I've only been here a few days. You brought me yourself, you should know that."

Kane pursed his lips thoughtfully. "But . . . the man in the dining room. The way he stared at you, as if he knew you."

"But Neall only meant to frighten me!" she burst out. "He's confined to a wheeled chair. He's paralyzed!"

"Neall, is it? Then you do know him."

"No, no, I don't! I—" She fell silent.

"You'd better tell me."

"No. I can't. There isn't anything to tell."

"I think there is. Do you think he came in here for fun? He could have killed you. You were just damned lucky I was downstairs and able to run up so quickly." He was shouting, his eyes blazing at her.

"It . . . it's true that I knew Neall before, but I can't tell you about it."

"And why not?"

She turned her head away from him, and stared stubbornly at the rough plaster wall. "Because I can't. My father made me promise."

"But your father is dead now. This has something to do with your life in Ireland, doesn't it? Tell me about this Neall. What's his last name? And don't think I can't find out for myself, because I can and I will. If I go to the man and demand to know what connection he has with you, he'll tell me fast enough."

"No!" she burst out. "Don't do that!"

"Why not? I want some answers, Brenna!"

"Because," she whispered. "He was my . . . my husband."

Her voice shaking, she told Kane everything. When she

had finished, she didn't dare look at him. She could only hear his feet angrily pacing the floor.

"I see," he said. "I see it all. Your father sold you—that's what it amounts to. And Urquhart blames you for his paralysis, doesn't he?"

"Yes."

"Then I've heard enough! I'll be back soon." He left, slamming the door to the veranda behind him.

"Kane—" she cried. Dread filled her. Kane must have gone to find Neall Urquhart; there was no other possibility.

Kane, oh, Kane, she thought. *What foolish thing are you going to do?*

She sat up, almost crying as the room began to reel, black and white spots dancing in front of her eyes. But she couldn't faint again, she told herself. She got off the bed and went out to look for Kane.

They were at the far end of the veranda just outside Neall's room. Neall's chair was a solid dark block of shadow, Kane's body was silhouetted against the moonlight. Brenna quietly walked up to them. They spoke in low, fierce whispers, and neither noticed her.

"You were going to kill her!" accused Kane.

"You are a bastard of the lowest order even to suggest such a thing," Neall hissed.

"You're lying!"

Neall Urquhart laughed, low in his throat. "Why not call me out? Perhaps that would satisfy you, to challenge a crippled man, a man in a wheeled chair whose legs are just lumps of flesh."

Kane took an involuntary step backward, and Brenna sensed his dismay and revulsion. He, who was so healthy, was facing a ruin of a man.

Again Urquhart laughed. "I was the victor in four affairs of honor, and two of my opponents lie in their graves at this very moment. Of course, that was before I lost the use of my legs, through the fault of that little slut—"

"Leave her out of this."

"Now, be reasonable, my dear man. How can I leave her out of it when she is the central cause? *She pushed me!*"

Brenna sprang forward. "No, it's not true!" she cried.
"It was an accident! Kane, don't believe him, he's lying!
He—"

"Brenna, what are you doing here?"

"You've got to believe it's a lie," she insisted. "I would
never have done such a thing deliberately, I—"

"Shut up, you accursed little bitch!" Neall's hatred
emanated from him, an almost palpable force. *"You*,
with your lovely body and tantalizing breasts. I can picture
you lying in bed with Fairfield, your body squirming under
his . . ."

Neall's hand went to his side, as if searching for something. He lifted the long dueling pistol.

Brenna gasped.

Slowly, deliberately, Neall raised the pistol. His left hand
scrabbled awkwardly on the wheels of the chair as he tried
to maneuver it into a better position. "Now I'll finish what
I started," he sneered.

Kane leaped forward in quick reflex, and wrested the
gun out of Neall's hand.

"Urquhart . . ." Kane began. Brenna knew what pent-up
fury must be in him, screaming for release. Yet he stood
quietly at her side, holding the pistol, as Neall shouted
threats.

"I'll get you, you bitch, I'll slash your face to ribbons.
I'll—"

"Brenna, let us go back to the room. He won't follow."

"But, Kane . . ."

"He is mad." Pity and anger mingled in Kane's voice.
"Now, let's go."

As they walked away, neither of them turned to look at
the figure in the chair, impotently shaking his fists at them.

❧ Chapter 21 ❧

"BRENNA, ARE YOU AWAKE?"

It was three days later. Kane rolled over in the bed, flinging an arm across Brenna's nude body. Early morning sunlight filled the room, casting striped shadows across the mosquito netting. From the street sounded the ringing of church bells, the shout of an oxcart driver, the rumble of his heavy wagon.

"No," she mumbled, burrowing into the pillow. Her body felt so warm, so satisfied, so comfortable. She didn't want to wake up and lose the feeling.

Kane had barely left her side during the past three days. And when he had, he had given her the brace of pistols and told her to shoot to kill if necessary. But it hadn't been necessary. Kane had spoken to Señor Tranquilo, who had ordered Neall to leave the hotel. They had not seen him again.

"Yes, you are awake, I can see your eyelids fluttering."

"No, I'm still sleeping," she told him, half-smiling. She snuggled closer to him, savoring the feel of his bare skin next to hers. They had made love last night, slowly, deliberately, and perfectly. She could still feel the glow in her, the swollen surfeit. How was it possible that she could love him and hate him all at the same time? She didn't know; she only knew that her body wanted him, as if he were some addictive drug that she had to have.

"Come on, sleepy, wake up!" Kane ran a hand over the curve of her hip.

"No . . ."

"It's another gorgeous day, and I promised to take you to mass in the cathedral."

"Today?" She sat up, pulling at her disordered hair. "But I have nothing to wear."

"Your new gowns came yesterday; you'll look wonderful."

Kane sat up, yawning. The sunlight caught his bare torso, making the smooth skin gleam, highlighting the white scar that cut diagonally across his chest. He had received it in a shipboard accident, he had told her once.

"I didn't tell you last night," he said, "but I have learned from Señor Tranquilo that Frontenac and the other witnesses may be staying in Marianao. It's a small village about eight miles out of the city."

"Really?"

"Yes, it's a pretty little village," Kane said absently. "Many of the rich Spaniards have villas there."

"Oh, could I come along with you? Please?" As he looked dubious, she added, "I've been resting for three days, and I feel so much stronger now, really I do. I need to get out."

Kane frowned. "I have to talk to Frontenac. And what I have to say won't be pleasant. I'd rather you weren't there."

"But I can't bear sitting idle here another minute!" she cried. She played her final card. "Besides, I hate staying alone. I worry that Neall might come back." She smiled at him, arching her back like a sensuous cat. "Please? I would wait in the carriage for you, or at a cafe. I can't stay in this room any longer, or I'll go mad!"

"Very well, then. If you promise to wait and not to interfere in any way."

"I promise. Anything to get out of these rooms!"

"Anything?" He pulled her to him.

"Yes . . . anything . . ." Languor swept over her. She abandoned herself to the sensuality of his kiss. At moments like this, all other thoughts flew from her head. It

was as if the two of them filled all the world; were the
world.

"Kane . . ." she choked. "I love you . . ."

Had she really said those words, or only thought them?
She didn't know. She was only aware that he rolled over
on his back, pulling her on top of him, that he guided
himself into her. Then she was moving in wild abandon,
a core of sweetness expanding at the center of her, ex-
ploding her.

They lay twined in each other, their skin moist with
perspiration. She could feel Kane's warm breath in her
ear, growing slower and more regular as the minutes
passed.

"You love me. I'm glad . . ." he said in a voice so low
that she could barely hear it. But before she could reply,
he had fallen asleep.

She sat in front of the small mirror, putting the last
touches to her hair, adjusting the veil that she would wear
to mass. The new gown gave her great satisfaction. A pale
muslin the color of fresh cream, its simple lines and
décolleté neckline revealed the fullness of her breasts.

"You look beautiful." Kane came into the room, adjusting his linen cravat. He, too, had ordered new clothing, and
today wore a green linen coat, its cut making his shoulders
look even broader than they were, his waist narrower. His
vest was of brocade, his fawn-colored pants skin-tight.

"Am I prettier than Coleen?" she dared to ask.

"Far prettier."

She laughed happily, conscious of his eyes on her, filled
once more with unmistakable desire.

Mass was fascinating, with twenty or more priests offici-
ating at the high altar. Through the folds of her veil,
Brenna looked about her at the floor of variegated marble,
the tall pillars, rich paintings and frescoed walls. Afterward, they ate a heavy Cuban breakfast, followed by more
sightseeing, another big meal, and a siesta.

It was after their shortened siesta that they finally left
for Marianao, in a rented *volante* with a driver.

As they bounced out of town, Kane told her about the
slaves he had bought the previous day.

"I bought twelve, each man a prime specimen," he said proudly. "They've already been fattened up and kept out of the cane fields, so they're in good physical shape. They should fetch a handsome sum in New Orleans."

"Oh?" The *Sea Otter* would be a slaver now, she thought uneasily, with all the evil that implied.

"Don't worry," Kane said, as if reading her mind. "These are prime men, and I'll be damned if I'm going to lose half of them by cramming them into the hold like beasts—or worse than beasts, for no one would treat an animal in such a way. I'll put them in the fo'c'sle, and the crew can string their hammocks on deck. That's where they sleep most of the time anyway."

He was going to treat the slaves decently. Brenna felt relieved.

"Of course, we'll have to do something with the female. We can't keep her in with the men."

"The female?"

"I bought a girl, too. She's probably about sixteen, and magnificent, with a face like an Egyptian princess. Her eyes are almost gold, like a cat's. One could almost imagine that they glow in the dark," he said enthusiastically.

Brenna felt a pang. Their past days—especially the hours they had spent in bed—had been so wonderful. And now here Kane was, talking about another woman. Slave or not, she sounded desirable.

"I suppose she is very beautiful," she said.

"Of course. I wanted only prime quality—otherwise, why bother with them?"

"What does she look like?"

"Well, she is tall and slim, and perfectly proportioned, with small, pointed breasts, and—"

"You have seen them?" Brenna asked stiffly. She was glad that the driver, a man named Carlos, could not speak English.

Kane threw back his head and laughed. "Of course I have, you little prude! How else do you think that female slaves are purchased—through the mail? I inspected her from top to toe. It's necessary," he added, as Brenna gasped. "I had to make sure she was free of disease or blemishes."

"Blemishes!"

"Naturally, her potential purchaser will care about things like that, since he is going to pay a very large sum of money for her."

"But to strip her naked, as if she hadn't any feelings . . ." Brenna felt the blood pounding into her face. What if it had been herself standing on the slave block, her own nude body revealed to strange men? She felt a spasm of pity for the unknown black girl.

"It was over quickly. Besides, disgusting as it may seem to you, it's the custom," Kane said coldly. "The advantage is that you'll have a maid during the voyage. Of course, you'll have to teach her English, but she seems bright and tractable enough. I'm sure you'll have no trouble with her."

"And . . . and what is her name?"

"I've decided to call her Glory. It's appropriate enough. Their African names are unpronounceable."

"So she can't even keep her own name."

"No, she can't. Someday I'll tell you why. Now, I think we've discussed this quite enough, don't you?"

"But I don't understand," she burst out. "You are kind enough to these people, you treat them well, and yet—"

"And yet I accept the fact of their slavery. Is that it? Well, I want you to know something. I have read some of the material written by the abolitionists, and I agree with a good deal of it. Do you think I like to see men and women being bought and sold like animals? But slavery does exist. The whole economy of Cuba and of the southern United States depends on slaves to work the huge plantations. How can one man fight that?"

"So you've decided to go along with everyone else, all the rich planters like Patrick and Monty Carlisle, who need men to work in the cane fields!"

"All right. Yes, I have. I'm a practical man, Brenna, not a wild-eyed dreamer. Leave the tilting at windmills to the idealists and the Don Quixotes of the world, not to me."

They rode on in silence, while Brenna seethed. Somehow, in New Orleans she hadn't seen slavery in quite this way. Aunt Rowena's servants hadn't bothered her as much as did the thought of an unknown black girl, inspected for disease and blemishes as if she were a mare.

They were in the countryside now. Ahead of them the road stretched a dusty red-gold under the arch of incredibly blue sky. A wild green profusion of trees and undergrowth crowded the road and gaudy flowers grew everywhere. Often the road ran along the sea, the breakers frothing white.

They left the sea, driving over a picturesque arched bridge. The road clung precariously to the sides of intense green hills. Once they passed a group of tiny palm-thatched hovels, the bare red earth outside them swarming with naked children, donkeys, cows, chickens and dogs. "These are the free black men," Kane said coldly. "The people who drive the city's oxcarts and sell bread, milk and fruit in the streets. Do you think they are any better off than the slaves?"

The village of Marianao, when they reached it, was charming. There was a wide main street lined on either side with two-story, white-pillared villas. Overhead stretched the green of cocoa palms, banana and magnolia trees. South Sea roses, pink and white camellias, and filmy carnations all grew in riotous profusion.

"You'll have to wait in the carriage and look at the flowers while I go and try to find Frontenac and the others," Kane told her. "I have it on good word from one of Señor Tranquilo's friends that he is staying in one of these villas. Perhaps the other witnesses are with him. At any rate, we shall see, won't we? Don't leave the *volante*," he added. "Carlos will wait here with you. You'll be quite safe."

Her wait was short enough. Within ten minutes Kane stormed back out of the villa, his face flushed with anger. "Damn! Just as I was so close! Apparently, Perrier and Cardell died at sea from the fever, and Frontenac left yesterday morning for New Orleans." He slammed his fist onto his knee in frustration. "If I had know where to look from the beginning, if he hadn't covered his trail so well, I might have caught him. Now I'll have to go back to New Orleans, where he'll have a hundred friends who will hide him and lie for him, and where he'll be right under Rynne's thumb again. Damn! This is like trying to catch smoke rings with your bare hands. Just as you think you've grasped something, it all fades away into thin air."

"I'm sorry," she said.

"Sorry! Yes, I am, too. Sorry for a lot of things. If I hadn't decided to hare off to Cuba like this, perhaps young Jemmy might still be alive. Damn, the waste—'"

The late afternoon sun was casting long shadows on the street. Irritably, Kane ordered the coachman to take them to a small inn in the village where, by bribing the owner, they were able to get coffee and a light meal. Kane ate silently, his face so forbidding that Brenna did not dare to talk to him.

As they left the village, Brenna glanced behind them, and was surprised to see a dusty yellow cloud. This meant that another carriage was behind them. They had seen little traffic on the way to Marianao. Save for oxcarts and an occasional donkey laden with produce or fodder, the road had been empty.

"Someone else is driving back to Havana, too," she said, trying to sound cheerful.

"I suppose so," Kane said savagely. "What difference does it make?"

"You needn't take out your frustration on me. It's not my fault that you missed Frontenac!"

After this they fell silent again, and by the time they came to the hilly area she had quite forgotten about the other carriage, and was conscious only of her own discomfort. For the seat of the *volante* was hard. It was not built for long-distance travel, and each rut and bump sent a jarring sensation up through her spine. She felt numb from the constant pounding. The driver, Carlos, seemed oblivious to any hardship, and broke into cheerful singing, his voice floating out over the road until it was swallowed up by the green foliage.

Dusk was upon them. The low hills cast long shadows over the road. Idly Brenna turned to look behind them again. The carriage that was following them was now only a half-mile away. She stared at it, surprised. It was a big, black, English-style carriage, drawn by two matched dark bays and elaborately trimmed with brass.

Strange, she thought uneasily. Most people in Havana seemed to prefer the little open *volantes.* Surely there could not be all that many English-style carriages in the city. Perhaps Neall Urquhart ...

But quickly she squelched the thought, telling herself that she was being foolish. Kane had done a thorough job of scaring off Neall. Neall had left the hotel and was due to leave Havana soon.

At the next curve, when she turned to look, the other carriage seemed slightly closer, its wheels sending up long plumes of dust.

Then, abruptly, almost as if a giant's hand had passed in front of the sun, it was dark. The tops of the trees nearly met over the road, and the carriage seemed to be passing through a black tunnel. Brenna drew in her breath, oddly frightened by the thought. The sharp, hoarse cry of a night bird added to the eery feeling.

A wind sprang up, whipping the branches of the palms back and forth.

"The wind has been blowing all day, but it's stronger now," Brenna said.

Kane did not answer.

They reached the sea again. Great rolling breakers crashed on the white beach, the biggest breakers Brenna had seen since their arrival. Then the full force of the sea wind hit them, blowing Brenna's hair out of its ribbons and lifting the hem of her muslin gown in wild disarray. The noise of the breakers filled their ears, nearly drowning out even the sound of the horse's hooves.

Suddenly Brenna glimpsed a dark shape to their side. The carriage that had been following them was now nearly abreast. Its boxlike shape loomed out of the night, its coachman only a silhouette. Even the pair of horses were nearly invisible against the curtain of trees.

Brenna turned to Kane. "I think that other carriage is trying to pass us!" She had to yell against the noise of the sea.

Kane shouted something to Carlos, who obediently pulled the *volante* to the far right, giving the black carriage room to pass. Like a ghost it drew alongside them, all sound blocked out by the tumbling surf, so that it seemed to move in utter silence.

Why had it followed them, Brenna wondered? And why, only now, as the side of the road sloped precariously down to the sea, had it decided to try to pass them?

The carriage was directly beside them now. The bays'

eyes were shielded with blinders, so that they could only see straight ahead. Their sides heaved with the effort of sustaining their mad pace. The coachman was half-crouched on his box, lashing at the pair with a whip.

Abruptly the black carriage veered toward them, so close now that Brenna could see the white outline of a hand in its side window.

"Kane!" she screamed. "It's going to hit us!"

The *volante* lurched violently as Carlos tried to maneuver it as close to the edge of the road as he could. Their horse's hooves skidded in the loose gravel and shell mixture at the edge, a sickening, slithery sound.

Brenna clutched the wooden sides of the *volante*, her heart hammering inside her. The black carriage veered toward them again, its coachman slashing at his horses until they galloped like mad creatures, froth bubbling from their mouths. Horrified, Brenna heard their own animal's feet slip. Then slip again. The horse would soon lose its balance, pulling the *volante* over with it.

Brenna thought she caught a glimpse of a white face in the interior of the English coach. But it was only a blur. Perhaps she hadn't seen it at all, perhaps it had been only a flash of moonlight.

"Kane! Kane!" Was that her own voice screaming?

Suddenly, the matched pair, maddened by the whip, lunged to the left to avoid a boulder in the road. The coachman lurched, fought to maintain his balance, and then fell. His scream, if there was one, could not be heard.

Driverless, the black carriage thundered on, finally passing them and taking up the whole road, its wheels bouncing wildly. Then, like a creature gone berserk, it swerved toward the right, where the treacherously soft shale fell downward to the beach.

Even over the pounding of the surf, Brenna heard the scream of the terrified horses as the black carriage overturned, flinging its occupant out onto the sand.

❧ *Chapter 22* ❧

THE OVERTURNED CARRIAGE was a dark shape against the sand, moonlight glinting off the brass trim. But Brenna caught only a glimpse of it, for their own horse, maddened with fright, plunged on, dragging the *volante*, its driver and passengers behind him.

Carlos shouted at his horse, trying to slow it. Brenna was slammed from side to side, the hard wooden sides of the *volante* smashing into her ribs. Yet the *volante* plummeted on, lurching from one side of the narrow road to the other, totally out of control.

Only some blind instinct kept the horse on the track. If he slipped, if he made a mistake, the *volante* would overturn, probably killing them all.

Abruptly the road began to climb. Again the *volante* jerked with such force that Brenna bit into her tongue, sending a warm spurt of blood through her mouth.

"Kane!" she screamed. "Kane!"

The crazed little horse bolted away from the road, away from the sea. They were headed for the trees! With incredible slow clarity, the black mass of the palms grew nearer. Brenna could only stare, her throat gone too dry now for screaming. They galloped straight toward the thick trunks. The *volante* would soon crash, dashing their lives out—

The horse stopped.

Sides heaving, breath strangling and whimpering in his

throat, he stopped, and the *volante* creaked to a halt behind him. For an instant there seemed to be only silence, then Brenna heard the distant sound of surf, the screech of a night bird, the choking gasps of the horse.

Carlos broke into a wild gabble of prayer, crossing himself repeatedly.

"We stopped! We're all right!" Brenna brushed back her hair with shaking hands. They were alive. She could barely believe it.

"I knew he'd tire eventually," Kane said. "Especially pulling uphill like that—if he didn't drop dead first. But thank God the animal had a bit of sense remaining in his foolish head. We won't be able to use him further, of course. He's completely spent."

Brenna looked at him. Kane was calmly adjusting his coat. "Weren't you even frightened? I was terrified! We . . . we were almost run off the road. And then our own horse, running away—"

"Of course I was frightened. But there isn't time for talking now. You'd better wait here with Carlos while I go back and see what happened to the other carriage."

"Oh, no." She pulled up her skirts and climbed out of the *volante* unassisted. "I am coming with you. If that was Neall . . ." She licked her lips. "I want to come with you. I think I should. I owe that to him, at least."

"It's quite a walk for someone in kid slippers."

Brenna looked down at herself. Her muslin dress was badly crumpled, ripped at the midriff where she had smashed into the side of the *volante*. Already her ribs hurt with a dull, aching throb, and she knew she must be badly bruised.

"I don't care about my shoes. I'm coming with you. I'm not some pale lily of a girl who's never walked more than a few paces in her life. And you can't stop me," she said loudly. "I can walk just as fast as you can, and you can't prevent me from coming!"

He did not reply, but turned and walked off toward the road. She took his silence as assent, and began to hurry along beside him, trying to match her paces to his. She was a grown woman now, she told herself rebelliously. She didn't want to be babied and protected and coddled. She wanted to see what had happened.

The moon had risen full and pale, so close that she could see the pitted features of its face. Perhaps the old man in the moon had had smallpox, she had time to think, forcing back a nervous laugh.

They knew they had reached the overturned carriage long before they actually saw it, for one of the horses was screaming, high and tortured.

Horrified, Brenna staggered to the grass at the side of the road, turning her back to the overturned carriage and fighting back the metallic acid that rose in her throat.

There was the sound of a pistol shot. Brenna's body jerked as if the bullet had gone into her. The screaming stopped. There was only the noise of the night insects, scraping and whistling in the underbrush.

"Well, that takes care of him, anyway, poor devil." Kane came toward her. "The other horse was already dead —a broken neck. Poor beasts—it's a damn shame that anyone should have used them so hard. They deserved better." He peered at her. "You look a bit shaky."

"I'm fine," she gasped. "Just a little . . . sick . . ."

To her relief, Kane did not say *I told you so,* but merely touched her arm, then drew his other pistol. "You'll be all right. I'm going to see what else there is. You stay here. This is nothing you'll want to see."

Brenna struggled to overcome her sickness. She wiped her mouth on the hem of her gown, feeling a pang for the lovely muslin, ruined now by dust and perspiration. She stood breathing deep gulps of the tangy sea air.

At last, trembling, she picked her way over the sand to the overturned carriage silhouetted in the moonlight. Kane was not in sight, evidently hidden by the bulk of the carriage.

There was a faint sound.

She stopped, her heart twisting.

The sound came again, a thready, bubbly kind of breathing. A gasp that went on and on, fighting for air.

Slowly she walked around the carriage, the sand giving way beneath her slippers. Kane was kneeling near something. Something black, something that lay hideously twisted and crumpled, something that struggled to breathe.

"Neall."

She looked down at him. He lay grotesquely curled around a large, pointed boulder, cradling it to him like a child. The tip of the boulder had crushed his chest, and oily spurts of blood stained the sand. He was conscious, his emaciated face coated with a sheen of perspiration. His eyes focused toward the sea, as if he listened intently to the sound of the breakers. His clothing, so black against the sand, made him look like a monstrous spider, half-crushed.

Brenna took a step backward, stifling a scream.

"I told you not to look," Kane said. "But don't worry, the blackguard can't hurt you ever again. He hasn't got long now—probably only a few minutes more. But he won't give up. After all he's been through, he still wants to live."

The breathing noise continued, a rattling, struggling whistle. It all seemed unreal, Brenna thought suddenly. The whole scene—the black carriage, the bodies of the two horses, the man crushed like a spider. Yet this was Neall, the man she had married. The man who had possessed her body without love, who had twice tried to kill her.

Virginity, she thought. All of this for virginity. And for pride.

And she didn't feel anything. Not anger, not hatred, not even disgust. She could only stare down at him, at this man with the crushed chest, dying before her eyes. Yes, she thought. Dying. The thin face looked more skeletal than ever, the high cheekbones brutally shadowed.

Something made her step closer and kneel down beside him. The sand felt hard and cold through the fabric of her skirt.

"Neall," she whispered. "Can you hear me?"

The labored breathing changed tempo, paused. The eyes flickered.

"Neal, I . . . I'm so sorry. Sorry it turned out like this."

The bloodless lips twisted ironically. The scar on the left cheek was slashed with silver. "No . . ." Words came out of his mouth. "No . . . you . . . bitch . . ."

Brenna pressed her lips together until they hurt. Absurd, monstrous, that she should feel anger at a dying

man. But she did. Anger surged in her veins like the force
of the breakers. She was powerless to stop it.

"You are dying for your own mistakes, not mine!" she
cried in a low, intense voice. "Your paralysis was your
own fault. This accident was your own fault. You paid that
coachman to run us over the cliff, didn't you?"

"You . . . deserve . . ." Neall struggled for another
breath, his mouth working. "I curse . . . you. . . . May you
be . . . used for the rest . . . of your . . . life like a . . ."

Feather words, barely whispered. She had to lean close
to hear them, nausea choking at her again.

". . . like a pig . . ." His black eyes were slits of triumph, catching and reflecting the face of the moon.

May you be used for the rest of your life like a pig.
The words hung in the air like a poisonous fog. Quickly
she glanced at Kane. He hadn't heard; he was frowning,
staring across the road at the forest as if thinking of other
things.

"You can't mean that," she gasped. "Neall, whatever
happened, you can't—"

"Do . . . mean . . . it . . ."

Had she really heard those last words? The lips had
barely moved. And now a film spread over the staring eyes.
A hand twitched against the boulder, then was still.

"Neall!"

"He's dead," Kane said. "You didn't think he could live
long with a wound like that, did you?"

She was crying wildly, unable to stop herself.

"For God's sake, Brenna, what are you crying for? The
man tried to kill you at least twice. And he treated you
horribly as your husband. You should be glad he's dead.
You're free now. Free."

Sobs racked her, painful and tearing. She didn't know
why she was crying. The reasons were buried somewhere
inside her, beyond all rationality. But she couldn't stop.
All the horrors of the past weeks and months were bursting out of her in one torrent.

A slap stung her face, and another one.

"Brenna, don't you dare collapse into hysteria on me
now. Don't forget the other man, the coachman. He's lying back there on the road somewhere. I'm going to go

and see to him. You can stay here if you wish. With the body of the husband you seem to be mourning with such passion."

"No," she said. "I'm not mourning him. I—"

"Then get yourself under control. And wait here. I'll be right back."

She clung to his arm. "No, no, don't leave me. I'll come with you."

"Very well. Come along, then. It shouldn't be far."

They found Neall's coachman lying like a twisted heap of rags in the center of the road.

"He's dead, too," Kane said. He poked at the corpse with a foot. "I can't tell how. Maybe a blow on the head, maybe a broken neck. At any rate, he got what he deserved."

"No . . ." she whispered.

"Regrets for him, too? The man brutalized those horses and tried to kill us. Can't you understand that? As far as I'm concerned, he isn't even worth burying." Kane pressed his lips together, and looked about him, as if deciding something. "Well, there's nothing further we can do here. We'll have to walk back into the city. It's only a few miles."

"But we can't just . . . leave them . . . here like this!"

"We certainly can. These men tried to murder us, Brenna. Why should we worry about their remains? As a matter of fact, I intend to do nothing further about them."

"Nothing further? But the authorities—"

"The authorities, dear girl, are Spanish. You've seen some of the charming fortifications they have here. I, for one, don't intend to find out if any of the torture devices are still in use."

"But this wasn't our fault! How could they possibly blame us?"

"Who knows? At any rate, there could be an investigation that might last three or more days. I want to leave right away. Carlos will keep quiet if I pay him; the whole thing will look like just another carriage accident. Runaway horses are common enough. In the morning the bodies will be discovered, and probably thoroughly looted by the peasants. By the time they are finished, the authorities won't be able to tell what happened."

Brenna shivered. "But we'll be seen walking. Someone might ask questions."

"Not if we hurry. We can always explain that our horse went lame. By the looks of him, that won't be a lie. Now come on, Brenna, let's go. I want to get as far away from here as possible."

His hand pushed at the small of her back, and she walked, one foot stumbling in front of the other. She felt numbed by what she had seen. Surely it had been only an ugly nightmare, to be forgotten as soon as she awoke, safe beside Kane in the iron bedstead.

But it was no dream. Her aching feet told her that, as her thin-soled shoes began to wear through, carving out blisters on the toes and heels of her feet. Beside her Kane seemed quiet, glum. When they reached the *volante*, Kane spoke sharply to Carlos, who answered in a flood of Spanish.

"What is he saying?" Brenna asked.

"He wants me to spare the animal—it's the only source of income he has. He's a free man of color, and he has a family depending on him. The horse will collapse if it's forced to work."

"What are we going to do?"

"We'll walk," Kane said shortly.

It was very late when they reached their hotel; Kane had to pound on the door for Señor Tranquilo to come and unlock it. The plump little man did not ask them any questions, but rolled his eyes and pursed his lips, as if he had caught them doing something nasty. Brenna hid her anger, and followed Kane upstairs.

As soon as they got inside the door of their rooms, she stooped to slip out of her shoes and ease her burning feet. But Kane stopped her.

"I don't care how tired you are or how much your feet hurt. You can't go about these rooms barefoot."

"But my feet hurt so."

"They'll hurt worse if you get a festering wound and your foot has to be amputated." Then Kane's voice softened. "All right, then, we'll soak your feet. That should help. Sit up on the bed."

Obediently she sat on the edge of the high bed while Kane lit the oil lamp, Then he half-filled the basin with tepid water. Kneeling, he took off her shoes.

"You're blistered," he said. "You should have stayed with Carlos, as I asked you."

It was very late, they had seen a man die, she had walked miles, her feet hurt. "Perhaps I should have!" she snapped at him. "But I didn't. And now my feet are all blisters, and it's my fault, right? All my fault!" She could have wept.

"No," he said shortly, lowering her feet into the tepid water. It felt so soothing that she almost gasped with relief. "No, it's my fault. I was thinking of this as we walked back. I shouldn't have brought you to Havana. I was a fool. But unfortunately, now I can only take you back to New Orleans as soon as possible. You're free now, Brenna. The bargain's over."

"Over?"

He stood up, and went to the window, where he carefully closed the shutters. He didn't look at her.

She stared at him. How many times had she longed to hear those words? How often had she hated Kane, resented him, loathed him? And yet now she felt abandoned. She felt as if everything important in the world had been taken away from her.

"That's right, it's over," he was saying. "It was a damn fool thing I did, snatching you from under Rynne's nose like a child grabbing candy from a bully. And you've suffered for it. You nearly died of the fever—it was a miracle you pulled through. Here in Havana you were nearly killed. If I hadn't brought you away, none of it would have happened." He fastened the shutters with a sharp click. "So, it's all over. I'll take you back and deposit you at your uncle's. Let him decide what to do with you. Let him have the responsibility. I'm through."

She stood up, her feet still in the water. Her whole body was shaking. She felt as if she could cry and shout and scream, all at the same time.

"You're tired of me, then. Is that it? You always said you'd get rid of me when you grew weary of me."

His back was still to her, his hands clenched into fists at his sides. "No. I'm not tired of you. I . . . but I can't marry you, Brenna. I've told you that, and I've told you why. I shouldn't have taken you away under those circumstances. I just couldn't stand the thought of Rynne using you as the central attraction for one of his perverted little circuses—oh, yes, circuses!" he snapped, as she drew in her breath sharply. He began to strip off his jacket in swift, bitter motions. "It's common enough knowledge in New Orleans what that man does for his pleasure."

"No!" She felt as if he had hit her.

"Nevertheless, it was one of the few damn-fool things I've done in my life, going off with you, and I thoroughly regret it. Oh, you needn't worry, I'll provide for you amply. I'll leave you sufficient funds so that you can move to another city with your brother, buy some property and start over again. You'll be able to live comfortably for the rest of your life. You'll have to call yourself a widow, of course. But that shouldn't be much of a problem. With your looks, I'm sure the men will be standing in line to marry you—"

She stepped out of the basin, water flying, and smacked him across the face. She hit him so hard that her own palm stung. "How dare you! How dare you treat me like a common whore? I'm not a . . . a woman like Maud Sweet, to be paid off. I don't care about money!"

Kane did not even touch his reddened cheek. "Oh? You don't care about money? I thought you did. I thought you went with me to get money for your brother, so he wouldn't be killed for his gambling debts."

"Well, I hadn't anyone to turn to, I had to! But that was *then*, Kane. Now I . . . now it's all different!" *I love you*, she wanted to scream at him. *I never could love anyone else, ever. Only you.* But the words choked in her throat.

"Different? I hardly think so. Things are still the same. Our bargain has been discharged satisfactorily—more than satisfactorily, wouldn't you agree? After all, my settlement will leave you and your brother well provided for the rest of your lives. That is much more than originally agreed upon. As for you, you've given me your body, and I've found the arrangement to be . . . quite nice. Quite thoroughly pleasant."

"Pleasant!" Brenna backed away from him. "Get away from me!" she screamed. "Get away, get to the other room, go anywhere. But just leave me alone!"

He looked at her for a long moment. Then he went into the second room, and closed the connecting door.

❧ *Chapter 23* ❧

SHE HAD FALLEN ASLEEP, exhausted from crying. But even her dreams were full of Kane, his strong arms sponging her after her fever, touching her as they shared a small joke. *Kane . . . Oh, please. . . .* She turned in her sleep, reaching out for the man who should have been beside her in the bed and wasn't.

Gradually she passed into a deeper sleep, a sleep that mercifully erased all dreams. She was a stone, falling into blackness, small, round, and cold, and very alone.

Then something warm touched her. From the depths of her sleep she felt it, something warm stroking her back, pulling her out of the deep well of loneliness.

Darling, I didn't mean . . . I didn't mean to hurt you like that . . .

Was that Kane, whispering to her so softly? Or was she still caught in the heaviness of slumber? It was a dream, she was sure of it. A torment devised by her grieving brain to show her what she had lost. She stirred in the bed, feeling a rain of soft, light kisses on the places where her tears had dried.

She sighed and turned over. She was warm velvet. His hands cupped her breasts, massaged them, stroking her nipples until they were erect and sensitive. The strokes became softer, yet more intense, each one drawing a thrill of pleasure from deep in her groin.

His fingers savored her, running lightly over her skin until she could feel herself moistening, could feel herself ready, her legs opening, her hips arching to receive him.

Not yet, darling. Not yet, the soft whisper came. She felt his hands on the flesh of her inner thighs, stroking her, each touch a spurt of flame, until she almost exploded before he put—

He was inside her. Their bodies moved together, and quick joy crescendoed in her. But he was not finished yet. Slowly, inexorably, he drew her up again. Drew her trembling and moaning with him upward and upward, until she nearly screamed with dizziness. Up higher still, and then he was plunging into the deep center of her, into the very core of her being. Again she exploded, her body molten, burning in red-hot arcs, her climax deeper and more powerful than anything she had known before.

She never felt him leave her, or roll over beside her on the bed. She had fallen asleep again instantly, like a stone falling into that heavy dreamless darkness.

It was morning. She felt sunlight against her eyelids.

"So you're awake. You slept long enough, my sweet." She stirred in the bed, conscious of a full, swollen feeling in her groin. She opened her eyes. He was standing naked at the basin, washing himself, his body lean and perfect as an animal's. Men were not supposed to be beautiful, she knew. But he was. There was not an ounce of fat on him, not an ugly thing about his body. Even the faint scar across the ribs did not mar the powerful lines of his chest.

"Yes, I'm awake." She did not know what to say to him. Her eyes were still swollen from weeping. And she had had a dream last night—or had it been a dream? By the feel of her own body, she knew it had not been. And looking down at herself, she saw that she was nude, her skin still flushed where he had touched it.

"Do you feel better this morning?"

The events of last night flooded back to her. Neall's death. Kane's announcement that their bargain was completed, that he would never marry her.

"Better?" she asked shakily. "Yes . . ."

He had finished washing. He turned and began pulling on his smallclothes, his movements brisk. "Good, because we have much to do today. We're setting sail in a few hours, and I want you to be packed and ready. Scroggins has been signing on crew and gathering supplies. I sent a message to him this morning. We should have a good voyage."

"Today? We leave today?"

"Why not? I must get back to New Orleans, and the sooner the better."

"But what about me? What will happen to me?"

"I will take you to your uncle's. Then you can make whatever plans you wish."

She turned her face away from him. *Dear God*, she thought. She thought of Uncle Amos, his face puffy with rage. Aunt Rowena, her lips tight. They must hate her by now, she thought. She had thwarted their plans and humiliated them publicly. How could she crawl back to them? As for Toby . . . she shivered.

Well, she would think of something, she decided with sudden resolve. There was a long voyage ahead of them. Perhaps she could get Kane to change his mind and marry her. *Why not?* she thought defiantly. *Why not?*

The remainder of the morning was hectic. They ate a quick, light breakfast of fruit and coffee in their room. Afterward Brenna pulled on the pale yellow organdy gown, the only one of her new dresses that had not been ruined. Carefully she packed their clothes, and bribed the maid to bring her a crate of oranges, plantains and bananas to take aboard ship with her.

Kane had gone to see to last-minute details, so when her packing was completed, Brenna sat gazing out the window at the street, waiting impatiently for him. In a way, she would miss Havana, she realized with surprise. The narrow, cobbled streets, the high brooding walls of the convents and cathedrals, the pastel houses, the flowers—she would never be able to think of these without remembering Kane and the moments they had spent together.

An hour later, they were aboard the *Sea Otter*. A straggling group of black men was lined up on the foredeck, under the supervision of Scroggins, who had a pistol at his belt. Dressed in crumpled white garments belted at the waist with rope, the men seemed oddly alike, all tall, all black, all with faces beaded with perspiration from the hot sun. Heavy iron chains secured them, linking one individual to the next. *A chain gang*, Brenna thought with dismay. A chain gang aboard the ship.

"So these are the slaves," she said to Kane.

"Yep," Scroggins said before Kane could answer. His gold teeth flashed briefly. "Waiting to be inspected afore going to the fo'c'sle. I still say we should put 'em in the hold where they belong—they're going to stink up the whole ship, sir, begging your pardon."

"No, they won't. The *Sea Otter* is no slaver, and I'll be damned if we're going to smell like one," Kane said.

"Aye, sir." Scroggins' face tightened slightly; his dislike for the slaves was plain. "And what about the girl, sir? Surely she could be thrown in with the rest of 'em. It ain't as if she's a great lady or nothing like that."

"I said she's going in a separate cabin, and that's what I meant. She's valuable property and I don't want her savaged. Now bring her aft, and let's get these men stowed away, too. We'll put them in lighter chains so they can move about. And don't worry—you and the rest of the crew will be amply paid for your inconvenience when we reach New Orleans."

Scroggins withdrew a key from his pocket and released the last man in line, giving him a shove in the small of the back that sent him stumbling forward. Clad like the others, in wrinkled trousers and loose, ragged shirt, the man stood with bent head, staring at the holystoned boards of the deck.

"But, Kane. You said there was to be a girl aboard. I don't see her," Brenna said, puzzled.

"There." He pointed. "That's Glory. When I bought her she was wearing a dress, but evidently they kept that, and put her in those rags she's wearing now."

"You don't mean . . . that's she?" The figure moved slightly, and the wind pushed against the shirt, revealing firm, round breasts. The baggy clothing seemed to conceal a slim figure, delicately constructed with long bones and a long, slender neck. The girl's skin was velvet brown, her mouth curved but firm, her nose straight. Her short, kinky hair clung to the lines of her well-shaped skull, giving her an exotic look. In other clothes, she would have been lovely.

"But she's dressed as a man—!" Brenna blurted.

"What do you want me to do, strip her naked right
here just to prove she's female? Take my word for it,
she is. Now, if you don't like what she's wearing, why
don't you take her to our cabin and find her something of
yours to wear. I guarantee you she'll look more civilized
in some decent clothes."

Slowly, unsure of herself, Brenna gestured to the black
girl. The girl looked up, her brown-gold eyes blank.

"I'm Brenna. *Brenna.* Come with me. I won't hurt you,
I promise you that."

The girl still stared, not understanding. Then Scroggins
gave her another push, and reluctantly Glory followed
Brenna. She moved with a sinuous muscular glide that
made Brenna think of a wild creature.

They went down the companionway, the girl clinging
fearfully to the support rope behind Brenna.

"Don't worry, we're just going below. I won't hurt you,
truly I won't. No one here will hurt you." Brenna tried to
make her voice soft and soothing. Even if the girl couldn't
understand her words, she might understand the tone.
When they reached the passageway, she reached out and
gave the black girl's hand a quick squeeze. The girl looked
at her, her dark eyes solemn and reserved. A faint sheen of
moisture glittered in them.

"I don't like those clothes you're wearing," Brenna
went on, feeling slightly silly, as if she were talking to
herself. "You look exactly like a man, like a—" She
stopped. She had almost said *slave.* She hurried on. "I have
some old dresses which might do for you very nicely.
They're not very colorful, and I'm afraid they might be a
bit small for you—you're taller than I am—but perhaps we
can alter them to fit. We'll try, anyway."

She pulled open the door to the cabin, then stepped
backward, gasping. There was someone in the saloon—a
tall, slim woman dressed in sea-green silk that clung to
every line of her figure, her red hair burnished in the light
that streamed in from the porthole.

"Welcome aboard," said Coleen O'Reilly. "I've been
wondering if you people would ever get here."

"What are you doing here?" Brenna cried.

"Why, waiting, of course. What else would I be doing?"

"But Kane doesn't know you're here. I'm sure he doesn't. You're a stowaway, aren't you?"

"A stowaway?" Coleen smiled slowly and deliberately, showing her perfect teeth. "I'm not so foolish to think I could hide on such a small ship. Kane would only have to turn back and put me ashore. No, I have a much more simple and direct plan. I will simply ask him to give me passage. After all we have been to each other, he can hardly refuse me."

After all we have been to each other.

"No. Oh, no, you're not coming aboard this ship! In the first place, we're not going to Boston but straight to New Orleans. Secondly, Kane wouldn't do such a thing to his friend Patrick. You're the wife of a very ill man—you have no right to be here!"

"My husband is not a 'very ill man,' as you call him. He is dead."

"What?"

"Patrick died early this morning of an extremely bloody and unpleasant hemorrhage. And I decided to take this opportunity to get out of Cuba right away. I stayed with him while he was alive, didn't I? I listened to his horrible coughing, I socialized with his ghastly friends and pretended I didn't know he was dying. Well, it's all over. He's dead now, and I don't owe him anything. I hate the sight of this city—the very sight and sound and smell of it. I won't endure it another second."

"But, the funeral. The arrangements, the plantation, the house—you can't just leave it all and sail away!"

"I can't? I already have. Don't worry, a friend of mine, an attorney, will handle my financial interests. I trust him; he'll sell the estate and send me the money. He'll even attend the funeral for me. I hate funerals, why should I have to put myself through it? I didn't love Patrick—I won't mourn him. I've done my duty by him, and no one can demand any more from me!"

"But Kane won't take you along! He—"

"Are you so sure of that? Leave the cabin at once—you and that black creature. Send Kane down here. I'll talk to him, in the privacy of the cabin. And you needn't worry. I'll persuade him. I know exactly how to do it."

Pulling Glory with her, Brenna left the cabin and slammed the door behind her. For a moment she stood in the passageway, too angry to speak. How dare Coleen do this? How dare she! Stowing herself aboard the *Sea Otter*, expecting to bend Kane to her bidding. Well, she couldn't. She, Brenna, would see to that. She would see to it that Kane put Coleen ashore at once.

"Wait here," she told Glory, gesturing to the girl.

The black girl looked at Brenna, her eyes dark with fear.

"I said wait here. No one will hurt you, I promise. And I'll be right back. And I'll get you the gowns just as I said. Oh, I wish you could understand me!" Had she reassured the girl? Brenna didn't know. But Glory stood where Brenna had left her, her body pressed into the bulkhead, her face resigned.

On deck, Brenna found Kane in the fo'c'sle.

"Kane—" She pulled him aside. "Kane, I've got to talk to you."

"Can't it wait? I want to get these slaves settled."

"No, it's got to be now. Please, Kane."

"Very well, then." Kane spoke quickly to Scroggins. "Make sure you put pallets on the deck, so they have something to lie on. And I want them well fed—no swill. We'll give them exercise twice a day, and a bath on deck every morning. And buckets, Scroggins. I want buckets in here for them to relieve their bodily functions. I'll be damned if I'm going to have this ship smelling like an outhouse. We may be carrying slaves but we don't have to smell like it. Now, what is it, Brenna?" He guided her toward the rail. "This is a busy time for me. I've got gold to secure—Señor Tranquilo is sending a shipment to New Orleans to be invested. And we've rum aboard as well. Why don't you wait for me in the cabin? I'll be down as soon as I can."

"But I *can't* wait there," she said desperately. "Someone is already in the cabin."

"Someone there? What are you talking about? Do you mean one of the crew?"

"No, I mean—" She paused, all of her resolve shrinking.

"Then what are you babbling about? Are you trying to tell me that someone has come aboard this ship without my knowledge?" Kane turned toward Scroggins, who had just emerged from the fo'c'sle. "Scroggins, Brenna tells me there is someone aboard ship. What do you know about it?"

"Why, I . . . she promised she wouldn't stay long, sir. She said she had something to deliver to you that couldn't wait, sir, that's what she told me. She said she'd leave, sir, before we sailed. I made her promise to that, I did."

"You made *who* promise?"

"Why, the lady. I don't know her name, sir. But she said she knew you."

"Well, see to the ship. I'll just go down and see who this woman is. I'm growing rather curious." A light glinted in Kane's eyes. Was it amusement? Expectation?

As he turned toward the companionway, Brenna grasped his arm. "Kane, don't let her come aboard. She'll cause nothing but trouble, I know she will. She—"

"Don't tell me what to do aboard my own ship, Brenna."

Helplessly she watched him disappear below deck. He couldn't let Coleen remain aboard, she thought wildly. He just couldn't!

It seemed hours that she stood by the rail, the ship still at anchor, gazing out at the massed boats in the harbor. Why, she thought rebelliously, couldn't Coleen have decided to take some other ship, instead of the *Sea Otter?* And what were they doing down there, she and Kane, closeted together for so long?

The minutes passed. She heard Scroggins shouting out orders to the crew, who were raising and securing the sails, clambering in the rigging like deft monkeys. She saw some new faces—undoubtedly men Scroggins had signed on in Havana. A fresh, steady wind blew on her face, lifting strands of her hair and blowing them against her cheeks.

I know exactly how to persuade him, Coleen had said.

Brenna shivered. No, she thought. She couldn't stay here anymore, waiting like a dismissed servant. She had to know what was happening.

She turned and hurried toward the companionway. She ran down the steps with quick resolve. Glory still stood in the lower passage, pressed against the bulkhead, her eyes shining white in the semidarkness.

"It's all right," Brenna whispered. She gestured to the girl to wait. Then, swallowing hard, she crept toward the cabin door.

She stopped outside the door, her pulse beating loudly in her ears. No sounds came from behind the heavy wood. Yet she knew they were there. It was the only place they could be.

Silence.

What were they doing?

Suddenly her hand found the handle of the door and pushed it open. She stepped inside the saloon. The room was in semidarkness, its brasswork glinting. The mahogany table where Kane wrote his log, and where they ate their meals, was bare.

She stood listening. There were sounds coming from the cabin beyond. Intimate sounds.

She felt the blood pushing through her veins like a sudden cold wash of seawater. She drew one quick, gasping breath, then turned and fled. In the passage, she stopped and collapsed against the bulkhead, helplessly sobbing.

❧ Chapter 24 ❧

FOR A LONG TIME Brenna stood shuddering, unable to stop weeping. But at last she felt Glory pulling at her sleeve, urging her up on deck. Numbly, she followed, no longer caring where she went or what she did.

They stood together at the stern, the Irish girl and the slave, watching the sea glitter at the mouth of the harbor. They were going home, Brenna thought dully. But what did that mean for her? She no longer had a home. Her place, such as it was, had been with Kane. Now that was gone. After the sounds she had heard—

No, she must stop thinking about that. She must try to get control of herself, or she would throw herself into the shark-infested harbor. And no matter what happened, there was too much life in her for that.

"B-na?" Glory was pointing to her, trying to say her name.

"No, it's Brenna. *Brenna*. And you . . . you're *Glory*." Carefully she repeated the name.

"Glo-ry."

"That's right. Oh, Glory, I think you're going to learn very fast. By the time we get to New Orleans, perhaps I can have you speaking some English. Would you like that? Oh," she sighed. "I wish you could talk to me. It would help so—"

She heard Kane's voice behind her. She turned, the words freezing in her throat. Kane and Coleen were com-

ing up the companionway. Coleen daintily held her dress
down so the wind would not lift her skirts. Her eyes looked
flushed, bright and triumphant.

"You have another passenger," Coleen called out, her
voice lilting.

Brenna stared back stonily. Had they heard her in the
saloon? Had they known she was there? Well, it didn't
matter. She hated them both. Hated them. A hard knot
pushed at the back of her throat. She would never be able
to forgive Kane.

Kane adjusted the set of his jaunty coat, looking as
composed as ever. He smiled at her as if nothing unusual
had happened.

"We are taking Coleen to New Orleans with us," he
explained. "Against my better wishes, she has persuaded
me. From there, she assures me she can secure passage to
Boston."

"It does not seem like the most direct route," Brenna
said coldly.

"It isn't, and I'm well aware of that." Coleen smiled,
her triumph complete. "But I need to get away, to take the
fresh sea air, to be among friends—I am among friends,
am I not?"

"Accommodations will be extremely crowded, Coleen.
I suppose you hadn't thought of that, had you?" Brenna
asked angrily.

"I had." Kane's eyes glinted. "Since we have three females aboard, I will simply vacate my cabin and leave it
to you. We have extra bedding and hammocks. You should
all be comfortable enough. I will share the mates' cabin
with Scroggins."

"Both of us, in the same cabin?" Coleen gasped. She
and Brenna turned toward Kane, their faces equally dismayed.

"Enough." Kane was laughing. "The Sea Otter is small,
and not built for passengers. If either of you is displeased
with your accommodations, there is still time to put you
ashore." He paused. "No? Neither of you wishes to stay
in Havana? Then you'll accept the arrangements I have
made. Coleen, you may stow your gear in the cabin.
Brenna, I would like to talk with you a moment, privately."

Pouting, Coleen went below. Glory stood waiting, her features unreadable.

Instantly Brenna turned upon Kane. "So the three of us are to share your cabin!"

"What do you mean?" Kane's fingers bit into her upper arm.

"Please let go of me, you're hurting!"

"Not until you tell me what this nonsense is about. Are you angry because I offered Coleen passage back to New Orleans? Well, you've no right to be."

"I'm angry because . . . oh, Coleen told me she had ways of persuading you to take her along, and I guess she did. She certainly was persuasive, was she not?"

"Coleen and I are old friends. What we had together is none of your concern."

"Oh, it's none of my concern, is it?" Her voice broke. "You sleep with me, you hold me, you . . . and then you turn to her. To someone else, after what we had. . . ."

His face softened. "Whether you choose to believe it or not, I did nothing with Coleen but hold and comfort her. It wasn't important—just an act of friendship, if you can understand such a thing. The girl has gone through her husband's long and wearying illness, she's had no friend, no one to turn to—"

"Isn't that too bad!" Brenna stormed. "What you and Coleen did was not important, you say? Well, it was important to me. It hurt *me*. But you don't care about that, do you?"

"Brenna, Brenna, you are beginning to sound exactly like a fishwife." His hand caressed her back lightly. Even in her rage, Brenna felt a betraying curl of sweetness somewhere inside. "Is this what I'd get if I married you? Harridan scoldings and tongue-lashings?"

"No!" she sputtered. "No, of course not! Do you think I would . . ." She drew a deep breath, clenching her fists in helpless fury. "Oh, you make me so angry, Kane Fairfield! I . . . I could hit you!"

"Don't. Once we put to sea, I'm captain of this vessel, and I might construe your actions as mutiny. What would you think of that, eh?"

Was he laughing at her? Did his dimples flash in amusement? Brenna whirled and ran to the foremost part of the bow, where she stood trembling as the ship lifted anchor.

The weather held, although Kane said that the barometer was falling, and they might expect a storm within the next day or so.

"Storm?" quavered Coleen, looking at Kane appealingly.

Brenna turned stonily aside. She didn't care if there was a storm. And she would not ask Kane for anything, even for reassurances.

The captain's cabin, thanks to Coleen, was no longer a refuge. Brenna spent as little time there as possible, preferring to be on deck, gazing out at the endless, white-capped waves. Grimly she wore her sunbonnet, and fashioned a rude covering for Glory out of a torn petticoat. Without the dark girl, Brenna did not know what she would have done. For it was Glory who gave a purpose to the slow days. Standing or sitting near the rail, Brenna coached her in English for hours at a time, pleased that the girl mastered the language so swiftly.

In two days, Glory learned hundreds of words, and began to put them in sentences, smiling proudly with each achievement. Her accent was soft and faintly burry, like Brenna's own. Dressed in Brenna's altered brown merino dress, Glory was attractive. In a dress of more flattering color, with a proper fit, she would be stunning, her exotically sculptured face giving her the look of some foreign princess.

As perhaps she was. It was said that many of the slaves claimed to be royalty of some kind or another. But of course, once captured, that made no difference to their owners, Brenna thought ruefully. They were slaves all the same.

To Brenna's relief, Coleen spent most of her time in the cabin, lying on the bunk or working at embroidery. She showed no signs of seasickness, even though the ship pitched heavily in the rising sea. The first day aboard, Coleen had claimed the bunk for her own. Brenna and Glory, she said, could occupy hammocks in the saloon.

"Very well," Brenna had said coldly. "What difference does it make?"

"None, none at all," the other had replied, smiling but not relinquishing her place.

Brenna had forced back an angry reply and left the cabin, wishing for the hundredth time that Coleen had chosen any ship but Kane's. If it had not been for Coleen ... but she refused to think about that now. She and Kane were barely speaking. For all Brenna knew, Kane and Coleen were sleeping together every day. But it didn't matter anymore. Everything was over between herself and Kane.

The storm crept up on them gradually. Throughout the day the waves grew higher. While they were eating supper in the saloon, a sudden pitch of the *Sea Otter* slid all the dishes and crockery onto the floor in a sloshing mess.

Later, on deck, Brenna stood with Glory amidships and watched the huge rollers, pushed by a fierce wind that had whipped them up into terrifying small mountains, some bigger than the *Sea Otter* herself. The ship had started to roll in the troughs of these waves, each dip of her bow bringing a torrent splashing over the deck. Exhilaration swept through Brenna. The sea was so powerful. If it chose, it could shake the *Sea Otter* off its back, as a dog dislodges an ant.

Glory, too, stared out at the waves. Sea spray showered both of them until their gowns were damp, and heavy with salt. "Brenna? Ship . . . go . . . ?" She made a dunking motion with her hands.

"No, Glory, no. Of course not," Brenna said. "Nothing is going to happen to us. It's merely a storm, that's all. It will blow over in a few hours, I'm sure."

As she spoke, the deck tilted under them, and she staggered, grasping one of the stays for support. An enormous sweep of gray water flowed across the deck, covering their feet, as Kane came back from the bow, dressed in an oil-skin slicker, his face wet with spray.

"My God, what are you doing up here, Brenna? Haven't you any better sense?"

"I wanted to see the storm. I like to watch it."

For an instant she thought she saw a flicker of understanding in his eyes. Then his face twisted impatiently. "You're a fool, then. Don't you realize that the deck is the

most dangerous place to be during a storm? The waves
are getting bigger by the minute. Any second now one of
them is going to sweep over this deck waist-high. Waist-
high, Brenna! Do you have any idea what that means?"

"But you are here. You—"

"I am the captain. I want you and Glory below immediately. Both of you! Go to the cabin and secure anything that might move. Wait there until the storm is over."
Spray glistened on his hair and face, and there was a glitter
in his eyes.

"But what about you? Aren't you coming too?"

He laughed harshly. "I have the ship to see to. Now,
get below!"

Obediently Brenna and Glory fought their way to the
companionway and descended into the darkness. They
stumbled to the cabin, the floor lurching beneath them.

Inside the saloon, Coleen was sitting at the mahogany
table, her embroidery spread out before her in the light
of the oil lamp. She looked up as they entered, her hands
shaking visibly. There was a spot of blood on her finger
where she had pricked herself.

"What is happening?" she asked. "Is it getting worse?"

"Yes," Brenna said. "We are to stay below." In spite of
her dislike, Brenna had to admire Coleen for trying to
sew while the cabin pitched frighteningly.

Slowly, shudderingly, the ship righted itself. Then it
began to slide again, in the opposite direction. The oil
lamp skidded off the table and Brenna lunged for it, managing to catch it just before it hit the floor.

"We're going to have to put the lamp out," she said.
"I'm afraid it will set the cabin on fire."

With the flickering light out, the darkness was thick and
moist, so black that it seemed it would smother them. In
the dark the movements of the ship seemed exaggerated,
and with each pitch it felt as if they were turning over.

"It's this . . . this darkness I don't like," came Coleen's
voice. "As long as I could see . . . but now . . ." Her
words trailed off and Brenna sensed the effort she was making to control her fright.

"We'll be all right," she said.

"If only I hadn't come," moaned Coleen. "I should have stayed in Havana with Patrick. I should have stayed and mourned him. Gone to his funeral and . . . and done all the things a widow is supposed to do . . ."

Brenna could think of nothing to say. What would it be like, she wondered dully? Would the water rush in swiftly to drown them, or would there be time to know what was happening? Time to struggle in desperate fear?

"It's so dark . . . God, so dark . . ." Coleen's voice went on compulsively. "When I was a little girl my nurse locked me in the wardrobe once, when I'd misbehaved. She was a spiteful creature, she left me there for hours, while I sobbed and beat my fists against the door—" Her breath caught. "I wonder if we shall die here. If we do, it'll be God's punishment to me, won't it? Punishment for leaving Patrick—"

"It doesn't matter," Brenna heard herself say. "He's dead now. He doesn't know." She still hated Coleen, but somehow that wasn't important now. They were all three locked in this black, pitching box of a cabin, and any minute the *Sea Otter* might pitch so far she would never right herself. Then the sea would rush in, silencing all their fears and hates.

"I don't want to die," Coleen wept. "I've always hated death, hated anything that made me think of it. I . . . I was meant to live . . ."

"Enough of that sort of talk," Brenna said sharply. "You're not going to die, and neither am I. Kane is on deck right now, seeing to that. We'll just have to wait until the storm is over, that's all."

They waited most of the night, while the floor of the cabin tilted and pitched, first one way, then another. There was no hope of putting up hammocks; the three of them sat wedged together on the bunk, gripping its wooden supports as best they could when the cabin began to tip, the woods and timbers of the ship shrieking under the pressure. From overhead came sudden smacking noises, shouts, bangs. Coleen had long ago stopped talking, and now sobbed softly to herself, uttering snatches of prayer. Brenna could hear Glory, too, talking to herself in some unknown language. Was she praying too?

She herself prayed silently, asking help not only for herself, but for Kane. If they below were in such terror, what must be happening up on deck, where the waves could roll across, shoving everything in their path? She remembered Kane telling her of Cape Horn. *I know of ships where one whole watch—that's half the crew—were swept overboard within minutes, just like that—*

Was Kane all right? Was the crew? She longed to go up there and see what was happening for herself. Nothing could be worse than this helpless waiting, this feeling of being trapped in a dark, tumbling box.

At last she heard a thumping noise in the passage. She rushed to the door and pulled it open. It was Kane, and he dripped water.

"Are you all right? What's happening up there? I've been so worried!" she cried.

"Worried? Have you?" He spoke softly, pulling her out into the passage, out of earshot of the cabin. "How are they taking it? Glad you put the lamp out—I should have told you."

"They're fine. Coleen is a bit frightened, but we're managing. How is the crew?"

"It's not been good. Four men have been swept overboard, and there wasn't a damned thing I could do about it, not a damned thing. One minute they were here, and the next—" He smacked his fist against the bulkhead. "It was impossible to turn back for them, not in this wind. We've taken in sail, we're running before the wind. We're headed toward the coast of Florida. Maybe, if we're lucky, we can shelter there, behind the islands. I don't like doing it, but it appears I have no choice."

Florida. All the coasts were dangerous, Brenna remembered, yet anything would be better than this.

"The slaves?" she managed through shaking lips.

"They're having a rough time of it, but they'll survive. Poor devils, I think they're praying to whatever gods they have—not that I blame them. Myself, I've been too busy to pray, so you'll have to do that job for me." He laughed, then gave her a kiss, his lips wet and tasting of salt. "Tell Coleen not to worry—we'll get through this somehow."

He was gone. Brenna went back to the bunk feeling

obscurely warmed. He had wanted to talk to her, not Coleen.

It was morning before they reached the shelter of the coast. Brenna woke from a cramped position on the bunk, jammed against Glory's sleeping form, to discover that the cabin was no longer pitching, but merely rocking slightly. Sunlight streamed in through the porthole.

Leaving the other two asleep, Brenna slid off the bunk and climbed up on deck.

The sky was a blue bowl, with only a few high-scudding clouds to indicate there had been a storm. The sea was choppy, but the waves were small, and seemed almost peaceful after the fury of the previous night. To her right was land, to her left more land, close enough so that she could see tangled jungle trees and a white strip of beach.

She found Kane standing on the poop deck, looking at the closest island with a frown. He had taken off the slicker and wore only a white shirt, the sleeves rolled up, the fabric wrinkled and salt-stained. His face showed the strain of the night before, and there was a stubble of beard on his cheeks.

"I can't believe that the storm is really gone," she said. "It's as if it never existed."

"It existed, all right. It left us with four dead and a lot of torn rigging. We're going to have to lay over for a day and make repairs. Damn—if only Phelan were here. We lost our new carpenter overboard last night." Kane passed one hand over his eyes and she realized how exhausted he was.

"You'd better get some rest, hadn't you? And leave the repairs to Scroggins?"

"Perhaps, when the work is well started. But this is my job, Brenna. I won't desert it as long as I'm needed. I'm holding a service for the men we lost, in an hour."

"I . . . I'll come," she said.

"Breakfast ought to be ready soon," Kane added. "If everything in the galley hasn't been ruined. Will you go down and see that Coleen is all right? I've been worried about her."

"Indeed?" The warm feeling left her. She turned and

walked toward the companionway without a word. On her
way she passed Scroggins, who had a livid black and blue
mark across his face and was limping slightly. He must
have been injured during the storm, she realized. He was
lucky to be alive; they all were.

The day inched by. She and Glory spent the time practicing English, the other meticulously imitating Brenna's
pronunciation. She was growing very fond of Glory,
Brenna realized with a pang. She dreaded the moment when
Kane would put the girl on the block again and sell her to
someone else. Perhaps he would give Glory to her.

By early evening the repairs had been completed and
Kane, who had rested during the afternoon, said they
would push on as quickly as possible.

An hour after they had left the shelter of the island,
they spotted a sail astern of the *Sea Otter*, blending with
the glitter of the late sun on the water.

"I don't like that sail," Kane told her shortly. There was
still a weariness about his eyes. "I'll feel better when we're
away from here."

After supper, Brenna came on deck to breathe some
fresh air, prompted by a feeling of unease that she couldn't
explain. It was already twilight, the night descending even
as she watched. There was a pale, partial moon, often hidden by rapidly moving clouds. The sea seemed black and
oily, the waves lit by occasional sparkles of light.

Was the strange sail still behind them? Squint into the
darkness as she would, Brenna could not see it.

Back in the cabin, they all settled themselves for the
night. But Brenna turned uneasily in her hammock. She
couldn't sleep; her muscles felt tense and jumpy. After a
few hours she got out of the hammock, pulled on her
gown, and went back up on deck. It was about midnight,
she thought; maybe later.

The sea was flatter than it had been earlier. A group of
sailors were gathered on the fo'c'sle, speaking in low
voices. Their voices, however, sounded wrong—too low,
with no laughter.

"Brenna, what are you doing on deck? I thought you
would have been asleep by now." Kane came toward her
out of the darkness, his face pale in the moonlight.

"I was restless. I couldn't sleep."

He nodded.

"Kane, am I being silly, or . . . I feel something. Something isn't right."

"No, you're not being foolish. I feel the same thing. So do they." He pointed to the men on the fo'c'sle, who were shifting about, looking toward the sea.

"Is it . . . that other sail?" she whispered.

"I'm afraid so. I've armed the men. I think that ship is following us—I think she's been behind us all evening. I've seen the moonlight glinting off her bow wave."

"But why? Why would she be following us?"

Kane gave a small, laconic shrug. "Pirates, perhaps. Who else?"

"No—"

And it was just then, staring out into the night, that she saw a strange flash of light, and heard a muffled noise, like a musket being fired. A musket from across the water, from a ship that was not their own.

❧ Chapter 25 ❧

NOTHING Brenna had read or heard about pirates had prepared her for the reality. The pirate ship had followed the *Sea Otter* until dawn, then suddenly had launched a small boat filled with men armed with muskets, pistols, swords and cutlasses. Their howls and curses had ripped into the clean dawn air, frighteningly animal-like.

The battle had been futile. The *Sea Otter*, using her mounted guns, sunk the first little boat, sending pirates scrabbling into the water. But, as if her supply of men were inexhaustible, the pirate ship had immediately launched another boat. Then another.

They had fought, all of them, but the pirates had boarded the *Sea Otter* all the same. Brenna had used one of Kane's pistols, firing at the bearded, dirty, dark-skinned men in their odd scraps of clothing. But she and many of the crew were not used to guns. And pistols were not very accurate, reloading slowly, and sometimes firing in the pan.

Mercifully, she had not seen all that had happened, but the sounds alone had been terrifying. From the stern had come a high, agonized scream. More shouts and screams had sounded from the fo'c'sle, where dark forms had sprawled on the deck. Kane had stood grappling with three small men in pantaloons and red sashes.

Horrified, she had buried her face in her hands. This was how they had captured her, shoving her backward onto the deck and quickly tying her hands with rope. Then she had been dragged below to the captain's cabin. A few minutes later, they had brought Kane as well, tying him tightly to her back.

Now they sat trussed up in the cabin, listening to horrifying sounds coming from the passage outside the cabin. "No . . . no. Oh, God, please, please. . . . Oh! No! No!" Coleen's voice was high, piercing, half-crying and half-screaming. It was the most frightening sound Brenna had ever heard.

"Please . . . *No! Oh!*"

Male laughter, guttural grunts, more screams.

"Kane," Brenna whispered. "They are—oh, isn't there anything we can do? We can't just sit here and . . . and listen!"

"What would you suggest we do? We're trussed up like pigs. We can't move. And stop struggling, Brenna. You'll only chafe your wrists. Better save your strength."

"Save my strength! But I can't, not when Coleen—" Her hatred for the red-haired woman had evaporated. Now she could only remember Coleen's fears and prayers during the storm, her regret and guilt at leaving Havana. "Kane, I can't bear to listen."

"Then think of something else," he said coldly.

"I . . . I can't—"

Within a few minutes, however, the screams in the passageway died down to a low, whimpering sobbing. More shouts and thumps came from overhead, and Brenna realized that the pirates had abandoned Coleen in the corridor.

"Kane, do you think she is all right?"

"I don't know. From the sound of it, she probably is. Rape isn't the end of the world. Women do survive it."

"How can you be so callous?"

"I'm just being realistic. You might as well accept the facts, Brenna. The *Sea Otter* has been taken by pirates. By now, the crew is dead. When they are finished, only the slaves and the women will remain alive."

"But there's Scroggins," she said rapidly. "And . . . and the cook. Surely Scroggins can help us. He—"

"Scroggins is dead. They strangled him. The last I saw of him, they were smashing away at his gold teeth."

Her gorge rose. "I can't believe it. I can't believe this."
She stopped. *Only the slaves and women will remain alive.*
"But Kane, what about you? What's going to happen to
you?"

Even as she spoke, she knew.

"They will kill me," he said.

"Kill you!" Her heart constricted. She tried to swallow,
but couldn't. "But they can't! How can you say it so
calmly! As if . . . as if you can't do anything about it?"

"How else can I say it? I'm a realist, Brenna. You saw
how they overpowered us. There must be more than a
hundred of them. Do you wish me to go out of the world
gabbling and begging for my life? I am prepared to die,
Brenna. I wish my death had been different, I wish I had
had a chance to clear my name, and to . . . to do some
other things, but I will have to accept the fact that I cannot. Don't be concerned about me, Brenna. You have your
own life to live. You must go on and live it."

But I can't! Not without you! she wanted to scream.
But she couldn't. He had given up, she realized suddenly.
Despite his tremendous vitality and violent energy, Kane
had given up.

Well, she wasn't going to let him. Sudden anger pushed
through her. *She* wasn't ready to die yet!

"I have no intention of living my life without you," she
said. "I don't think we're finished yet. We can't be! Somehow we'll get away."

"We'll do nothing of the sort. Soon they will come in
and ask me where the gold and valuables are. That's why
they've saved me this long. I'll resist, but eventually they'll
make me tell. Then they'll kill me. You they'll take as a
captive—probably back to an island camp. They'll hold you
for ransom."

"Ransom! But there is no one who would pay money
for me."

"Toby Rynne would, I'll wager. You told me he is obsessed by you. You must use his name to influence them.
Tell them that he will pay thousands of dollars for your
release, but if they harm you they will have to answer to
him. Don't worry, they won't touch you if they think you
are Rynne's woman. At least, they won't kill you."

"But I couldn't use Toby's name—"

"You little fool, you can and you will. It isn't a matter of what you want or don't want. It's a question of survival."

Just as Brenna was about to answer hotly, the door of the saloon opened and they heard the tread of heavy boots.

"Well, what have we here? A handsome young captain and a beautiful girl, tied together in enforced intimacy?" The voice had a Spanish accent.

It had to be the chief pirate, she was sure. He was clean, his black, curly beard freshly washed, his pale blue broadcloth coat immaculate. Beneath it Brenna could see a brocaded vest, ornate ruffled shirt, white linen cravat. Diamond rings adorned his fingers, and a gold watch hung prominently across his vest front. His eyes were brown and glinted at her almost humorously, the full lips slightly smiling. He was a fine figure of a man, with a marked sensuality about him. If she had met him in a drawing room, Brenna realized, she would have found him attractive.

How could a man like this be a pirate? Brenna didn't dare to imagine. But perhaps, she thought rapidly, he was more intelligent than the others, more humane. Maybe he could be used. Even if Kane had unaccountably given up, she hadn't.

"Please . . ." She looked up at him appealingly. "Please, could you untie us?"

His eyes raked over her. For the first time, she was conscious of her own appearance. The front of her gown was torn, revealing the creamy skin of her breasts. Her hair had fallen in wild abandon about her shoulders.

"I am Gasparilla," he said. "Now, what makes you think you and the gentleman here should be released?" He regarded her with amusement, his arms folded across his chest, rocking slightly on his heels. He reminded her of the dandies she had seen at Aunt Rowena's, all clothes and style and manner. If there was killing to be done, he would delegate it to others. Yet he was still dangerous.

"Because it is to your profit to do so," she said quickly, her mind working fast.

"Profit? Yes, as you may have gathered, I am not averse to profit. But what do you suggest, my dear? How can I profit through you and your captain here?"

She smiled at him, willing herself to be charming, even though her heart beat like a trapped rabbit's. But this had to be done, she thought. If they were to live.

"Perhaps if you would untie me, we could talk," she said. "It's very uncomfortable here on the floor. And I . . . I would like to be able to see you better."

The man called Gasparilla gazed at her for a long moment, assessing her. Then he pulled a long, thick blade out of his belt and, bending, cut the ropes that bound her hands and feet.

Trembling, Brenna got to her feet. Her wrists and ankles were throbbing with the return of circulation. "Thank you," she said. "You've no idea how frightening this has been for me."

"I'm sure it has." He lowered his gaze, and she stood very still, permitting him to look at her, at the ripped cloth, at her breasts pushing against the damaged fabric.

"For one thing," she began, "I'm sure you have Captain Fairfield tied up here for one purpose—to learn where he keeps the gold that he is carrying."

Gasparilla nodded. "You are right."

"Well, I am afraid there is going to be a slight problem." Behind her she sensed Kane's startled movement. "You see, Captain Fairfield is rather a greedy man himself, but he is also very brave, a man who would not be likely to tell you where that gold is, even under the worst . . . worst conditions." She licked her lips.

"We shall see about that."

But now Gasparilla was looking speculatively at Kane, who stared back at him, his eyes cold blue stones, revealing nothing.

"Captain Fairfield will not tell you because he hopes to keep the gold himself. But I could persuade him to tell you," she whispered. "Under the condition, of course, that you allow both of us a share in . . . in the business at hand. You see, Captain Fairfield has already killed many men. Only recently he murdered one in a duel. And he is the owner of more than one hundred ships," she lied recklessly. "He could turn his entire line over to you, and his crews, too. They are very loyal to him. He could even help you dispose of your goods in New Orleans. He has influence there, much greater than Toby Rynne, and he would cost you far less."

The man nodded when she mentioned Toby's name, and Brenna felt a cold shiver go through her. So, Kane had been right. Toby really was involved in piracy. But she had no time to think of that now. She had to keep talking, had to keep Gasparilla's interest.

She slid her arms around the pirate's neck, pressing her body into his. "Naturally," she whispered into his ear, "He would like to keep everything for himself. But I think I could persuade him to join you. You and he would make a fine team—"

"I've always operated alone."

"There are better things than being alone." She amazed herself by rotating her hips into his, ever so slightly, as if by accident. "You might like my idea if you would take time to consider it. And meanwhile, if you would release Captain Fairfield, I will find out from him where the gold is, and I will tell you."

"I have no intention of releasing Captain Fairfield," he said emphatically. Her heart sank. And then—she couldn't believe it was happening—she felt the pirate lift the hem of her dress, and push his hand between her thighs.

She forced herself not to cry out, and pressed her body even closer to the man. "You'll see," she whispered. "You won't be making a mistake. And I . . . I could use a bit of that money myself. I like the things money can buy."

Had she convinced him? She didn't know. She only knew that his hand was still under her dress, that he had penetrated beneath her petticoats and drawers to the warm, moist secrecy of her body. Stroking, urging . . . a warm little flower of pleasure began to grow in her. Involuntarily, she pushed him away.

"Now, why are you doing that?" he murmured. "You like me, don't you? You really do, you aren't pretending. You'd like to know me better, wouldn't you?"

"I . . . I don't know—"

Blood pounded to her face, burned through her. She was

acutely conscious of Kane, still bound and tied at her feet, his face a stony mask. He had seen everything, she thought in agony.

"I won't tell him where the gold is," Kane said abruptly. "So don't bother with all of your schemes, dear Brenna. I, too, prefer to work by myself. In a few years, I will rule these waters."

Brenna stifled a smile of relief. So Kane was going to support her story. He was going to fight back after all.

"I will see to this," she told Gasparilla. Quickly she bent by Kane, making a show of whispering persuasion in his ear.

Kane was silent for a moment, his eyes veiled. "Put your ear near my mouth," he said.

Obediently, she did so.

"Under the floorboards by the bunk is the gold scrip Señor Tranquilo gave me—ten thousand dollars' worth. There are also ten cases of Cuban rum in the hold if they haven't found them already. And . . . good luck, my little wildcat. If you want me to be savage and greedy, then that's what I'll be. But, remember, save yourself. Do what you must to survive. You know what I mean."

You know what I mean. He'd spoken so quietly that she was not sure she had really heard those last words.

Gasparilla was watching them, his head tilted to one side. Quickly she got to her feet. She felt the man's eyes on her body and she knew that in his mind he had already stripped her naked. But much as he wanted her body, his greed for money was greater.

"I will tell you where the gold is," she said.

They were alone in the cabin again, Brenna retied to Kane's back as if nothing had changed. Gasparilla, with two of his men, had pried up the floorboards by the bunk, and extracted Señor Tranquilo's gold. Then he had gone, to look for the rum and see to the slaves, Brenna presumed. She hoped Glory was all right; surely they would realize she was valuable property and would not harm her. They had heard no further sounds from Coleen. Evidently she had been dragged up on deck. They could only pray she was still alive.

"Well," Brenna said shakily. "At least we are both still breathing. I have accomplished that much."

"And the gold is gone."

She was suddenly angry. "Of course it's gone! Are you complaining because I told them where it was? Which is more important, gold or life?"

"Life, of course." Kane paused, and then added, "But I am afraid, Brenna, that you didn't succeed with your fantastic little ruse. It was a noble try, but you didn't convince him."

She bit her lips, part of her confidence seeping away. "We can't know for sure. He left you alive, didn't he?"

There seemed nothing further to say. They sat, their wrists burning in the tight ropes, listening to the noises of the ship. Sails flapped, spars banged. There was the pounding of boots, the sound of men shouting. The pirates, she thought numbly, were going over the ship inch by inch, looking for spoils. She wondered if they had found the rum. And where was Glory? Was the black girl lying on the deck, her body bruised and raped?

Kane's voice broke the silence. "I should tell you, Brenna, you'd better do what this Gasparilla tells you to do. He may seem affable enough, and he may be cleaner than the rest, but believe me, he's the same as they are. I've seen his type on Grande Terre. He's not above rape, and he enjoys brutality just as much as his men do. He likes this kind of life, Brenna. Better get that through your head."

Brenna thought of the clean and handsome Gasparilla, with his black, curly beard and full, soft lips. The heavy knife he had pulled out of his belt. The way his eyes had raked over her. Yes, she thought dully. He would be capable of anything.

You really like me, you aren't pretending, Gasparilla had said. Was it true?

She shuddered and closed her eyes.

❧ *Chapter 26* ❧

THE PIRATES HAULED Kane and Brenna up on deck, and put them into a small boat. An island loomed close, its headland covered with palm trees, its sandy beach wide and blindingly white. Coleen was dumped unceremoniously into the boat with them. Her face was red from crying, her dress soiled, and her hair streamed raggedly about her face. She sat muttering snatches of prayers, cries and curses. Brenna tried to touch her hand to give what comfort she could, but Coleen shook her off violently.

The slaves were herded into a second boat that had come out from the island to meet them. Glory was among them, her dark face twisted with fright. But she seemed physically unharmed, and Brenna felt relief.

Two of Gasparilla's men rowed the boat that held Kane, Brenna and Coleen—wild-looking bearded men with pistols and cutlasses. Both exuded a foul body odor as if they had not washed in months. As the wind pressed her gown against her body, their eyes widened with lust, and Brenna felt panic stirring. The pirates numbered nearly a hundred. If they decided to rape her . . .

But it wasn't going to happen, she told herself quickly. She was under Gasparilla's protection. She must try to keep her courage up.

"Where are they taking us?" she asked Kane in a low voice.

"To the island. I am sure they have a camp there, and

probably a stockade as well. There is plenty of shelter for their ships in these coves. They probably steal all the fresh supplies they can get, and live off the land for the rest, if they are not too lazy to fish."

The two pirates kept rowing, but looked at them suspiciously.

"Do you think these men speak English?" Brenna asked.

"I don't know," Kane said. "But I would keep quiet for now. We don't want to excite them."

But there was something Brenna had to know. "Kane, the crew. The men of the *Sea Otter*. What has happened to them? Surely they can't *all* be—"

She stopped and swallowed, seeing in Kane's expression the answer to her question. The crew was dead, every one of them. She, Kane, Glory, Coleen and the eleven slaves were the only survivors.

The water near the island was shallow, broken irregularly by sandbars. The beach was wide and flat, littered with thousands of shells and dead sea animals, the smell of them strong and acrid. Seabirds swooped in the air, and skittered along the edge of the water. The pirates pulled the dory into a cove, and one of them gave Brenna a rough push, indicating that she was to get out of the boat.

She stood up, balancing awkwardly, for her hands were tied behind her back. The pirate gave her another push, and she stumbled out of the boat, falling to her knees in the sand. Glancing behind her, she saw the two pirates throw Coleen out of the boat, tossing her face-down on the sand and broken shells.

"Please untie me," Brenna begged. She held up her bound hands, trying to look harmless. The taller of the two pirates stared at her greedily, his tongue moistening his lips. His beard was tangled and dirty, crusted with dried food and salt.

"Please?" She tried to smile, extending her hands again, this time toward him.

He hesitated, then stepped forward and unknotted the rope.

"Thank you," Brenna said. Quickly she went to help Coleen up from the sand. The girl made little effort to assist herself. Her body was so slack and listless that it took nearly all Brenna's strength to get her to her feet.

"Coleen!" she panted. "You've got to help yourself. I can't carry you. You must walk for yourself."

As she was about to speak to Kane, the bearded pirate shoved her again, indicating that she was to go toward the trees that lined the beach. Kane, however, was to remain where he was.

"Kane—" she cried frantically, turning to him.

"Brenna, don't worry." Kane's face was calm and confident. "They'll release me after I have a talk with Gasparilla. You'd better go with the man for now. I've heard that Gasparilla makes an attempt to protect his female captives, and has built a stockade for them. You're better off there. And . . . take care of Coleen for me, will you? I'm worried about her."

Worried about Coleen? What about me? Brenna thought rebelliously. But quickly her anger vanished as the second pirate gave her a push that nearly sent her sprawling. She took Coleen's arm and pulled the other girl along as they stumbled over heaped-up deposits of shells. Among the trees she could see log buildings, even a fence enclosing chickens, pigs and cows.

"No . . ." Coleen muttered. "No . . . tell them to stay away from me . . . please . . ." Coleen's sea-green dress was now a ruin. Her face was pasty white, her once-glorious hair tangled and dull. She did not look like the same person who had smiled so seductively at Kane.

"Please, Coleen," Brenna begged. "Everything is going to be all right."

The women's compound stood in a small clearing chopped out of the jungle growth. It consisted of a spiked log fence surrounding a long, low, open building built crudely of logs and thatched with palm leaves. The walls were woven palm leaves, and inside Brenna could see palm mats, and rough blankets spread out on the floor. In front of the building sat a small group of women dressed in dirty, ragged gowns. They looked up hopefully as the women from the *Sea Otter* entered, then broke into a torrent of wild Spanish. Several dropped the palm mats they were weaving, and jumped to their feet.

As Brenna hesitated at the door of the compound, the pirate pushed her inside. Hastily, she pulled Coleen with her. Coleen seemed frozen in some mental paralysis, without will of her own, only moving if pulled or pushed.

The log gates swung shut behind them, but almost immediately reopened to admit Glory, her eyes glazed with fear.

"Glory . . . oh, Glory!" Brenna embraced the slave girl, feeling absurdly glad to find a friend here.

"Bren-na." Through the dull brown merino Brenna could feel Glory trembling.

"Don't worry, Glory, everything will be all right, I promise you," Brenna said reassuringly, trying to hide her own doubt.

On the other side of the log gate, a man cleared his throat, and Brenna realized that he must be their guard. She had glimpsed water through the trees as she had approached the compound, and she speculated that the island must be long and narrow, with the other shore lying close by.

The day passed slowly, marked off only by the lengthening shadows of the log walls of the compound. The Spanish girls, most of them Brenna's age or younger, welcomed them eagerly, but could only communicate with the newcomers by sign language. Were they from Mexico? Or, perhaps, Cuba? In vain Brenna tried to get Coleen to translate. But the red-haired girl was immersed in a private nightmare of her own, and only sat staring off into the distance, her eyes blank.

There was a cooking fire, with a frame over it supporting a cooking pot. One of the Spanish-speaking girls was cleaning fish for the noon meal, while another husked a coconut. In sign language Brenna offered her help, and a young girl showed her how to wrap the cleaned fish in leaves and lay it on the coals to cook.

At first Brenna did not think she could eat. But Glory firmly put food in Brenna's hand, motioning toward her mouth. Then she herself began eating methodically, as if forcing herself for the sake of survival only. Looking at Glory more closely, Brenna saw white streaks of tears on her cheeks. Her dress was ripped under the arms, and Brenna thought it likely that she, too, had been raped.

What lay ahead for all of them? Glory, she knew, would be sold as a slave. She and Coleen would be held until ransom was paid for them—if anyone could be found to pay it. Meanwhile they would be kept here, in this log enclosure, at the mercy of Gasparilla and his men.

The worst thing, she decided, was the waiting. In the hot afternoon air she could hear sounds coming from other parts of the island—shouts of wild, drunken laughter, the occasional bang of a musket. She saw the Spanish girls whispering together, their faces grim, and fear began to grow in her. The pirates had captured ten cases of rum. Shivering, she remembered how the two men in the boat had looked at her. It was a good thing she was inside this stockade. . . .

Anxiously, she thought of Kane. The pirates were growing drunker each minute, and he was in their hands. Again she heard a musket firing, a sound almost immediately repeated. More shouts of laughter arose.

Was Kane all right? *What was happening?*

The sun rose higher in the sky, fiercely hot. The pirates' shouts grew louder. There was another gun shot, and a scream of pain. Was it Kane? In spite of the heat of the day, Brenna felt icy-cold.

At the other end of the enclosure, one of the Spanish girls squatted in the dirt with a crude rosary made from seashells. Her lips moved as she touched each shell reverently. Brenna, too, tried to pray, closing her eyes and trying to summon a picture of God. But she could only see Kane, his face jauntily confident, his dimples flashing. *Dear God,* she said in her mind. *Please help him. I love him so.*

Suddenly she looked up. The gate of the compound swung open, and Gasparilla stood silhouetted against the green of the palm thicket, his shoulders so wide that they nearly filled the aperture. He looked over the compound as if searching for someone.

Brenna sat very still, feeling, foolishly, that if she did not move he would not see her.

He motioned to her.

Slowly she got to her feet, feeling acutely conscious of the rip at the bosom of her gown. In the fall from the boat, it had torn further and now exposed the upper half of her breasts completely. As she walked toward him she tried to cover herself with her hands.

"Miss Laughlan, I am wondering if you would like to take a light refreshment with me."

The pirate must have learned his English from a gentleman, for, although he had a Spanish accent, he spoke with sauve confidence, as if in a fashionable New Orleans drawing room. It was ludicrous, Brenna thought wildly. For he had changed his clothing, and now wore a pale green broadcloth coat with mother-of-pearl buttons, and black, shiny Wellington boots. Dressed like a popinjay in the Florida jungle? She wanted to laugh hysterically. Instead, she kept walking toward him, feeling his eyes on her, burning through her dress.

He repeated his invitation.

"Refreshment?" She forced herself to smile.

"Yes—and might I call you Brenna? It is a lovely name, and you are a lovely girl. Much too beautiful to belong to an American." He smiled at her, revealing a row of even, white teeth, marred only by a space between the front two. His beard had been freshly combed, the moustache waxed into stiff points.

He led her toward a sturdy log building with a palm roof, taking it for granted that she had accepted his invitation.

"I . . . I didn't realize that you had such a large camp," she said. It was the first thing that came into her head.

"Yes. These are my quarters. I also entertain guests here."

Entertain guests. As he spoke, he squeezed her arm intimately, pressing his forearm against her breast.

She couldn't help herself. She had to ask. Yet she didn't want to sound pleading. "Tell me. Were you able to persuade Captain Fairfield to join forces with you?"

Gasparilla smiled, his teeth contrasting white against the dark hair of his beard and the sun-brown of his skin. "We have not settled that yet. He is alive, if that is what you mean. We gave him a small . . . shall we say, test? To discover if he is indeed courageous."

Her heart sank as she remembered the muskets firing, the scream of pain. But she couldn't let the man see her fear. "Indeed?" she asked cooly.

The pirate regarded her closely. "You are wondering whether he passed the test? He did, I am happy to tell you. And unscathed as well. It was one of my men who was injured. You were right, Miss Laughlan. Your Captain Fairfield is very skilled at dueling . . ."

Dueling. They had forced him to duel. But he was still alive. She wanted to weep with relief.

"But enough of such talk," Gasparilla said. "I want you to see my home here. It may not be as grand as the establishments in New Orleans, but it is very comfortable, and well-furnished. I am sure you will like it."

He pulled her inside the building. After the harsh sunlight, the room seemed dark. It was furnished in almost ridiculous luxury. The floors were entirely covered with Bokhara carpets, their variegated patterns assaulting the eye. The walls were even hung with carpets, like an Arabian tent. Ornate carved furniture, crammed with bric-a-brac, filled every corner and wall. Heavy tables were heaped with leather-bound books, delicate porcelain vases, Irish crystal, and English bone china. Brenna shivered, wondering how many lives had been lost so that Gasparilla might have hand-blown crystal cluttered tastelessly on the tables.

"Do you like it?" he asked. She sensed his childish pleasure in the room.

"To come from the women's compound to . . . to this, it's like another world," she told him, truthfully enough. "Not that the compound is uncomfortable."

"I am glad you are pleased with your treatment here. It would disturb me if you were not."

She felt his hand in the center of her back, guiding her toward a far corner of the room. Dominating it was an enormous four-poster bed, draped in green velvet, its mosquito netting drawn aside. And on the table beside it was a bottle of Cuban rum and two Waterford goblets.

She tried to hang back. "Please . . ."

He smiled, ignoring her protest. His hand slid down to cup her buttocks.

"No . . . please, I didn't realize—" She stopped, angry at herself for sounding so surprised and helpless. What had she expected, after all? Coleen had been brutally raped by these men; Glory too. By those standards, she herself was lucky. *Do what you have to do,* Kane had told her.

Kane. The thought was sharp in her. He was alive now, Gasparilla had said, but how long would he remain so in this nest of savage men who tortured before they killed. If she angered Gasparilla, if she refused him, what might happen then?

Gasparilla picked up the bottle of rum and poured some into a glass. He held it out to her. "Have some Cuban rum—it's the best."

She choked down the hot, gagging liquid. Almost immediately a warmth began to spread through her, tingling in her bones.

"Do you feel better now? A drink is good for a woman. It makes her relax." The big pirate pulled her to him and kissed her, his beard bristling against her face. Then he pulled her toward the bed.

"Take your gown off for me," he said. His breathing was heavy. "It's something I would like to see."

She closed her eyes. Her heart was thumping. "I . . . I don't think I can."

"Of course you can. You like me, don't you? And I like you. You will be more comfortable without that heavy dress, will you not? And besides . . ." Gasparilla's expression hardened. "Besides, you have no choice, do you? With your friend, Captain Fairfield, still in my power . . ."

He was right. She had no choice. Slowly she fumbled with the back buttons of her gown. He did not offer to help her, but stood back, rocking on his heels, one hand stroking his beard. After one glance, she did not dare to look at him again.

At last the gown was unbuttoned.

She let the dress drop in a heap at her feet, and rapidly pulled off the petticoats, corset, camisole and underdrawers, flinging them beside it. Then she faced him, naked.

"Beautiful . . ." he breathed. Slowly, as if fingering a flower, his hand touched her left breast. With his fore-finger, he drew a circle around the nipple. Brenna drew in her breath sharply.

"You liked that, didn't you?"

"I . . . no . . . I don't know." She was frightened, badly frightened, by the man's soft insistence, by his ability to draw pleasure out of her against her will. She loved Kane, she told herself desperately. It was Kane who had brought her body to such ecstasy in the past. No other man could give her that . . . no one.

"If you will lie down upon the bed . . ."

"I can't. Oh, please—" The words burst out of her before she could stop them.

"Of course you can. You do not have to fear me, my little bird. I am only a man, not a monster. I will not hurt you. I will only love you. What is wrong with that?"

She could not answer.

"Go to the bed," he repeated.

Silently, she obeyed. Her heart was beating so quickly that she thought it would pound through her throat. She settled herself on the heavy velvet bedcover and closed her eyes, hearing the sounds of the man undressing himself. She thought how his body would look, massive and ridged with muscle, covered with dark, curly body hair. She knew he was close to her, but she could not look.

"Open your eyes," he said.

He was standing by her, and she had been right. Dark curls of hair covered his chest like a thatch, trailing down over the flat belly to the enormously, erect organ . . .

"Touch me," he commanded.

Slowly, her hand shaking, she did. He was hot and hard and dry, thrusting himself into her hand.

"I am going to make love to you. We have all night, and will not be disturbed. It is not often that I get the chance to have a girl like you, and I won't hurt you. I promise you that. We will do only pleasurable things."

All night. Fear pounded in her. But in spite of herself, she felt a curling little flicker deep within her. This was wrong; she knew it was wrong. But her body, her treacherous, hateful body betrayed her. Her body was going to be unfaithful to Kane, and there was nothing she could do to stop it.

She did not know how many hours had passed. Darkness had fallen, and from outside came the pirates' drunken shouts and screams as they continued to drink the *Sea Otter's* rum.

Gasparilla had made love to her three times. Or was it four? She had lost track in the rum's consuming dizziness. He had forced her to drink often, holding the goblet to her lips and laughing as some of the golden liquid dribbled down onto her breasts. "I will kiss it off . . ." he had said, and then his lips had been all over her, the beard prickling her, the teeth nibbling, the soft tongue probing.

There was nothing about lovemaking he did not know, no part of a woman's body that he could not excite into pleasure, over and over again. Yet, she thought, her head whirling from the drink, there was something cold and wrong about it. Because, although Gasparilla paid elaborate attention to her body, she sensed that he cared nothing whatsoever about *her*. She, her mind, her feelings, meant nothing to him.

Now he was inside her again, his full, thick organ filling her, drawing involuntary gasps of pleasure from her. With Kane, she thought despairingly, it had been different. There had been pleasure, but there had also been something more. In some subtle way, they had joined, they had become one.

And even as her climax approached, sweeping her forward with elemental power, a tiny thin thought remained at the edge of her consciousness. *Kane. Oh, Kane, where are you?*

Gasparilla had fallen asleep. With the rum bottle emptied, he lay sprawled naked on the bed, his snores loud. In the light of the guttering candle his bulky form was totally inert, a mound of bare flesh. Carefully Brenna sat up and slid off the bed. She pulled on her clothes, wishing she could bathe. The smell of his body was all over her.

Just as she was stepping into the gown, she heard a movement at the door of the building. It was one of the pirates, his eyes and teeth shining white in the darkness. How long had he been there? How much had he seen?

She shrank back toward the bed.

"Come with me. I will take you to the women's stockade." He spoke a rough, gutter French that she found difficult to understand. His eyes were gleaming, and, unaccountably, she feared him more than she had Gasparilla.

"No. I will wait here."

"You will come." He approached her and took her arm. "He will not want you here when he awakes. He does not like women here then."

"Oh, he doesn't, does he?" But she had to follow him, for his fingers were digging into her arm, and she could see the flash of the cutlass blade in his belt. Fervently, she hoped he would respect Gasparilla's ownership of her. If he, too, tried to rape her . . .

But she made it back to the women's compound without incident, the man guiding her carefully around the drunken pirates, as if he had done this before. At the log gate, he spoke shortly to the guard, who opened the gate and shoved her in.

The enclosure was dark, the fire only glowing coals. She found Glory and Coleen huddled at the far end, both asleep. She could not find a blanket, so she lay down on the palm mat. In spite of the mosquitoes, she fell asleep almost instantly, her body totally exhausted. She could sleep for days, she thought as she closed her eyes. Weeks. . . .

She slept four hours. It was still dark when something nudged at her arm.

She stirred, moaned, pushed it away.

"Dammit, Brenna, wake up, will you?" The whisper was sharp.

She sat bolt upright, her pulse jumping. "Kane! Where . . . how did you get here? Are you all right?" She began to cry, reaching for him blindly, pulling him to her.

"Shh! You can't cry now, for God's sake. We've got to get out of here."

The rum had left her with a heavy, cottony feeling in

her brain. She shook her head, trying to clear it. "But how? There are nearly a hundred of them. They—"

"We'll manage. Now, come on. Quickly." He pulled at her, lifting her to her feet, urging her toward the gate.

"But," she whispered, "the others. Coleen and Glory, and the other girls here. We can't leave them."

"Don't be a fool. Two might get away. But we can't escape this island with nine or ten helpless women in tow, and one of them sick in the head. We'd never make it. We'll send a military ship back after them. I guarantee you, they'll be all right."

"No," she said firmly. "I won't do that. I won't leave without Glory. And Coleen . . . we can't just leave her here!"

"Brenna." He touched her urgently, whispering into her ear. "Can't you see we haven't time for this? I've killed the guard. The rest of them are so drunk they don't know what's happening. But we can't be sure they'll stay that way. We've got to get out of here right now."

"No. We'll leave with all of us, or none of us."

"Brenna, talk sense, will you? I've told you—"

"And I say I won't leave without them."

"Very well," he sighed. "Wake them, then. But for God's sake, hurry."

❧ *Chapter 27* ❧

THE MOON RODE LOW in the sky, partly obscured by clouds. The breeze was moist, full of salt tang and the scent of wild beach grasses. It was the kind of night Brenna had always loved. She could have stopped to stroll along the shore, to listen to the sound of the surf pounding against the sand.

But there was no time for that. *How strange,* one part of her mind had time to think as they raced out of the stockade. How strange that there could still be part of her that longed to savor the beauty of the evening.

With sign language and whispers, Kane herded them toward the far side of the island, through a palm grove crowded with palmettos and tropical undergrowth. Hurriedly they pushed through the foliage, which was frightening in the darkness with its sharp leaves and fronds ready to snap back and slash them in the face.

Brenna gripped Coleen's hand, pulling her along unmercifully. Behind them struggled Glory with the other girls. Once a girl tripped over a creeper and fell, crying out in sobbing Spanish. But she was helped up, and they hurried on, driven by their need to get away before the pirates woke and found them.

In the occasional glimmers of moonlight Brenna saw that Kane carried a pistol and had thrust a short, heavy, curving sword through his belt. His coat was gone, his white shirt torn in several places. With his quick, stealthy movements, he looked like a pirate himself.

Suddenly Kane stopped, signaling the others to do the same. They had reached the beach. Only a short distance away lay the dark mass of the Florida mainland, brooding and silent.

Kane whispered, "Look. They've got their ships moored here. It's as I thought."

Brenna stared out over the water, where a few silver waves reflected the half-hidden moon. The dark shapes of boats bobbed in the water.

"There's a dory pulled up on the beach," Kane was saying. "We'll use that. But this won't be easy, Brenna— they may have guards on the boats. And I'll need a boat we can manage. It would be suicide to try the *Sea Otter*, we haven't enough crew."

She took a deep breath, trying not to think what would happen to them if they were caught.

Kane spoke a few sentences in Spanish, and the girl with the shell rosary nodded quickly.

"I've told them to wait," he said to Brenna. "Come on. We'll have to row out there and see what we can find. You can hold the pistol, but for God's sake don't fire unless you have no other choice. I don't want every man on the island awake. I'll use the cutlass if I can."

They dragged the small boat into the water, Brenna's shoes and gown getting wet nearly to her knees. Awkwardly she climbed in. Then Kane rowed out, his face grim and intent. "Tell me if you see anything," he whispered. "I'm hoping even the guards came ashore to sample that rum. They had women, as well. Gasparilla provides generously. Too generously, in this case, since it was one of the women who untied me."

Women, always women. She felt like letting out a wild giggle. Instead, she peered into the night, looking apprehensively at the shapes of the boats around her, the waves slapping against their sides with sharp, clunking sounds. They passed the *Sea Otter*, looking ghostly and derelict, her sails furled and her deck empty. At least she hoped it was empty; deep shadows covered most of the deck surface, making it difficult to see.

They floated by another shape, this one smaller, slimmer and more graceful than the *Sea Otter*, its twin masts pointing to the moon.

"A staysail schooner!" Kane exclaimed. "I wonder where they stole it. It's our chance, Brenna. She's light, and she's got lots of sail—she'll be fast. We can outrun them if we have to, if we get a good start."

On their way back to shore to pick up the other women, the clouds again moved away from the moon, and silver light spilled onto the water.

"Kane!" Brenna pointed toward the *Sea Otter*. "I see a man on deck!"

They both stared.

"It's either a sleeping guard, or one of the bodies they forgot to remove," Kane said at last. "At any rate, he's quiet, isn't he? We haven't time to think of him now." If he regretted the loss of the *Sea Otter*, his face did not show it.

It took two trips to get all of the women on board the small schooner, but at last they were all standing on her deck, the wind lifting their skirts and rattling the canvas sails.

Kane again spoke in Spanish. The girl who had made the rosary—Brenna was to learn her name was Rosalia—inclined her head, her lips pressed together grimly.

"What are you telling them?" Brenna asked.

"I told them they've got to be my crew—all of you must, if we expect to get home. You'll have to do what I tell you without question. It may be a rough trip—I haven't any idea how many supplies are on board—but this boat is our only chance. We've got to be well away from here before sunrise, so they can't spot our sail and follow us."

Brenna's heart sank. This was a group of young women, not experienced sailors. Several of the Spanish girls were as young as fourteen or fifteen, barely out of childhood. And there was Coleen, completely removed now to some inner world of her own.

"We'll manage," she told him. "Please, quickly. Tell us what to do."

Never had she worked so hard. They hauled up the heavy iron anchors, and let out and secured the sails, the thick ropes harsh and strange to their hands. Brenna worked until the sweat ran down her sides and between her breasts. Her skirts impeded her at every turn, until, in desperation, she pulled her skirts up and tied them at her waist, as the Spanish girls were doing.

But at last all was ready. Incredibly, the sails filled with wind, taut with power. The boat began to cut through the water, its wake foaming silver behind them. They were off. Brenna felt like laughing with triumph. They had done it. She stood at the stern and watched the long, low island shrink behind them.

They were lucky. The breeze was brisk, and when they reached the open gulf, the wind pushed at them with insistent strength, bellying out the sails and scudding the boat across the water. Later, Kane would point out to her the schooner's various sails—the mainstaysail, forestaysail, fisherman and others. But now she knew nothing of that— only that, by some miracle, they were flying over the water as if the ship were a seabird.

Below deck, the facilities of the ship were primitive, consisting of two cramped, untidy rooms. One was fitted with four bunks and a few salt-stained brown wool blankets; the other held a crude table and benches, a food and water safe, and a primitive stove. Everywhere was evidence of the pirates—rotten fruit peelings, a ragged coat flung across a bench and forgotten. A film of grease and grime covered everything. As she took stock, Brenna's heart sank. Would there be any food and water here at all?

The food safe was dirty, and it smelled. With trepidation she opened it. She found a small sack of cornmeal, a supply of salt and sugar. There were four loaves of bread, their dried crusts rock-hard. There was a leather bag that contained about eight gallons of brackish water.

She went back on deck and told Kane.

He frowned. "I didn't expect better. Well, we'll have to take on some supplies, that's all. We've escaped Gasparilla, that's what matters." He hesitated. "Speaking of the man, are you all right? Did he——?"

"I'm fine." Numbly she turned away from him, to hide the tears which glistened in her eyes.

He touched her, his hand lingering on hers. "Go and divide up the bread. We'll use some as bait. I've found some fishing gear—you and Glory are about to become fishermen. And I will tell Rosalia to air the bedding. It stinks of pirate."

Time had never seemed to pass so quickly. Always before, when sailing, Brenna had been a passenger, with hours of time on her hands. But now there was real work, enough to keep her busy most of the day. First, of course, was the fishing. They trailed their line, baited with bread, from the end of the boat, and several times were rewarded with the plump, silvery, flapping fish on deck which meant there would be food for supper.

The entire ship had to be scrubbed and cleaned, for Kane insisted he would not travel on a filthy vessel; their health alone demanded it be kept as clean as possible. They hauled up seawater in buckets and scrubbed the decks and cabins until they shone, polishing the corroded brasswork. The ropes, or working lines, of the vessel were ragged and untidy, a potential danger, Kane explained. So Brenna learned to whip and knot and splice, her fingers growing tougher and more calloused as the days passed.

She fashioned a sunbonnet out of some old rags they'd found—it made a sort of crude babushka. Kane insisted that both she and Coleen wear them. They, he said, had the lightest skin of the women and were most vulnerable to sunburn.

As the days wore on, she found it cooler and more convenient to shed her petticoats, save for the inmost one, and to wear her dress hitched up with a makeshift belt. With a sail needle she mended the bodice of her gown. Each mile they traveled was partly due to her efforts, to the ropes she pulled and knotted and secured, to the scrubbing and cooking she had done, to the fish she had caught and cleaned. It was a heady, triumphant feeling.

Even Coleen seemed affected by the peace of the voyage. She had stopped screaming and crying in her sleep in the crowded cabin, and now would actually help scrub the deck, her eyes staring dreamily out to sea. She ignored Kane now, looking at him as if he were a stranger.

"Are you anxious to be home, Coleen?" Brenna asked her once.

"Home?" The red-haired girl repeated this word with such tremulousness, that Brenna turned away.

They stopped at a small Spanish settlement that Kane called Pensacola. Kane bought water and fresh food, paying for them with some gold coins he said he had stolen from one of the pirates. "Most of them bury their share of the spoils in a secret spot as soon as they receive it," he explained. "But this fellow liked his rum a bit too much, and passed out first. When he awakes, he'll think one of his comrades took his cache."

They now had oranges, grapefruit, yams, salt pork, oatmeal, dried peas, pickled beef, and five live chickens in a crude crate. Rosalia, smiling, showed Brenna how to make a kind of bread atop the cookstove, and demonstrated how to kill and pluck the chickens.

The Spanish-speaking girls, Kane had learned, were from Mexico. They had been the servants of a Spanish lady with a long and unpronounceable name, who had been sailing back to Spain when Gasparilla captured her ship.

"But what happened to the Spanish lady?" Brenna asked.

"She was old and ugly, with a weak heart, Rosalia says. They probably tossed her overboard to the sharks. They don't like ugly women."

"Oh!"

"They are animals, Brenna. Animals who only live to eat and drink and copulate and kill. Gasparilla eventually would have tired of you and killed you. He had done it before—I heard his men talking. Or, worse, he would have thrown you to them. That was what they were hoping for."

She shivered, turning her face.

Her concern now was for Glory. As a slave, she knew Glory would be quick, intelligent and tractable. But what if she were sold to a cruel master, someone who would beat her, or . . . or worse? She couldn't let it happen. Brenna decided to talk to Kane about it as soon as possible.

Her opportunity came the next evening when supper was finished. Kane was at the wheel of the small schooner. His beard was growing, and his cheeks were covered with short,

blonde-brown hairs. Brenna wanted to touch them, to feel
the texture beneath her fingers. Instead, she twisted her
hands together behind her back, to remove the temptation.

"Kane, there is something I would like to ask you."

"And what is that?" he asked formally. He had been
only distantly courteous to her for the past several days.
Her only consolation was that he treated the other girls
the same way, his manner toward Coleen heavily laced
with pity.

She went on hurriedly, "It's about Glory. I have grown
fond of her. And she likes me. Kane, I . . . you said that
when our bargain was terminated you would give me
funds to start a new life . . ."

"Yes?" His eyes regarded her sharply, their blue as intense as she had ever seen.

"I would like Glory to be a part of that life. I . . .
I can't bear to think of her being put on the slave block.
She's too shy and dignified for such treatment."

"She's a slave, Brenna. A valuable slave."

"Yes. I know she is." Brenna turned to look at the sea,
at the waves topped with shining, curling foam, spanking
against the hull of the ship. She would not beg; pleading
would not work with Kane anyway. Nor would angry
words. What he would do, he would do.

She waited.

"Do you know you are as tanned as a sailor?" Kane
suddenly said.

"Am I?" She touched her cheek. "I suppose so. I've
been working in the sun enough."

"If you were a man, I'll wager you'd make a good
seaman." He was smiling at her, his look so warm that
her heart begin to hammer. "All right, Brenna. You can
have Glory if you want her. She'll be my farewell gift to
you."

Farewell gift. Something twisted within her chest. She
lowered her eyes so he would not see the pain in them.

"Very well, then. Thank you. I appreciate it," she said
in a low voice. Then she turned and fled below.

They sailed into New Orleans harbor on a gray, over-
cast day, the air humid with the threat of rain. Brenna

was absurdly glad to see the long docks lined with their varied collection of boats.

"Well, we're here at last." Kane seemed in an odd mood, expansive, yet irritable. She knew the thought of Toby Rynne weighed heavily on his mind.

"Yes, I suppose we are."

"What is that sour expression for?" he asked. "Are you thinking of that uncle of yours? Well, I've been considering. You don't have to go to him. I'll give you money —you can take Glory and ride a riverboat north, to some other city, and start over again. Somewhere where no one knows you. And where Rynne can't find you."

She had been thinking about this for the past two days. Where she would go, what she would do. "I've already made my decision," she told him. "I'm going to stay at my uncle's for a short time, if he'll have me. Until I . . . I see what happens with you."

"The duel? The witnesses? But I can write you about that." Kane scowled.

"I know. But I want to be here. I've been thinking. If I go to my uncle's, I may see Toby again. Perhaps I can talk to him, learn something about him to help you clear your name."

"You would be willing to do that?" He stared at her.

She forced her eyes to meet his. "Yes."

"But, Brenna, the man must hate you! You jilted him, for God's sake. Don't you remember?"

"I know that, but still, I . . . I want to stay. Perhaps I'm wrong, but it is something I want to do."

"Why?"

"Because I . . ." She sought for the right words. "Because I have come to believe you are innocent of murdering Ulrich Rynne. I'd like to see it proved. That's all." *And because I love you,* she wanted to add. *Because I want to be near you, because I can't bear to let you go out of my life.*

"Perhaps you regret leaving Rynne? Is that it?"

"No! Nothing of the kind! Do you think I . . . no, never!" She stopped, remembering Gasparilla. Oh, she had learned so much from the pirate. She had learned that her body could respond even to a cruel man, to a man she didn't love. Her body could find pleasure with a murderer. Hot shame filled her.

"You're foolish even to think of this!" Kane had turned away, so that she could not see his face. "I want you to leave New Orleans immediately. I don't want Rynne near you again. I forbid this."

"You have no right to forbid me anything!" she said sharply. "I can go anywhere I wish. And if I choose, I can go back to my uncle's house. And if I should see Toby again, it's no one's business but my own."

There was a long silence, broken only by the sound of the sails flapping.

"Very well, then," Kane said coldly. "I plan to go about the city as a riverboat man. The streets are crawling with them, and no one will recognize me, I'm sure. If you wish to get in touch with me, you can send a note to Maud Sweet's. She'll see that I get it. You may take Glory to your uncle's with you. I'll make out the necessary papers. As for Coleen and the other girls, I will provide money to send them all home. You must arrange their passage, since I will not be available."

"Yes."

"I will have money sent you. Give some of it to your uncle. It will placate him and pay for your board." He put some gold pieces into her hand. "Take these, as well. They will pay for a hotel for the others."

They docked with much confusion. Kane, in his ragged shirt and salt-stained trousers, immediately blended into the crowd and disappeared, leaving Brenna standing on the jetty with the others. They made a strange party: eight Mexican girls; a tall, exotic-looking slave, and Coleen, clutching at Brenna like a lost child. Dock workers and black roustabouts stared at them, but no one spoke. They were ragged and poor-looking; women of this sort often traveled on the riverboats. It was nothing unusual.

Brenna, looking about her, felt her first prick of doubt. What was she going to do with them all? Certainly her uncle would be in no mood to offer them shelter. At this point, a dray driver, rattling close with his ponderous wagon, stared directly at her and made a suggestive remark. He had mistaken them for whores.

Quickly Brenna turned and marshalled her group into some sort of order. They would find a carriage, she decided instantly. And a hotel.

By waving her hands frantically, she managed to stop an ancient-looking carriage driven by a coffee-colored *gens de couleur* who, after seeing her gold coins, agreed to transport them. He would even, he promised, obtain a second carriage so that all of the girls could ride. He also knew of a cheap, decent hotel. Of course, all of the young women would have to sleep in one big room, but the meals were good, the food plentiful, and the bedbugs few. What more could they wish?

Awkwardly, in the dark, cramped lobby of the hotel, they parted.

"Brenna . . . oh, Brenna, I will miss you!" Coleen blurted, to Brenna's astonishment. She pressed her hand. "I hated you once, did you know that?"

Brenna nodded.

"If you ever come to Boston . . ."

"Yes, of course." The two embraced, feeling strange with each other. Then Rosalia gave Brenna a swift hug, and pressed the shell rosary into her hand.

Back in the street, Brenna and Glory climbed into the waiting carriage. For the first time Brenna was conscious of the stares of passersby at the remnants of her once-lovely muslin gown, now soiled beyond recognition.

"Where we going now?" Glory asked in the soft voice with the accent so like Brenna's own.

"To my uncle's home. I . . . I hope it will go well there."

The black coachman looked at her questioningly. "To Prytania Street, please," she told him. She drew a deep breath and squeezed Glory's hand, trying not to think about what lay ahead.

❧ Chapter 28 ❧

THEY DROVE THROUGH the Creole section of the city, and memories of Brenna's last days in New Orleans came flooding back to her. Arbutus in her wedding dress. Arbutus as they had seen her near the docks, looking like a young, contented matron. And Kane's disturbing words. *Her name is Yvette and she's one of the loveliest quadroon women in the city . . .*

Brenna had not spared many thoughts for her cousin since leaving the city, she thought guiltily. So much had happened that those in New Orleans had seemed to fade into the distance, like figures seen at the bottom of a deep well.

But now images of Arbutus came pouring back; the warmhearted, bubbly, chattering girl she had known.

Impulsively she leaned forward and spoke to the driver. "Please, I've changed my mind. I'd like you to take us to the Carlisle plantation . . . Carlisle Oaks. You know where that is, don't you, on the river road?"

As the carriage changed direction, Brenna made hasty plans. Instead of going directly to her uncle, she would go to Arbutus. Surely, no matter how much scandal had erupted here, Arbutus would not refuse her shelter. And at Carlisle Oaks she and Glory could get a change of clothing and send a message to Uncle Amos, so they would not have to arrive on his doorstep in rags and completely unannounced.

The Carlisle plantation had been named for two rows
of live oaks, standing like sentinels along the avenue leading to the house. As the carriage pulled into the long,
straight drive, Brenna was struck by the beauty of the
great white-plastered house, glimmering through the trees.
Many slim pillars supported the encircling upper balcony,
with its delicate wrought-iron railing. Palms, flowers and
vines grew in profusion next to the house and up over the
walls, so that the building looked natural in its setting, as
if it might have grown from the earth.

This, Brenna thought slowly, was Arbutus' home. She
was mistress here.

She saw that Glory, too, was staring at the house, her
hands pressed tightly together, so that her knuckles were
pale. The driver pulled the carriage around to the back,
obviously expecting them to use the servants' entrance.

"No, no, driver. We'll use the front entrance. Please
turn your carriage around."

The driver turned and scowled at her, looking over
her ragged gown, the crudely mended bodice, her hair
pulled back into a wispy knot.

"Brenna! Oh, Brenna, is it really you?" A voice seemed
to float disembodied in the misty air.

Brenna turned, startled, to see a woman and a child
emerge from a wild, overgrown garden. The woman
clutched at her wide-brimmed white hat as she limped
toward them over the lawn, pulling the child so fast that
it nearly tripped over its long, white dress. The little girl
held a flat basket of flowers, blossoms spilling out.

"Arbutus!" Brenna jumped out of the carriage.

"Brenna, I couldn't believe it when I saw that carriage
coming in, and then there you were, just like that! Oh,
I've thought of you so often, wondering what had happened to you—"

The two girls embraced. Even through the fabric of
Arbutus' gown, Brenna could feel her new, bony thinness.
Her shoulder blades felt like chicken wings.

The cousins pulled away and looked at each other.
Arbutus wore a plain white cambric day gown which gave
her a look of utmost fragility. Her hair was dressed in an
elaborate cascade of curls peeping out from under her ex-

pensive bonnet. Her face, with its clear, pale skin and pansy eyes, was as delicately beautiful as ever.

"Mama!" The child, a dark-haired, round-faced little girl, plucked impatiently at her stepmother's skirts.

"You're so thin!" Brenna cried.

"And you . . . that dress, Brenna! And your skin, it's so brown! Haven't you been wearing your bonnet?"

They clung to each other and laughed, barely aware of the whimpering child beside them. At last Arbutus said, "I'll attend to you in a moment, Monica, darling. Do be patient. You had better come inside the house with me, Brenna. You'll want to freshen up. And shall we dismiss the carriage? Your driver looks positively surly. And is this girl your servant? Oh, there's so much to talk about! If you could only know how much I've missed you."

Continuing her flow of chatter, Arbutus, over Brenna's protests, paid the driver with a coin taken from her own apron pocket. She lifted the child and hugged her to quiet her complaining.

"Do come into the house, it will be cooler there. The air is so thick and muggy today, I'm sure it's going to rain any minute." Insistently, Arbutus pulled Brenna along to the side veranda, where a plump, dark servant took charge of Glory. "Feed her well, Dulceen, and find her some clean, presentable clothing. And do take Monica to the nursery. It's time for her nap, isn't it?"

Arbutus took Brenna's arm again, and urged her into the house. "The both of you in rags, Brenna! I declare, what has happened to you? We will go into my sitting room and you can tell me all about it. Monty is in town," she added, her expression shadowing slightly. "We will have plenty of time to talk and decide what to do before he arrives. I am sure he will welcome you as much as I do." But somehow Arbutus' voice did not carry full conviction.

Feeling as if she were moving in a dream world of polished flooring and crystal chandeliers and rich paneling, Brenna followed her cousin into the small, first-floor sitting room. It was a charming room with a high ceiling. Tall French windows opened onto the back veranda and the overgrown garden, with its wild masses of flowers and shrubs. The walls were white, and there was pale yellow carpeting, and dainty yellow brocaded furniture, so that the room seemed full of sunlight and the outdoors.

"This is a beautiful room!" Brenna exclaimed.

"Yes, I like it, too. I am having many of the rooms completely redone," Arbutus said. "But I don't want to talk about that. What about you? What happened to you? Where have you been? Did you really run away with Captain Fairfield, as they say? Are you married to him? Oh, I have so many questions! Please do sit down so we can talk as we used to. Those days seem so long ago, don't they?"

Brenna hesitated, then lowered herself onto a delicate chaise. In this sunny, luxurious room, against the contrast of Arbutus' perfect costume and hair, she felt soiled and untidy.

"I don't know where to start," she said slowly. "I suppose you must think the worst of me . . . and of course, you have every right to. I . . . I have done some things which would shock you . . ." She let her words trail off, all at once feeling unutterably tired. So much had happened. But there would be so little that this delicate, eager girl could understand.

Arbutus pulled a small armchair close to the chaise and sat in it. She leaned forward, and Brenna saw violet shadows under her eyes. "Please . . . won't you tell me? I . . . I won't think the worst of you, really I won't. I am not a young girl anymore, but a married woman. And I love you, cousin. I wish only the best for you."

So, Brenna began to pour out all that had happened, leaving out only Neall's death and the night spent with Gasparilla, events that she would never be able to share with anyone.

"Oh." Arbutus looked down, her lips quivering slightly. "You do love Kane, don't you? Yet he is going to leave you," she said heavily.

"Cousin, is anything wrong?"

"Wrong? Of course not, everything is fine with me. I have lost a bit of weight, of course. But I will probably gain it back with the baby, Doctor Bradley says. Isn't it wonderful? I do love children so, and Monty is hoping it will be a boy. He wants an heir for Carlisle Oaks."

Arbutus was blinking back tears, an incongruous contrast to her cheerful words.

"Arbutus, are you sure nothing is wrong?"

"Pardon me for . . . for weeping. I didn't mean to, I was trying not to. But I have recently learned something that I would rather never have known. Monty has a quadroon mistress. And he has children by her. Three of them. He is probably visiting her at this very moment. Remember, Brenna, we talked about such things, we whispered about them. But it didn't touch us—it wasn't real. And now it is."

So Arbutus knew. Brenna didn't know what to say.

"I will go on as before, of course," Arbutus continued. "There is Monica . . . and the baby to come. And the house. I love Carlisle Oaks, Brenna. I feel as if I belong here, as if all these years the house has been waiting for me to come . . . is that so wrong of me, to love the house?"

"No, no, of course not. Oh, cousin . . ."

Quickly, Brenna changed the subject, and asked Arbutus for fresh clothing and for her help in dealing with Uncle Amos. As if in relief, Arbutus concentrated on the problem of sending a message to Amos, and sorted through her wardrobe for a gown that would fit Brenna.

She held up a light green striped gingham with gabrielle sleeves. "Yes, this should do. It will fit, and it's sober and meek enough to please Mama." Arbutus giggled, then grew serious. "I do hope you know what you are doing, cousin. There has been much scandal over your running away. People whisper about you. No doubt some of them will cut you."

"I don't care about that. Let them say what they wish."

"You really love him very much, don't you, Brenna?"

"Yes."

"I love Monty, too, although I know I could not be so brave as you are." Arbutus turned away to hide her face.

Brenna and Glory left late in the afternoon in one of the Carlisle Oaks carriages, a fine brougham pulled by matched chestnut bays. Glory wore a dark gray cotton dress, a white *tignon* and apron, and looked fresh and neat, although the dark shade of the dress did not compliment her skin. She would look best in gay colors, Brenna decided. And she would give Glory her freedom. The thought of owning another person made Brenna feel uneasy.

She occupied herself with these thoughts on the long drive back to the city. Arbutus' words ran through her mind. *I do hope you know what you are doing.* Perhaps she was being a fool. But she couldn't bear the thought of leaving Kane behind when she still might be able to see him. Touch him, help him . . .

By the time they arrived at her uncle's house, she was perspiring with nervousness. They were greeted at the front door by the tall butler, Domo, who eyed Glory suspiciously. Brenna learned that, although the message to Amos had been received, he had not been home to read it. He was still at his office.

Her heart sank. She would have to present herself to him without advance preparation. She could not help noticing that the house smelled musty. Domo's livery was not altogether tidy. It was odd, she thought, for Aunt Rowena had been a fussy housekeeper.

"May I wait for him?" she asked at last. "Or, if Aunt Rowena is at home, I'll talk with her."

"She in her bed. She not well," the servant replied.

"Oh. My cousin, Jessica, then?"

"Miss Jessica, she in Natchez now, visiting friends. She been gone three weeks or more."

"Then may I wait in the drawing room? I would like to speak with my uncle. I am sure he will not mind if I wait."

"Yes, ma'am. But she, she go kitchen." Domo indicated Glory with a contemptuous incline of his head. The girl gave Brenna a quick, pleading look, and Brenna nodded. Reluctantly, Glory left with Domo.

The minutes ticked by, marked off by an ormolu clock on the white-painted mantel. Brenna sat on the red velvet couch looking about her. This was the room where she had seen Kane for the first time, and where Toby Rynne had first proposed. But now the room looked unused. The pianoforte was dusty, and Arbutus' harp was gone. A shaft of late sun streamed through the window, to lie in bars on the Turkish carpet, motes of dust floating in it.

It was odd, she thought, that her aunt did not come down to greet her. Perhaps she was seriously ill. That would explain why the house seemed neglected. Well, she would find out soon enough from Amos. Or from Mary. Surely her old Irish nurse must be somewhere about, and could tell her what had been happening.

She had been sitting nearly an hour when Amos arrived, slightly out of breath and smelling of whiskey.

"Brenna!" He seemed to recoil when he saw her. "What are you doing here? I thought you were off with your paramour. Or is it husband now?"

"Uncle Amos." She got up and forced herself to walk toward him, to face him without flinching. "Uncle Amos, I have nowhere else to go at present. Can you allow me and my servant to stay here for a week or so until I can make other arrangements? In a few days, I expect to receive enough money to pay you for my board."

"So. You expect to come back, just like that. After all the scandal and heartbreak you have caused? A ruined wedding, your poor aunt taken to her bed with shame over what you did?"

"Is Aunt Rowena ill?" Brenna tried to steady her voice, and hide her nervousness.

"She took to her bed a few days after the wedding. She has grown steadily worse. And it is your fault, you slut! I should have known better than to allow you to enter my home at all. We had to send Jessica to Natchez because of the scandal. And Arbutus' life has been most difficult. Only because of Mr. Carlisle is she received in polite society at all."

Brenna flushed. Arbutus had not said a word of this. "I . . . I'm sorry," she said. "I didn't think—"

"Of course you didn't think!" Amos said furiously. "We arranged an excellent marriage for you with a man who wanted you despite your penniless state and already dubious reputation. But you spurned all that to run away with a disreputable fly-by-night—a man accused of murder!"

"Kane did not murder anyone! And he . . . he's determined to prove it!"

"Oh? And where is this fine Kane Fairfield of yours? Out killing more innocent men? Or, perhaps, seducing more pretty girls? Is he the one who will pay me for your board? He did not marry you, I gather, did he? And now you expect us to shelter you."

He was so close to her that she could see beads of perspiration among the hairs of his moustache, and little red, crooked veins along his nose. He gripped her shoulder. "Well, let me tell you something, miss. You are here now, and you owe us something for what you put us through. You will stay here, and you will repay your debt. I am going to notify Toby Rynne that you are here. We shall see what *he* has to say."

"No . . . please . . ." Brenna flinched back from him. "I . . . I do wish to see him, of course, but not like this."

"You'll talk to him as *I* wish. Remember, I am your legal guardian now. I have every right to make you do as I desire."

"No, I'm sure you're mistaken. My brother, Quentin, is my guardian now, is he not? He . . . he was twenty-one recently, I am sure."

"Your brother Quentin is a drunk, lying unconscious in the streets for all I know," Amos said harshly, spittle flying from his mouth. "He lost his lodgings, and he's been living from pillar to post, depending on handouts. He's no fit guardian for anyone. The scum of the city, that's what I would call him!"

She was horrified. "But . . . the money! The money we gave him!"

"Money? The faro table took that, my dear. What did you expect from such a wastrel? The two of you make a fine pair!"

"But didn't you help him?" she whispered. "Surely you could have done something. So at least he could have kept his lodgings!"

"I haven't the money to throw away on hopeless causes. Besides, I believe some octoroon girl has taken him in and feeds him now and again." Amos threw back his head and laughed. "The milk of human kindness appears in unlikely places, does it not?"

Brenna lowered her head, unable to speak.

"So," Amos concluded pompously, "I am your guardian. And I have decided that you will stay here."

"But . . ."

"Go upstairs, Brenna. This is no longer your concern. I plan to send a message to Toby at once. After all, it's only his right after the way you mistreated him!"

Brenna tried to think, but her mind seemed full of hopeless, skittering thoughts. "My slave, Glory. She is waiting in the kitchen. She needs a room."

"She is a slave? She shall go in the quarters with my own people. And perhaps I shall sell her. After all, you do owe me something for all the trouble you put me through."

"But Glory is mine! Kane made the papers over to me!"

"I am your guardian, and I shall decide how to dispose of your property. Now, enough of this. Up to your old room with you. And do freshen up a bit before Toby arrives, will you? You look ugly with your hair screwed in that makeshift bun. A pity, isn't it, that we had to get rid of that hairdresser of yours, Mary, or whatever her name was."

"Mary? She's gone?"

"With Rowena ill and Jessica and Arbutus out of the house, do you think we could keep an extra mouth to feed? We let the woman go to another family—they have five daughters and I am sure they keep her very busy."

"But . . . she was my servant! I brought her from Ireland with me. She—"

"You should have thought of that before you ran away, my dear. Now, upstairs with you. At once. I have work to do."

Stunned, Brenna went upstairs, clinging to the railing. For one wild moment she thought of rushing out of the house, of running away. But Glory was in the kitchen, trusting her to return.

She gripped the bannister, feeling dizzy. So much had changed, she thought. In only a few months. Quentin a drunkard now, Mary gone to another family. Aunt Rowena ill and Jessica gone. Arbutus a wife and mother.

And now Uncle Amos wanted to steal Glory, she thought feverishly. She reached the top of the stairs and turned down the corridor toward her old room, her footsteps echoing on the bare flooring. How empty the house sounded.

She was about to open her own door when she heard a silken, rustling noise behind her. She turned to see a white-clad figure at the end of the corridor, silhouetted against a window.

"Aunt Rowena!"

Her aunt had been a small, precise person with gray-beige skin, always dressed in immaculate muslin and a starched cap. But now, clad in an untidy and wrinkled nightgown, Rowena looked old and obviously ill. Her skin seemed grayer, and soft, like a chamois skin. Her hair, capless, was disheveled.

"Is it you? Gwenyth?" Gwenyth. Her mother's name. Her aunt passed one hand vaguely in front of her face.

"No, no, I'm Brenna. Gwenyth's daughter. Your niece." What was wrong with Aunt Rowena? She acted drugged, groggy. And she was gray—gray all over.

"Oh. Brenna. But I thought . . . where is that Hattie girl? I want my bath, I was supposed to have it, it's far past the time . . ." she said petulantly. As she moved, Brenna caught a whiff of staleness.

"I don't know where Hattie is, but I'm here," Brenna said. "I've come back. May I help you to your bed, Aunt Rowena? Since Hattie hasn't come yet?"

"Help me? No . . . no, I don't need help. I can walk by myself. You say you're back. Did he marry you, that good-looking Fairfield man? Or did he just take you and throw you away?"

The sharp words, after the woman's fogginess, set Brenna aback. "Why, I—"

"He didn't marry you, did he?" The ill face brightened in a malicious smile. "I didn't think he would. No, I didn't think so. I thought you'd come back, ruing the day. I thought someday you'd be back on our mercy. And so you are."

Brenna did not reply, but grimly took the stick-thin arm and helped Rowena into her bedroom, which was a clutter of untidy bedclothes, liniment bottles, strewn books, empty trays, pillows, orange peelings and coffee cups. She stood and waited while the older woman climbed unsteadily onto a low stool and then into the four-poster bed.

"I have female troubles, you know," Rowena said, settling herself. "Or at least that's what the doctor says it is. Myself, I suspect it's a tumor, down there, growing like a melon. A tumor." She touched her belly and closed her eyes. The lids were white and papery. "I'll probably die soon—it wouldn't surprise me in the least. But at least I lived long enough to see you crawl back, looking like a little mouse. A very sorry little mouse. Oh, yes, your mother never paid fully for the wrong she did me. But perhaps you will. Perhaps you will indeed."

❧ *Chapter 29* ❧

BRENNA WENT TO HER ROOM, where she paced back and forth. A few minutes later there was a knock, and the maid, Hattie, came in, looking weary.

"Miss Brenna, you wants a bath or anything? I hears you come back."

"Why, yes, Hattie. A bath sounds wonderful. And could you bring some egg shampoo for my hair? After you've looked after Aunt Rowena, of course."

The bath was warm, scented and luxurious, the most relaxing moment she had spent in weeks. For the first time, her spirits began to rise. Kane was resourceful; he would clear himself and get the necessary facts to convict Toby. Together, Kane and she would save Glory, and take care of Mary and Quentin. Brenna began to feel that things might go well, after all.

Her bubble burst when Hattie came panting back upstairs to say that a gentleman was waiting in the drawing room to see her.

Quickly Brenna dressed, coiled her damp hair into a thick knot at the base of her neck, and covered it with a lacy day-cap. She hoped he wouldn't notice her hair was not yet fully dry.

He was standing at the bottom of the stairs, gazing up at her as she descended. Uncle Amos was tactfully out of sight. The candles were already lit, and Brenna knew she looked lovely and slim, her breasts temptingly revealed by the low neckline of the gown she had chosen.

At the bottom of the stairs, her courage faltered. "Toby . . ."

He had changed. His coat was somber black, and he was thinner now, harder. His face was longer, leaner—somehow more dangerous.

"So. You are back—and you are as lovely as ever."

"Yes, I'm back," she said awkwardly.

"Fairfield has grown tired of you, has he?" She felt his hand digging into her upper arm, and then he pulled her into the drawing room. He shoved her against the white-painted fireplace mantel.

"Please! You're hurting me!"

"I intend to. You have hurt me, why shouldn't I hurt you?"

"I . . . I guess there is nothing I can say to that," she managed. "I couldn't go through with the marriage after all." She moistened her lips, and tried to swallow past the cold lump in her throat. "You can't blame me for everything that happened, Toby. You and I . . . we didn't have love together. All we had was your obsession to marry me."

His eyes widened slightly, and a flush stained his cheeks. "You were mine, Brenna. I'd marked you off as mine. You wounded my pride, and I'm not going to let you get away with it."

"Please, you're holding me too tightly. It hurts. Please let me go!"

"Not until you give me a few facts. Where is Fairfield? Where is he? I'm going to kill him."

"Kill him? You can't! You—" She stopped, remembering all the deaths Toby had been indirectly responsible for —Kane's murdered crewmen, the old Spanish woman . . .

"I have every right to revenge what the man did to me."

"Do you?" Brenna narrowed her eyes at him. "Well, I can't tell you where he is because I don't know. He left me at the docks and went off somewhere. He didn't tell me where he was going or what he planned to do. And I didn't ask. As you said, he has tired of me."

Toby scowled. "I can find out, you know. If he's in this

city, I'll find him. The man owes me a great deal. He owes me my brother's life, and my wife. I'll see he repays that debt."

"But I was never your wife."

Slowly Toby released her arm. "Perhaps that's true. But you will be my wife. You will come to church and marry me, and this time it will be real. Very real indeed."

She walked over to the pianoforte, and sat down at the bench. She played a few chords, loud, smashing ones, expressing her anger and frustration.

"I don't feel I owe you the rest of my life because of that one day," she heard herself saying coolly. "I can't marry you. I—"

Suddenly, before she could move or react, Toby was behind her, his hands cupped under her breasts. His face pressed into the back of her neck.

"Brenna, God help me, after all you've done, I still desire you. I don't care what sort of lover Fairfield has been to you, I'll be better. I'll love you properly, I'll love you as no one has ever loved you before . . ."

She struggled, but he twisted her around, and pressed his mouth against hers, devouring her.

At last she managed to pull away.

"You've changed, Brenna." He was smiling. "You're a woman now. I can tell by the way you kiss me. You can learn to love me, your body can respond to me. It already has. I know it. We'll be married, Brenna. I'll take you to bed. Then I'll show you. I'll show you all the things that a man and a woman can do together . . ."

She slid away from him, along the bench, her heart slamming with horror. For it was as if she had heard Gasparilla's voice again: *I am only a man, not a monster. I will not hurt you.*

It was two days later. Brenna had spent the time resting, visiting Arbutus, and making arrangements for Coleen and the other girls to return to their homes. Glory had settled in the slave quarters, learning household duties. Toby Rynne had called a second time, leaving the house with his face flushed, almost jocular.

For she had told him she would marry him.

Even now, after nearly two days, she couldn't believe
it had happened. Had she really pressed her hands into his
and agreed to his demands?

It had happened so suddenly. She had gotten up from
the pianoforte bench, her head pounding, wanting only to
get away from his presence. Again he had grabbed her,
pressing his body against hers.

"Did Fairfield love you like this? Did he? Did he?"
He had covered her face with his kisses.

Kane. The thought had been like a bucket of ice water
poured over her shoulders. It was Kane she loved, Kane
she was trying to help. If she could manage to get close to
Toby, to win his trust, then she might be able to get the
information Kane needed.

If she said she would marry him . . .

Of course, it would be a lie. He would surely be exposed, perhaps within only a few days. So she would never
have to carry out her promise. She had pushed down a
twinge of conscience, telling herself that the lie wouldn't
matter. After all, Toby was a pirate, and had been responsible for many deaths.

"P-Perhaps you are right," she said at last. "Perhaps I
do owe you something." She pulled away from him and
smiled, trying to stop her lips from trembling.

"Yes?"

"Perhaps I can marry you after all. I . . . I don't love
you, of course. You know that. But maybe I can learn to
be fond of you . . ."

This was the best she could do, but it had been enough.
He had whooped victoriously, lifted her high, and whirled
her about. She had sensed the enormous strength of his
beefy arms. In bed he would be a strong, aggressive lover.
He would keep her aware of his power . . .

Toby had begun making plans, but she had put him off,
saying that she was tired and wished to consult with her
aunt first. She had not been well, she had told him truthfully enough. She had suffered from yellow fever and had
been very ill. She needed time to rest and recuperate; later
they could plan the wedding.

She had listened to her own voice saying these things
with a kind of numb wonder. Was that really Brenna

Laughlan, laughing softly as she conveyed the impression that she had been swayed by Toby's lovemaking? That she was willing to try to make amends?

After he had left, she had gone up to her room in a jangle of confusion, dismay and self-disgust. Again she had acted impulsively, thinking only of how she could help Kane. She felt a flood of foreboding. What if things went wrong? What if she were forced to fulfill her promise?

But things wouldn't go wrong, she assured herself. In a week at most, she and Kane would have collected the evidence needed to convict Toby. For now, she must coax him to talk of his business, his plans for the future, his daily routine. She would listen carefully, writing everything down so she could send it to Kane. If there was only some way, she thought feverishly, to follow Toby about the city, watching what he did and where he went.

This had to be the right thing she was doing. It had to be.

It was the morning of what promised to be another hot, moist day. Brenna was in her room, impatiently waiting for the carriage to be brought around. She had two purposes for going driving today. She wanted to go and assure herself Mary was all right. And she wanted to speak with Tiny.

There was a knock at her door. "Carriage ready, Miss Brenna," Hattie said.

"Thank you."

She hurried downstairs to find Tiny waiting in front of the house with the small two-seater. She sagged with relief. It was Tiny she wanted to speak to, not any of the other, older, slaves. Tiny was a boy in a man's huge body, but there was something about him she trusted.

She ordered him to drive to the Rydells' house, where Mary was in service. However, as soon as the carriage was underway, and had passed down the avenue far enough to be invisible from the house, she leaned forward and asked Tiny to stop. He pulled up under the shadow of an enormous live oak.

"Tiny, I must talk to you for a moment."

"Yes'm?" Tiny turned to look at her. She sensed an

eager, restless quality in him. It must be difficult for him to stick to the slow, placid routine of Aunt Rowena's establishment.

"Tiny, remember the brooch I gave you, before I left? On the day you drove me down to the docks?"

"Yes'm."

"Did your girl like the brooch?"

"Yes'm, Miss Brenna, she did." His smile was wide.

"Well, Tiny, I have a gold piece here in my bag that I will give you if you will do something for me. You and, perhaps, someone else you might hire to help you."

Tiny's face grew immediately serious; she was aware that a few of the slaves tried to save up money to purchase their freedom. At the very least, there would be trinkets, food or clothing that Tiny might wish to buy.

Hastily she outlined to him what she wanted done. He was to follow Toby Rynne and report to her. She wanted to know where he went, whom he saw, and the locations of any property or buildings he owned. If necessary, Tiny should hire another boy, perhaps a freeman, to work with him. She would give him one gold piece now and another later. Carefully, she emphasized the secrecy of what they were doing. If he were to be caught . . .

The boy nodded. It was clear that he grasped the danger.

"Do you think you can do it, Tiny? I know it might be hard for you to do alone . . . that's why I thought you might want to get someone to help you. But I don't know anyone else to ask. If you can't help me, I don't know what I'll do."

"I can do it, Miss Brenna. And I can get help."

"Can you?" She felt like laughing. She leaned forward and unobtrusively slipped the coin into his hand. "But it has to be soon, Tiny. As quickly as you can."

"Today's Saturday. Most of us going to Congo Square for the dancing. I have a friend and I see him then. It be all right."

With that, she had to be content.

The Rydell home was an imposing Greek revival structure with white pillars in front, and a lawn clipped and trimmed to a perfection unusual in this city of rampant growing things. Brenna had been here several times during her first months in the city. Anne and Celia Rydell, the two older girls, were vivacious and popular.

She presented her card and stood waiting in the huge, tiled foyer, hearing from the second story the muted sounds of young girls giggling, probably from the schoolroom.

She waited what seemed like a very long time before the butler returned to tell her that Mrs. Rydell was resting at the moment and could not receive her today.

"Perhaps tomorrow, then? I . . . I must have an opportunity to speak with Mrs. Rydell about my servant, Mary."

The butler, a tall, thin man with flaring nostrils, regarded her coldly, his dark eyes flickering. "She be resting tomorrow, too."

"Oh—" For an instant, Brenna stood stunned. Then she realized what was happening. She was being cut by Mrs. Rydell. No longer received. And, she thought wildly, even the servant knew of her predicament and was gloating about it. Everyone had passed judgment on her.

She turned and rushed from the house, nearly stumbling in her haste to leave.

"Home, Tiny!" she ordered recklessly. She got into the carriage before he could assist her, her face and neck burning. As they drove away, she looked up to see a corner of a curtain in an upper window move furtively. Someone was watching her leave.

❧ *Chapter 30* ❧

SHE SAT AT THE SMALL TABLE in her room, struggling with her note to Kane, frowning at the two blots she had already made. In her haste, she had pressed down too hard upon the quill. But there was so much to tell him. So much had happened.

I have learned that my servant, Mary Flannagan, has been taken in service by the Rydell family. Bleak lines to express that painful moment.

I am worried about my brother, Quentin, to whom I have sent three letters. But each time, Tiny returns saying that Quentin cannot be found. I fear something has happened to him.

She laid down the pen and looked out the window at the hot, brilliant blue of the sky. A smell of wisteria and honeysuckle drifted up from the courtyard, almost sickeningly sweet. She had wanted to go and look for Quentin herself. But Aunt Rowena, propped in her bed against piles of goose-feather pillows, had flatly forbidden it.

"We tolerate you in our home for the moment, but we will not countenance any more of your scandalous undertakings. Do you possibly intend to search every alley and gambling place for your brother? It would be a disgrace! I will have Amos look into it. I am sure you need not concern yourself longer."

"But, Aunt Rowena—"

"You must live as circumspect a life as possible, Brenna,

until some of your notoriety has died down. Fortunately, you have agreed to marry Toby Rynne. With his influence, I am sure it will not be long before you are fully accepted, at least in the American community. For the sake of Jessica and Arbutus, I wish this to happen as quickly as possible. Perhaps we can smooth over some of the consequences of your rash and heedless act."

"Why will I be accepted?" Brenna had asked. "Because everyone is afraid of Toby and what he can do to them?"

"Enough of that sort of talk! Or I will have you confined to your room until the wedding." In spite of her illness, Rowena's eyes had snapped with some of their old power.

"But I'm sure Quentin means no real harm," Brenna had protested. "If only I could talk with him, assure myself he is all right—"

"I am sure Amos will do the best he can. If Quentin is still in the city, he will turn up like any bad penny." Rowena had shrugged, and had reached for one of the novels littering the tables in her room. Red fluid in a medicine bottle had gleamed warm in the sun, medicine Rowena took less often now that Brenna was here.

Angrily, Brenna had turned away. If she knew Amos, his help would be worse than useless. No, she would get Kane's assistance. Or Tiny's.

Now she went on with her letter. *I have arranged passage on the* Sarah Lang *for Coleen; she is to leave in three days. The other girls have already departed on the* Temple *for Mexico City; I gave them some of the money you sent me to speed them on their way. I hope that meets with your approval.*

She stopped, tapping the end of the quill with her fingertip. What should she say next? She had to tell Kane of her engagement, of course. If she didn't, he would surely hear of it anyway.

As a ruse, I have agreed to marry Toby Rynne, in order to gain his trust and secure information from him. Therefore. . . . No, she didn't like the sound of that. *I must leave the city as soon as your name is cleared, since I do not plan to go through with the ceremony.*

She had made a list of the information brought her by Tiny and his friend, Raoul, most of it consisting of names

and addresses which were not familiar to her. The two
boys had been able to locate several old houses converted
into warehouses and owned by Toby, or at least visited by
him. Carefully she copied out these addresses. Toby had
mentioned something about "another big deal" just accomplished, and she wrote this down as well. She stared
gloomily at the paper. Was all this worth anything to him?
There was no way she could know.

She bent her head to the letter again, wanting to add
something more. *I still hear talk about you, so I am
hoping this matter is settled to your satisfaction. Please
be careful and do not take any risks. Yrs. with deep affection, Brenna Laughlan.*

She wasn't pleased with the letter; she hadn't said what
she wanted to say at all, and there were two dark blotches
of ink to mar her otherwise acceptable handwriting. But
it would have to do. Tiny was waiting near the quarters for
her to appear in the courtyard and deliver it to him.

She was just affixing a seal to the envelope when there
was a knock at her door. Hastily, she slid the letter under
her pillow, then opened the door. It was Hattie, with the
announcement that Miss Melissa Rynne waited downstairs
to see her.

Melissa!

As soon as Hattie had left, Brenna rushed to the mirror
to stare at herself. How flushed she looked, her cheeks
burning in two bright spots of red. Her hair, shining red-
gold with rich highlights, was pulled into a simple coil at
the nape of her neck. If only Mary were here to dress it
elaborately with ribbons and feathers!

She frowned at herself, wondering if she should change
from her day gown of amber striped gingham. But the
dress, new just before she had left New Orleans, was
trimmed with rows of lace, its cut emphasizing the fullness
of her breasts and the perfect slope of her shoulders. She
would not change, she decided.

She found Melissa pacing back and forth in the large,
tiled entrance hall, toying with a watch that was pinned
on a long chain to her belt. She wore white muslin and
a small, white bonnet trimmed with feathers and lace. If
anything, the girl was more lovely than before, her com-

plexion milk-pale, her hair done in gold ringlets which shone in the sunlight. Yet there was an agitated look about the small, lush mouth.

"Brenna, I have my carriage waiting outside, and would like to invite you to take a short drive with me. Would not some fresh air do you good this morning? My maid will accompany us."

"Why, I . . . I suppose I could," Brenna said, realizing that Melissa wanted to speak with her privately. "I should consult with my aunt, first," she added.

"Very well."

Brenna hurried upstairs to Rowena's room, where she found her aunt sitting up in bed, wearing a green velvet wrapper that accented the grayness of her skin, writing letters on a board. But if anything, her aunt seemed to be more energetic recently, as if Brenna's presence stimulated her.

Rowena granted permission with a dip of her long, sharp nose. "Why shouldn't you go? Melissa will be your new sister-in-law, will she not? Minx as she is, she's accepted here by American society. And you need all the acceptance you can get."

"Yes, ma'am." Angrily, Brenna excused herself, went to her room for a lace shawl, and then hurried downstairs.

Melissa's carriage, one of Toby's, was black and shiny, with gold *fleurs-de-lis* painted in gilt on the panels. Waiting inside the carriage was a small black girl of about fifteen, obviously brought along as chaperone.

"Agnes is my maid," Melissa said, adding something sharp in French to the girl that Brenna did not catch. "Don't concern yourself with her. She speaks only French, and will not be able to understand what we say if we speak English."

They drove at a slow, dignified pace past the gracious homes. Some were still in varying stages of construction, workmen swarming about the sites.

"You know, of course, why I am here," Melissa began.

"No, I don't believe I do," Brenna said as coldly as she could, remembering Kane's presumed attachment to the girl.

"Surely you don't think it is to welcome you into my

family! I would hardly do that! It is wrong, wrong for you to marry my brother, after what you did. Still, I suppose it doesn't matter. Toby . . ." Her voice broke off.

Brenna sat quietly, watching the sunlight flicker on the leaves of an oak tree as they passed it, long Spanish moss eerily draped from its branches.

"I hate my brother!" Melissa muttered under her breath.

"Hate him?"

"Of course I do!" With a dramatic gesture, Melissa jerked back the long sleeve of her gown to show black-and-blue bruises on her arm. "He did that—he!"

"Toby did that? But why would he? You're his sister."

"His half-sister," the girl corrected bitterly. "We did not meet until we were adults—I was nearly sixteen. And he has never been fond of me. Ulrich and I . . . we liked each other well enough. But Toby can think only of himself and his plans. And now he plans to kill Kane Fairfield!" The last words were spoken in a whisper. "He knows I would hate that, he knows that Kane and I have been . . . more than friends. And yet he won't listen to me, he won't listen . . ."

Melissa slowly pulled down her sleeve, her mouth twisting. "I have seen Kane since he came back. Did you know that?"

Brenna jerked around to stare at the other girl, the blood rushing to her cheeks. "What? You have seen him?"

"He knew where to find me. He wanted to see me. So he came."

"I . . . I trust he was well?" Brenna could hardly conceal her shock and dismay that Kane should seek out Melissa. She remembered the possessive way he had smiled at the girl at Aunt Rowena's party, when they had first met. Did he, after all, still love her?

"He was very well. Although I must say I do not like that beard he has grown. I will ask him to shave it off for me later, when things are settled."

When things are settled.

"And what did he tell you? What did he say?" she heard herself ask.

"Why, I don't believe it is anything I wish to share with you," the other girl said. "You thought you could take him away from me, didn't you? But he is mine now, more than ever." Antagonism hung between them sharply. "Anyway, I came to ask you to keep quiet about where Kane is. Toby has already tried to force me to tell." The blue eyes glinted. "I would rather die first."

"Of course I won't tell! What kind of a person do you think I am? Anyway, I don't know where he is. He . . . he has not been in touch with me."

For the first time, Melissa smiled. "Good. I was not sure." Her voice purred like a satisfied cat.

Brenna drew her back up straight. "I should like to go home. I have had quite enough fresh air."

They rode the short distance to her uncle's house in silence.

The days crept by, each filled with an uneasy mixture of boredom, strain, worry and waiting. Brenna still had not heard from Kane, although Tiny assured her he had delivered her letter to Maud Sweet's exactly as ordered.

Where was Kane? Had something gone wrong? Why hadn't he written her at least one letter? He could see Melissa, she told herself bitterly, but he hadn't time for her.

Worry permeated her day. She was barely able to touch her food and grew thinner. Quentin, too, filled her thoughts. Was he lying somewhere in a gutter, as Uncle Amos had declared several times? No, he couldn't be, she told herself staunchly. Quentin was too young for that. He still had his entire life ahead of him . . .

Toby, also, was a constant problem. Each day it grew harder to put off the marriage. One week had become nearly two. And Toby was so demanding, so insistent, as if having her had become the sole purpose of his life.

"I want you, Brenna," he had told her. "And I want you now, not next week or six months from now. You've had time enough to recover from the fever—you look healthy enough to me. Why shouldn't we marry immediately? Why should we wait?"

"I . . . I must rest," she had said lamely. "I am not sleeping well, and I am still weak. Also, I must have time to grow accustomed to you, to change my thinking toward you. Surely you can be generous enough to grant me that?"

"You can grow accustomed to me after our marriage,"
Toby had given her a slow, hot look that seemed to strip
the very clothing from her body. "If you are not careful,
I will creep into your bedroom some night and steal you
away, just as Fairfield did. If you could run away with
him, surely you would not object to me, the man you have
twice agreed to marry?"

A threat had hung in these words. Or was she mistaken?
She didn't know. Toby was a stranger, and his thoughts
were unreadable to her.

They were to be married in the cathedral. Not, of course,
that she planned to go through with the ceremony. Surely
Kane would come for her before then. *Please, please, let
me hear from him,* she would pray before she fell asleep
each night. *Let me know he is all right . . .*

Without Jessica, Arbutus and Mary, the house seemed
empty and dead. With Rowena confined to her bed, the
affairs of the house faltered. Floors needed waxing, upholstery needed beating. Brenna took to eating most of her
meals in her room. She seldom saw Amos. Since Rowena's
illness, he spent most of his time at the office or elsewhere,
as if trying to escape what waited at home. He treated
Toby with an uneasy reserve. Had Toby threatened him in
some way, to make sure the wedding would take place as
scheduled?

Brenna sank into a nervous depression, unable to con-
centrate on the novels she borrowed from her aunt or the
embroidery she had forced herself to start. Even teaching
Glory English no longer brought her satisfaction, although
she insisted on spending as much time with the girl as she
could. She had set aside some of the money Kane had
given her; if necessary, she would buy Glory back from
Amos. But so far her uncle had not mentioned selling her
again.

They had heard nothing of Quentin, although Amos
claimed to have hired a man to search for him. Then one
morning, on her way back with Glory after a fitting at the
dressmaker's, their carriage paused at a corner, where a
shrimp vendor was calling out his wares. Clustered about
him was a group of women, their *tignons* gleaming white
in the hot morning sun.

Idly Brenna watched them, thinking how lovely some of

them were, with their slim, yet voluptuous bodies, their
exotic features so like Glory's, although their skin was
much lighter—the color of coffee diluted with cream. One
girl, wearing a red dress, was truly stunning, her skin so
light she could almost be mistaken for white . . .

The girl turned, holding a basketful of shrimp, swaying
her hips in a careless way. Brenna stared, thinking how
familiar she looked. Almost like the girl she had seen that
day outside Quentin's apartments . . .

"Tiny! Please stop the carriage!" she called, without
stopping to think. She jumped down, paying no attention to
Glory's startled exclamation. She lifted her skirts and ran
after the girl, who had turned a corner and was hurrying
along the uneven sidewalk.

"Stop! Wait, please!"

To her dismay, the girl didn't turn, but only hurried
on faster, clutching her basket.

"Please stop! I only want to talk to you for a minute!
Just for a minute! I won't hurt you—"

The girl looked around, then started to run, a difficult
task on the irregular, sloping sidewalk, riddled with rotted-
away spots. But in spite of this, the girl was graceful and
surefooted.

But Brenna had spent her girlhood on horseback and
running across the hills behind Quentin and his friends,
always struggling to keep up. And she did not have a
basket loaded with shrimp to hamper her, for, even in her
haste, the other girl was too practical to drop her purchases.

The girl stumbled, and before she could begin running
again, Brenna caught up with her. She grabbed the girl's
arm.

"Please—I only want to ask you one thing and then
you can go. Are you Quentin's friend? The girl who was
taking care of him?"

The girl shrank away as far as she could. Seen at close
range, she was truly beautiful, with brown eyes flecked
with gold, and a creamy, even complexion the color of milk
shaded lightly with brown. Her lips were full and defiant.

"I won't tell you anything!"

"Then you know where he is. You are that girl, the one

I saw outside his apartments, the one he called . . . was
it Lucille?"

"No . . . no—" She was frightening the girl, Brenna
knew, and she didn't want to do that. Yet every instinct
told her that this was the girl who had been caring for
Quentin.

"I know you are Lucille, because I recognized you. Now
I don't plan to hurt you or Quentin. I'm his sister, Brenna.
Surely he's told you about me? I'm his family, the only
real family he has left now, and I wish only good things
for him."

The girl stared at her. Down the street the vendor raised
his voice as he moved to another corner. Carriage wheels
rattled, a dog barked.

Lucille seemed to relax. "He's somewhere safe," she
said. "I'm not telling you where that is."

"Good." Brenna released the girl's arm. "I'm glad he's
safe because I've been so worried about him. Lucille, is he
still drinking and gambling as he was? I must know."

"No, ma'am, he isn't. I'm not letting him."

"You're not?"

"No, ma'am," said Lucille. "I don't want him to be like
that and he doesn't want it either. That's why we're getting
ready to leave this city. Day after tomorrow, we're going
on a riverboat, as far as it'll take us. No thanks to you
and the likes of you," she added fiercely. "Coddling and
cosseting him, letting him feel that someone will always
be there to clean up after him. . . . Well, he's getting
away from that, him and me both are. Getting away from
you. We're going west. We're going to homestead out
there, just the two of us and some land, it's all we
need . . ."

"But . . . Quentin's never farmed."

Lucille's gold-brown eyes hardened. "Yes, I know what
you're thinking. He's soft and weak, never farmed in his
life, and I'm nothing but a dark-skinned girl, can't even
read and not good enough for him. Well, we don't care
about that. It's a chance for us, and for him, better than
we got in New Orleans, anyway. Here there's nothing but
faro and monte and . . . and whorehouses and men like
Billy Love ready to kill a man if he can't pay back the

money he owes. Out west, Quentin isn't going to owe
money to anybody. He'll be free. We both will. I can pass
for white, and if I can't, we don't care. We're going anyway."

Brenna remembered Quentin as she had last seen him,
raddled and unkempt, ready to sell his sister to save his own
skin. And now here was this girl with skin the color of an
eggshell, willing to take Quentin and go away with him.
*I don't want him to be like that and he doesn't want it
either.*

"I . . . I wish you luck," Brenna said slowly. "I won't
try to see Quentin. I can see he doesn't want that, and
perhaps I don't want to see him either. But maybe sometimes you can let me know how you are. I'd like very
much to hear."

"Yes."

"Would you object if I gave you a little money to help
you on your way? I have some money that Kane Fairfield
gave me . . ." Brenna fumbled in her reticule.

"Kane Fairfield?" Lucille stared at the proffered money
without taking it.

"Why, yes. Do you know him?"

"I know that he's dead."

"He's what?" Brenna swayed. The low, stucco buildings,
the mucky street filled with refuse, seemed to sway and
twirl in front of her, in a kaleidoscope of blurred colors.
In the distance, the voice of the shrimp vendor mocked
her.

"A man was fished out of the canal near where me and
Quentin are staying. He was dead all right, stabbed through
his belly. He was all bloated and swole, but they said he
was Kane Fairfield. That's what Quentin heard them say,
and he told me. He said you . . . he said it's common
enough, a dead man every day in the streets, it's nothing
unusual . . ."

But Brenna did not hear the last of what Lucille said.
She had fainted.

❧ *Chapter 31* ❧

DIMLY SHE WAS CONSCIOUS of the hard wood of the sidewalk against her hips, of the slippery feel of the mud film on its surface. Faces bent over her, one of them Lucille's.

"She just passed right out . . ."

"Must be the heat, you think? Or the typhoid. You think it the fever?"

"She getting all dirty laying there . . ."

Their voices mingled in a clamor of sounds without meaning. Brenna stirred, moaning slightly.

"She moving now—"

"Miss Brenna! Miss Brenna!" Glory was kneeling beside her, wringing her hands. "Wake up!"

"Glory . . ."

She felt hands grip her shoulders, pull her into a sitting position. From somewhere came a tin cup filled with water. Glory pushed it to her lips, held it there until she drank. The water was lukewarm and full of sediment; she nearly choked on it.

"Miss Brenna, I get Tiny and we take you home right away."

"Kane . . ."

It was all a nightmare. This wasn't happening at all, none of it was. It wasn't real. It couldn't be. Kane wasn't dead, not that vital man with the superbly muscled body and gentle heart. No, it couldn't be!

She allowed herself to be helped up. She hardly be-

longed to the stumbling, shaking body that wept so convulsively. They rode home quickly through the streets. She
felt Glory pressing her cold hands between her warm ones.
She heard Tiny calling out to the horses, his voice harsher
than she had ever heard it, as if he, somehow, were
angry.

Then they were home, and Tiny carried her upstairs to
her bedroom. "I find out," he muttered as he left.

Glory undressed her, and thrust Hattie away angrily
when she came in to see what had happened. Glory slipped
her into her white, lace-trimmed, cambric nightgown and
tucked her underneath the coverlet as if she were ill.

Sick. She was sick, Brenna told herself, wearily. Sick of
all the dying, of all the lives taken away for no reason
whatever. Her father, the cabin boy Jemmy, the crew of
the *Sea Otter*. And now Kane.

Sobs ripped through her.

She didn't know how many days had passed. Was it only
one or two, or was it a week or more? Time had lost all
its meaning, empty hours inched by, one after the other,
in a gray fog. Meals, baths, bed . . . none of it touched
her, none of it seemed to matter. Her eyes were swollen,
her chest ached, and all her tears were gone. She could
only sit in the chair by the window and look out at the
courtyard, at the willow and the stone cupid, frozen permanently with his foolish smile.

Glory didn't leave her, even to sleep. Always the black
girl was there, to press her hand, to help with the dinner
tray, to look through the wardrobe for a fresh gown that
might please her. Once she heard Tiny's voice outside the
room, and Glory left for a moment. When she came back
her mouth was grim. *He told Glory that Kane is really
dead, that it is no mistaken rumor, but truth,* Brenna
thought. *He is dead. Dead.*

Arbutus came, filling every corner of the room with her
bright chatter, so that after she left the silence was heavy
and leaden. Uncle Amos looked in on her, clearing his
throat officiously. She had no right to grieve over Kane
when she was betrothed to someone else, he told her, his

small eyes puzzled and resentful. She would only bring trouble on them all.

Even Rowena came, leaning heavily on Hattie's arm, for she had not been walking well for some days now. Was there a flare of triumph in those sharp blue eyes? But Brenna didn't know, didn't care, and soon her aunt was gone. It didn't matter. None of it at all.

Another week went by. There was a pile of letters on her dressing table, unopened. At some point Brenna began to be aware that it was Tuesday. Then Wednesday. Her hair was growing oily and lank, and one morning she asked Glory to help her wash it.

"Miss Brenna, I tell you of M'butu, my man," Glory said, as she pulled a comb through Brenna's long, damp hair, untangling the snarls. "I was his . . . his wife. I loved him. And he loved me. He taken with me by the men of the big ship. He taken, put in chains with the other men of our village. We all like this . . ." She made a gesture to show how they had been jammed up together, like spoons in a row. "We lie in our . . ." Glory made another motion of distaste, and Brenna knew she meant excrement.

"Then he die. Dead in his chains. He lie dead there for many days. I think I die. I want to die like him. But I don't, I live. Then I know I am strong. I can go on and I can live . . ."

I know I am strong. I can go on and I can live.

"I . . . I didn't know, Glory." Brenna turned to look at the black girl, seeing the finely shaped bones of her face, the firmness of her jaw. "Glory," she whispered. "I . . . I wish I had died, too. I don't want life without him."

"You strong, too. Like me. You will live."

"Oh, Glory." She buried her face in her hands, feeling Glory's arm around her.

Glory had been right. Brenna's body clung tenaciously to life. In a few more days she was tasting her food again, reaching once more for the embroidery she had discarded, sewing frantically, as if her salvation were to be found in a needle and a skein of brightly colored yarn. Her stitches were awkward, but as she worked, snatches of Mary's childhood instructions came back to her, and soon her

knots and leaves began to take on a semblance of neatness. So this was why they did it, all of those women with
their needlework, one small part of her mind mused. To
keep themselves from weeping . . .

Then one morning Hattie knocked at her door and told
her that Toby Rynne was waiting downstairs for her. Toby!
Brenna pressed one hand to her throat. The past days had
slipped by like beads on a necklace. And Toby hadn't been
a part of them. His letters lay ignored on her dressing
table. Her mind had blanked them out.

"He waiting, Miss Brenna," Hattie prompted.

"Yes, I . . . tell him I will be down in a few minutes."

She went back into the room and stood in front of her
opened wardrobe, looking at the gowns within. Then
slowly she turned away. It didn't matter what she wore to
see Toby. She was thinner now, she knew, and her skin had
lost its pale-peach bloom. But it didn't make any difference.

Toby was waiting for her in the drawing room, the room
that held so much significance for her. He wore a tight,
impeccably tailored black coat that made him look taller
and more muscular than she remembered. A gold watch
chain glinted across his vest front, and there was a gold
seal ring on his left middle finger.

"So, Brenna, you have finally consented to see me. You
have hidden from me all these days because you are mourning that gutter scum, Captain Fairfield. Isn't that right?"
Toby's face was flushed red. An acrid smell emanated from
him, as if his very anger were seeping out through his
pores.

She looked at him. He couldn't frighten her anymore.
Nothing could.

"Yes," she said. "Kane is dead now."

"You have no right!" he burst out. "All this time . . .
why, I am the man you are going to marry. Not that
murderer, who died in the gutter like any river rat."

"I loved him."

"Love! You don't know anything about love. But I
intend to show you. Whether you like it or not."

In spite of herself, Brenna managed a brief laugh.
"Toby, that's foolish. You can't force a person to love
you, no matter how much you want them to. And I don't

love you. Not in the least. I . . . I am afraid I can no longer marry you."

He looked at her. She could see the brocade of his vest expanding, as if he were about to explode.

"Brenna, I am going to give you the benefit of the doubt and pretend that I did not hear those last words. That I did not hear you telling me for the second time that you would not marry me." He moved closer to her. She could see the moisture shining on his full lips, his nostrils pale and bloodless. "Because I . . . if I thought you were planning to disgrace me again, I would pick you up and carry you out of here whether you liked it or not."

She backed away from him. Something made her say, "Haven't you always damned the whole world? Now, if you would please excuse me, I have a headache and wish to rest."

"Headache! Vapors! Mourning!" Toby was shouting now, his voice bouncing off the plastered walls and white-painted moldings, filling the whole house with his fury. But who was there to hear him, she thought wildly. Rowena was in bed with her red medicine, Amos at his office. There were only the slaves, who could do nothing.

He raged on. "Do you think that I will stand for any more of your nonsense? Do you?"

Before she could formulate a reply, he grabbed her and was shaking her violently. "You say you loved him. Well, you are going to learn to love me, you little slut! Don't think that it can't be done. I felt the way you twisted and writhed under me. You'll like me yet, you little—"

"No!" She pushed back at him. "Glory! Tiny!" Her voice rose in a scream.

"Be still!" He clapped his hand over her mouth. The palm of his hand smelled of sweat and tobacco, and the metallic taste of money. "Two times you have refused me, you little bitch—two times! And all over that bastard Fairfield, the one my sister is crazy about, too. She begged me not to find him . . . said she'd do anything, if I'd only leave him alone—"

Toby dragged her easily toward the door, as if she were a doll. In vain she kicked and struggled. Out of the corner of her eye she saw Glory, poised horror-stricken on the stairs.

"Do you think a slave will help you, my girl? Don't you scream out, or I'll come back here and I'll buy that wench and I'll sell her to a brothel—"

"No!" she screamed. "Not Glory!"

He was panting as he pulled her along. Desperately she made her body a dead weight, but he merely scooped her up and carried her, his words pouring out in jerky spasms. "Marriage, my little Irish wench? You no longer have a right to that. If you can be Fairfield's mistress, you can be mine as well. And don't bother to struggle. Do you think there is anyone in this house, or in this city, who would dare stop me?"

His laugh was sharp and ugly, making her think of the unkempt, wolfish pirates. "As you are well aware, Fairfield is dead. There will be no one coming to rescue you this time. No one!"

He pulled her out the door, muffling her screams with his heavy, thick palm.

❧ *Chapter 32* ❧

TOBY HAD LEFT THE ROOM, had gone somewhere, thank God. It was midmorning, and already hot, the air thick and moist. Brenna lay naked in Toby's bed, her flesh bruised and throbbing.

She looked around her at the high-ceilinged, ornate room, thinking how like Toby it was. All of the furniture was heavy, its finish dark and ugly. A cabinet held an array of crystal and silver decanters, each filled with rich amber. Two tall windows overlooked a courtyard. On the wall was an enormous, gilt-framed painting of a harem girl, reclining on white pillows, her body sensuously tinted in shades of peach and rose. Her eyes looked into the room knowingly, as if she had seen what had happened last night, as if she knew.

Brenna looked down at herself with disgust. On her upper arms were the bruises made by Toby's fingers. Even her breasts held marks of him; near her left nipple was a reddened tooth mark.

She turned and buried her face in the pillow, shivers rippling through her. His red mouth, eating her body like some greedy animal. . . . He had forced liquor into her, his hand tipping the glass cruelly into her mouth. The whiskey had burned through all her veins, and soon everything that Toby did to her was just part of the nightmare, the bad dream that went on and on and on, beyond grief and beyond screaming.

Anger, cold anger, had been her only sustaining force. That and her memory of Gasparilla. For now, in a kind of desperate relief, she could see that Gasparilla had at least tried to give her pleasure. He had used his knowledge of a woman's body to pull her, in spite of herself, to heights of orgasm. But Toby had used her like meat, and she had been able to withdraw into some cold, small center of herself where he could not follow.

Kane . . . Kane . . . she thought, even as this small kernel of herself rejoiced that Toby had not been able to pleasure her. He hadn't touched her, not any of the part that mattered. And he never would. Never, never would she ascend those heights with any man again. There was a shell around her now, and no man could get through it, no matter what he did to her body.

She lay in the bed, listening to the sounds of the household. From somewhere a servant shouted, crossly. She heard dishes clattering, and realized that they must be preparing breakfast in the kitchen. The thought of food filled her with distaste. She knew she would never be able to eat. But the rattle of crockery meant that someone would soon come to the room. Whoever it was, she couldn't let them find her like this, naked and bruised.

With effort, she pulled herself out of the bed and stood swaying for a minute, the room whirling about her. But after a moment the dizziness passed, and she looked around for the clothing she had worn the night before. A plain blue day-dress it had been, with a high neck and narrow bands of nainsook edging. She walked about the big room, wondering where it could have gone. He had pulled it roughly off her body, she remembered, along with her underthings. But she had been screaming. She hadn't seen what happened to her clothes.

She walked about the room more quickly now, pulling open drawers in the dark mahogany bureau, finding them oddly bare. They looked as if they had been emptied in a hurry. Through an alcove was a dark-paneled dressing room. On a dressing table she saw a leather and boar-bristle hairbrush, jars of pomade, a gold stickpin, a cravat flung carelessly away. She pulled open another drawer. It, too, was empty.

Her heart began to beat more quickly. This didn't make sense. Why would all of the drawers be empty?

In a panic, she jerked open the big cypress wardrobe looming against one wall of the dressing room. Bare. Empty. She stepped backward, the blood draining from her face as understanding sank in.

Then, frantically, she ran to the bedroom door, and pulled and jerked at it with arms suddenly strong with fright.

The door was locked. And Toby had taken all clothing —his as well as her own—out of the room so there would be nothing she could use to cover herself. She was locked in the room, naked, for Toby to do with as he pleased.

She couldn't believe it. She sat huddled in the bed, wrapped in the satin sheets, her limbs shaking convulsively. Surely, surely, he couldn't get away with this, she told herself over and over. Her uncle and aunt would learn from the servants what had happened to her. They would contact the city militia and send someone for her . . .

Or would they? Aunt Rowena hated her. As for Uncle Amos, Toby had some sort of hold on him, she was almost sure. Perhaps Amos, as attorney for several shipping companies, had given Toby information about cargos and ships that were sailing. She realized she couldn't expect help from that house.

She thought of Arbutus, then reluctantly abandoned the idea. Arbutus, for all her warm heart, was under her husband's control now. Besides, Brenna thought slowly, Amos might tell Arbutus that she had eloped with Toby. If Arbutus believed him . . .

Brenna sank back in despair. Even the slim prospect of help from Melissa was gone, since Melissa had left her brother's home and moved into a hotel recently. Toby could lie to her, anyway.

A rattling at the door made her sit upright in panic, the sheet falling away from her breasts. A key rattled, and then the door opened to the clatter of dishes. Hastily she pulled the sheet over herself and sank back onto the bed. At least she could salvage her pride and pretend that she was still sleeping, that she didn't know about her situation yet.

She smelled hot, savory, chicory coffee, and warm, yeasty croissants. Heard the noise of a tray set beside her on the bed.

"Breakfast, miss," a woman's voice said. "While it hot."

Then soft footsteps left the room, and she heard the careful sound of the key in the lock.

She sat up and looked at the tray. They had given her a linen napkin but no cutlery, save for a spoon. The croissant was still warm from the oven, filled with rich raisins and covered with sugary frosting. A halved orange overflowed with juice.

Her stomach growled. Abruptly she remembered how Glory had made her eat in the pirate compound, slowly, methodically, to survive.

Well, she did have to survive. She would eat, to give herself whatever strength she could. When Toby returned, she would not face him weak and faint with hunger, but with all the courage she could muster.

It was nearly two hours before Toby returned. She spent the time lying in bed wrapped in the sheet, staring up at the hairline cracks in the white plastered ceiling, seeing strange and disturbing pictures there. The outline of a two-masted brig, a brooding Spanish castle . . .

The door opened so abruptly that she was startled. Toby came in, his cheeks flushed, but otherwise bearing no trace of the previous night. He wore a fawn-colored coat with an embroidered vest and silk cravat. His pants were skin-tight, showing off his powerful thigh muscles.

"Good morning, my dear."

She pulled the sheet around her shoulders, looking up at him without speaking.

"Well? Aren't you going to answer me?"

"Why should I speak to you? You are nothing but a—"

"Careful, my little Irish slut. You might say something you would regret."

"I regret nothing I said to you! You are a . . . a pirate! Do you think that because you stole me away, that you can really possess me? That I could really belong to you? Well, you are badly mistaken—"

"Be quiet, or I will slap you." The words came from Toby's mouth very quietly, menacingly.

She stared at him, frightened.

"You called me a pirate," he said. "What did you mean by that?"

"You *are* one, aren't you? You and that . . . that man Gasparilla have your arrangements. You help him dispose of his goods here in New Orleans, don't you?"

Toby's eyes narrowed. "You don't know what you are talking about."

"Don't I? Kane told me—" She stopped, horrified.

But instantly Toby sprang forward, his hands tossing aside the sheet and grabbing her upper arms. "Kane told you what?"

"Why, he—"

"Kane Fairfield is dead, very dead indeed," Toby said coldly. "So it matters very little what he told you about me, or what impossible theories he may have concocted. No one can prove anything. And even if they could, they wouldn't dare. I have power in this city, more power than you could imagine. Power, perhaps, even of life and death."

"Of life and death?" She stared at him, horror flooding through her. "You don't mean . . . Kane . . ."

"Perhaps. And perhaps not. Why should I admit such a thing to you? Such discussions are not to be held with women. Especially not with women as beautiful as you." He looked down at her body, at her full, glossy breasts.

She tried to pull away, and hide beneath the satin sheet, but he stopped her. "Why do you cover yourself? A woman's body is one of the loveliest sights in the world. I have waited so long for this moment, and I want to savor you as long as I can."

"Savor me!" Her voice was furious. "I am not a piece of cake or a sweetmeat! And what's more, I resent being treated like this! Do you realize that I . . . I am confined to this room without a stitch of clothing to put on my back? I have only these sheets to cover me. An animal would be treated better!"

"Animals do not wear clothing," he told her with a grin.

"That's not what I meant, and you know it! Please give

me my gown back," she stormed. "And let me go back to my uncle's home at once, or I will—"

"You'll what? I'm interested to hear just what you plan to do."

"Why, I . . . I'll kill myself if you don't release me," she told him wildly.

"I doubt that. You're too much alive for that. Last night you were cold to me, but I guarantee you'll warm up as the days—and nights—pass. Soon I'll have you willing enough —more than willing."

"I'll never be willing!" she snapped. "And I *will* kill myself. What does it matter?" she added dully. "Kane is dead now, and I have no other reason to keep on living. Especially with you."

Toby's face reddened. "You didn't kill yourself when Gasparilla seduced you—why should you now?"

"How do you know about Gasparilla?"

"Someone told me."

Brenna stared at him. There was a glint of triumph in his eyes.

"Who?"

"Someone you're very fond of, my sweet. Someone to whom you've been close recently, and about whom you've talked a great deal when you've been with me. In your attempts to make conversation, you revealed a great deal about yourself. Your likes, your dislikes, those to whom you have given your affection . . ."

"What are you talking about?"

"Why, your slave, Glory, of course. You see, the reason I have been gone so long this morning is that I wanted to make a special purchase."

"What?" She could feel the blood leaving her face. She felt cold, cold all over. "You don't mean that you have . . . bought Glory?"

He nodded.

"But she belongs to me! Kane gave her to me, and made out the papers himself. I have the papers in my reticule."

"Papers? Your uncle found no papers."

"But I . . . my reticule was—" She stopped. When she had gone down to see Toby, she had left her personal effects in her bedroom. And now the papers of ownership were most certainly destroyed.

"Did you buy her from my Uncle Amos?" she asked furiously.

"I did. He is your guardian, is he not? I told him that you elected to go away with me, and wanted your own servant with you. I paid a pretty penny for her, I might add. Your uncle drives a hard bargain."

Glory, here in Toby's establishment. A cold, hard feeling seemed to expand in her belly.

"I wish to see her . . . at once!" she demanded.

Toby smiled. "I am afraid that is not possible just now."

"Why not?"

"Because I don't want you to see her. She is *my* slave now, Brenna. Get that through your head. She is mine, to do with as I will. And, I might add, she is a luscious piece of black flesh, most desirable. Almost as lovely as you are, my sweet, although in a different way, naturally."

"But Glory is *my* servant! You said you bought her for me! You said—"

"I said many things. The truth is, my dear, that the fate of that little black sweetmeat depends entirely upon you. If you are, shall we say, cooperative, then I will give the girl to you as your maidservant, and all will be well. If you do not . . ."

"Yes?" She felt sick. Glory—the beautifully sculpted features, the long, slim neck, the soft, dark skin. The black hands that had reached out dozens of times to help her, to offer comfort, even when Glory herself must have been full of misery, fear and bewilderment.

"If you do not cooperate, I could keep Glory here, for my own use. She is delectable. I am sure she would make a most enjoyable addition to my establishment. And she could be easily trained for everything that I would require of her . . ." Toby paused and examined Brenna's reaction before he went on. "Or, I could sell her to a brothel. Perhaps one of the cribs down in the Swamp. Or one of the many places that feature only black and mulatto girls. Dark meat is extremely popular in certain quarters of the city . . ."

"You wouldn't do that!"

"Of course I would. On the other hand, if you were to cooperate . . . I want you to marry me, Brenna. I've decided it isn't enough to have you as my mistress. I want

you for my wife, publicly. Beyond doubt or question or
gossip, and in the eyes of everyone. Those damned society
bitches clattered their tongues enough when you jilted me.
Now I want to give them something more to gabble about.
The fact that I got you, after all. That you belong to me.
You're mine—my property, my possession. Do you see?"

She saw. "I am surprised that you care what those . . .
those . . . people in drawing rooms say about you," she
managed to say, coolly enough.

"I hate them. I hate their very guts! But, yes, I care.
Do you think I worked my way up from those filthy New
York tenements for nothing? I want to mingle with people
like that, the best people. Not only to be accepted by
them, but to be better than they are, to laugh at them if I
wish. As they once laughed at me."

His hand released her arm and slid down to cup her
breasts. "You. Me. Perhaps we're more alike than you
think. I've got to have you, all of you. And I'll do anything to make it happen. Anything. Do you follow me?"

"Yes. I see." She could hardly speak. Her mouth was
so dry that her tongue adhered to the roof of her mouth.

"Are you going to marry me?"

Glory. Oh, she couldn't let Glory be thrown away in a
brothel like human garbage. She would wake up screaming
for the rest of her nights if she did that. Suddenly Brenna
thought of Neall Urquhart, and the last words he had
said to her: *May you be used for the rest of your life like
a pig.* A curse of malevolence from a dying man.

And now, she thought wildly, that curse was going to
come true. How Neall, wherever he was, must be laughing.

"I can't desert Glory," she told him coldly. "I will marry
you. But don't think you can ever possess me. I'll never
warm to you, never."

He smiled. Then he ripped away the satin sheets and
threw them to the floor. He forced her legs apart brutally.
Without even removing his clothes, he took her.

After slaking his desire on her, Toby subjected her to
the humiliation of having to stand, naked, while two female
slaves came in and stripped the bedroom of all sheets,

clothes, sharp objects. Even the pull-cord and the decanters of whiskey were removed. There would be a slave sitting below in the courtyard, Toby told her, to stop her if she tried to climb out of the window.

Brenna stood watching, her skin covered with goose bumps, her hands and feet unbearably chilly. She could still feel the discharges of his body on her skin, disgustingly unclean. How she wished she could scrub herself! But she could not bring herself to ask. She stood proudly, her back straight, her hands at her sides. She would not cower and huddle to hide her body. And she would not even acknowledge the curious looks of the two black women, who worked so efficiently to insure that she could not kill herself.

"There," Toby said at last, inspecting their work. "The room is suitable."

"Suitable! For what? A madwoman? Really, Toby, do you think that I would impale myself on your . . . your stickpin, after I have given my word to marry you? Or drink down all that ghastly whiskey?"

"I don't know. I'm only making sure. Don't worry, my dear, if you prove cooperative, I'll return your clothing fast enough. It'll be something to look forward to, won't it?"

He was smiling with amusement. To him, this was all a joke.

"You . . . you beast! You pirate!"

"I told you I would slap you if you said that again. I mean that. Do you want to test me?"

"No. I don't want to test you. But may I . . . may I at least have a bath?" She hated herself for begging. But she had to be clean. She had to. She had to wash her body free of all traces of him or she would go mad.

"A bath? Why not? I'll have Scylla bring one up as soon as she is finished here."

"Thank you," Brenna said sullenly. "I'll try not to swallow the bath water. Or choke on the soap."

He looked at her. "If you think that I am going to deny you food, or simple cleanliness, you are mistaken. I have no intention of being cruel to you. I only want to humiliate

you a bit. I want to make you realize that your body does
not belong to you anymore, it belongs to me."

"My body may belong to you, but my soul does not."

"We'll see about that."

He turned and left the room, taking the two slaves with
him. Brenna heard the sound of the key turning in the
lock. The harem slave looked down from the wall mockingly, as if to say, *we are sisters.*

Brenna threw herself on the bare goose down mattress
and began to sob.

To her utter relief, Toby did not approach her sexually
again. He left her alone in the grotesquely bare room,
with nothing to do but stare out at the patio, where, as
Toby had ordered, a slave sat on a stool watching her
window. Once she saw Glory walking gracefully across
the courtyard, her eyes downcast, her lips pressed tightly
together. She wore a yellow gown Brenna had never seen,
a charming dress trimmed with embroidery, in a shade
that set off the glow of her skin exquisitely.

Seeing her, Brenna caught her breath. Toby had bought
Glory a new dress while allowing her, Brenna, to have no
clothing whatsoever. *That little black sweetmeat,* he had
called her. Was it remotely possible that he was already . . .

But she refused to think about that. If she did, she
would lose her sanity.

On the third day one of the slaves, Charybdis, came in
with her petticoats, underthings, and a blue muslin gown,
and told her to put them on. "The seamstress, she coming
to fit you for your wedding dress," Charybdis said shortly.

"What?"

"That's what Master Toby say. He say you get dressed
quick, hear?"

Gratefully Brenna scrambled into the clothes, vowing
that, now she had them, she would not relinquish them
easily. It was odd, she thought, how much of her pride
and self-esteem depended upon having clothing to wear.
To be the only one naked was truly diminishing to the
spirit.

She stood and suffered the attentions of the quadroon
seamstress, a fat, grizzled woman in her fifties, who barely

spoke to her and acted as if she were frightened of her. And no wonder, Brenna thought despairingly. Toby had probably threatened her somehow, or told her that Brenna was mad.

The woman had brought no swatches of material with her, and Brenna gathered that Toby had already made the selections. Knowing him, she thought bitterly, the dress would be the most grotesque gown the city had seen in a generation, loaded with ribbons, feathers and jewels; a monstrous parody of a gown designed to show the world Toby Rynne's power.

But what did it matter, she asked herself dully? She hardly cared. She would marry Toby, if she had to. She would gain his confidence. Then in a few weeks or months, when his vigilance began to relax, she would take Glory and run away.

If, she thought soberly, Toby would let her.

After the seamstress had left, Brenna sat waiting, wondering what was going to happen next. She was not going to give up her clothing, she decided, without a fight.

Almost immediately, Scylla was back, letting herself in with the key. A twin sister of Charybdis, she was a tall, slender black woman, with two missing teeth on the left side of her mouth, which gave her face a rather crooked, raffish look. But she had been kind enough to Brenna, bringing her carefully laid meal trays and seeing to it that her baths were warm and prompt.

Before the woman could speak, Brenna got up and faced her, her hands doubled into fists at her sides. "If you think you're going to take this dress away from me again, Scylla, you're badly mistaken. I'm not going to give it up."

"Miss Brenna—"

"I am not giving up my clothing, Scylla. And if you try to approach me, I . . . I'll fight." She raised her fists at the astonished servant, and fixed her with a cold look out of narrowed eyes.

"But Master Toby, he say you—"

"I don't care what Master Toby says. I'm not giving up this dress. It's inhuman, Scylla, keeping me this way, like an animal, and you know it!" As the woman hesitated,

Brenna added, "You can go and take the message to Mr. Rynne, if you wish. Tell him I have been cooperative, I've done everything he asked, and now I want my clothing back. What's more, I intend to have it."

"Yes'm." Scylla gave her a long look, her lips twitching, as if she were trying to hold back a smile. She left the room hastily.

Brenna sank down on the bare mattress, her heart pounding. Soon, she had no doubt, Toby would appear. It was easy enough to threaten a slave, but Toby was another story. She would have to face him down as best she could.

It was nearly two hours before Toby came. And when he did appear, he was in an oddly jubilant mood.

Instead of raging at her, he complimented her gown. "Blue becomes you, my dear. After we are married, I will give you a gown of blue-green silk. It will bring out the color of your eyes."

So, he was going to allow her to wear the dress. Brenna could hardly conceal her elation. "I would like that," she said quietly.

"Would you like to hear the plans I've made for the wedding?"

"Yes," she said, not wishing to anger him.

He told her that they would be married in the cathedral —he had had to pay well for this privilege—and then leave for a magnificent reception and ball at the Orleans ballroom, the scene of many of the city's finest social functions. "After we are married," he went on, "I plan to build a house, would you like that? I've already spoken to the architect. It's going to be the biggest and most magnificent house this city has ever seen. We're going to have pecan paneling, hundreds of crystal chandeliers, and a beautiful suspended staircase down which you can descend, your chin held high, looking beautiful and haughty—"

"It will be a house to which no one will come," she said.

Toby reddened. "They'll come—never you worry about that. I'll make them come. You wait and see. They'll come, and they'll drink my wine and sit at my table, and I'll be secretly laughing at them for the fools they are."

"You must realize, Toby, that I will never be accepted in polite society here after all that has happened."

" 'Polite society,' as you call it, can swallow a lot without choking. Don't worry, they'll swallow you. I'll make them."

Toby's eyes shone intensely. For a moment Brenna could almost—but not quite—feel sorry for him. Was she really so important to him? But, she thought with a chill, he was right. For wasn't it the God-fearing merchants of New Orleans who purchased the pirated goods, the merchandise stained with blood? Where money was involved, people could overlook any number of high principles.

"We will, of course, adhere to our original wedding date," Toby was saying.

"But . . . we hadn't set one."

"We have now. It's day after tomorrow. A little soon, but what does that matter? All the plans are made. You have only to relax and rest so that you will look your loveliest. I have engaged the finest hairdresser in the city for you. I had to pay a great deal of money to get her away from the family that had her, but she'll be worth it, I'm sure. And I'll see to it that she gives you a coiffure far surpassing anything she ever gave the Rydell girls."

"Rydell?" Brenna felt her heart give a sudden jump. "You don't mean . . . Mary?"

"Why, yes, her name is Mary Flannagan. Do you know her?"

"She . . . she was the servant I brought with me from Dublin," Brenna said weakly.

"Oh? Yes, I remember now. Well, what matters is that she's going to make you the most stunning bride this city has ever seen. They'll be talking about our wedding day for ten years."

"If not longer," Brenna said. She shivered a little.

❧ *Chapter 33* ❧

IT WAS, AGAIN, her wedding day.

Sometimes Brenna felt as if she were moving in a dream. At other times, the reality seeped sharply into her mind like freezing rainwater. Then she would pace up and down the bedroom, feeling like one of the yellow butterflies she and Quentin had trapped in glass bells when they were children. She beat her wings, and flew about, but hit the glass hopelessly on every side.

She was going to marry Toby, and there was nothing she could do about it.

If only she could slip out and run away! But Toby had made this impossible. The guard still sat on his stool in the courtyard, watching. Her door was always kept locked. And now, since her threat to Scylla, the two sisters came together to attend to her needs.

Besides, there was Glory. She was sure Toby would make good his threat to send Glory to a brothel. Brenna had been in New Orleans long enough to realize that, in spite of arguments and bills introduced in Congress, many people did not consider slaves human. And she was sure Toby fell into this group. But Glory was human, she told herself. She couldn't just abandon her.

So she let the hours slip past, trying not to think about Kane, for when she did, she collapsed into tears and weeping. If only she were marrying him, instead of Toby! Then how happy she'd be, with what joy she would plunge into the wedding preparations.

The day had dawned hot and clear, the sky a cloudless blue bowl, the banana trees in the courtyard swaying fitfully in a light breeze. As Brenna sat before her untouched breakfast, she heard the key turning in her door.

"Miss Brenna? Is it you?" Mary stood in the open door, with Scylla and Charybdis behind her. Mary looked just as she always had, a gray dress neat on her angular body, a wicker basket of curling irons and implements in her hand. Her long, pockmarked face was smiling.

Brenna jumped up, nearly knocking over her laden breakfast tray. "Mary!" She threw herself into the Irish woman's arms.

"Brenna, why, what is it? You're trembling. And is it that you're crying, too?" Mary held Brenna at arm's length, looking searchingly into her face.

"I . . . Oh, Mary, Mary, I think I am crying." Brenna was laughing through her tears as she pulled the older woman to her again. "Oh, it's so good to see you! I didn't realize how much I missed you."

"Child, child. You leaving, running away as you did, ruining your reputation . . . oh, I missed you, too. Things have changed so very much . . ."

The smile left Mary's face, and Brenna saw a muscle at the corner of her mouth twitch. She remembered how angry she'd been when Mary had championed her marriage to Toby. But Mary hadn't known, she told herself now. She hadn't understood the situation.

"Brenna, are you truly happy about marrying Mr. Rynne now? I felt so bad before when I saw how upset you were. And then when you disappeared as you did . . . well, I was frantic, frantic. And when we finally heard . . . oh, I worried so about you. And now you're back, and you're going to marry Mr. Rynne after all. So it must be for the best . . ."

Brenna stared at Mary, at this woman who had been a mother to her for so many years. Didn't Mary see that she was a prisoner here, that she was being forced into marriage? Or didn't she want to see?

"After learning about poor Quentin and his drinking

and gambling, it would break my heart if anything bad happened to you," Mary said brokenly.

"I . . . I'm fine," Brenna heard herself reply. "Don't worry about me. I'm sure that Toby and I will be . . . happy," she finished lamely.

But Mary didn't seem to notice her hesitation. "Oh, Brenna, I'm so relieved. It's the best thing for you, the way it's all turned out. You'll see as the days pass. You need the protection of a husband, you do. I suppose you'll want me with you now, won't you? Not that I didn't like the Rydells," she added. "They are fine people, I'm sure. But not family, the way you and Quentin are."

"Of course I'll want you with me! If you want to stay. Or I'll have Toby give you the money for your passage back to Ireland. Would you like to go home?"

Mary pressed her lips together. "I do miss Dublin, and I don't think I can ever love this sinful city with its flowers growing so shameful lusty, and its smelly, muddy streets. But it's with you I'd rather be," she said firmly.

"Oh, Mary." Brenna was in Mary's arms again, hugging her as if clinging to the days of her childhood. "Mary . . ."

The Irishwoman took nearly three hours to transform Brenna's hair into an elaborate coif of red-gold splendor, with shining puffs of hair at the temples, and ringlets cascading down, artfully interwoven with white satin ribbon encrusted with seed pearls. Brenna sat and endured the pulling, tugging and backcombing, trying not to wince when an occasional hair was tweaked too hard.

"Mr. Rynne said to make you into the most beautiful bride this city has ever seen," Marry murmured in her "working" voice. "And I think I'm going to succeed. Not that you need dressing up to look lovely. I only hope Mr. Toby Rynne appreciates what he's getting in you."

"I . . . I'm sure he does."

At last her hair was finished. Mary laced Brenna into her corset, pulling it so tightly that she felt breathless. Then Brenna stepped into the gown, heavy satin weighted down with tiers of flounces trimmed with French lace and more seed pearls. She felt Mary buttoning the small, mother-of-pearl buttons into the satin loops, with an uncanny sense of having been here several times before.

Any minute now, Hattie would knock upon her door, and tell her there was a man waiting for her in the courtyard. She would feel a wild leaping of her heart, a sudden rush of blood to her cheeks. Then, gathering up her heavy skirts, she would run down the hall toward the back staircase . . .

She stared at herself in the mirror through a film of tears, seeing only a white, shimmering blur. Kane would not be coming to carry her away, because he was dead. Dead, forever gone. There would be only Toby to welcome her, to take her cold hand, to strip the dress from her trembling body.

"My, and aren't you a sight?" Mary said with obvious pleasure. "None of the Rydell girls, or Arbutus or even that little prig of a cousin of yours, Jessica, could hold a candle to you now. You're far prettier than any of them could hope to be."

"I shall please Toby then," Brenna said woodenly.

"I am sure you will. Now, you must not sit down, or you will crease your train. And don't move about too much—you don't want to stain your gown with perspiration."

Brenna fought the wild urge to laugh. Practical Mary, so ready with down-to-earth advice but able to overlook the most important things, like love. She felt a hot prickling behind her eyelids. But she blinked rapidly until the moisture was gone, and the face she turned toward Mary was smooth and pale.

They were leaving the altar. A blur of white, staring faces passed on either side of them, whispers rising like the humming of bees. Brenna felt Toby's hand on her arm, pulling her along, forcing her to move. Organ music blared, coughs reverberated against high ceilings. Behind them followed the rest of the wedding party. Melissa Rynne, dressed in pale yellow, with a sullen, angry face. Matt Watson, others whom she didn't know, friends of Toby or people who owed him favors.

She forced her legs forward, one by one, the heavy gown seeming to drag her down. She was married now, the wife of this stranger in the tightly fitting black coat

and trousers, this man with the full, red lips who kept looking down at her, his eyes glinting. She wore his ring upon
her finger like a mark of ownership.

She saw Arbutus. Beside her was Mrs. Rydell, the
woman who had cut her. Mrs. Rydell was resplendent
in Spanish lace veil and pink silk, and she stared at Brenna
resentfully. *Don't worry, they'll accept you,* Toby had said.
She wondered what he had done to get Mrs. Rydell here.
And what he would do to insure that the opulent house
he planned would be full of people.

Nausea surged into her throat, and she swallowed
desperately, nearly choking on the hot, sour bile. Then
they were outside on the steps. The bright sun glared into
her eyes.

A crowd of people were waiting. She had the impression of army uniforms, men's dark suits, women's bright
dresses, children's frocks. Many of the onlookers had black
or brown skin, and jostled each other cheerfully as if this
were a holiday. A mulatto woman bore a huge tray full of
cakes, and was hawking them enthusiastically.

And all of them were here to see her, Brenna thought
half-hysterically. The infamous Brenna Laughlan who had
once run off with the murderer, Kane Fairfield, and who
now was brought to marriage with the man she had jilted.
She could sense their eyes boring into her with good-
humored curiosity. Hear their whispers, their laughter.

She felt Toby's hand on her arm, pulling her to him.
Then, in front of everyone, he embraced her and kissed
her, his tongue moving urgently. She felt dizzy, drowned
in whispers. Behind them she heard the wedding guests
emerging from the cathedral, laughing, buzzing . . .

Toby finished his kiss, held her away. "You look as
white as that dress of yours," he said. "You're not going
to faint, are you? Better not do that to me, Brenna, or
you'll answer for it later."

"I wish I could faint. But don't concern yourself. I'm
not going to."

His arms were about her, his lips nearly against her
ear. "Good, because we still have the ball to get through.
Then it's home and to bed . . ."

Bed. With Toby. She thought of the night she had spent with him and wanted to scream.

He pulled her down the steps toward the big, gilt-embossed carriage waiting for them, the coachman ready. The crowd pressed closer, their voices rising in excitement. A man in ragged clothes pressed forward to get a better view. His blonde-brown, curly beard glinted in the sun. She paused, struck by some aspect of him.

The man turned toward her. Abruptly she stopped, shock pounding through her.

It was Kane! Kane with his beard long and curly now, his face thinner, the cheekbones jutting and prominent, as if he had been ill. His eyes were fixed on hers, holding her in their intensity. She felt her heart slamming in her chest. He was alive!

"Kane . . ." She started toward him. She felt as if she could scream, could cry, could weep with sheer joy. Behind her, Melissa Rynne gave a sharp cry.

"Don't come any closer, Brenna, not yet."

She stopped, bewildered. Around her people were crowding closer, shoving to get a look at this new development.

"Toby Rynne, I hereby accuse you of collusion in the piracy of the brig *Sea Otter*, and of responsibility for the deaths of twenty men in her crew." Kane's voice, strong and low, carried throughout the crowd.

"But . . . you're dead—" Toby muttered.

"No, I'm very much alive. Which is more than I can say for my men, and for my first mate, Andrew Scroggins. Would you believe that I found his gold teeth in your secret warehouse? And as if that isn't proof enough, there are goods from my own cabin, some of them still streaked with dried blood—"

"No! It's all a lie!" Toby, his face reddened, backed away from Brenna and edged up the steps toward the other members of the wedding party who stood, transfixed, staring at this extraordinary scene.

"It's no lie, but the whole damned truth," Kane said angrily. "What's more, I'm here to clear my name. You couldn't bear to think that a Rynne might have been bested fairly, could you? So you bribed the witnesses to say otherwise."

"But . . ." Toby's face worked. Brenna could see streams of moisture running down his temples into the high collar of his shirt. "They pulled you out of the canal! They told me you were dead . . . they swore it—"

Kane's grin showed a flash of white teeth. "A man was pulled out of the canal who looked like me. I let people go on thinking that . . . why not? It was more convenient for me to move about the city as a dead man. Unfortunately, the typhoid hit me. If it had not been for Maud Sweet, who nursed me, I might have ended a corpse after all."

So that was why she had not heard from Kane, Brenna thought. He had been ill with the typhoid fever that constantly swept the more disreputable areas of the city. And loyal, blowsy Maud Sweet had kept his secret.

"Fever!" Toby shouted. "I wish you had died, you . . . you scum!"

"I am sure you do. You could not accept the fact that I killed your brother in a fair and equal meeting, and had to take revenge by destroying my name. Well, here in my pocket I have proof of your dishonor. The dying statement of Raoul Frontenac, lately of Havana, signed and witnessed by reliable people. You thought your money had taken care of him, didn't you? But when he was stricken with typhoid even as I was, his conscience got the better of him. He died only an hour ago, but his statement stands."

"It's a lie, all of it! A lie, do you hear me?"

"No. You are the liar, Rynne. Your entire life has been a lie. You, the prominent New Orleans businessman, accepted in all the best drawing rooms? No, you are nothing but a gutter rat from the stinking tenements of New York, and a filthy pirate . . ."

"*No!*" Toby was standing directly in front of the wedding party. Brenna saw his hand slide backward, toward Matt Watson. Was an object passing between them?

"Kane!" she screamed. "He has a pistol!"

Never take a pistol lightly, Kane had told her when he had taught her to use one. *When you fire, chances are about fifty-fifty you'll miss. But a gun is power, Brenna. Don't you forget it.*

Kane reached for something in his own belt, and the

sun flashed on polished metal. Brenna stood frozen, knuckles clamped to her mouth. Someone jostled her and she realized it was Melissa Rynne, the other girl's eyes wild in a chalk-white face.

The two men circled each other, each seeking the best position. Kane moved with the same quick, athletic grace she remembered. But his face was much thinner, and there were dark smudges beneath his eyes. He was physically weaker than Toby, Brenna realized with growing dismay. Even from here she could see his legs trembling slightly. In contrast, Toby looked in ruddy good health, his chest filling the linen fabric of his shirt. His tongue shot out to moisten his lips, but his small, blue eyes did not leave Kane's face.

"Kane!" Melissa's high, clear voice rang out. The girl started to push her way toward the two men.

"No, don't!" Brenna held her back, hearing the angry swish as their full skirts brushed each other. "Don't go out there!"

"But we've got to stop this! Can't you see that Toby will kill him?"

For the first time, Brenna felt a quick sympathy with the blonde girl. "But you can't distract his attention, Melissa. If you do, you will be responsible for his death." She heard her own fierce words with a dim surprise. She held Melissa's arm with all her strength, holding her back. She, too, wanted to scream and fling herself between the two men. But she knew that if she did, she would upset the delicate balance between them.

Seconds ticked by, fragments of time in which the two men circled, their bodies slightly crouched, their eyes locked. Brenna was horrified to see Kane's legs shaking, his pallor growing more noticeable.

Then Toby fired his pistol. The crowd screamed. The explosion seemed to echo, then dissipated into the warm, moist air. Toby was reloading quickly.

Kane raised his own weapon. His eyes, fixed on Toby's, did not waver, although the miss had been a near one. "Rynne, don't fire in this crowd," he said. "You might hit someone. Let's go outside the city. We'll duel fairly. This time without any lying on your part."

"Be damned. We'll have it here. And I'll have you dead."
Toby fired the pistol again.

Brenna could not suppress the scream that tore out of
her throat. For now Kane staggered, his knees crumpling
as a red bloom spread from his shoulder to stain his white
shirt. The pistol drooped from his hand, seeming almost
ready to fall from his fingers.

"Kane! Oh, God . . ." Was that her own voice, frantic
with fear and anger? Or was it Melissa beside her, screaming too? Just as Brenna started forward, Kane's fingers
suddenly closed about the pistol he held. He fired.

In front of her, Toby Rynne looked down at his chest
with shocked eyes, at the place where a raw circle of red
bubbled and frothed.

"Kane . . . Kane . . . oh, dear God, Kane. . . ." Brenna
didn't know what she was babbling. Toby and Kane lay
on the cathedral steps, Toby slightly above Kane, like two
piles of discarded rags. Every detail seemed as night-
marishly clear as a tinted lithograph. Above, a seabird
circled in an updraft. The cake vendor had dropped her
tray, and was staring down at her wares scattered in the
mud. Toby's pistol lay in a puddle.

Brenna ran toward Kane. Around her the crowd pushed
and shoved, some trying to get forward to see what had
happened, others trying to flee. She saw Arbutus, her face
filled with horror under a poke bonnet.

She threw herself beside Kane, and turned his face
toward her. Her hands reddened with his blood.

He was still alive. His face was paper-white, his eyes
enormous staring holes, his lips bloodless. Perspiration
was clammy on his forehead. But his eyes moved, his lips
tried to speak.

Her breath caught in her throat. Blood was flowing
from his shoulder, staining his shirt with red. He might be
alive now, she thought quickly, but he would die soon from
loss of blood. Desperately she jerked off her wedding veil,
heedless of the metal pins holding it on, wadded it, and
pressed it against his wounded shoulder. She held it there,
feeling it grow wet with blood.

Melissa knelt beside her, screaming at Kane, shaking
him.

"Rip off a strip of your petticoat," Brenna snapped at the other girl. "Hurry!"

"But—"

"He'll die if you don't, you fool! Do you want that?"

She heard Melissa sob, and the sound of fabric ripping. Brenna took the cloth and pressed it against the already blood-soaked veil. The creamy satin of her own gown was covered with ugly red spatters and smudges of dirt. As if a dress could matter, she thought frantically, trying to summon a prayer. *God . . . please . . .*

Then he stirred, his eyelids flickering. Although Melissa was still beside her, his eyes were fixed only on Brenna. "Sorry . . . little wildcat . . . I got here too late . . ."

"No, it's all right, Kane. You'd better just rest now."

"Got to tell you . . . heard of the wedding. Was going to . . . steal you away again . . ." A shadow of a smile transformed his face, then was gone.

"Oh, Kane . . ." Joy thrilled through her, to be replaced by fear as he faded away into unconsciousness.

Then Arbutus pushed her way up to them, elbowing the stunned Melissa aside, her delicate face determined. "Keep pressing those cloths onto his wound, Brenna. We'll take him to Carlisle Oaks whether Monty likes it or not. We'll pick up Doctor Bradley on our way out of town."

From out of the crowd came helping hands to lift Kane into Arbutus' carriage. Only as they were pulling away, did Brenna look out of the carriage window at Toby, lying still and dead on the steps of the cathedral.

"If it hadn't been for you, young lady, he wouldn't have lived this long." Doctor Bradley sighed as he wiped his hands fastidiously on the damp towel Arbutus handed him. "I've removed the bullet, but unfortunately, the man has lost so much blood that I frankly doubt he is going to live."

Dr. Bradley was a comfortably portly man, with a waxed moustache and plump sideburns. But his eyes were weary with too many deaths.

"But . . . he's a strong, healthy man, doctor," Brenna protested. "He has a strong constitution. Surely he will live through this!"

"Perhaps. The wound has a chance of healing, I'll admit, but the man is so weakened that I doubt he has the strength to survive. You told me he'd had the typhoid fever, didn't you?"

"Yes, but . . . he's got to live!" They stood in Arbutus' sunny sitting room, yellow bars of light lying across the carpet in great rectangles. Brenna knew she must present a sight, with her hair straggling and her gown stained with blood and dirt. The doctor looked away from her.

"Now, Brenna." Arbutus squeezed her hand. "You mustn't worry. I'm sure Dr. Bradley is doing all he can—"

"Then let him go upstairs and help Kane!" Brenna shouted. "Let him try everything there is to try. Kane has got to live, he must!"

"Miss Laughlan, there is nothing more to do but nurse the man, and you can do that as well as I. Or, if you wish, I'll send a nurse. Now, I have other patients to see. A woman is in labor with her first child and I must go to her."

"Go? No, you can't! You can't leave . . ." Brenna tried to hold the doctor back, but he stepped aside to avoid her and then was gone.

"Arbutus." Brenna sank against the edge of the doorway. Her knees trembled beneath her. "Arbutus, I've got to do something. I can't let him go from me like this. I . . . I never really told him that I loved him. I . . ." She swallowed. "He said he was coming back for me. He was going to take me away . . ."

Arbutus' face was pale with sympathy. "Go upstairs and stay with him, Brenna. Pray. Perhaps . . ."

Brenna never knew how long she sat there, in the upstairs bedroom at Carlisle Oaks, while the shadows in the room got longer and longer. At last a slave came in with candles, which flickered in long shadows against the walls until they burned themselves down to stubs. Hours. Hours of sitting and watching that beloved face, spooning water through the pale lips, sponging the perspiring forehead. Others came in and out of the room—Arbutus, servants, even, somehow, Mary. But she barely looked up, so intent was she on the prayer which kept running through her mind like a litany. *Let him live. Please, God.*

Slowly the sky outside the window turned a translucent pink, like the inside of a shell. Dawn. Brenna shifted in her chair, feeling the sudden ache in her back. He had lived nearly fourteen hours now.

Then she saw his lips move.

"Brenna . . ."

"Yes?" She bent close to him to hear the bare whisper of sound.

"I'm still going to . . . to do it, you know."

"You're going to do what?" She stared at him. Was it her imagination, or was there the barest hint of color in his face? Or perhaps, she thought dully, it was only the reflection of the pink glow of morning.

"Why, I am tired of seeing you in a wedding dress . . . time after time. Haven't you anything better to wear?"

"What?" She looked at him, bewildered. Under his beard the twin creases of his dimples flickered, and for a moment he looked almost like his old self, confident and aggravating.

"When I saw you . . . coming out of that cathedral on his arm and knew that I was too late—" Kane stopped to cough, wincing with pain. "Knew I had to have you . . . steal you if necessary . . ."

"Oh!" There was a swelling of happiness in Brenna's chest. As Kane sank back into the pillow, too weak to speak further, she took his hand. His pulse was stronger than it had been in hours.

"Very well," she said. "But on my terms, this time. Not yours. And my terms include marriage, with a nice gold band and a quiet ceremony somewhere—no cathedrals, ever again. We'll buy back Glory and set her free. And then I'm going with you, wherever your ship sails, to Boston or California, or China or . . . or wherever."

Kane's eyes glistened. "My love, you drive a hard bargain."

Brenna smiled. Outside the window the sun came up, a perfect globe of pure gold.

AVON PRESENTS THE BEST
IN SPECTACULAR WOMEN'S ROMANCE

Kathleen E. Woodiwiss

The Flame and the Flower	35485/$2.25
The Wolf and the Dove	35477/$2.25
Shanna (large-format)	31641/$3.95

Laurie McBain

Devil's Desire	30650/$1.95
Moonstruck Madness	31385/$1.95

Rosemary Rogers

Sweet Savage Love	28027/$1.95
Dark Fires	23523/$1.95
The Wildest Heart	28035/$1.95
Wicked Loving Lies	30221/$1.95

The achievement of Avon's authors of original romances has been nothing less than a phenomenon—sweeping, passionate, beautifully written adventures that have thrilled millions of readers—the focus of the national media, and a whole new trend in publishing.

Captive Bride

**She knew no master
until a desert sheik
claimed her heart.**

Johanna Lindsey

On a night
made for love,
there was only terror
for beautiful Christina Wakefield.
She who had recklessly followed her brother
from London to Cairo on a whim was
now made prisoner by an unknown abductor
who carried her off to his hidden encampment.

Soon she would share his bed,
know his touch, growing ever closer to
the man who owned her as a slave.

And soon she would learn to want him
as he wanted her—to share his soul,
his being—her body aching for him alone.

 AVON 33720 $1.95

BRIDE 8-77

Of Love Triumphant and Passion Ablaze!

MYSTIC ROSE

PATRICIA GALLAGHER

A sweeping historical romance
by the author of CASTLES IN THE AIR

Across a fiery landscape of slave revolt and the tumult of war,
the rapturous love story of the beautiful, high-spirited
Charleston belle Star Lamont and the virile, dashing Yankee
sea captain Troy Stewart sweeps from the magnificent ball-
rooms of sumptuous Deep South plantations to the tempestu-
ous dangers and emotions of the high seas.

Theirs is a blazing saga of pride against passion, of burning
hatred and volatile desire. And it is the story of a plantation
called Mystic Rose—a place of mystery and enchantment—
where a young woman never dreamt that emotion could be so
glorious, so overwhelming, until she met the one man fated
to bring her unbounded love!

AVON 33381 $1.95   MYST 9-77